Norman Creek has a destiny: to save the world.

Earth has been almost lifeless for forty years, since a mysterious disaster caused most of the world's population to vanish. With the greatest famine in decades at its peak, thousands lay dying in the ruins of once-great cities.

A high-ranking member of England's last true society, Norman will soon have to take up the mantle of leadership, and keep the ways of the Old World from becoming lost forever. But being a leader was never a life he wanted.

As starvation grips the country, and Norman becomes ever more desperate to escape his fate, a hostile coalition emerges; one that heralds the coming of a second Apocalypse, hell-bent on ending the Old World forever.

Subscribe to the newsletter to hear about new releases and future titles: http://eepurl.com/V4niL

For Mum and Dad

THE RUIN SAGA

VOLUME 1: RUIN

Harry Manners

1

THE END

Listen, I tell you a mystery: We will not all sleep, but we will all be changed—in a flash, in the twinkling of an eye, at the last trumpet.

— **1 Corinthians 15:51-58**

1

Norman Creek was hunting. Through the rifle's scope the streets below him were magnified tenfold. Pale, late-afternoon light fell upon the tarmac and his prey.

His pulse quickened, and his throat grew tighter, but a deep breath saw to his nerves and calmed his trigger finger. Adjusting his position upon a high ridge with creeping increments, he settled into a recess in the scree. His muscles ached, but the discomfort was dull, without edge. The sharp pinches of pebbles against his skin seemed a thousand miles distant. He only felt hunger, a maddening beast growling in his gut, driving him forwards.

Allison and Lucian were perched on either side of him, ready. Their quarry was close.

Below, a thick mist prowled the streets. Ringing silence filled the air, stark and naked. Rivers of cars lined the roadside, rusted skeletons, often crushed together into mangled balls of twisted metal. Bearing down on them were the remains of houses, office blocks and shopping centres. All crumbling, all faded, mere shadows.

Most buildings stood without roofs, hatless. The slate tiles and supporting beams had collapsed and sent upper floors crashing to the dirt long ago. Possessions were scattered in the rubble: lamps, telephones, pots and pans, the occasional sofa.

Norman paid none of it any attention. Things had always been this way, ever since the End. And those old enough to remember the Old World were growing fewer. He only had eyes for the dark figure milling at the intersection below the ridge.

Amidst decayed bricks and mortar echoed the steady clip-clop of hooves on concrete, those of a foraging stag busying itself with a clump of grass thrusting through the tarmac.

The old Red had been gorging himself. His bulk was distended almost a foot, bulging and round. But he was no picture of health. His aged body was decrepit, and the herd had long moved on; his tired legs were no match for the spring in their step.

He gave a low grumble, chewing his pulpy meal, oblivious. As Norman squeezed the trigger, the stag snorted a plume of morning vapour with an attitude that could have been weariness and turned to face his death.

A low whine filled the air, followed by a wet splattering sound. A plume of red matter soared from the side of the stag's head, spewing against the cracked window of a burned-out Prius. Stiffening in a sudden spasm, it sank to the pavement, twitching and jerking in a spreading pool of crimson.

The gunshot's roar reverberated against walls, trees and stones, rolling out across the landscape, but its might went unappreciated. There was scarcely anything left alive to recoil from the racket. The sound died away after only a few diminishing echoes to be replaced by the same deep quiet as before.

In the distance, a bird chirped in the English spring morning. The door of a nearby fast-food restaurant blew in the wind, jostling against the wall behind it. Otherwise, the world was silent and the town lifeless once more, just as it had all been for almost forty years.

Norman lowered the rifle and checked his companions. Lucian, wrinkled and squat, was already climbing over the ridge, sending a cascade of stones rolling end over end towards the junction, taking soil and grass with them. Norman clambered over the ridge's lip and followed, descending towards his prize, stopping only to help Allison to her feet. She rose in a cloud of dust, her usual squeamishness hidden behind a disciplined mask.

They fell into step with Lucian without a word and made for the stag, peppering the street with rubble. Once the ridge levelled out, Norman took a deep breath, working the knots of tension from his shoulders. His senses slowly came to life again. He'd been so focused on the stag that he'd forgotten the distant roar of the North Sea and the salty air clinging to the back of his throat.

They crept low and fast, skittering over uneven ground. A sharp gale blew through the streets, lifting some of the mist for a moment, giving them a view of the coast and the remains of Margate. The quaint little town had once catered to seafront tourists, but it was a far cry from its heyday now. Seagulls still took flight from towering white cliffs nearby, diving to catch fish from the surging waves, but that alone remained unchanged.

The wilderness had retaken much of the land since the End. The relics of the Old World had been overgrown and smothered by grasses, vines, and moss, painting the grey and white stonework a speckled green. The wiry trunks of sapling trees thrust their way through foundations, crumbling concrete and tearing plaster. By now, no surface remained untouched by the encroaching foliage.

Though the fallen stag lay only twenty yards from the base of the rise, it took them almost a minute to reach it. Every movement was calculated, necessary. They maintained their rigid stances until they stood over the corpse, and then stood for a further minute in silence, turning in a wide arc to survey the town's many shadows.

Once satisfied that they were alone, their wariness evaporated.

Allison Rutherford's cherub-round face contorted. "I miss beef," she said.

Lucian grunted. "You ain't going to see another cow for a long time—if you ever see one."

"They can't all be gone."

"They bloody well can. Same thing happened with the sheep, Allie, before your time."

Norman watched without saying a word, but couldn't prevent his stomach from rumbling at the thought of steak.

They had all grown thin of late. Most had fared far worse, and by comparison they had enjoyed a luxurious diet. Yet it was becoming ever more difficult to ignore their pronounced cheekbones, their pallid skin, or the manner in which their clothes hung in loose folds around their waists.

Norman glanced down at his hands, filthy and stiff with dried detritus, protruding from grimed sleeves. His fingertips were numb to the coastal breeze, oblivious to its caress. There was no denying it. He was falling apart.

Allie was still looking at the stag resentfully. "It's not the same," she muttered.

"It's food," Lucian said. "Be thankful you have some."

She looked down at him with distaste. Although of average height, she stood almost a head taller than him. Yet her gaze was laced with respect. "All the same, I'd rather not butcher an animal in the street."

Lucian shared no such qualms, and with a flick of his wrist drew a knife across the stag's hide, exposing the crimson tissue beneath. Blood oozed from the open wound.

"I don't know about you," he said, "but I can't wait to get back. What do you think?"

Norman nodded and bent to help. "Let's get it done. We're sitting ducks," he said, trying to ignore how weak and clumsy his own voice sounded. The mud on his face cracked as his cheeks tightened with lines of concentration. Cutting with broad strokes into tendon and gristle, he set about removing the stag's hindquarters.

If they didn't eat they would grow careless, and their efforts to remain hidden over the last few days would have been in vain.

The road was soon deep rouge and their hands became slick with gore, but they were quick and cut with expert care, never wasteful. The carcass deflated as they removed the liver, kidneys and the flesh of the upper limbs, but apart from their incisions, the stag didn't look brutalised.

The three of them pulled out ragged sacks from their trousers, letting the sea breeze blow them open. They stowed the meat, binding the sacks in knots that were given loving attention lest anything escape. Then they stood and looked about, wary once more.

To have their prize stolen now would be too great a loss, especially today.

Watchful of the looming hills, they took up the sacks and fled the bloodied junction, darting over the wreckage of the Old World, into roadside mist.

*

"Do we have everything?" Norman said. He hefted one of the bags of meat onto his mount's back, struggling under its weight. The stallion snorted and shuffled, restless, but took the load. He patted its muzzle, despite himself eyeing the rippling lean meat of its shoulders.

If we didn't have to forage so far from home just to scrape by, you'd be only so much stew, he thought. *And, if things don't pick up, that's exactly where you'll end up.*

Allie was hunched over a small pile of yellowed paper, crouched atop a large, smooth stone. She rifled through the pages, muttering to herself, pointing from each sheet to a corresponding bag or package, ticking things off.

A small fire crackled in the centre of their makeshift campsite. Lucian was boiling some water in a billycan suspended from three sticks wedged at opposing angles. The clearing was shielded from view by a thick shrubbery on one side and by the sheer edge of a large cliff on the other, forty feet from where they sat. Three horses were tied at the edge of the clearing, chewing away at the sparse grains in the bags hanging from their snouts.

Allie looked up and shook her head. "Heather needs more supplies. Bandages and sutures, mostly, but we can't afford to go over to the chemist. It's on the other side of town. Besides, Ray said that it was picked clean a few weeks ago. Somebody must have passed through. But we definitely need more food."

"We'll go back tonight and come for the food tomorrow," Lucian said.

"There is no food," Allison said, and the pages tumbled from her hands.

"It's a bad year, that's all."

"We've had bad years before. This is different," Allison muttered. She pulled an ugly face. "We can't keep doing this. All we're doing is moving up the coast and taking all that we can carry. That's not a survival tactic, it's just buying time."

"We're alive."

"There won't be enough for anybody else. They're starving as it is, and here we are swooping in and taking it all for ourselves."

Lucian was quiet for a moment. "We don't have a choice," he said.

"We can't keep it up all year." She turned to Norman. "What should we do?"

Norman started. "What?" he said.

"What should we do?" she demanded.

Lucian also looked over, but his stare lacked the deference of Allison's. The two of them watched and waited for a reply while Norman shifted uncomfortably.

"Why ask me?" he said.

Allison looked taken aback. "It's your job," she said. "You'll lead when Alex is gone. Lead all of us. It's in all the stories."

"I know the stories!"

"So, what should we do?"

"It's not my job to make decisions."

"It will be, one day."

Norman drew his coat closer about him. "Not yet," he said.

"Soup's up," Lucian said, lifting the billycan and pouring three portions into cups of ancient steel. "I had to get the water from the stream. If you swallow it fast enough you won't taste the mud."

Norman took his ration and walked around the edge of the camp, making final checks.

This would make the third supply run of the fortnight. An ordinary year usually saw a group being sent monthly for razors or clothing, but this year they needed food, and lots of it.

There were many mouths to feed.

He drained his soup and turned the cup skyward, coaxing out the last few drops. It tasted of grit and rotting plant matter, but it was warm. For that, he had learned to be grateful.

The ferns ended at the tree line, and he emerged onto a patch of grass lining the cliff edge. Behind him, Allie and Lucian stamped out the fire, each of their footsteps meeting the ground with a sharp crackle of dead leaves. He watched them break the sticks that had held the billycan and throw them into the underbrush. They then set about hauling the last of the sacks from the ground.

Norman looked at the sea, hundreds of feet below. The air was fresh out in the open and untarnished by the smell of horse manure or unwashed bodies. The chilled sea breeze brushed his hair away from his dirt-stricken face, ruffling his stiff clothes.

The grass was long and scattered with rough brambles, peppered by a handful of vibrant, vivid flowers. He hadn't seen such things for countless weeks. He took a deep breath, absorbing a momentary peace.

It would be some time before he'd get another chance.

Looking out at the rugged, rubble-strewn landscape, it was hard to believe that human beings had once reigned supreme.

Norman had never seen it with his own eyes—at twenty-nine, he hadn't even been born when the lights had still burned. Forty years before, the Old World had ended. Now, so much time had passed that most were too young to know how things had once been. All they had were the elders' stories—stories of power, of knowledge, of bustling billions.

They said the planet had been silenced in a single instant. That towns, cities—entire countries, even—had been emptied without warning. That less than one in a thousand lives had been spared, the rest cut short in the space of a single second when the vast majority of the world's population had, quite suddenly, vanished without a trace. Left behind, the few scattered survivors had been faced with a struggle for survival, bewildered and alone.

Now, after forty years, just when everything had been on the verge of recovering, famine had arrived. And it was taking its toll.

The world, or what was left of it, was fading.

What had for so long been green and wild was now brittle and wilting, starved of life. Instead of continuing its merciless advance, retaking arable land and smothering the remains of the world's towns and cities, vegetation lay limp on the ground, drying in the sun. Stems cracked open in the heat and creepers rolled in the wind, crumbling to dust underfoot.

The previous autumn had brought with it a plague that had levelled forests and great fields of wheat alike. What the last of the world's farmers had worked to cultivate over the decades since the End had been felled in mere weeks— had become blackened and rotten before hungry eyes. Only the grasses, a few species of trees and the hardiest of shrubs had been unaffected, none of which bore sustenance. Nobody knew why the underbrush and forests had been spared and continued to flourish, lush and thick. It was another mystery, another danger, another worry.

In a world already reeling from disaster, the population had been sparse and scattered, numbering in the thousands only, but still people had starved. What had been a trifling hunger in early winter had by New Year almost become a death knell for the human race. No end to the spreading devastation had lain in sight.

That had been months ago. Summer was now on the horizon, and the crisis had passed its zenith. In its wake it had left the world emptier and darker.

Decades before, there had been bustling metropolises, surging channels of traffic and airwaves alive with voices. After the End, there had been whispers, a shadow of civilisation that had endured for over a generation.

Now there was only a deep silence.

Norman sighed and turned away from the sea, retreating back into the shade. As soon as he faced the forest once more, he realised that something was wrong. At the same time, the horses became agitated, stomping and whinnying, pulling at their tethers. They trampled some of the sacks at their feet, spilling their contents onto the ground.

Lucian and Allie leapt away from the flurry of hooves. They landed without a single rustle, and silence fell over them as they crouched low to the ground. They dashed to the trunk of an old elm, snatching their weapons from a notch in its gnarled roots.

At once the horses quietened and stopped midstomp, their whinnies caught in their throats. They snuffled and milled, turning back and forth, straining against their tethers and watching their masters.

Men, woman and beasts waited in silence, until muscles ached and sweat broke out on the backs of their necks. Somewhere high above, a crow cawed and took flight. The sound of movement was carried on the wind, off to their right. Something was pushing through dense shrubbery not sixty feet from them. It was moving through towards the junction, towards the stag's corpse.

Norman, Allie and Lucian tracked the noise with pricked ears for over a minute before it died without warning, to be replaced by an anguished groan.

Norman shuddered as the hairs on his neck stood on end despite the stifling heat of the campsite. But it wasn't until a second source of rustling emanated from the opposite direction, followed by yet more groaning, that the beginnings of fear stirred in his gut. The noise carried and echoed in the forest, warped by the breeze into a ghostly wail.

Lucian gestured to the horses, then to the small path they had cleared, leading away from the camp and along the edge of the cliff.

The groaning had once again been replaced by the sound of movement. But it was pitiful now, a mere rustle, and grew no closer. Then from the distance came a single pained cry, deafening in the strained hush. For a moment there was silence, save for the chattering of a flock of passing gulls and the booming of the waves far below.

And then another cry answered, far louder and nearer than the first, emanating from just a few yards away— beyond the screening of ash and elm that shielded the campsite from view.

Norman took a steadying breath, glancing at the horses, and then looked to Allie and Lucian. He raised his hands, moving them in a deft series of predetermined signals:

What do you see?

After a pause, they both signed back:

Nothing.

Norman cursed.

Which way?

Lucian replied:

Straight ahead.

Norman stared into the trees until his eyes ached from the strain, but he too could see nothing. Despite the slithering fear in his gut, he began to inch towards the trees, followed closely by Lucian, with Allie creeping at the rear. Now even the tiny and unavoidable noises that he produced seemed amplified, and each one made him wince with dread.

The groaning came again, and this time it was very close—only feet away. They froze in the underbrush and listened until it came again, so near that it sent them flinching backwards, solid as a gale.

Once again, despite his apprehension, Norman found himself moving forward. Lucian's harshly whispered warning did nothing to slow his pace, and together the three of them advanced on the source of the noise.

When Norman heard the groan a final time, he gasped. It had come from directly below him. He looked into the ferns at his feet and saw somebody staring up at him through a screen of underbrush.

It was a man, or at least had been. His body was deathly pale, so emaciated that his face was no more than a skull clothed in skin, his ribs protruding at an extreme angle.

The three of them looked down at him as he met their gaze. A tiny groan escaped his throat. He reached forward with skeletal fingers but could scarcely manage a few inches from the ground. "Please," he said. His voice was tiny, defeated. "P-Please…help us."

Another groan rang out from behind them. Norman whirled to see another deflated body, prone beside the trunk of a nearby tree, too ruined for its gender to be discernible. Then he saw the others—over a dozen people strewn across the ground. Some lay still, putrefying, but others called out, reaching for the newcomers.

In the distance, he could hear the whimpers and groans of many more. Norman backed away from them, unspeaking.

"Please," the man below him repeated. He was still trying to reach for them, but could no longer lift his hand from the ground.

Norman turned to the other two:

Let's go.

Allison's young, rounded face softened. This time signing was unnecessary. Her response was obvious from her eyes alone:

We can't.

Lucian and Norman exchanged a glance, and Lucian gave him the tiniest of nods. Together, they took Allie by the shoulders. She began thrashing against them, tears seeping from her eyes, but she couldn't have weighed more than a hundred and twenty pounds, and so they dragged her away from the bodies without hindrance. Their silent struggle raged as they walked, fighting back towards the horses. Soon, Allison's waving arms were accompanied by a stifled gargle in her throat.

They dragged her nonetheless, leaving gouges in the ground as they went, hushing her with warning glances and fingers mashed against their lips.

Her protests lessened as they neared the horses and she was pushed up onto the back of her mare. She then abandoned the pursuit and took to haughty silence, but her eyes remained trained in the direction of the helpless creatures. She pointed to the floor, where split packages of food lay tangled around the horses' hooves.

Norman climbed onto his own mount's saddle and answered with shaking hands:

Leave it.

He took hold of his reins, ignoring the self-hatred that welled up in the pit of his stomach. He wanted nothing more than to rush back to the fallen and drag them to safety, but their supplies would do no good for so many mouths, and the people in the clearing were already past the point of no return.

He lingered a moment to close his eyes and take a breath, and then kicked at the horse's sides. With a snort the steed burst from the tree line, racing out over the fields that bordered the cliff, with Lucian and Allie's mounts thundering along behind.

The bags strapped to Norman's saddle jostled, their contents threatening to bounce free and fall out of sight. Norman did his best to close those nearest to his hands, but had limited opportunity, snatching wild grabs only when the ground was even enough. He saw several pieces of fruit spiral away into the grass, each worth more than its weight in gold.

The wind streamed against his face as Lucian and Allie pulled up beside him. Once abreast one another, they hurried along the edge of the cliff. The ground ahead soon levelled and cleared of foliage, carpeted only by yellow grass cropped short by the stag's former harem, which scattered in a blur of fur and hooves. It was getting late. Fading light was dancing on the waves near the horizon.

Looking left for a moment, Norman saw Lucian's silver-haired figure bouncing atop his equally silver stallion. He was pointing behind them, bellowing something made incomprehensible by the whistling wind.

Norman looked over his shoulder. The forest beneath the tree line was dark and thrown out of focus by their galloping pace, but he could still see the black shapes amongst the shadows, edging out into the field.

The emaciated people were crawling in pursuit of their fleeing chance of salvation. From a distance it was difficult to make out any detail, but nonetheless Norman felt a chill run down his spine.

He cursed, turning to face the road ahead. He could feel Allie's gaze burning into his temple, but didn't dare look at her. Instead, he tugged on his reins and steered his mount until they rode parallel to a small stream, and headed home.

FIRST INTERLUDE

The day of the apocalypse started like any other: a lazy mid-June Tuesday in the late noughties that passed without incident until, at precisely 08.15 Greenwich Mean Time, the End struck.

There were no warnings or signs, nor was there hysteria or panic. The people of the world were waking in their beds, watching their favourite soaps, sitting in traffic, laughing, eating, or fast asleep. Perhaps for a single moment, as one, they felt an odd sensation in their bones and a chill in their lungs, coupled with a white-hot pain in their extremities.

Unfortunately, there wasn't enough time for them to react before their bodies dissolved into vapour and they vanished from existence.

Then it was over. The disaster had come and gone, the clocks had stopped ticking, and the world was changed forever.

An instant later, upon the lawns of a backwater Cumbrian village, a young man fell to the ground, screaming and alone.

*

Cold. Raw, gnawing agony.

Alexander Cain was surrounded by darkness. He was suffocating on a vast, viscous something that filled his mouth, throat and lungs. Whether he was spinning and falling, or whether the world was spinning and falling around him, he couldn't tell. All he knew was that *something* was moving at breakneck speed, tearing at his body amidst an endless void.

Here, there was no time. Forever was now, now was forever, and nothing new could ever be. He would remain here until the infinite had grown small, and everything had faded completely.

And yet, eventually, something emerged from the ether, something that seemed to consume all else: a light. The faintest, most distant light. It was above. There was no direction here, and yet Alex was certain that the light was *higher*—was *up*.

He thrashed and fought his way towards it. The void shrank back and his body pressed against a great barrier, one that stretched and ripped at him with vicious talons. He was being pierced by icy tendrils. The void was pulling him back, desperate to hold onto him.

For the briefest of moments it was over—he didn't exist at all—and then he broke into the world beyond.

*

The first thing he became aware of was his own screaming voice. The next was the agony, which had followed from the void. The spinning ceased with a jarring jolt, slamming his eighteen-year-old body against unseen ground with bone-crushing force.

The darkness had been replaced by blinding light. Dense fog surrounded him on all sides, and above was a sky of midmorning baby-blue tones, complete with wispy tracts of stratocumulus.

From every direction came an ear-splitting ring, pressing in on him with percussive force, a decibel short of perforating his eardrums. His jaw clenched hard enough to pop a filling free from a premolar. The tendons on his neck, arms and legs tensed to breaking point, drawing him into a ball upon freshly cut grass.

He was shivering—no, quivering. It was cold enough for a layer of frost to have accrued on his body, puckering his skin and clinging to his hair in icy shards. Through double vision and barely opened eyes he could make out his own hands, gnarled and curled into claws akin to those produced by advanced arthritis.

He was granted a small mercy then, a momentary lull—a split second during which the fabric of existence seemed to undulate, almost to pulse. The sky rippled with ribbons of impossible colours, auroras that dwarfed any that had ever been seen over the Earth's poles. With those colours came intense sensation: the grass caressed his skin with a passion that surpassed that of the most dedicated lover's.

And then pain washed over him with renewed vigour, blanketing all else as the ringing reached an unbearable crescendo, driving him across the floor as though with a booted foot. An unbroken wail stormed from his throat, but he heard no trace of it. If the noise persisted he would go mad. He was certain of it.

He wished for death, for peace. As he writhed and bellowed upon the grass, the sky lost its ribbons of absurd colours, and the screech intensified a final time. A small part of him registered a sudden, crushing absence in the world, and he realised with horror that the screech was not artificial, not alien or cold-minded, but the product of billions of screams no different from his own.

This was the last moment, the brink of insanity. He was at an end—

...

...

Silence.

The world was still, without pain. Warmth kissed his skin.

Alex blinked.

High above, the sky was blue—just blue. His hands fell from ears accosted by nothing but the chirps of a distant chaffinch. The frosty glaze upon his skin was gone. He was dry, no longer shivering.

He took a hesitant breath, heard his strained throat whistle with the gentle inhalation. He kept still for over a minute, too afraid of the nightmare's return to move an inch.

When nothing came, he tried moving his fingers. They wriggled feebly, brushing fresh grass cuttings. Once he had grown confident enough to sit up, a great many aches and pains shot through his body, but he scarcely noticed.

The thick, swirling mist remained. A few feet of visible ground lay in any one direction before the blanket of fog took over. All that he could make out through its depths were the ghostly outlines of nearby trees, and the faraway fence that skirted the park—

The park.

With a sudden rush of recollection, Alexander remembered: the morning school rush, the last-minute revision for the finals, the mad dash through the park in the blind hope of a shortcut…and then darkness.

He had been on his way to the last exam of the summer, the one upon which his entire future pivoted. And now he was certainly late, perhaps too late.

It must have been a fit. He'd heard of people having stress-induced seizures before.

But the exam boards wouldn't let a little thing like a nervous breakdown keep them from starting on time.

The emergency room could wait. For now, there was a desk nearby with his name on it.

Ignoring his injuries, along with any thoughts of the macabre dream-void, he pushed himself into a standing position and hefted his bag—laden with the great tomes of Hardy, Faulkner and Steinbeck that had been decreed as the year's set texts—onto his shoulder.

He wobbled on his feet and put a hand to his eyes, squeezing his forehead as a wave of nausea washed over him. He looked around again, spitting the remains of his popped filling into the leaf litter, tasting blood.

The mist encircled him, unbothered by wind or the heat of the still-rising sun. There were no signs to indicate that anybody or anything lay near him. He was alone on the slight rise that marked Lovers' Leap, which overlooked the town of Radden.

He paused, speechless. His memory of the morning was clearing. He should not have been alone. The park was a popular cut-in point for those late for the eight o'clock bell, and he had been surrounded on all sides by over a dozen stragglers, each as desperate to make the exam's sit-down time.

Now they were gone.

But there was something else, something all the more jarring: there had been no mist as he'd entered the park. None at all. Only moments ago, it had been a perfect, clear summer morning.

Alex cursed, spinning on the spot. His head was as clouded as the air around him, and so only two possibilities presented themselves. Either the fit had been more serious than he'd thought, and he'd been unconscious for some time—long enough for bad weather to have rolled in off the coast—or something terrible had happened.

The latter struck him as infinitely more likely. There was something about the absolute silence and the soupy nature of the mist that suggested something was very wrong.

He was on the verge of setting off down the hill, while his mind's eye offered him images of the town having been levelled by a terrorist bombing or freak storm, when he began to pass piles of clothing.

The first few he registered as only shapes in his peripheral vision, but within a few steps a dozen or so had emerged from the mist, not quite neatly stacked in the grass: jackets, shirts and blouses, denim jeans and skirts, underwear of every shade and pattern, and socks of all lengths, tucked into the inners of a dozen pairs of shoes. A few were topped by objects unique enough to set them apart, and to allow Alex to identify their owners: Simon Wells's flat cap, Connie Black's spiked choker, Sally Macklintock's nose bar and hooped earrings, and nearest to him was a pile topped by the headphone wires of Jerry Peter's iPod. Beside them were heavily stuffed bags all too similar to Alex's own. They lay precisely where his fellow stragglers had been before his blackout. But their owners were nowhere to be seen. It was almost as though they had stripped naked, calmly dropped their belongings in perfect head-to-foot sequence, and walked away into the mist. Or they had quite simply vanished.

Disbelief throbbed in his head, which had set about a fantastic panic. Only the sheer strangeness of what his senses were telling him kept his eyes from rolling back in their sockets.

"Hello?" he called. His voice bled away down the hillside, utterly alone except for the twittering of faraway songbirds. An echo returned from where the trill of the town's morning traffic should have emanated. That was enough to send him running.

Alex left the stacks of clothing behind. Within a single bounding step they'd disappeared into the mist. He ran with his arms outstretched, fearful of running into a lamppost or fence at full speed. He tripped every other step, and was sure he would break an ankle any moment, but was powerless to stop his own advance. His thoughts had abandoned him, leaving a baser part of his mind to operate on instinct alone.

Distantly, he was aware that he remained parallel to the slope, still moving towards the school. The notion of still trying to make the exam on time was so bizarre that he almost laughed—but he was sure that if he did, then the wild scream of terror lurking behind his tongue would break free, and hysteria would swallow him whole.

He was less than a hundred yards from the gates of Radden High when the mist departed. It did so without warning, as though a gale had torn across the land and peeled it away. The lifeless mass of thick whiteness seemed to expand, wither and twirl upwards simultaneously, revealing Radden and the great moorland in which it sat.

Alex froze. "No," he whispered. He shook his head, as though he could jar the world back to making sense. But the absurdities before his eyes remained.

The town was untouched, pristine. The cliffside gathering of Victorian terrace-rows twinkled in the morning light, along with an outlying halo of ancient cottages and farmsteads. Together, they were a twee mass of autumnal-shaded roof tiles and rustic brickwork amidst the moor's vast reaches. The town appeared as it had done on any other day, and at first he could have expected the distant whistle of the Marshall-Aimes Quarry over in Bleak to ring at any moment, kicking off the morning shift.

But then he saw that there was a very good reason for the silence.

The town centre was still a considerable distance away, but Alex could make out thousands of piles of clothing strewn across Radden's streets, arranged in little piles identical to those in the park.

Not a single person was in sight. All was still and lifeless, frozen in place.

Alex did scream then. Once. It broke free from his lips as a single, ragged cry, not dissimilar to that of a wounded animal.

And then he was running once more, moving on legs that seemed a million miles away. The school forgotten, he made for home. If he could make it back to his room, back to his bed, then he would surely wake from this hellish double nightmare—for that was all this could be: a delusion brought on by fatigue, twelve-hour study marathons and one too many cups of coffee.

It wasn't until a final blow had been dealt that this last semblance of hope died a quiet death.

When the great blaze on High Street burst to life, it reached some sixty feet into the air. Alex had made it to the first of the outlying terrace-blocks when it roared forth from the twisted wreckage of a severe road accident, which had involved over two dozen vehicles. Their crushed and shredded aluminium shells were cast in the brilliant light of igniting fuel, and then a fireball enveloped the mass, blowing out every window for thirty feet and throwing a great column of jet-black smoke into the sky.

Alex didn't pause, not this time. He kept running while the flames began to lick higher. Around him the alarms of shop fronts and parked cars honked and trilled, the only sounds other than his ragged breathing and the hollow slapping of his shoes against the tarmac. He drew closer, and from even a hundred yards away began to receive mouthfuls of acrid smoke, along with the first waves of heat.

The bulk of the accident appeared to have been caused by a twelve-wheeler that had fishtailed at the intersection and then toppled onto its side. It had from then on acted as a solid wall, stretching across the breadth of the street. Vans, cars and motorbikes had proceeded to splatter against its underside like flies against a swatter.

Alex coughed, stumbling as a gag reflex wracked his upper body, but pressed on, driven by a surge of adrenaline. While the bellow of the fire enveloped the trills and honks, and his breathing became laboured due to the growing heat, he threw desperate glances around at the upper-floor windows on either side of the street.

By the time his lungs seared in earnest and he was mere feet from the first of the flames, nothing had stirred. Not a single curtain had been disturbed by a parting hand, nor had a concerned face graced one of the many doorways.

He passed into the column of acrid smoke, and the world was whipped away under a sheet of black. Holding his shirtsleeve to his mouth to keep out the worst of the fumes, he gagged without pause, blinking tears from his eyes. Flames reared up on either side, and the hairs on his arms began to char as his sweat evaporated, leaving behind a tightly packed residue of salt and grit. His throat and lungs soon became lined with ash despite his makeshift sleeve mask, and he choked most of the way to the first of the cars.

The flames were almost too bright to see through, and had rendered most of the windshields translucent. While a great many tyres melted and unexploded fuel tanks threatened to extinguish his life any moment, Alex skirted the edge of the pileup and scanned the wreckage for any sign of survivors.

Flaming headrests, billowing airbags, crumpled steering columns. But no bodies. Nothing. Through the few panes of glass still transparent, it was quite clear that each vehicle was devoid of occupants.

Alex froze, dumbstruck. Somewhere distant, he told himself to move, that his now oxygen-starved mind was stuck trying to cope with what he was seeing, but he had to *move*. With superhuman effort he forced shaking limbs to send him leaping to the other side of the street. Choking, he emerged into fresher air and cast another desperate search around him. He put his hands on his knees and bent over, spitting tendrils of blackened saliva onto the curb. By the time he could straighten again he was still breathing raggedly, but the urge to vomit had eased.

Then a scream of pain rang out behind him. He winced instinctively. The very tone of it—the shrill, panicked trill of a trapped animal—cut at him like glass. "HELP ME!" It was emanating from the heart of the flaming wreckage, from the carcass of a yellow executive saloon sandwiched fast to the bulk of the eighteen-wheeler.

Alex was already springing forward when he spotted a figure across the street, just beyond the pavement, beneath the shadow of an old oak. His impression of it was fleeting, but detailed enough to send shivers of relief coursing through him. It was a man in his mid thirties, dressed head to toe in what looked like a black overcoat. Upon his lupine, marble-coloured face were two streaks of purple-black directly beneath his eyes—maybe eyeshadow, maybe not. A strange half-smile was plastered over his face, his gaze fixed resolutely on Alex, almost as though the blaze between them weren't there at all. Despite his relief,

Alex felt something stir in his gut: an irrational fear response, one that nudged at him with alarm bells ringing.

What was wrong with him? There wasn't time for turning help away, oddball or not. Help was help. Pushing suspicion aside, he fished his mobile phone from his pocket. "You! Hello? Help!" he called, waving his arms over his head, heading for the saloon. "There's somebody trapped! Give me a hand!" As the fire licked at the passenger window, a hand struck against the translucent glass, followed by the profile of a terrified face.

At the driver's door there were no flames, and so without hesitation Alex grabbed the handle. He screamed as the scolding metal ate at his flesh, and drew his hand back up his sleeve, cradling it against his side, cursing. Before the pain could set in and send him reeling away from the wreckage, he bunched what remained of his sleeve further over his burned arm, gritted his teeth, manoeuvred the swelling hand back towards the door, and pulled it open.

A young man dressed in a cheap suit and matching tie tumbled out onto the ground, his jacket trailing a carpet of flames. He had been brown-haired from what Alex could tell, but his eyebrows and most of his crown had been burned clean away. All over his body the skin was blackened and had taken on the texture of charcoal in palm-sized patches. He shivered in teeth-chattering judders, as though freezing.

Alex recognised him. It was Paul Towers, a junior partner at Aimes & Logan Law. He had been quite the town mascot of late, having turned away from a bad path of heavy drinking a few summers before. Paul had been the focus of attention for the Moor's crop of young women since hitting puberty due to his floppy fringe, striking good looks, and sharp '*I know what I want*' stare—something that was now almost impossible to believe.

Paul tried to move away, but simply whimpered and collapsed onto the bubbling tarmac. Alex grabbed him by the arm and dragged him from the crash site, towards the side of the road. Struggling, he felt yet more grit and ash cling to his face, caking him in a thick paste, adhering to the rivulets of perspiration streaming down his cheeks. By the time they reached the kerb, the fire had burned his eyes dry, and streams of tears had joined the grimed rivers of sweat. Even here, waves of heat still buffeted his body.

He glanced up at the man he had seen across the street, expecting to see him making his way over to their side. But the figure was standing in precisely the same spot, still staring at him with that same half-smile. He didn't seem at all concerned, nor did he even seem as though preparing to step forwards. Instead, he merely cocked his head, as though fascinated by their scurrying.

"HELP!" Alex bellowed.

The figure cocked its head the other way, but moved no more.

Alex felt his heart skip a beat from sheer disbelief.

Had the man not heard him? Surely he had. Perhaps he'd been struck dumb by the sheer oddity of what was happening. Or maybe he just didn't care.

The figure's gaze pressed hard into Alex's temple as he fumbled with his mobile phone. The hell with him. He hit dial, blinking until his vision cleared. But the screen was blank. He beat against the phone's underside, but there was no response. It was dead.

He cast it aside with a curse of fury and bent over Paul, who was shaking on the ground. "Can you hear me?" he said.

Paul merely whimpered.

Alex glanced up again, saw the figure still standing beneath the tree—now staring across at him with an expression closer to a jeering leer—and then looked away. He didn't bother to call out again.

"I have to turn you over," he said. He meant to sound confident, but his voice cracked, trembling in the air. In the back of his mind he knew he shouldn't touch Paul until an ambulance arrived. With those burns, he could do more harm than good. But a firm voice from somewhere even deeper told him there would be no help coming anytime soon. And so, before Paul could protest, Alex grabbed him and turned him over in a single swift movement.

Alex saw the pain in his eyes. Paul's mouth opened in what could only be described as beyond screaming. Tears dripped down his face onto the pavement as a tiny sound escaped from deep in his throat. Blood was oozing from a slash across his forehead, revealing the startlingly white skull beneath. Alex checked his body and saw that the front of his shirt was gone. The flames had eaten through the flesh of his belly, such that a horrific mash of charred skin and blood-red muscle tissue lay where his navel had been.

Alex flung his hands to his mouth as a wave of nausea swept over him. He turned away to the grass and vomited with a great heave. Fighting black rings encroaching in his peripheral vision, he fought his way back to Paul, who now had only one eye half open, unfixed and catatonic.

"I don't know what to do... I'm sorry," Alex breathed. "I'm sorry, I'm so sorry... There's nobody here. I—I..."

Hyperventilating, he looked around in desperation for the figure once more, ready to surge to his feet and drag the static onlooker from the shadows. But his eyes were met only by the sight of the old oak, unblemished by the figure's presence. He'd vanished, just like everyone else.

Alex accepted it without argument, too blank and addled to cope with any more. He was spared instant insanity only by Paul's sudden bout of gargled choking. Alex grabbed him by the collar. "Hey," he yelled. "Hey!"

Paul's eyes flew open. For the briefest of moments he stared skyward, his face blank, almost peaceful, and then he began to vibrate against the ground. With his feet hammering the floor, he whined while his head snapped back and forth in vicious spasms.

Alex could only moan, clinging to the writhing body. "Are there others?" he cried. "Are there others? Please, tell me!" He was wailing now. "Tell me there's somebody else!"

No answer. It took almost a minute for Paul to become still. Alex checked for a pulse, then stumbled back, sat on the kerb, mouth open with shock, and put his head between his knees. "This isn't happening," he whispered to the grass. "This can't be happening."

When he finally stumbled away from Paul's body, he didn't bother searching for the eyeshadow-wearing figure again. He probably hadn't even been real. Instead, he wandered back towards the rise of Lovers' Leap.

He stumbled back through the streets and across the park. Countless piles of clothing and jewellery passed underfoot, occasionally accompanied by handbags, briefcases and infants' pushchairs. It all seemed to glare at him, daring him to stray too close.

He skirted each item in a daze, ascending the hill without as much as a single glance from his path. His mind was muggy, enamelled, too shocked to register much of anything. In what seemed only moments he was scaling the steep incline that marked the crest of the Leap.

It would be fine. He would signal for help. By now the government or army had mobilised a response to the terrible accident in the Moor, and were on their way in full force, accompanied by herds of gabbling reporters from around the world. He would be surrounded by press, harried by intelligence officers for an explanation, tested for alien probing, and dragged into the limelight as the sole survivor of the Radden Moor Disaster.

But he would be alive. He would be safe.

He sobbed as the desperate, paper-thin sentiment cracked and fragmented in the face of what he knew awaited him just on the other side of the rise. As he tore his way over the crest of the Leap and looked down upon the lands below, he saw that his imagination's worst predictions hadn't been far wrong. But that did nothing to lighten the blow.

From here he could see for miles over the countryside—the entirety of Radden Moor and a crowd of neighbouring towns, along with the stretch of dual carriageway that snaked between them.

Far away, nestled in a nook of coastal mountains, was Bleakstone Down, and perched directly above it the village of Lorndale. On any other day they would have appeared as little more than distant smatterings of antiquated spires and chimneys. Today, they were invisible behind a column of smoke as black as the one rising from Radden Moor, courtesy of a blaze that seemed to have consumed Lisey's Bar 'n Grill in Bleak. Alex suspected that the morning run of the good lady's famous bacon-and-mushroom omelettes had charred to combustion point without her there to flip them.

Alex's gaze swept across the moorland lakes, which glistened silver-white in the sun, and every other settlement in sight—Chester Walden, Stanfield, Eppinsborough, Langlebridge, Finstynne, Tinners' Lodge, and, nestled between the slopes of Porters' Pass, at the very edge of visibility, the twinkling lights of Milton Percy's radio tower—scanning farther back into the distance until his line of sight met the horizon.

Every one of them was utterly still. Unattended toasters, gas hobs, careening motor vehicles and hair straighteners had sent at least three of them up in flames along with Radden Moor and Bleak.

There was not a single person in sight. Thousands of cars, trucks and coaches sat on the dual carriageway, most in pieces, torn into great mountains of shrapnel and shattered glass. Some had careened through the centre divider or into the wooded ditches that ran downhill on either side of the tarmac, having by chance avoided total destruction. No attempt at braking had been made, for their drivers had vanished along with everyone else. Their motors still ticked amidst the fields and creek beds where they had come to rest.

Alex sank to his knees, covering his eyes with his hands, and let loose a wail of bewilderment. Once that first cry had escaped him, he was powerless to stop those that followed, and merely sat watching the flames, clutching at the grass. His screams rang out until his throat had become raw, the distant smoke columns had blossomed into rippling firestorms, and the monstrous carcasses of transcontinental airliners had begun to fall from the sky.

No screams answered his, nor did anyone cry out to be rescued from the burning wreckage. The world had grown still and silent.

He was alone.

Norman called a halt and pulled the reins towards his lap. His mount took a single step farther before coming to a stop, snorting in the evening gloom.

Allie stopped beside him but said nothing. Her mouth was pulled into a tight grimace.

"You're still mad," Norman said.

She was quiet for some time before responding, "How could you do that?"

He leaned from his saddle until they were almost face to face. "There was nothing we could have done. We can barely feed ourselves."

She rounded on him, her eyes flaring. "We could have helped. We could have done something. We could have given them something."

Norman shook his head as he watched Lucian ride across the field behind them. His steel-grey hair and horse to match made him difficult to miss amidst the meadow of browning grass, even when he stopped abreast the posts of an ancient wooden fence, scanning the horizon.

"We knew that people were starving," Norman said, sighing.

"That doesn't make it all right."

Allie took an apple from one of the bags swinging beneath her saddle and looked at it for a while. She soon took a bite, but her expression was disgusted.

"You ought to save those," Norman said, motioning to the bag. "We had to leave a lot behind."

She swallowed with a heavy gulp, as though to make a point of defying even so small an order, but when she replied her voice had fallen to a mere whisper. "At least they have that much."

"Allie…"

"How could we leave them?"

Norman turned to her. "What do you want me to do?" he said.

"I don't know. *Something.*"

"It's not my job to make those kinds of decisions."

"It's going to be."

"I'm not a leader," Norman hissed. "I didn't ask for this."

There was a pause.

"For what?" she said.

Norman gestured to the sacks beneath them. "For this!"

Lucian, over by the fence, held up his hand to give the all-clear signal. He then wheeled around and rode back towards them, turning his head occasionally to peer over his shoulder, as though fearful of taking an arrow to the back. His face was creased into an ugly frown.

He pulled up beside them and grumbled to himself, brushing a tangle of iron-wool hair from his face. He looked to Allie, and then the apple in her hand. "Got another one of those?"

She threw him her own. "You didn't see anything?" she said.

He shook his head, taking a bite. "There's nobody there."

"They couldn't have followed us anyway," she said. Her eyes were swimming with sorrow.

Lucian's gaze settled on her. "We were stealing from them, don't forget that," he said.

"I'll never forget that."

Allie turned her mare towards the slight rise before them. Norman and Lucian followed without question, sharing a meaningful look. Lucian put on an encouraging voice, addressing her in an upbeat tone entirely unlike his usual grumble, "Those people had been starving for a long time. We didn't do any harm."

She didn't answer, but Norman thought he saw her shoulders relax somewhat as they reached the foot of the hill.

The horses snorted to each other as they began to climb, their hooves slipping on wet mud, uprooting tufts of gnarled, dead grass as they went. They lost traction and slid backwards several times, but they were urged on by swift kicks to their flanks, and soon crested the ridge.

Norman felt a weight lift from his chest. Raised high over the landscape, they could now see for several miles in every direction. The sun was dipping below the horizon, sending the world into a deeper state of shadow.

Below were the remains of what had once been Canterbury. Surrounding it on three sides were wild fields and barren farmland, growing darker by the second, being consumed by a monochromatic haze. On the remaining side were cultivated fields, but the crops lay limp and dying, close to the ground, in various stages of decomposition.

The city itself looked much like it had done many decades before. Most of the buildings were crafted from solid stone, and had been built long before the previous century. In the mere forty years since the End, they had changed little. The jagged architecture was lent a stark beauty by the dying light; the winding streets and quaint cobbled roads rendered in a picturesque golden tint. After the horrors of the coastal ruins, it was a sight born of fairy tale and dreamscape, brought forth by the magic of dusk.

The city was now home to eight hundred people, the largest settlement for at least thirty miles. As the trio watched from the hilltop, distant booms echoed from the riverside, and a portion of the city became illuminated by sharp artificial light. The lampposts of the north-eastern labyrinthine streets blinked to life in rapid succession, leaving the uninhabited, unlit remainder to darken further towards obscurity.

Snaking through the city's centre, the river Stour reflected a thousand twinkling lights—a thin ribbon of silver-white, meandering its way through the city's heart. In the distance, the great cathedral was outlined in profile against the sky, its innards emanating a spectral glow through its many-coloured windows. Its mighty spires thrust towards the sky, towering above their surroundings, monuments to a bygone era, lording over their own private Lilliput.

They simply sat for a while and watched. Norman sighed, comforted by the sight of the city's lights rallying against nature, pushing back the shadows. In his twenty-nine years, he'd never seen anywhere quite like it.

Here, at least tonight, nobody would starve. Here was home.

It had only been a few days since he'd last laid eyes on it, but it felt as though it could have been years.

Ablaze with light, the inhabited pocket of the city looked like a glowing torch, suspended in fading limbo. In the growing darkness it was becoming quieter atop the hill, and the lights drew them like sailors to a siren.

"I need a shower," Allie said, setting off down the hill.

Norman and Lucian watched her go until she was out of earshot.

"She's right. The time's now. You need to start taking charge," Lucian muttered.

Norman ground his teeth, but kept his voice level. "I've told you… I've told all of you: I don't want this."

"We're going to need somebody to step up soon. Alex isn't going to be around forever. And you need to be ready to take over when the time comes."

"If somebody needs to step up so bad, then why don't you do it?"

"Because it was always going to be you. Alex has spent the better part of twenty years getting you ready for it."

"That's just it: he *picked* me. I didn't ask for this."

"Your parents thought you could do it. They died as much for Alex as they did to save you, to make sure you had the chance to be what we need. You might have your doubts now, but it doesn't matter. You *are* going to lead." Despite his emphatic delivery, Lucian's words were flat, regurgitated. Not his own, but Alexander's.

Norman had heard it all a million times over. He whirled on his saddle, his teeth gritted. "This conversation's so worn that it's like a bad joke. But no matter how many times you spit out that same old speech, there's some part of me that thinks maybe you don't believe it at all. The others might think I'm some kind of saint, but not you."

Lucian didn't reply. A breeze kicked up, casting a cascade of long-dead leaves against their calves. He drew a ragged breath and, for the briefest of moments, looked as though he meant to say something. Instead, he merely kicked at his horse's sides and descended the hillside.

Norman watched him go until the hairs on the back of his neck stood on end, and the brute that inhabited the base of his skull prodded him forwards, towards the light. He followed soon after, a curse passing his lips.

The Stour trickled seaward, glassy-smooth in the evening hush. Only occasional shallow wavelets sprayed the cobbled street running parallel to its meandering path. A small wooden rowboat rocked close to the water's edge, against archaic stonework, its oars jostling within its depths with each resounding bump. This part of the city was not directly illuminated, but only caught the glare of the streetlamps across the river.

Alexander Cain stood alone at the edge of the path, where stone gave way to water. From even here he could identify Lucian McKay, with his slim build and steel-grey hair scintillating in the youthful twilight, which made him recognisable at a fleeting glance.

Two more dark forms were also descending into the city, and soon the snuffling of horses was on the brink of audibility. They were still some distance away, but they would reach him shortly.

Alexander had crossed the river only minutes before, rowing up from the cathedral as the streetlights had spluttered alight. People had seen him go, but none had questioned him. Nobody had thought to doubt him for a great many years.

Enough time had certainly passed since the End to have cemented the kind of look that people gave him: the downcast gaze, aimed not at his eyes but the ground over which he walked; the respectful nod—in some more of an awkward bow; and the slight trace of awe, as though he carried in his pockets not fluff and lint, but tablets inscribed with divine wisdom.

Long ago, when his struggles to unite the fractured tribes of the Early Years had begun to gain traction, he had tried to dispel the special status that people had awarded him. But the more effort he'd made to sit around campfires and work in the fields along with the everyman, the stranger the looks had grown, until eventually all eyes had turned to him whenever he made an appearance, and he had stopped bothering.

He had been forced into a costume and mask to match, to play Fearless Leader to the masses for year upon year, until now he was to the people of New Canterbury naught but a wandering Messiah.

Keeping even this tiny corner of the world from slipping into ruin had demanded it. Time had done the rest, just as surely as it had ravaged his body. He was a sprightly teenager no longer. Weathered by years of hardship, his cheeks now hung lank upon his skull, and his hair sprang from his head in a heavy thatch, heedless of brush or scissors.

He'd never been one for complaining about the ageing process—there hadn't been time to slow down, not for a single waking moment—but right now, surrounded by wilting plants and half-starved critters, he felt old.

Before he could dwell on it, he forced his gaze towards the city—his city—and searched for the returnees. As the snuffling grew closer, the smallest of smiles played upon his lips, but was quickly replaced by a frown. Tonight, away from the city lights, he felt unnerved.

The feather clutched in his hands had driven him here. Wreathed in shadow, its delicate edges curled and parted at his fingers' touch. He had been holding onto it all day, and whenever he became aware of holding it, a thousand emotions reared up in his chest, the most prominent being acute disbelief. The gut reaction was so strong that he found himself suspecting it had a lot to do with the unsettled rumblings in his stomach.

But he knew better than that. The rumblings were down to hunger, pure and simple.

The smell of a cooking meal was dancing across the water, making his stomach ache with longing. They had sent parties out foraging for scraps in all directions during the months of hardship, and Alex was sure that many had suffered due to their pilfering, but they had felt the effects of the famine nonetheless. Even the meals he had eaten lately had been sparse at best. Now that the last of their stores were truly depleted, they were all fast becoming undernourished.

The snuffling continued to grow closer, but the scavenging party would be hidden by the narrow, winding streets until they were right on top of him. Eventually, he could hear the telltale clip-clop of hooves emanating from somewhere nearby.

They appeared a short time later. He recognised Norman instantly: the slightest of the three shadows, tall and lithe, with an angular jaw and an unruly crop of black hair. Beyond, he glimpsed a flash of silver, and knew that Lucian was close behind. The last figure resolved into a young woman he vaguely recognised, one of the newer arrivals from a few years before. He tried to remember her name, and settled on Abbie, but that didn't sit right.

Norman paused momentarily as they rounded the corner, but his surprised expression was replaced by brief warmth, which itself then sank towards an even, polite smile—the one Alex knew, and had always known, hid a distant resentment. In turn, Lucian simply nodded, while the young woman—*Allie*, that was her name—gave one of the respectful bows he hated so much.

"Evening," Lucian said. He looked towards the illuminated oasis across the river and then back to Alex, as though questioning his presence. He then turned his head a fraction, enough to reveal his furrowed brows, but not enough to catch the attention of Norman or Allison.

Alex shook his head minutely, and Lucian turned away, accepting the message.

The four of them began to move along the street, towards the distant lights.

"You're leaving the boat?" Allie asked.

"I'll get it in the morning," Alex answered. "My arms hurt from all the rowing."

In truth, he felt the unbearable need to accompany them. Despite the lazy atmosphere of the riverside, even the short distance between them and the stables now seemed fraught with unseen dangers. It wasn't safe, not tonight, even within the confines of the city.

He felt their eyes on the nape of his neck, and so made a concentrated effort to keep his voice casual. "How was it?"

There was a brief pause, during which the hoot of a lone owl floated towards them from the spires of the cathedral.

"It went fine," Norman said, "but we still need more food."

"We need a lot more," Lucian growled. "Whole world's running on dregs."

Norman sighed. "We'll go back tomorrow. There has to be more somewhere."

Allie interrupted in a hurried, high-pitched babble. It was as though a great swell of words had dammed behind her tongue and they were now spilling from her mouth in a torrent. "There were others."

Alex stopped and looked at her. Under his gaze she grew timid. He waited patiently for her embarrassment to wane. "Just like we've seen everywhere else," she continued. "They're all starving. Everybody's starving."

Alex was quiet. They skirted the edge of the river and headed towards the illuminated portion of the city. Voices calling from near the cathedral were now reaching their ears, bouncing off ancient slate chimneys and reverberating along the intervening cobbled alleyways.

When he glanced at her once more, he saw that her embarrassment had been replaced by a dazed frown. "There were so many," she said thickly.

"We're not going back, not there," Norman said. "We'll go somewhere else. If we take anything more from the coast then we'll be killing them."

Alex shook his head. "It's too late to worry about that."

A strained silence followed, but Alex made a point to keep his steady pace. The feather in his hand kept him moving, even as they passed beneath the first of the illuminated streetlights.

"We saw a lot of people today," Lucian said.

Alex cleared his throat. "How did they look?"

"Skin and bones."

They rode along in silence for a moment. They were now only a hundred metres away from the row of restored buildings that the people of New Canterbury had come to know as Main Street.

"We shouldn't go back," Norman said.

Alex sensed the tension in his voice. By the sound of it, they'd had a rough time in Margate. He decided to offer no resistance this time. If things were about to take a turn for the worse, he needed to keep Norman on his good side. "Alright, not yet," he conceded. "But soon we'll have to."

There was more to say, more to argue over and report, but none of the three men said a single word further—not in Allison's presence. He might not have known her name, but people had pointed her out to Alex before; it was common knowledge that the art of subtlety was as alien to her as the greater good. As it was, the least that they could expect was for the story of the encounter with the coast's natives to be distributed overnight, as if by some infectious magic, to all ears within the city. The last thing they needed was gossip diluted by the hundred reiterations that would occur along such a chain of whispers.

And so their conversation petered out as quickly as it had begun. They each withdrew into their respective thoughts, their shadowed faces sheer white and bowed against the harsh glow of spluttering streetlights.

*

Norman was disturbed.

Guards—ghostly sentinels, hidden amidst shadow in the alleys overhead—were now appearing as they crossed the perimeter of Main Street. The detail, usually composed of one or two crack snipers, had swelled to a party of over a dozen. Norman had lived in the city for a long time, and not once had there been the need for such a heavy overnight guard.

Nevertheless, there they were, perched on roofs and balconies like fleshy gargoyles. To the casual eye they would have appeared to be no more than insomniacs staring out at the night. But from their stances and rigid orientation, spaced in a strategic barrier along the pool of light thrown down by the streetlights, Norman could spot them.

This was no doubt Alexander's doing. Norman almost spoke of it, but then laid eyes on Allison, still haughty and quiet beside him, and the words died in his throat.

It was rarely loud, even here, and at night it was often just as quiet as the surrounding dead city. The sound of the horses' hooves was accompanied only by the chatter of the few who remained in the street, standing outside what had once been a storage facility.

They used it as a town hall and kitchen of sorts.

As the gathering turned towards the returnees, familiar faces began to appear. The gaggle of night owls was gathered close to the main body of occupied housing, farther towards the cathedral.

A communal meal was afoot for those who had been lumbered with the night shift. Norman caught the deep, gamey aroma of roasted chicken and the tangy flair of stewed fruit.

To smell such luxury after only days of rotten soup flooded his mouth with saliva, and his mind with feelings of extreme guilt. To indulge in such things when thousands were dying of starvation beyond their walls seemed almost absurd, even callous.

Their arrival was heralded with great enthusiasm. Cries of welcome rang out in the night. Despite himself, Norman smiled.

Allison, the most sociable, leapt to the ground and was immediately immersed in conversation, disappearing into the crowd without a moment's hesitation.

Alexander was also subsumed into their midst, beset by curious onlookers, but he merely spread his hands until they parted, wielding their attention with practised ease. He answered a few questions, smiled a few smiles, and then proceeded without further impediment. Norman watched with jealous awe. In similar situations, he was usually apprehended for what seemed like hours, tongue-tied and aghast.

As they reached the storeroom, Lucian jumped down from his mount and began transferring the bags of food and supplies from its saddle with the help of Robert Strong, whose coal-black skin and navy engineer's jumpsuit had blended seamlessly with the shadows until he'd moved. Now in motion, however, he couldn't be missed. He towered at least a foot above everybody else, built like a tank.

"I'll take these over to Heather," Robert said, hefting their small packet of liberated medical supplies. "She'll need them. Bumps and scrapes are getting infected left, right and centre. She says it's our immune systems, shot because of the crappy diet, but I don't know…"

He disappeared into the darkness, hurrying in the direction of the clinic.

"You're coming in, aren't you, Lucian?" Allie asked.

"In a moment," he said. He clearly had no intention of joining the gaggle of chattering well-wishers, and continued his task of moving the remaining food with his head down, brow furrowed.

Unsociable to the bitter end, Norman thought. He considered helping to unload the mount, but another look at Lucian's ugly grimace convinced him to pass on by. He was left looking down at the welcoming party, and realised that he wanted no more part of it than Lucian. He could sense their eyes upon him, silently expectant. They were waiting for him to follow Alexander's lead and descend into their midst to give the latest on what was happening outside the city, dispensing wisdom and comfort along the way.

Even Allison's earlier deference, however, had been more than he could manage. After the horrors of the day, he couldn't stand being beset by a rapturous audience.

Before an uncomfortable stalemate could set in, he bade them each goodnight and turned his mount towards the stables, hurrying lest they replied or protested. A brief silence followed, but soon after he heard the others move inside.

"We'll talk at breakfast," Lucian said to him as he passed.

Norman nodded, firing off a brief temple-flick salute as he moved away. A moment later Alexander appeared at his side, leading Allie's horse on foot. As soon as they were out of earshot of the storeroom congregation, the atmosphere between the two of them shifted to one altogether more frank and familiar. They were quiet at first, growing accustomed to their privacy, and then Norman sagged, breaking the silence. "So, what do you really think?"

"Of what?" Alex said.

"Of everything." They led the horses into the gloom of the stables, and a concentrated odour of hay and manure filled his nose. "We work day in, day out to convince everybody that we're the endgame, that we're the ones fighting the good fight, and then…then we go and steal food from people's mouths as soon as the going gets rough."

There were around thirty horses nearby, snuffling somewhere in the dark. Each had been kept fed and watered at great expense, with food taken from far-flung lands. How many human lives had they cut short to keep their stables full?

Dozens. Maybe more.

Alex shook his head as he shut the stall's gate on Allie's horse. "I don't know what to think," he murmured. "I can't afford to."

Norman stroked his own steed's mane as he attached a bag of grain to its muzzle. He followed Alex back into the streets, looking over the dormant city and the ruins beyond. "This has never happened before," he said. "We've never been so close to the brink, even before we settled here."

Alex locked him with a steely gaze. "No."

"We *will* kill more people if we keep going out."

"We'll die if we don't."

Norman paused. The echoes of his footsteps took a long time to dissipate, returning time and time again from the winding maze of crumbling bricks and mortar.

Alex shook his head, having grown stern in an instant. "It's not a question of right and wrong. We go out and we take what we can, or we starve instead of them. It's that simple."

Norman said nothing. His mind's eye was busy once again, wriggling the skeletal fingers of the fallen before his eyes.

Alex watched him carefully until the silence between them had grown taut. "There's nothing that you can do until morning." He made to turn away, hesitated, and instead laid a hand on Norman's shoulder. He smiled, and although the expression was rendered monochromatic and twisted by the deepening darkness, Norman felt better. "Welcome home," he said.

Norman nodded, then frowned. "People are starting to look to me," he said. "All of them. It's like they expect me to grow a white beard and lead them into the desert."

Alex laughed for far longer than Norman thought appropriate; it was as though he had been privy to a hidden joke. After some time, wiping his eyes, he said, "Norman, they look to you because they can. You have something that they don't. You have a des—"

"Destiny," Norman muttered. "I know."

Alex's hand loosened somewhat on his shoulder, but his gaze was steady. "That's right," he said. "Destiny."

"You've told me that every day since I can remember." He looked over his shoulder to make sure that they were alone. "But I don't know if I'm the right person. I can't do this, Alex. I'm not ready, I'm not… I can't save anyone."

Alex's expression didn't change. Instead, he merely clapped a hand against Norman's cheek. "Nobody ever wants to lead," he said. "And anybody who does is the last person for the job. But that's what people need: somebody to look to. In fact, it's all they ever need. And"—he looked down at himself and laughed once more—"I'm not always going to be here. They need a fresh face, to know that somebody's ready to step in and take the reins when… when the time comes. They need you to be that person, Norman. I need you to be that person."

Norman's words caught in his throat, the same ones that had lodged there every time he'd tried to argue his case. Day after day, year after year, they had festered in his bowels.

I'm not you.

Instead, he forced the falsest of smiles onto his face— one he hoped was hidden by shadow—and nodded.

Alex patted his shoulder once more and turned away towards the hall, becoming a mere silhouette against the flare of the streetlights. "Get some sleep," he said. "We'll talk in the morning."

Norman stood alone for some time outside the stables. He peered in through the hall's windows and watched Allison talk with haunted eyes. Although it was against orders, he was sure that she was recounting their tale, and his stomach sank. He no longer felt hungry at all. He sighed and headed home, his footsteps echoing through empty streets.

*

Alexander waited in the gloom while the supplies were packed away. He paced back and forth until the job was done and the others stumbled away into the night.

By then, Lucian was taking a last look around at the pavement for forgotten scraps. He then affixed the storeroom door with its enormous padlock and stowed the key in his pocket with great care. It wasn't until he was on the verge of turning for home that Alexander stepped from the shadows.

"Thought you'd gone home," Lucian said, apparently unsurprised to see him materialise from the darkness.

Alexander said nothing—Lucian had always had a sixth sense about being watched—and approached until they were no more than a few inches apart; close enough for Alex to smell the several days' worth of perspiration that had accrued on Lucian's body. "Welcome, brother," he said.

They embraced, but for a moment only. Lucian stepped back and frowned at the proximity. "How are things?" he said slowly.

"They're fine," Alex said.

"Did something happen while we were away?"

"No. It's been quiet here."

Lucian's eyes narrowed. "Then what's wrong?"

"I can't give my brother a hug when he comes home?"

"You haven't given me so much as a handshake since I got old enough to piss without sitting down. And don't call me 'brother'."

Alex was quiet for a moment. Then he merely nodded, ignoring the unsettled lump in his throat, and held out his hand. "Here."

Lucian received the perfectly kept pigeon feather, a silver slick upon his palm in the artificial light.

The two of them looked at it, frozen in place for a long time, uttering not a sound. So quiet had it become that the trickle of the Stour seemed deafening. Alex could almost see the cogs turning in Lucian's mind as the atmosphere around him took the long road from bemused surprise to confusion, through disbelief and finally to a muted, distant fear.

When Lucian spoke, his voice was cracked. "What's this?"

Alex swallowed hard. "I found that on my doorstep this morning," he said.

Lucian's stance remained unchanged by the news, and yet to Alex's eyes his entire manner had shifted. His eyes were suddenly trailing the edge of their sockets, his lips parted and his breathing quickened. Alex knew to exactly what extent Lucian's inner calm had been shattered, because the very same thing had happened to him that morning.

"You're sure that it isn't a coincidence?"

"I'm sure."

Lucian ran a hand through his hair and grumbled to himself. He turned in a wide circle and threw myriad glances out into the night. "This can't happen," he whispered. "It can't."

Alex said nothing and watched him whirl on the spot, distantly pleased to see him react so well, and slightly ashamed that he himself hadn't taken the news with quite as much grace.

After only a minute, Lucian was standing still again and was looking down at the feather. "It's not possible," he said. "It's ridiculous… It's not poss—" He muttered to himself for a while longer. His whispering dissipated only after several emphatic grunts, and his voice began to come back to him. Soon after, his usual irritability returned.

Still, Alexander said nothing, and watched while Lucian paced and ranted, waiting for the storm to quell itself.

Eventually, Lucian stood still again, and they were staring into each other's eyes.

"What do we do?" Lucian said.

Alex exhaled through his teeth and looked away, along the road, to where Norman had been not long before. "I don't know," he said.

IV

Donald Peyton kicked at the horse's ribs, urging it on. As they accelerated, the icy rain bit at his skin without mercy, driving numb fingers closer to coming out in chilblains. Sheer panic kept him moving, but for the last mile he'd been on the brink of falling into a senseless stupor.

When lightning flashed, the valley below was cast alight. Gnarled branches devoid of leaves loomed and clawed at the air above his head. The remains of a winding road cut across the land, stretching away into the unknown.

Somewhere behind the roar of the storm, a distant rumble stirred on the brink of audibility. To Don's ears, however, it was a deafening racket, dangerously close. Whenever it punctured the din of the tempest, he mercilessly beat at the horse's sides. The road ahead straightened, allowing him to chance glancing over his shoulder.

All he saw was the tarmac, shimmering behind a curtain of rain.

He pushed on, navigating the winding road, allowing his instincts to guide him. The horse was reluctant and exhausted, but yielded under his beatings.

After ten minutes he could see through the trees ahead, to where the Celtic Sea surged back and forth beneath wicked, black clouds. The beginnings of dawn were afoot, casting the water in an ugly grey hue. The waves slammed against the crumbled sea wall, spraying the remains of County Cork's most south-western barony—the name of which had slipped from the world's memory—with chunks of rusted detritus.

Don raced parallel to the sea for what seemed like an age, but couldn't have been more than a further five minutes. The sea wall was soon left behind and the land buckled into the shape of what had been the harbour. Innumerable yachts and motorboats had once been moored, but now in the churning water only the tattered remnants of as many masts bobbed in their place, bearing fabric torn and limp.

Don peered into the maritime mausoleum and picked out his destination: a tiny rowboat bobbing along the jetty like a twig in a puddle—a violent, turbulent puddle. The rumble grew louder and niggled at the back of his head until he could no longer resist the unbearable urge to glance over his shoulder once more. Again, all he saw was rain-soaked tarmac.

But in his mind's eye he saw the assortment of orange lights that had hung between the trees like fireflies, before the storm had descended and limited his view. They had remained in pursuit for mile after mile, defying his efforts to escape them. He was sure that as soon as he stopped, they would regain the ground he'd won, but for now they were only ghosts of the mind and a rumble in the night.

He left the trees behind and descended into the ruins of Schull, clad in shadow under the moonlight. The horse's hooves clattered on uneven cobbled streets and Don was forced to grip the reins tighter to maintain control. He passed by abandoned houses and shops, sending fleeting glances into darkened alleyways.

Then the cobbles gave way to the water's edge, and he was riding out along the jetty, towards the rowboat. A single figure popped up from within and disrupted its black silhouette. The figure didn't move an inch until he was directly beside it. He disengaged himself from the steaming mount and worked his arms until the faintest sliver of feeling returned to his frozen, claw-like hands. Grunting, he rubbed them against his chest until they prickled with the heat of fresh blood.

The figure rose from the rowboat and stepped onto the jetty. In the midst of the harbour, the footsteps of the old man were audible in every crevice, cellar and attic, even over the crash of the storm. But, just as was so everywhere else, there was nobody left to hear them. He crept up to the shuddering steed and took the reins, pulling its head close and whispering calming words into its ear.

Don fought the urge to let his knees buckle and gripped the stirrups for a time, watching the old man soothe the exhausted mount. Schull's withered ruin sat quietly beneath the looming hulk of Mount Gabriel, but he kept it within his peripheral vision, wary of its many shadows.

"You were gone a long time," the old man said.

Don tried to answer, but his lips had become an exotic form of rubber. He shuddered and stamped along the concrete until his feet were burning in his boots and he felt enough strength to answer. "I had trouble."

The old man didn't break the horse's dull stare. "What kind of trouble?"

"They came for our things. The house was raided by the time I got back."

"What was left, we didn't need."

"I know. I just told them what I wanted. But one of them already had the locket."

"And?"

"He wouldn't hear me."

"Did you tell them who you were?"

"They weren't interested. They knew we weren't coming back. They must've been watching us pack up for days."

"You shouldn't have gone alone. People never respect a man on his own."

"I had to. There wasn't time."

"You should have said something. I had to wake up to find you gone. I had to look after Billy. What would I have done if you hadn't come back?"

Don fumed. "I had to get it," he said. He touched the locket, now hanging from his neck, and his gaze fell to the ground. "It's all I have left of Miranda's."

The old man abandoned his testiness, and was quiet until Don raised his head once more. "I know," he said. "You were saying?"

"They were taking it all," Don began. He made to say more, but hesitated.

The old man caught his eye. "What happened?"

"They thought I was there to do the same, so they got rough. I tried to make them see sense, but they wouldn't listen."

"And?"

Don could meet his gaze no longer, and instead addressed the jetty as he said, "Dad, I killed one of them."

The old man's mouth drew into a sharp line, but he continued to caress the horse's mane. After a while he gave the tiniest of nods.

Don knew he would get no more. "I grabbed for the locket, but he wouldn't let go." He paced, grunting. "Argh…we fell, and it was dark. I picked up the first thing I could lay my hands on and beat him over the head with it, and…it was your old claw hammer. I killed him," he murmured, uttering the last words in a harsh voice unlike his own.

"You did what you had to do."

"I killed a man."

The old man seized his arm. Don stared down into his sunken face and was subjected to the ravages of his frank, searching eyes. "Yes, you killed a man," he said. "Smashed his head in, no doubt. And then what?"

Don swallowed. "And then I ran. I took the locket and ran."

The old man nodded impatiently. "Yes, you ran. And *then?*"

"They followed me across our fields and through the forest. But I think I lost them."

"You think." Two words, only two, but more than enough to make Don's heart skip a beat.

The old man searched his face. Then he said, "Get in the boat. We can't be seen in the harbour."

Don moved closer to him. "I lost them, I swear."

"Get in the boat."

Don glanced back at the village a final time—and then he saw them. The distant orange glow turned his chest to ice and sent his knees shaking. He made to alert the old man, but he'd already noticed, and was in the process of loosening the boat's tether, his ancient hands a blur.

"They followed me. I shouldn't have come back!"

"Be quiet now," the old man hissed.

The orange lights were in the lower parts of the port, bringing the dead buildings to life, shining ghostly light through long-weathered glass. The rain was thinning as dawn approached. The storm was moving up the coast, leaving the harbour in relative silence. The rumble that had plagued Don in the forest had once again become audible, and was growing louder by the second.

Don sat in the boat and laid the oars over his lap, flexing his arms for a last time. He rubbed them until his tingling skin screamed in protest before taking hold of the oars again, preparing to push off from the jetty.

And then he paused, eyes bulging from their sockets. The dull pain that had persisted in his chest for the last few weeks—which he'd forgotten all about during the night's chaos—suddenly pulsed, sending daggers shooting along his throat.

No, he thought. *Not now. Please not now!*

But despite his efforts to stifle the ugly sensation, a guttural groan forced its way up from his lungs. He doubled over as a deafening cough flew from his mouth. The racket echoed across the harbour, followed by a rapid succession of gags and cries. He tried to stop the flow of spittle as it fell from his lips, tinged with darker shades of blood, but his lungs were doing their best to rid themselves of any residual air.

"Be silent!" the old man said.

Don tried to answer, but his body had no intention of allowing it. He dropped the oars, his vision blurred by tears as unbearable pain wracked his body.

A shrill cry issued from the awning in the stern, young, feminine and frightened. "*Daddy!*" The flap jostled as its occupant shifted within.

Don whirled, gagging, and flapped his hand at the old man.

Billy couldn't see him like this. She couldn't see how close they were to oblivion.

The old man rushed to the awning's opening. "No, no, Billy! Stay there. Stay hidden. No matter what, you stay under there."

"Grandpa, I—"

"You stay there!"

A whimper filled the air, but the jostling ceased.

The coughing subsided after half a minute. By then Don was on the floor beside the abandoned oars, taking great gasps of the fetid blanket of air surrounding the rowboat's hull. The old man said nothing more. After a while Don had caught his breath and sat up. Rubbing his chest, he waited for his breathing to settle, and blinked tears from his eyes.

The coughing fits had been getting worse, but that had been the worst yet. He suppressed a distant pang of fear and forced himself to focus.

He struggled over to the stern and steadied the tarpaulin draped over it, checking the lashings and tightening the knots until he was certain it wouldn't collapse in the high winds blowing in off the North Atlantic.

"Daddy," Billy whispered from within. Through a crack in the tarp, a pair of owlish eyes peered out at him, ocean-blue, watery, and afraid. "Daddy, what's happening?"

"Quiet," he hissed. "We're leaving. Stay hidden, now. Stay safe."

The old man whispered a few final words to the exhausted horse before leading it a small distance down the jetty and slapping its hindquarters. It gave a startled huff and shuffled away, towards the orange lights. It wasn't long before it disappeared into the town, no doubt in search of food and rest. The old man's shoulders slumped at its loss.

The orange glow now permeated the village, and Don all but pulled the old man into the boat. He threw the loosened tether into the bow and thrust them from the jetty with a great heave, ignoring the pain that still wracked his lungs. Then they were rolling on the calm waters of the harbour, and he fixed the oars in place moments before giving his first, smooth stroke. It was hard going, and his muscles trembled against the drag, but the second was easier. By the third, they were moving.

But he had set off before the old man could get into position. Without his aid, the rowboat wandered off course until it was dangerously close to the mast of a sunken yacht. Don winced, but then the old man sprang into action, displaying an agility that Don had thought lost to him for many years. Together, they steered around the ragged shadow of the wreck.

The orange lights were a single street from the jetty. They would be upon the water within the minute, and the rowboat would be spotted immediately.

They made slow progress through the water. Don and the old man divided their time between weaving between wrecks and casting terrified glances over their shoulders, still buffeted by the last of the rain and ice-cold gales.

They reached clear waters just as the orange lights reached the jetty. Don rowed with such force that his shoulders shuddered under the strain, and the rowboat jumped to a greater pace—but they were still only twenty metres from the water's edge.

Dozens of figures on horseback rushed out along the jetty, lanterns held high, hollering and shouting. Hooves roared upon the rickety planks, which squealed under their combined bulk. Axes, knives and hatchets filled the air above their heads, but Don was eternally relieved to see no guns. They kept up their galloping advance until they reached the very edge of the jetty, where they yanked on their reins and piled up, row upon row, until the mounts in front were in danger of being pushed into the freezing water.

"Daddy, what's happening? Who's there?" Billy whimpered.

"Stay down, Billy," Don wheezed. There wasn't a rifle to be seen, but that didn't mean they didn't have bows. "Get as low as you can, make yourself into a ball. Don't move!"

"O-Okay." As her shuffling emanated from beneath the awning, Don's heart skipped a beat. Images of an arrow soaring over his shoulder and plunging through the tarp leaped into his mind's eye. He cursed, certain that at any moment the first volley would be fired.

But no arrows came.

He didn't dare look back again, concentrating only on the next stroke. The raging hollers washed over the rowboat as they slipped away from the harbour, slowly fading, until the ruins had dimmed to a distant smattering of darkened shapes.

Still, he didn't look at the jetty. He was afraid of what he might see—afraid that instead of the mindless faces of a group of country bumpkins, he would see a band of grieving neighbours, robbed of a loved one by a foolish brawl.

They passed the broken breakwater and left the harbour. The sun was still below the horizon, and in the shades of grey his tired eyes had trouble finding distinction between land and sea.

Without the harbour's protection, they were battered by monstrous waves. The stern climbed some four feet in a single moment, followed by the bow. Before Don could regain his balance, they were falling down the other side of the crest. He and the old man cried out as their stomachs fluttered. Under the awning, Billy screamed.

Despite the fact that the storm had moved away, the waters had yet to settle in the slightest. Don tried not to look at the giant, froth-capped rollers colliding with the sea wall farther along the coast. Nevertheless, his imagination subjected him to flashes of their tiny boat slamming against concrete and being shredded in an instant.

The wind was colder on the open water, but the salty air and proximity to the sea was somehow warming, robbing the gale of its icy bite. This distant warmth, however, could do nothing to ease the chill that had stiffened Don's bones.

The orange lights had become as indistinct as the shrinking hillside, and Don felt his stomach begin to settle.

From then on they worked in shifts. Don rowed until his arms seized and he could move no more. The old man then pushed him into the bow and took his place. He himself rowed feebly, but kept them moving.

The old man said that there would be more land elsewhere, even claimed that it lay just over the horizon, but Don couldn't bring himself to trust such an ancient memory. Something in his gut shirked the possibility of so much more lying so close, just beyond sight. Despite laying eyes on so many maps and hearing stories from so many people, he still couldn't quite believe that there was anything but water beyond the harbour.

Yet there was no option now. The farm was lost. Every farm was lost. This was their only chance.

As the first hour wound to a close, only a brief glance back to shore made it obvious that they had made little progress. Land was still very much in sight—the very same land from whence they had come, the only land he'd ever seen with his own eyes—a mere two miles distant. Their one saving grace was that the water had grown almost glassy-smooth. The rowing from then on was easy enough for Don to let the old man take a double shift, allowing him to recover his strength.

Billy wept quietly under the awning, but Don kept her there for the time being. She couldn't see him this weak. He needed to rest first.

He sat in the bow, staring up at the lightening sky as his arms took on an agonising ache. He tried shaking them again to keep them from swelling, but that made his joints ache, and so he was forced to compromise with a pathetic shuddering.

The ugly sensation in his lungs came again soon after, washing over him in an unstoppable wave, and the coughing returned. He doubled over the side and retched, spitting a bloody mixture into the water while his body was overcome by a spasm. The old man kept a watchful eye on him until the worst had passed, his brow furrowed and his eyes shimmering with stifled tears.

Don collapsed back and tried to catch his breath. For a while each inhalation was accompanied by a high-pitched wheeze.

"I loved that horse," the old man said. He sounded conversational, if not sorrowful, but Don knew nonetheless that it was an attempt at distraction. "Raised that one from birth, you know."

Don nodded and spat over the side again. "I know, I was there," he said.

"He was beautiful."

Don nodded, grasping at the threadbare material over his chest, still gasping. After a while the pain lost its edge, and his breathing settled. The throbbing ebbed, ever more dim, until he felt it no more. He watched the clouds pass overhead and drank in slow, deep breaths of coastal air.

Sometime later, a tentative clatter jarred him from a dazed stupor. It had come from the awning. He waited for it to come again before sitting up, composing himself.

Billy muttered from the dark, mousy and tearful, "Daddy?"

He smiled. "Come on out."

In the youthful morning light, a little girl of no more than eight years poked her head from the canvas flap and peered about the stern. She took stock of their swaying motion and the surrounding waves, and then looked into Don's eyes. There wasn't yet enough light for anything colourful, but to Don she was cast in the deepest rouges and the softest pinks. She clambered underneath the working arms of her grandfather and settled herself amongst the folds of Don's mud-spattered coat. "Hi, Daddy," she said.

"Hi," he said, brushing a lock of hair behind her ear. "I'm sorry I kept you under there so long. It wasn't safe." He gave her a squeeze. "How do you feel?"

"Okay." She hesitated. "Why wasn't it safe?" She indicated the sea. "I didn't get to say goodbye to home."

He stroked her cheek and smiled. "I'm sorry, Billy. We had to leave in a hurry. Somebody was…upset. But you can still see home, over there. See?"

He pointed towards the gap in the distant grey cliffs where the harbour lay. He shielded her eyes from the glittering water and turned her head until she followed the line of sight he'd drawn out for her.

"It's so far away," she said, agape.

"It looks farther than it is."

"How long have we been moving away?"

"Not long."

Billy looked around at the sea. She leant over to inspect the gentle swell of the waves and then sat back, as though to take in its grandness. "Where are we going?" she said.

Don sighed and slumped lower, feigning exasperation. In truth, he was bordering on breaking into a laughing fit, but he made sure to keep his face level. "Billy, we've been through this hundreds of times…"

Her eyes glittered, every bit in on the play-talk as he. "I know, but I like to hear it. Where are we going, Daddy? Please, tell the story."

Don sat back, wrapped an arm around her, and recounted the tale he'd built up over endless twilight story times: they would travel to a new place, away from home, where there would be other people who spoke strangely; where there would be more boys and girls for her to be friends with, thousands of them, and they could start again; and there would be food there—all the food they could eat.

"And we're going now?"

"Yes."

She purred, settling into his coat. "I like that story," she said.

Don frowned, but let it pass. It was all still a mere fiction to her. He decided to keep the truth close to the chest for a little while longer. At least there would be no disappointment in store for her if the tale turned out to be a fantasy after all.

The old man rowed for a long time, his arms moving back and forth hypnotically. Father and daughter watched him from their heap in the bow as the land shrank upon the horizon. Meanwhile, darkness drained from the sky and the clouds blossomed from grey whiskers to enormous, fire-red streaks.

Billy soon fell asleep. From then on, Don divided his time between watching her slumber and staring out at the far distance. It was another hour before he felt strong enough to sit beside the old man and take an oar again.

In the back of his mind he knew how far they had still to go, and was equally disheartened each time he remembered it. Occasionally, the old man brought out a rusted compass and consulted their grubby map, and the two of them would correct their course.

Hour after hour passed, during which time the two of them rowed, rested, ate and drank. By the time the cliffs disappeared, the sun had clawed a fair way into the sky, bathing the boat in soft light. The tiny, prickling warmth upon their skin provided just enough of a boost to keep them moving. Billy slept while they rowed well into the day. All the while the boat crawled along, heading into unknown waters, carrying them away from their homeland.

SECOND INTERLUDE

When Alex finally returned home, the fires had begun to extinguish themselves. The sound of the door slamming shut behind him was deafening. Before he'd even taken a single glance around, he was sure the house was as much a tomb as the world outside.

The dog emerged from its bed under the stairs and nuzzled his hand, whining. His heart almost broke at the sight of her—a companion. He sat against the wall facing the living room and allowed her to lick his face, whimpering at the contact. The tears finally came then, and he cried there beside his mother's wilted ficus tree, holding the mutt to his side. The hallway swam before him, but still his gaze was drawn to the kitchen, where he was sure his family had sat not an hour before.

He didn't bother to call out. They were gone.

Once his shuddering cries had abated and his cheeks had dried, he struggled to the living room and fell into his father's chair. He hesitated for a moment, keeping his gaze on the carpet until he felt strong enough to look at the brightly wrapped gifts waiting upon the mantelpiece.

They had been presents, early gifts for exams not yet passed. His parents had surprised him that morning, promising that he'd be opening them later that day. His father had ignored his protests—Alex had repeatedly insisted that it was entirely possible that he'd fail—and laid a firm hand on his shoulder. Alex had looked into his kind eyes and let his father's words crash over him: "Alex, some men have to put in the hours. They have to fight for everything they get. Men like me. But other men have something different, something else on their side. Some men have a destiny. And you got that, boy. You got that in spades."

Alex's throat constricted at the recollection. He would never hear that voice again, nor his mother's or sister's. The truth was beginning to sink in: They were gone, *gone*, vanished into thin air along with everybody he had ever known. The entire world had been pulled out from under him.

He continued to stare at the gifts, until the intricate spots and swirls of the wrapping paper were burned onto his retinas and he lost track of time. Despite the dog's occasional attempts to rouse him, he didn't move for what must have been many hours, for by the time he stood from the armchair, the sky had turned from a pale blue to a dull orange.

Dusk was approaching. An entire day had passed.

Alex hadn't heard a single siren or passing aircraft. He was sure the phone would ring any minute. A game show host's voice would come ringing out, telling him that he'd been a good sport while the walls of his living room slid away to reveal a studio, filled by an audience bellowing with laughter.

But, inwardly, he knew that it was all real, and that it had struck far more than just Radden County. Maybe the entire world.

Once the room's shadows had started to grow longer, for reasons that he couldn't fathom he moved to the mantelpiece, piled the gifts in his arms and returned to the chair. Slowly he began to unwrap them with great care, ignoring the throbbing pain in his burned hand. But before long, something stopped him. Try as he might, he couldn't bring himself to unveil their contents. After minutes of struggling he put them aside and instead opened the single envelope that sat atop the pile.

It was a joint card from his parents, adorned by his mother's long and flowing hand. Despite its beauty, what Alex enjoyed most was the manner in which his father had signed at the very bottom in an enormous, ugly scrawl. He kept the card in his hands, smiling through fresh tears until its charm waned. By then he had sunk to a new low.

Sunset grew closer. Still he didn't move from the chair. Without any real hope, he picked up the phone and dialled his mother's number. He waited, unsure of what to expect, but there was no response at all; not a dial tone, not a recorded error message—not even static. Just silence.

That was enough to rouse him. He set about the house, prodding computers, televisions, microwaves, radios and digital clocks. Each was dead to his touch.

Only the lights still worked.

Without thinking, he ascended the stairs to his bedroom, looking around at the carpet of detritus littering the floor. That morning he would have insisted that every piece was vital, that the clutter was an integral part of his identity. Now he felt as though looking upon it all from a great height. A profound sense of futility seemed to emanate from every surface.

The crushing weight of what had happened was cleaving a cavity in his chest. It was no dream. He wished it to be with all his might, but at the same time knew it wasn't. The look Paul had given him in his last moment had been something only reality could have conjured.

He had to leave immediately.

Grabbing the nearest serviceable bag, he set about packing. Scooping up clothes and underwear at random, he cast enormous volumes of his treasured belongings aside, never to be looked at again. Music, video games, textbooks and a great many novels parted in his wake. He continued his merciless assault until stopped by the sight of a single book, which lay in a tangled bed of ancient athletic gear. He dropped his bag and reached for it, sweeping away the heavy coating of dust upon it.

The cover was dark green, plain and very old, marked only by a delicate title of gold leaf: his father's copy of *Alice in Wonderland*. He took it in both hands, feeling the weight of it, taking note of the ancient stains and frayed binding.

"There's a story and a half about that book, let me tell you," his father had said once.

Alex had never asked to hear that story. Now he'd never know. As he stared down at it, his father's voice echoed in his head once more: *Some men have a destiny. And you got that, boy. You got that in spades.*

The book weighed heavy in his hands, heavier by the moment. He lowered it into his bag and forced his eyes away from it, swallowing to clear a solid lump in his throat. He finished packing the rest in just over a minute, and swept a long look around at the room, certain that it would be for the last time. Before nostalgia or hesitation could set in, he turned and descended the stairs. Returning to the living room, he then packed his still-wrapped gifts.

The dog emerged from under the stairs, sensing that something was about to happen, whining at the sight of his bag. He stroked her head, but still she yipped, her shoulders hunched, sensing something at odds with the world as surely as he.

Outside, the sky was beginning to darken as the day came to a close, and he became aware that he was set to sleep in the empty house for the night if he lingered any longer. There was no way he would be able to stand that.

"Come on," he said. "We're leaving."

The two of them left the house within the minute and marched away down the street. Alex was determined not to look back, but couldn't resist a final glance as they rounded the corner. The dog howled as it passed from sight. He, in turn, gritted his teeth against a fresh slab of heartache.

Then it was gone, and he was heading into the vastness of an empty world.

*

They walked for an hour before Alex decided to stop and check the nearest house. At first he only found cold coffee collecting dust, bread growing hard in the toaster, and a prepacked briefcase in the hallway. But when he looked closer, he found the owner's remains: a single bathrobe, still damp, spread in the approximate posture of a lounging person at the breakfast table. A pair of spectacles lay shattered near one of the chair legs.

He returned to the street with gooseflesh blossoming on his arms and neck. Hurrying away, he could no longer ignore the endless piles of clothing. He was walking over fresh, invisible graves.

From then on, as the hours passed, he checked larger and larger establishments, eventually making his way to police stations, schools and office buildings. He found nothing but more clothing, half-eaten food, and myriad half-completed tasks. Gas hobs blazed, air conditioners whistled, and cooling car engines ticked. But there was no hint of an evacuation, or abduction. Every shred of evidence indicated that people had simply disappeared, mid-action.

On several occasions he considered searching for the man he'd seen while Paul Towers had died at his feet. Where had he come from? Where had he gone? Had he even been there at all?

Each time he found himself shuddering with disquiet—the manner in which that lupine smile had fixed upon him had been almost predatory, as though Alex had been but a scurrying ant beneath a magnifying glass.

He never searched for the man. After a while, Alex even found himself pushing any thought of him from his mind.

He slept that night in the living room of a tiny bungalow, which had belonged to a couple of pensioners, judging by its many framed photographs, stagnant atmosphere, and the flock wallpaper hanging from the walls.

After that, he lost track of everything. Time became a dimensionless entity, settling somewhere between a trickle and a relentless cascade. Villages, roads, and towns passed by, one by one, but none yielded a single clue, just more of the same wreckage.

On the second day, the swarms flew overhead: enormous flocks of squawking birds that wheeled and swirled as one, stretching from horizon to horizon and blacking out the sky. He spent the majority of the daylight hours looking skyward. Millions passed overhead, hour after hour; every species Alex could name, and more. They cast shadows abound onto the ruined world of man, occasionally straying too close to the ground and committing suicide in their thousands, colliding with brick walls and plummeting through panes of glass without any attempt at evasion, as though blinded.

They plagued the heavens until dusk had fallen. When the sun rose the next day, they too had disappeared. Alex hoped that they had merely moved on instead of vanishing themselves.

He pushed on, still accompanied by the dog, which insisted on tossing around the bloody remains of brained birds whenever he stopped to rest. He was moving north, never once diverting from an arrow-straight course, following the roads.

At the end of the third day, while he was hopelessly lost in an area devoid of landmarks or signs of habitation, the sky grew dark and mist scaled the hills. Then the heavens opened, and rain began to hammer down over the carcass of the Old World.

Sunlight streamed through the curtains, bathing the bed in an orange glow.

Norman stirred slowly, his body cocooned in the sheets. It was some time before he could bring himself to move, listening to the din of the waking city.

The room grew brighter, and the shifting shadows danced to the birds' morning chorus. Against the far wall a chintzy sofa lay strewn with his muddied, half-rotten clothing. Surrounding it was a sea of trinkets and half-remembered trophies he'd liberated from countless ruined homes.

As the fog of sleep waned, he found himself disoriented. He could only distantly recall returning home, and had no memory of going to bed whatsoever. The previous day seemed far away and unreal, but the dirt of the wilderness still clung to his skin, matting his hair, and he could smell its concentrated stink high up in the fleshy parts of his nose.

They relied on a cacophony of hastily repaired knickknacks for power. Lighting the city at night commandeered what little they managed to store. Hot water was for daylight hours only, and so he had been forced to slouch away to bed after only a cold, cursory flannel wash.

As wakefulness set in and he hauled his aching body free of the bed, his stomach rumbled to the sound of thunderous growling.

They needed more food. What they had brought back wouldn't last more than a day or two, even with all the cooks' tricks and the pitiful portion sizes they had all grown used to.

Rubbing his gut and pulling on fresh clothes, he found his gaze drawn to the walls. Whenever they returned from the wilds, it all seemed more unreal—the fact that endless crowds of people, real people, had once walked the streets outside filled him with unease.

Before the End, his house had belonged to an elderly couple. Their personals spoke of a quiet, contented lifestyle, filling the house with a quaint and wholesome atmosphere that had outlasted not only them, but the entire world. He'd kept it all exactly as it'd been left, every picture and furnishing. It was a comfort to act as custodian to something so undeniably homely. Sometimes it felt almost as though the oldies had simply gone away on a trip, leaving him as housekeep.

Little fantasies like that made the lonelier days bearable.

He crossed the room to crack open the window, shivering as a frosty breeze brushed his cheeks, carrying with it the distant clink of cutlery upon plates and the chattering of sleep-addled voices. Those on field duty were having breakfast in the hall. He suspected that Lucian would be there too, watching for slackers like a hawk as usual—and waiting for Norman to show his face.

But there would be enough time for a shower. He was grimed enough to be stiff as a board. He'd make time. As he grabbed a towel and headed into the hallway, floorboards creaking in his wake, his stomach rumbled once more.

*

Lucian was staring at him as they sat down, his brow furrowed into its signature pockmarked streak—a wrinkled, vertical canyon between his eyes. Norman averted his gaze, intent on quelling the ache in his belly before the day's run of trouble began in earnest.

There were around three dozen people in the kitchen, all eating ravenously. Breakfast was eggs and toast, courtesy of their own chickens. Despite the menu's bold claim, the disappointment wrought by the sight of what actually lay on each plate—half a boiled egg and a single wedge of bread from the Mill's brittle loaves—pervaded the room.

The building was low and wide, with windows large enough to permit thick shafts of soft dawn light to splash down onto a patchwork of scavenged rugs. A hearty fire crackled in the inglenook at the far end, bathing the air in a woody punch.

But the environs did nothing for the mood. The summer morning was powerless against the grumblings of unsatisfied diners and the racket of empty stomachs.

Manning the cookers was a small group of acting chefs. The city's more mundane tasks ran on a rota system. Everyone took their turn. Those on the morning shift today looked drawn and tired, discontent at having had to rise before dawn only to serve such a meagre meal.

Norman took a bite of mottled crust, tasted sawdust— Rayford Hubble, the miller, had been adding bulk to make the loaves go further—and turned his gaze upon Lucian. "What do you think?" he said.

Lucian swallowed the last of his ration without complaint and leant back from the table. "I'm not sure we should risk it. We don't want anybody following us back here. We can't afford the attention. People are stretched thin as it is."

"I thought we needed the food," Norman said.

"We do." He shrugged. "Your decision. You're the 'future king'."

Norman grimaced. "I hate that."

Lucian's face remained set, but his eyes flashed with brief amusement. "I'm not going to help you make every little decision forever. Sooner or later you're going to have to do it all solo."

Norman sighed and bent closer, feeling more childlike by the second. "Well, what do you think we should do?" he murmured.

Lucian shot him a glance laced with exasperation.

Norman rubbed his eyes, gritting his teeth. If there was one thing he hated above all else, it was being put on the spot. "We need the food, simple as that," he said. "We'll have to risk it."

Lucian nodded. Norman thought the gorge between his eyes had become a little shallower, but it might have been the light. "Fine. But we need to go now, before it gets late. If we run into trouble, I don't want to have to retreat in failing light."

Norman cleared his plate, savouring the flavour for a moment. Eggs had been something he'd only recently begun to eat on a frequent basis before the famine. In his childhood they had been a rare treat. Now, they were once again a rarity.

Then he nodded, getting to his feet. "Have you heard from Allison?" he said.

"Not since last night."

Norman's gut rattled with disquiet at that. Lucian's eyes told a similar story.

"Just how short on supplies are we?"

Lucian belched, stretching skyward as he got to his feet. Despite his stature—his extended fingertips didn't reach much higher than Norman's crown—people rarely noticed. His perpetual scowling countenance made him seem a far larger, more dangerous creature, a silver-haired wolverine.

He thought a moment longer. "Hard to say. There are still half a dozen other scavenging parties out there. No telling what they'll bring back." He grumbled for a moment. "To be safe, six bags. That'll get us through the celebration."

"We shouldn't be gathering for the celebration this year. There just isn't enough to go around."

"Try telling Alex that."

Norman grumbled, made a quick estimate in his head, and cursed. "It just isn't going to stretch far enough. Birchington doesn't have that much to spare. Not half of it would have germinated by now."

"We could try Whitstable. And we should take Allison. She'll stir up a storm if we leave her here."

"She'll just slow us down. How many people could she talk to in a few hours?"

Lucian threw him a look.

Norman hesitated—

How many? The whole city, and the birds in the sky to boot.

—and then nodded. "Right. I'll get her and meet you at the stables." He left the hall and stepped out onto Main Street, holding up a hand to shield his eyes from the rising sun.

Beyond a rusted substation transformer from which wires spewed on all sides were three men dressed in blue overalls and hardhats, all looking up towards the top of a rusted pylon. For a moment Norman was nonplussed, until he saw the jagged silhouette of a bird's nest amidst the cables.

They'd had problems with birds doing that for months. People were shooting and snaring every winged creature they laid eyes on. As the crops had vanished and the forests been picked clean, hungry eyes had turned upon ravens and songbirds alike. Flocks now sought refuge in any crevices they could find. Those atop the city's electrical pylons had become a favourite.

Most people didn't mind them. Their songs were a welcome reprieve from the unnatural silence that had set in over winter—set in and never departed. They had almost become public pets—to the point that, despite their hunger, the city folk had come to frown on eating them.

The only problem was that they got caught in the wires when they tried to take flight and got themselves electrocuted, shorting out the power in the process.

For the most part it had been chaffinches and magpies that had discovered the elevated havens. Today's visitor, however, was unusual: a bird that Norman had never seen in the city before. The unmistakable profile of a pigeon bobbed upon the pylon before him, cocking its head and ruffling its feathers.

Norman waved to the overall-clad men as he approached. The rest of the street was empty, with most people either out in the fields or still eating breakfast. He had no trouble spotting Robert Strong, who stood as a giant beside his two young apprentices. As he drew closer, Robert appeared only larger by the second, until he began to blot out the building behind him.

His usual detail consisted of hauling ancient motor vehicles to the sides of the Old World roadways surrounding the city. Even with the aid of draught horses, it was tough work. To clear every road, even within a radius of a few miles, would take many more years yet.

"Morning," Norman called.

They turned to him and returned the sentiment.

"Another squatter?"

Robert's boulder-shaped head nodded, his gentle face—strikingly ursine—lost in the glare of the sun high above. The muscles beneath his overalls bulged, threatening to tear the fabric as he flexed his arm to shake Norman's hand.

"Any blackouts while we were away?" Norman said.

"None. This guy showed up just this morning."

"So what's the plan?"

"Buckshot," said one of the apprentices. "And then the oven."

"With a bit of cranberry sauce," said the other.

They were both grinning, but there was something lustful in their gazes that made Norman question whether their words were in jest.

Robert put his hands on his hips, and they fell silent. "We'll figure it out." He glanced at Norman. "You heading back out?" he said. His deep baritone voice resonated in the empty street, further adding to the impression of his great stature.

Norman nodded, continuing on towards the stables. "We're still a few bags short."

"Be home for pigeon pie," Robert said, which earned him a snicker from the boys at his waist. He began to turn away, but then paused, his brows lowered. "Hey, Creek," he called.

Norman, having almost passed out of earshot, stopped in his tracks. The sharpness in Robert's voice sent a twinge of unease snaking through his loins. "Yes?" he said.

"I heard you ran into somebody yesterday. Is that true?" His eyes said the rest—that which the young men didn't need to hear: *How bad has it gotten out there?*

Norman tried to keep his face level, but knew that his jaw had tightened despite his efforts. "Where did you hear that?"

Robert spread his arms, his face creased into an incredulous smirk. "Come on," he said. "Do you really think that you can keep a secret with Allie Rutherford around? If she knows, everybody knows."

Norman cursed inwardly. "It's true, but nothing to worry about," he said, more for the sake of the apprentices, whom he trusted no more than Allison.

The young had loose tongues these days, without enough crowds to teach them any better.

Robert drew away from his charges until Norman had to look straight up to make eye contact. His body now cut out the glare of the sun, allowing Norman an unmarred view of his face: small features set amidst vast tracts of forehead and pendulous cheeks, all of it weather-beaten, exuding a sense of frank pragmatism.

Despite his all-man appearance, his voice had fallen to a whisper that wasn't much more than a sigh on the wind. "Listen, Norman, what's going on? I mean, with all this?"

Norman blinked.

Robert watched him expectantly. "I mean, what's the plan? Alex has filled you in, right?"

Norman's stomach sank.

Robert was above playing sheep—was, in fact, one of the few who'd known Alexander since the Early Years—but in his eyes was the same look Norman had seen more and more often over the last year. Just like the others, Robert was fishing for guidance—as though Norman were privy to some deeper, hidden truth.

In that moment, he couldn't have felt less divine. But the look in Robert's eyes was too sincere, too trusting, to crush underfoot. He forced a smile onto his face. "I'll keep you posted," he said. "Listen, have you seen Allie this morning?"

Robert looked stricken. "Don't tell on me. She meant no harm."

"She's coming out with us."

Robert pointed down the street. "She was up at dawn. I stopped her before she could run her mouth too much. I left her with Sarah." He winked. "Go easy on her."

"No promises." Norman made for the stables once more.

*

Sarah Clarke was quite possibly the world's last librarian. She was also the last schoolteacher. And with such a ridiculous, inch-thick pair of spectacles as hers, she suited both roles to a tee. The warehouse behind Main Street was her domain, and everything beneath its high roof was under her protection.

To most, she was a kook to be avoided, hovering upon that delicious sweet spot between giggling lunacy and unbounded enthusiasm. To Norman, she was instead something to be appreciated, like a piece of experimental—if not overambitious—art.

An average day saw her flitting back and forth between the endless, sweeping towers of rescued books brought back from the wilds. The warehouse, an industrial-storage behemoth the size of an aircraft hangar, was filled to capacity; save for a network of narrow alleys, not an inch of floor space had been spared.

There were similar buildings for articles of art, electronics, and vehicles—but none as large as this. The Old World's books, which housed all its knowledge and secrets, lay strewn in the rubble of towns and cities, waiting to be picked up like nuggets of gold shimmering in a riverbed.

The city folk saved as many as they could—had been doing so for years—but there were always more to find, and time was beginning to take its toll on their vulnerable pages. Here, they were sorted before being moved to vast storage catacombs beneath the streets.

Norman gawped at a new, yellowed skyscraper of leather-bound volumes close to the doorway until Sarah's flowing figure rounded a bend in the aisle ahead and cried, "You're back!"

She approached from an unsorted heap of hardbacks, her bony face and tomato-red hair illuminated by the widest of smiles, which was occupied by her four million teeth. Hanging from her shoulders was a robe identical to those worn by the elders, a simple white cloth that billowed around the body and stopped just beyond the knee. Precious few younger citizens were awarded the cloth, Norman among them, though he only wore his during ceremonial times, when it was expected of him.

"Morning, warden," he said. "How are the inmates today?"

"Stale. Rotten. But still singing their sweet songs." She threw her arms around him and giggled. "Welcome home."

"Careful now," he said. "Robert catches us and I'll have a stump instead of a head before you can blink."

She drew back and glanced out the door, to where Robert's silhouette clambered the pigeon-infested pylon on Main Street, her eyes swimming with puppy love. "He's not the jealous type. At least, I don't think so. I suppose time will tell."

Norman forced himself to turn his attention to the task at hand, but did so grudgingly. He'd have liked to spend the day here. After the struggle, hunger, and horrors that lay beyond the city, the warehouse never failed to act as an all-curing tonic. In his youth, when Alexander had been working so tirelessly to keep society alive—when even his name had been but the stuff of legend to a handful of scattered tribes—Norman had spent his days in similar secret troves, his nose buried in books written by long-dead Old World writers.

In addition, Sarah was among the few who were unlikely to ever look upon him with any degree of hero worship. Her gaze never failed to penetrate the aura of godliness erected by the city folk, to see him for the clueless idiot he truly was.

She would never expect anything of him.

However, the thought of the maelstrom that was Allison Rutherford held his attention, and he peered around without another word, scouring the scale-model city of yellowed paperbacks and leather-bound tomes.

Sarah was wittering on, "Library running thin? We just got a new batch of first editions from a bank vault in Dover."

He shook his head. "I'm well stocked for the moment. I heard Allie was here. You mind if I borrow her?"

Sarah blinked, her lashes magnified to huge proportions by the slab-like lenses of her spectacles. "Not at all."

While Norman had spoken, as though summoned, Allison had poked her head from behind the stack of hardbacks from which Sarah had appeared. Her face was downcast and sheepish.

He beckoned her imperiously before she could disappear. "Come on," he said. "We have things to do."

She hesitated momentarily, reluctant to leave her sheltered hovel, but then her shoulders slumped and she stepped forwards.

"I'll be back to see those first editions," he called as he made for the door.

"Do keep a look out for more Tolstoy!" Sarah cried from the depths of the paper maze. "Our stocks are dangerously low." She paused. "But no more King! We already have enough to build a whole new ridge on the east side!"

Norman couldn't help smiling. "What's wrong with King?"

She made a noise of disquiet. "I don't play favourites when it comes to the world's heritage."

Norman's smile widened. "Prude," he said. "All work and no play…"

Sarah scoffed from the foothills of the pile he called Mount Fitzgerald and was gone, leaving behind a single resounding call, "Good luck out there, Gunslinger."

Norman led Allie back towards Main Street.

"I wasn't hiding," she said quickly.

"I didn't say you were."

"Yes, but—oh."

He turned to her. "What did you do?"

"Nothing."

"Who did you talk to?"

"Nobody."

Norman didn't speak again until they reached the stables, glad that Lucian had made his suggestion.

*

Norman darted between rows of plants, casting shrivelled fruits into a threadbare sack, his boots squelching in waterlogged mud. Nearby, Lucian and Allison filled their own bags. He worked at a feverish pace, pausing often to listen and look over his shoulders, hunched low to the ground.

The field in which they stood had long ago belonged to people who had enjoyed extra gardening and a steady supply of surplus greens. Quaint little plots, sectioned off in neat squares. The occasional dilapidated shed still protruded from the ground, sometimes adorned with a wisp of shredded tarpaulin.

When a sharp crack rang out, he instinctively crouched lower to the ground, turning on his heels to look for its source. He could see Allie and Lucian's knees through the fronds, but little else.

Sweat immediately began to form in large rivulets upon his skin, smearing the dirt on his arms and hands, falling past his brow and stinging his eyes. His fingers dug deep channels into the stinking mud as he began to crawl forwards.

Within four feet, the leaves parted before him to reveal a dark shape, amorphous and bristling. Norman flinched, pushing off from the ground in a moment of blind panic. He collapsed back into a tangle of decomposing creepers, spluttering and kicking for purchase.

Before he could cry out, a snort filled the air, one that made him freeze in place. He ceased flailing immediately and rolled forth onto his haunches.

Staggering to his feet, he stared down at the pink back of the fattest pig he'd ever seen. Its underbelly was covered with a thick paste of rotten plant matter and its nose twitched without pause in the morning sun, hanging from which were tendrils of rotten aubergine.

After considering him for a moment, it stepped forwards and nudged his legs with its snout. Norman put out his hand and patted its head awkwardly, glancing to the adjacent row of strawberry bushes as Lucian and Allie emerged from hiding.

Lucian crashed through the undergrowth, studying the pig. "We shouldn't have come out today," he said.

"It's just a pig."

"Look how close it got before we realised. People would kill us without a break in their step to get at this food."

"How is that different from any other day?"

Lucian shook his head. "That's not the point." He paused for a while, looking towards where the open gate swung in the wind. It backed immediately onto a main road. "We should leave," he muttered.

Allison turned to Norman out of what was clearly a knee-jerk reaction. She was awaiting not Lucian's word, but his.

A sliver of annoyance festered in his gut. In the past, those looks had come but once in a blue moon. Now, it seemed they waited for him around every corner.

With a grunt that wasn't quite devoid of chagrin, he nodded. A squall of shame lapped at his conscience, but Allie seemed satisfied, and to be rid of her demanding gaze was reward enough.

They made to leave, but before they could do so, a thought occurred to Norman. By the manner in which they turned back to face the pig in step with him, he guessed the very same had occurred to them.

The hog stared back at them with benign friendliness, apparently mistaking their attention for reciprocity.

But, as their stares endured, and Norman was sure that his gaze had become a leer of craving—or madness—something too changed on the pig's face. If it could have been smiling then, under their combined gaze, that smile would have faltered.

*

The sun beat down on the field without mercy as it reached its highest point in the sky. Blinding rays struck Norman's face as he struggled to focus on the middle distance, his eyes scrunched down to slits.

The tension was palpable. Gathered atop a slight rise at the periphery of an expansive field, all was still. Not man, woman or horse moved an inch, nor made a sound.

Norman adjusted his stance, bouncing atop bent knees as he concentrated on his target. A single bead of sweat made a break for his chin, escaping from its kindred upon his half-fried forehead.

And then, with practiced precision, he swung the club in his hands. "Fore!" he bellowed. His voice was rendered thunderous by the many echoes that returned from the valley floor.

The white ball soared skywards from the tee at his feet, becoming a mere speck and disappearing into the sun's glare. After several long seconds there was a distant thud as it struck earth somewhere out of sight.

"Slouching," Lucian grunted. "Try straightening your back more."

"Remind me why we're doing this," Norman said, turning to him and handing over the club.

"We have to wait. I'm not making a beeline for home if somebody's watching."

"There's nobody out here."

"We don't know that. Now stop your whining and move. It's my turn."

Norman stepped over towards his mount, from which hung what they'd managed to gather, along with the sack that contained the butchered swine, and felt the knot in his stomach loosen slightly.

They had risked lingering in the field for enough time to strip it bare. Most of the fruit would need culinary magic to make it edible—let alone palatable—but they had done well, and there was a chance the meat would add enough to the pot for the city folk to enjoy a decent dinner. The stag from the coast had been a prize in itself, but the pig had grown fat enough on the allotments' fetid slop to at least double their meat stocks.

At Lucian's insistence, they had taken a winding route home, and halted several miles from the city. They now stood in a valley that marked the northern edge of their territory, where they had stood watch for over an hour, waiting for any weary refugees who might have followed them.

Norman wasn't quite sure of when the golf had begun—only that at some point they had found the rusted club and basket of balls in the high grass, where some poor sod had left them forty years ago as he'd vanished from under his white flat cap—but in the midday heat it didn't seem to matter. He was glad for the distraction.

He sat on the grass beside Allison and the two of them watched Lucian take his swing, hunchbacked to the extreme, contrary to his own advice.

She sniffed. "Did you have to make me come out here all day?"

Norman looked at her for a second, found that there was nothing to say, and then turned back to Lucian.

He saw her eye twitch in his peripheral vision. "I don't believe in keeping things a secret. If people are starving, then everybody deserves to know."

"The whole world's starving."

"Not like them! My god, Norman, you can't be serious. We're living like spoilt royalty compared to them."

"We don't *know* anything," he said patiently. "We haven't even got reports from the other scavenging parties yet. We should just wait until we have all the facts before we go telling people about our…unfounded conclusions."

Allison bristled, but then seemed to restrain herself. "Fine. It's your decision. I just wish you'd tell us what we're going to do sooner rather than later."

Norman straightened, then looked down at his hands. It was some time before he could bring himself to say, "You shouldn't look to me for answers, Allie. I'm not a leader."

Allison looked taken aback. "But you will be," she said, frowning, as though stating that the sky was blue.

"I didn't ask to be."

Lucian cleared his throat and fixed Norman with a pointed stare.

Norman made to speak, but then registered Allison's confused expression and closed his mouth. "Don't listen to me," he sighed. "I'm just tired."

She looked relieved, and sank back. They lapsed into silence for a while and took turns swinging the club, sending ball after ball sailing down into the valley. After half an hour, Allison spoke up once more. "How did it happen?" she said.

Norman closed his eyes, dreading whatever was coming, lying in the depths of the wild grass. "How did what happen?" he mumbled.

"We've all heard the stories. People talk and whisper about you, but nobody's ever heard it from the horse's mouth." Her eyes scanned him carefully, and Norman began to wonder whether her name being drawn for scavenging duty in Margate had been entirely down to chance after all. "You said you didn't ask to lead us. So somebody picked you, didn't they? You were chosen."

She was staring at him with rapt fascination, as though she had been granted a private audience with a figure from a fairy tale. "It was Alexander, wasn't it? He chose you." She inched closer. "When?"

For a long time, he didn't answer, trying to catch Lucian's gaze. But Lucian kept his back turned to him, visibly rigid, wilfully deaf. Eventually, Norman bowed his head and nodded. "When I was a boy," he said. "Just after I lost my parents. At least, that's the first I remember of it." He picked at a stray blade of grass. "They tell me that my parents put me up for it when I was born, but...the accident that killed them... I got hurt too. I don't remember anything before it all that well."

Allie's voice was hushed, "What *do* you remember?"

He squinted skywards, recalling the flashes that sometimes invaded his dreams. He didn't mean to say a word—had a mind to tell her to mind her own goddamn business—but then his lips moved of their own accord. "A storm." His voice had grown cold, distant. Words formed without thought, as though somebody else were speaking through him. "I think it was just after the accident. I'm lying on my back...the rain is cold. My head hurts." Norman frowned as a twinge of genuine pain flashed just above his right ear—behind the twisted scar that lay just above his hairline—before that strange, detached voice continued, "Alex is standing over me. He's saying that it'll be all right, that he'll take care of me. And then he says something else. He has a secret. He says it's my destiny...my destiny to save it."

Allie's voice, a mere whisper, "Save what?"

"The world."

A brief silence rang in his ears before she answered.

"Just like that?" Allie said. "Right there and then?"

Norman nodded.

She hesitated before uttering, "Do you think you'll ever remember...what happened before?"

"Maybe." He shrugged. "Maybe not. It's been almost years..." He felt an ugly smile blossom on his lips and glanced up at her. "I'm not holding out for it."

Lucian was quiet, readying his latest swing, but Norman knew that he'd followed their every word.

Allison was still staring. "How do you tell somebody something like that?" she said. "That they're going to have to take care of everybody?"

Norman sat up and brushed his hair from his eyes. He looked away, towards a distant rise, where the wind turbines that powered New Canterbury revolved in the listless midday wind. Watching them made the words come easier, but he still spoke haltingly. "That's not what bothers me. I get that we need somebody to keep carrying the torch. I really do. It's that he used that word…told me it was my *destiny*."

Allie's eyes met his. "Why does that bother you?"

He laughed, but his wan smile slid from his face as he said, "Because there's no such thing as destiny."

VI

Don woke late in the afternoon. He rubbed his cheek, numb from being pressed against the lip of the prow, and groaned as the boat was buffeted by an errant wave, holding still until a spell of nausea had passed.

The day had been warm and muggy. Land was by now a long way off. A distant shadow that loomed where water met sky was all that remained of the heath-capped cliffs. He tried to judge how far away it was. It couldn't have been very far compared to what still lay ahead, but it certainly looked as though they had crossed an impossible distance.

The old man was snoring under the awning in the stern. With each honking breath he drew, the hull resonated. Only his feet protruded from the awning's shadow, but by their inclination it was clear that he was flat on his back.

Don sat up, groggy, and blinked sleep dust from his eyes. His skin felt leathery and his mouth was dry. He took one of their canteens and half-emptied it, but his thirst was unquenched.

He would need more soon if he was to retain his senses, but for now he returned the canteen to the awning's shade. Even as he did so, he felt the fresh moisture upon his chapped lips begin to drain away.

All of their planning, all of the time they had spent preparing for the trip, and they hadn't given a moment's thought to the fact that they'd need so much water. They'd used over half of their reserves already.

He cleared his throat, fighting cottonmouth and year-old hunger, and brought out the grubby folds of their map, which fluttered in the breeze while he checked their course against the old man's compass.

A shuffling eventually disturbed him. Billy's tiny profile had been invisible until she'd lifted her head, crouched beside the awning. Don blinked in shock, seeing her afresh. Her eyes looked enormous amidst her hollowed cheeks. She scarcely resembled the plump, freckle-faced munchkin he'd been raising a year ago.

His little girl was starving.

He beckoned her, and she crawled over to sit in his lap. Don continued to check the map with his arms looped over her shoulders. She peered at it for a while, bemused, and then said, "Are we there yet?"

"Not yet. Soon."

"I don't like the sea anymore. We've been away for too long. We should go back."

Don put the map down. "We've only been gone a few hours."

"I'm hungry."

"We're all hungry."

She wrinkled her nose and looked up at him, a coy smile touching her lips. "Where are we going?" she said.

"Billy…"

"Pleeaaase."

Don grumbled and then retold the story of their journey to the new land, embellishing it as usual with improvised speculative details. Billy listened in a trance and smiled at the fantastical legend of the New Land.

Afterwards, the two of them sat in silence and listened to the old man sleeping under the awning. They watched the sun begin to dip, rolling to the waves' rhythm.

"You were asleep for a long time," she said.

"Was I?" Looking at the sun, he made a rough estimation of where it had been before he'd dozed. "It can't have been that long."

"It was forever."

He smiled. "No, it wasn't."

"It's daytime. You always tell me not to sleep in the daytime."

"Grandpa and I were busy last night. We didn't get to sleep. You, on the other hand," he poked her ribs, drawing a giggle from her lips, "got a comfy twelve hours."

Billy's smile remained, but it soon grew thin. "I did?"

"Yes."

When she spoke again, her tone made him look away from the horizon. "I dreamed."

"You did?" Something about her expression made him press, "What about?"

A brief pause. Then she said, "Ma."

Don's throat clicked as he swallowed. They sat through the silence that followed in the same manner as they had many times before. He knew that he needed to say or do something to break the silence, to bring their thoughts away from Miranda. But nothing came to him. Her absence was still too raw, and the shock of her loss too fresh. He could only hold Billy closer to his side as his own tightened larynx failed him.

"I dream of her most nights," Billy said. Her voice had a hollow edge, devoid of engagement.

"You do?"

She nodded. "They're memories, though, from…before. When I wake up I can remember how she smelled. Do you remember how she smelled, Daddy?"

Don stroked her hair. "She smelled of lemons."

Billy frowned. "What's that?"

"A fruit. But I haven't seen any for a long time."

"Oh… I don't know what they smell like. Like Ma, I suppose."

"Yes, like Ma."

"I dream of her, but she has no face. It's fuzzy, like a drawing. Will she go away if I forget her face?"

"No, she'll never go away."

"But how can she be here if she has no face?"

Don sat back and sighed. "It's all still there, you're just not thinking about it right. You've got to think about something you did together." He kissed her forehead. "Try thinking about the Christmas before last," he whispered.

"You remember? How she cooked that enormous turkey, the one that grandpa fed double because it never shut up?"

She nodded, but was otherwise deathly silent.

Don's throat had grown narrow, but he pressed on, "We ate all those gooseberries by the fire. I've never been so full in my life..." He held back a laugh. "She taught you that dance... that..."

"Foxtrot," Billy muttered.

"Yeah." He kissed her scalp once more to hide the tears welling behind his eyes. "And we sang until the sun came up. You remember?" His voice wavered near the end of his sentence, but Billy didn't seem to notice.

After a long silence, a smile flickered upon her pale lips. "I see her," she whispered.

"Yeah," he said, looking out towards the reddening horizon. "Me too."

Sometime later, the old man snored himself awake in the stern. The awning was subjected to a vicious beating while he fought his way out into the open. There, he crouched, blinking and coughing.

Don handed over the half-emptied canteen, and the old man swiftly depleted it before he could say a word about rationing it, proceeding to peer in through its upturned neck with a dissatisfied expression.

Don laid a hand on his shoulder before he could reach for another. "We need to save the rest for later," he said.

The old man scowled, cradling his head in his wrinkled palms. "It's hot. I never thought it'd be hot on the water."

"I thought you'd been on the sea before."

The old man giggled feebly. "Yes, on a ferry, Donald. A big one. Not a…a…" He gestured to the rowboat around them, not bothering to finish. "I should have thought of water. Stupid."

Billy leaned over the side and skimmed the crest of a passing wave into her palms. She held it out to him. "There's water all around, silly," she said.

The old man shook his head, too weary to humour her, and turned away.

Billy looked to Don, her face blank.

"Throw it back, Billy."

"Why? Grandpa's thirsty."

"You can't drink seawater."

"But I've drank it before. It's not very nice, but it's still water."

"It makes you thirstier, throw it away."

She slumped and threw the handful back over the side, then peered into the water. "Where are all the fishes?"

"I don't know. Gone."

"When will they be back?"

"I don't know."

"In New Land?"

"Maybe. Hopefully."

She blinked, staring into the lifeless depths.

"What time is it?" the old man said, sounding wearier than ever. Don was frightened by how wilted and frail he looked.

"Half one, maybe two."

"We need to get moving if we're going to get there before we run out of supplies."

The two of them, stiff and aching, assumed their positions beside one another and took an oar each. They then began rowing once more, straining against the squalls.

Don fought the urge to cough several times, knowing full well that once he started he would have great difficulty stopping. Yet the urge never faded, plaguing him like an itch never scratched.

All the while, Billy sat opposite them and watched. The sun had become a fiery half sphere on the world's edge by the time her eyes started to droop and her chest began to sag. From then on, she swayed with the current until her shoulder made contact with the floor, and then she was still.

Don watched her sleep and knew that she was dreaming of a better time. He found himself wondering whether there was a person left alive who didn't do just that, whenever they closed their eyes.

VII

Row upon row of children moved in unison, their faces scrunched into expressions of intense concentration. Copying Norman's every move as he executed a series of oriental motions, they twirled and pivoted as one. Not once did their focus falter.

He watched them from the corner of his eye, forever fascinated by the manner in which their immaturity evaporated once their classes had begun. They moved with him, but at the same time they improvised, correcting his minute mistakes. Compared to them, he was a clumsy buffoon. The progeny of a hardened caste of survivors, their bodies and minds were honed to perfection.

Their weekly martial arts training was supposed to develop the stealth they'd need once they were old enough to scavenge and hunt. Going unnoticed was now paramount. Over the last year, remaining hidden had defused a great many potential shootouts.

But the children were already faster, quieter and more agile than any adult, and they all knew it. Having grown up around situations that demanded subtlety, they were each as lithe as birds.

Nevertheless, they were promptly lined up every week to hone their skills.

Teaching was something that Norman considered one of the less taxing duties on the rota system; the children were more or less self-sufficient already, and they seemed to like him. He suspected that his lax style appealed to their allergy to hard work.

And yet, he would still never see eye to eye with them. A distant but ever-present measure of respect nested behind their eyes, forging an impassable chasm between them. They too looked to him with a casual acceptance of his purpose in life. There didn't seem to be even a glimmer of doubt in their eyes that he would one day be the Big Man, the one in charge.

After half an hour of yelling, thrusting and twisting, the class was dismissed and the children dispersed. Their carefully crafted stances and disciplined silence fell away in an instant, and they were themselves again. They proceeded to poke, entertain and torture each other as they left the hall.

Norman was left standing alone in the gymnasium. They wouldn't be back for an hour, and he had little to do in the meantime. He wandered into the hallway, inspecting art projects tacked to the display boards—some new and some over forty years old; fresh paint right alongside the yellowed scrawls of the Old World's last students—and eventually found his way to Sarah's classroom.

The younger children were few in number, but sang merrily enough to make up for it, in a range of pitches that, together, sounded truly awful:

"The wheels on the bus go round and round,
Round and round, round and round.
The wheels on the bus go round and round,
All day long."

The rhyme—one of the few to have reportedly retained its original rhythm—echoed throughout the dozens of empty classrooms. Norman stopped at the doorway and looked in to see them gathered cross-legged on the floor, swaying from side to side to the din of their off-key wailing.

Sarah sat before them in a checked summer dress, the headband upon her crown framing her cheeks with curls of fire-red hair. She indicated the lyrics plastered upon her easel with a pointer, but the children scarcely glanced up, instead singing from memory.

Norman watched them sway, and couldn't help smiling. Eventually, Sarah looked up from her vigil and noticed his presence. She slid away from the easel. The children didn't seem to notice, and kept right on singing.

She tiptoed closer, bouncing on the balls of her feet so as not to disturb them, her face illuminated by an inner light, all gums and brilliant white teeth. She would have been beautiful, were it not for the gawky, disproportioned spectacles balanced on her brow.

"They're getting better," he said.

She smiled back at them, doe-eyed. "I prefer the sound of cats drowning in custard."

"Have you got time for lunch?"

"I'll be done soon." She was peering over her shoulder at the toddlers, transfixed.

"Come on, they won't notice if you take a break." He began to tug her from the room.

"Oh, I shouldn't," she said. "Norman—oh, all right."

A minute later they were eating tasteless bread in the hallway, listening to the ear-splitting singing and trying to ignore the grit and sawdust between their teeth.

After a while he realised that she was smiling at him. "You should come to an English class some time," she said. "I get all sorts to come along, not just kids. We could use a speaker every now and then—one who's actually been reading all the books that people have been bringing back from out there, one who isn't just following Alex's every word about *saving the world and all its wonders*."

"Careful. Enough words like that about the Chosen One are bound to get ye strung up by the village."

"I'll take my chances." Her smile was coy, puncturing his attempt at diversion with ease. "You'd be great."

Norman muttered under his breath for a while, pulling at his frayed sleeves. "I'm not one for public speaking."

She searched him with eyes magnified to insectivorous proportions by her ghastly specs. "I know it's been rough on you this year," she said, "all this…everybody turning sheep. But maybe you could try to see the other side of it.

You've got an opportunity to help them. It's all hand holding at first, but people are stronger than they look. All they're looking for is somebody to give them a purpose, a direction—something to live for.

"People look to you. They trust you." She hesitated, scanning him. "But you always shrink away. Why?"

Norman felt the light-heartedness of the conversation drain away. His throat had closed up. After a moment he could no longer match her gaze.

"Don't worry," she said. Despite his reticence, her unassuming gaze had only grown more amused. She smiled, observing him from behind hooded lids, and leaned against the wall. "I'll get to you eventually."

He was quiet for a moment longer. "So, you and Robert," he said.

She laughed, and her teeth brightened the hall once more. "Yes," she said. The comforting glaze had been wiped from her face. A flush touched her cheeks, and her chest rose and fell until she was almost breathless.

"Nobody saw that one coming."

She paused with her last crumb of sawdust-bread held to her lips, frowning. "Why?"

Norman shrugged. "If I were a betting man I'd have put my money on you having Richard in your sights. He lives for the written word almost as much as you do."

She glanced along the hall, brows raised. "Him? He's always got his head in the clouds."

"Funny, I always thought it was two inches up DeGray's arse."

She giggled, and hesitated before answering, "Robert's different. He's sweet, and kind," she breathed, her lids lowered further. "He doesn't despair about the End, doesn't fret about what's to come. He's a fixer. All he sees is something broken, something that only needs the right mechanic to make it work again." An inner light seemed to emanate from the rosy tones upon her cheeks and chest. "He's everything a man should be." She appeared to come back to herself, and trailed away into an embarrassed silence.

Norman couldn't help laughing. "Poetic."

"One tries." She then glanced back to him, her eyes growing sharp. "You need to change," she said.

He sighed. "I know," he said. "They're all looking to me now. I feel their eyes on me in the street." He paused. "I just need time."

She was smiling again, and flicked her head towards his midriff. "I meant your clothes."

Norman looked down at his martial arts robe. "I like it," he said after a brief pause. "I'm not sure why people don't dress like this all the time."

"The children seem to think along the same lines."

"At least I taught them something."

A hulking figure interrupted their joint smirk, blustering past with great bounding strides. The two of them parted to allow the portly man past, offering greetings that were promptly ignored.

"He's done it again," the man roared. "That boy will never learn!"

If Sarah was the last Librarian, then he was the last Professor. The sworn archenemy of all youth, John DeGray was a blimp of a man, and had taken it as his life's work to mercilessly educate anybody who strayed too close. Despite knowing more than most had forgotten, he was handicapped by the trifling affliction of hating almost everybody. In truth, were it not for Richard Maxwell, his one permanent student, he would have been at a loss for things to do.

Yet most thought them both indispensable, for they represented all that remained of the Old World's scholars. Afforded special status—owing to Alexander's most famous mantra, '*Knowledge is power*'—and yet unable to contribute anything tangible to the city, they spent the majority of their time in their hovel of a classroom.

Norman and Sarah exchanged bemused glances and, after a glance in the direction of the warbling young ones, followed him. They remained in pursuit until John disappeared into the second occupied classroom, at which point they were obliged to pause and recoil at the fountain of abuse whistling across the threshold. Approaching on tiptoes, they peered in. John, scintillating with rage, was in the process of verbally castrating a slight young man seated at the only desk.

Richard stared up at John's ranting form without the slightest trace of surprise or concern. Tiny in comparison to his mentor, crushed between his desk and a sizeable swathe of books and papers from Sarah's warehouse, he certainly looked to be little more than a child. Despite his foxlike features and intelligent gaze, he was still young enough to bear a fading smattering of acne. A faded red shirt that was far too big for him hung about him like a cloak. To Norman's knowledge, it was the only one he owned. Richard had adopted the Old World academics' hatred of fashion, and insisted on washing the same attire each night so that it could be worn the following day.

"You apologised to Hubble," John bellowed. His auburn eyebrows—tangled thickets upon his plum-red face—were pressed so close together that for a moment Norman was reminded of Lucian.

"I did," Richard said. He stared down at the chessboard before him, his hand poised above it. His face was a perfect picture of intense concentration.

"On my behalf?"

Richard moved an ivory bishop across the board with unflinching confidence, nestling it between a black pawn and rook. He then sat back and smiled, looking very pleased with himself. "Yes," he said.

John growled and leaned over the desk. "You had no right to do that."

"He's on catering duty. He was handing me smaller portions just for sitting in here with you all day. I'm not feeling faint all week again because you can't say sorry."

"He doesn't deserve an apology, he was wrong."

"You were both wrong. You got into a fight."

"It wasn't a fight."

"You punched him in the face while trying to convince him that violence was wrong."

"I was drunk," John blustered, flapping his hands. He glanced at the door and saw that he was being watched. "Oh," he said. "Hello."

"Afternoon," Norman and Sarah chorused.

Richard beckoned for them to enter, his gaze lingering on Sarah for a moment.

John, in a silent display of superiority, swept his hand across the chessboard and captured Richard's bishop, replacing it with a knight that had been previously invisible to everybody else.

"Wait, what?" Richard said, glancing down at the board, his expression one of absolute blankness. He stared from the victorious knight to the bishop clutched in John's hand, and then cursed.

John rubbed his chin and began pacing, a snide smile upon his lips.

Richard fumed, planning his next move. "You went out yesterday," he said to Norman, leaning forwards.

"That's right."

"Anything interesting happen?"

Norman sensed all ears prick up at once.

He sighed, now aware of how far Allie's words had spread. He cursed her and prepared himself for a swift bout of damage control. "Nothing. There's nobody out that way these days," he said. "The locals moved up the coast after winter set in."

"No trouble at all?"

"No."

Nobody said anything, but Norman could almost hear the indignation of their thoughts, almost as clearly as if they'd shouted into his ears. Their eyes told the truth—even Sarah's. They knew everything.

Allison Rutherford was clearly a force that needed to be contained at any cost.

Richard nodded with transparent, mock satisfaction. Norman braced himself. The door to further questions had been opened. "The scavenging details just seem so desperate, after all the effort that's been put into cultivating our own food supply. And frankly I'm shocked that there's so little out there. I haven't heard of a famine striking anywhere before this for… what? Twenty years? And now there's nothing left at all?" He looked to John for confirmation.

John grumbled in agreement.

"It never rains, it pours, I suppose," Richard finished.

John grumbled once more. "It could have been a lot worse for us if it had come even a year earlier. I don't think that our stores could have kept us going this long if it had."

Norman shrugged. "The land's stripped bare. We had to go all the way to the coast just to get a few bags of fruit and venison."

The two men frowned and shared a glance. Richard was still planning his next move, but his gaze now wandered the room, distracted.

"There's really nothing at all?" John asked. "Are you sure?"

"Yes. Even the sea's dead. No fish since winter…since Southampton went quiet."

He mused and muttered for some moments. "We knew the mass exodus from the south must have been caused by something, but still—*everywhere?*"

"I miss Market Day," Sarah said mournfully. "The bakers from Whitstable—so much better than Hubble's dusty loaves, theirs were—the millers from Blean, and the Torquay tea-runners. People used to come from all over to see us—see the libraries and the electric lights. Petham, Broadoak, Adisham… They can't all have gone away."

"They're probably all dead," John said.

Sarah looked wounded. "That's callous."

"It's not callous to state the truth. The trade routes are long gone. Whoever survived winter moved north, or away from the cities. The rest died. It's that simple." John shrugged. "And we killed them."

All eyes turned to him, stunned.

Norman felt a lump form in his throat, and found his gaze trained on the floor.

John's maroon pug of a face had creased into a thin smile, and he pressed on—though it seemed that he now spoke more to himself than them. "Our best estimates put the population at—what—fifty thousand? That puts about ten thousand over the South, who can only occupy land away from urbanised areas. But even a handful of communities like ours make up at least half of that number, and each one draws its food from the most productive remaining rural areas. When our crops were hit so hard last year, we took what we had to." John's brows flickered skywards. "Everybody else lost out."

There was a long silence.

"So why not group together, like us?" Richard said. "I can't get my head around the tribal mentality. There's safety in numbers: more hands to toil, more bargaining power, supply and demand, trade, mutual support—civilisation!" He frowned. "I just don't understand it."

"Of course you don't, you're just a boy," John mumbled, poised over the chessboard. "That's why I'm the Master and you're the Student."

"I'm still not happy with the title of 'Master'," Richard said with a heavy voice, his nose upturned. He moved a pawn and sat back, his hands behind his head. The smug expression remained upon his features long enough for everybody to have registered it, just in time for it to be swept away by the swift movement of John's queen.

"Get used to it," John said. "Western civilisation trumped the world's tribes, hands down, but getting it started took millennia. Without places like this, mankind would have already slipped into a new Dark Age."

Sarah tittered. "It's all very well and good coming off high and mighty, but like I said, just last year people would have walked a hundred miles just to look at a light bulb. It was…magic to them. This place was magical." She paused. "Our way of life hasn't exactly spread like wildfire, has it?"

John turned his gaze upon her. "People won't group together for a lot of reasons. First of all, it's dangerous: if you get into trouble, you can't run; you're a bigger target; and you're vulnerable to outbreaks of infection. And if that isn't enough, you've got all of the troubles of organising sanitation, security, food and water, a law system, and all the other things we're halfway through scrambling together." He spread his hands. "The bigger they are, the harder they fall."

"Look who's talking," said Richard.

"Careful, boy."

Richard shook his head, as though shaking off a fly. "It's still better than huddling for warmth in some mud hut somewhere."

"That's arguable. All of the problems that we have potentially outweigh the benefits. We just haven't noticed because we've had a run of extremely good luck, until now."

"But for nobody but us to even *try*…"

John waggled a finger. "Don't think that people haven't tried to do what we're doing before. There's been a lot of time for that—decades. I haven't been here as long as some. I've seen other places where the lights still burned. And I've seen every one of them fall. They've all failed, because none of them had what we have here."

"And what's that?"

"We've got Alexander."

At first, John's final words sounded strange, almost childish, plainly reverential. And yet, nobody felt the urge to mock them. As fresh silence settled, those words seemed anything but childish. They were what they were: the plain, naked truth.

"And we've got you, Mr Creek," John finished, gesturing to Norman with the slightest of curtseys.

Norman had been waiting for it, but warmth spread across his cheeks all the same. He did his best to smile. "Sure," he said, looking into the eyes of a genius, and seeing nought but another zealot.

John smiled, and turned to the chessboard. "Checkmate," he said, lifting Richard's king to his lips with a flourish.

Richard grumbled, and began to reset the board with a patience and dexterity that could have only come from a thousand repetitions.

*

By the time the final school bell rang, Main Street was thronged by workers coming home from the fields. Not a single murmur graced the air. All that was audible was the sound of clanking hoes and dragging boots. The field hands' drawn, hangdog faces had been made identical by exhaustion and malnutrition, their work-weary eyes never leaving the ground.

Norman reined to a halt, descending from his mount to watch the solemn procession.

He'd made straight for the school after returning from the wilds with Lucian and Allie, not even stopping to stable his mount or deliver his sacks to the storeroom.

Now, exhausted and ravenous, all he wanted was to crawl into bed with a loaf of the mill's bread—riddled with sawdust or not.

As the filthy folk passed by, a few glances were sent his way, pleading looks begging him for a word of comfort; forlorn and watchful, lest he'd become the prophet they craved during his few short hours in the wilds.

He could only blink and stare back at them, with shame pressing against the nape of his neck. Even as Sarah passed him, prancing off towards Robert—who stood silhouetted in the kitchen doorway—he remained slumped on his saddle, staring, clinging to the vague hope that his mere presence could buoy up the sullen droves.

He was eventually jarred from his trance by a grating racket.

"What's all this hush?" shrieked a high-pitched, ancient voice. "At this hour? You should all be home preparin' for End Day!"

Norman turned to see Agatha standing across the street, waving her cane at the field hands. A hunchbacked old lady with skin like sodden laundry and a face made dull and slack by advanced dementia, she struggled forth. On any other day she was perpetually dazed, always getting lost, but today she seethed with fury.

"It's our greatest festival, it is. Every year since the End, we've celebrated, and I'll not have a bit o' hunger see it forgotten." She stepped forwards and began clawing at elbows as they brushed past. "It's *tradition*. Get your heads up from the dirt and *smile*! Come on, now, dears. 'Tis End Day! Time to remember, to celebrate—"

"Hush your gums, you senile old coot! We're not celebrating nothing," exclaimed a sour-faced youth. His skin immediately drained of colour. It was clear that he had spoken before thinking, on impulse alone.

The comment nonetheless earned him a beating to the back of the head by no less than three nearby elders.

Agatha's face had fallen. Her grey, cataract-ridden eyes widened. "How dare you gab to me like tha', you little swine! Tomorrow's all that connects us to what we've lost, all tha' keeps the Old World alive. Are none of you going to take a stand?"

Some sent embarrassed glances her way. Most became only more fixed on the ground. None answered her. The procession sped along, trying to leave the wilted figure in its wake.

Agatha's protests continued, diminishing with each repetition, until her shoulders slumped and her cane slowly drooped to the ground, defeated.

Then a resounding, steadfast voice rang out over the cobbles, "Mr Singh, how are the pastry cases coming along?"

Norman whirled to see Alexander standing a few yards away.

He strode across the street and laid his hand upon Agatha's shoulder, then bent over her and whispered a few words that made her giggle like a little girl, looking adoringly into his eyes. Then he called Sarah and Robert from the kitchens and had them lead her home.

She went without a word, her eyes misty and vacant once more.

Once the trio had disappeared, he planted his knuckles on his hips and stared into the depths of the crowd. His eyes had become shards of flint. "Mr Singh?" he called. "The pastry cases?"

A weathered, white-haired man of Middle-Eastern descent answered with a wavering voice, "I have them ready, sir. Baked them firm yesterday evening—"

"Good man. Best get to it if we're to see the End Day pies good and ready."

The man jerked, as though struck. "But…but there's so little food, there is. I've heard nothing of any filling, sir. Everyone says there will not be any feast this year…"

But Alex had turned to another face in the crowd. "Mrs Hadley, is your dear father still happy to have his band play for us tomorrow?"

The procession had slowed to a crawl. Startled, watchful looks were being thrown every which way.

A dirt-streaked, mousy woman appeared to shrink under his gaze. "He's spoken of nothin' else for days, Misser Alexander. He and the boys have been keepin' me and the kids up for weeks with all their practissin! But…to be honest wi' you, sir, I told them to quit it. Said there wasn't going to be no celebratin' this year—"

But Alexander had moved on once more. "Master Ishadore," he cried, eyeing a passing boy of no more than eight years. "I trust you've been gathering mushrooms with your classmates, as I requested?"

The boy tittered at being addressed, but answered with pride, "For the last week. We've filled my Dad's shed full. But, sir…the End Day celebrations are cancelled…aren't they?"

Hundreds of pairs of eyes now turned from the ground just in time to see Alexander break into a good-natured laugh. "Oh, we'd never let a thing like a shortage in spuds scupper the most important day of the year. Now hop to it, all three of you. There's work to be done!"

Those he'd spoken to jerked, open-mouthed, and then chorused, "Y-Y-Yes, sir, Mr Cain!"

Mr Singh scuttled off at full pelt, dragging his hoe in his wake and parting the crowd ahead with stifled apologies. Close behind him dashed Hadley and young Ishadore. Their harried cries were soon consumed by the growing noise of the crowd, which had come alive.

Alexander watched them go, and then turned his gaze upon the rest. "That goes for all of you. We'll not let a poor harvest dampen our fair day, will we?"

A few muttered, "No."

Alex raised his voice, the wide smile still stretched over his cheeks. "A little hunger isn't going to keep us from celebrating what we've done—all we've accomplished."

A few more, "No."

"We'll never bow down to what life throws at us. Not this city."

Almost everybody, louder, "Never!"

"Are we going to forget the faces of those we've lost?"

"*NO!*" they bellowed.

"Then let's get to it. Hang the bunting, fetch the cider, slaughter the livestock, ready the china." He clapped his hands together with a deafening boom. "*We've got a feast to prepare!*"

Eyes lit up like lanterns festooned with oil. Morose sniffing had become wide-eyed glee in a single stride. The crowd rounded the corner buzzing with excited mutterings, half-suppressed giggles and a spring in its step.

Norman had watched the Shepherd wield his flock with mounting awe. *This is what they expect of me?* he thought. *What* he *expects of me? I could never do that—not in a million years.*

And yet, despite his admiration, as soon as they were out of sight and Main Street was deserted, his thoughts turned back to the questionable fruits they had picked. He lurched forwards, leading his mount, and pulled Alexander aside. "Alex, we can't go ahead with the celebrations." He reached into the sack nearest his reins and pulled out a handful of half-rotted fruit. "What we found today might not do us any good. We'll be lucky if it's fit to feed the horses…" Norman stopped, frowning. "Alex?" He wound down to a halt, his argument forgotten.

Alexander wasn't listening. He stood stock-still, and the plastic smile had fallen slack on his lips. His eyes were focused not on Norman, or the berry-red slush in his outstretched hand, but on the pylon above their heads.

He followed Alexander's gaze to see a bird perched upon the lines, silhouetted against the sky. A pigeon's silhouette. "Robert's been trying to get rid of them for days, but they keep coming back," he said, glancing between Alexander and the cooing figure. "What's the matter?"

Alexander's mouth bobbed without a sound. His cool composure had dissolved, and Norman thought that, for just a moment, he could see fear in his eyes. "We're not cancelling anything," he said. He sounded distant, unlike himself. Then he stammered, "I-I have to go." His hand had risen to his forehead, shielding his eyes. He suddenly seemed disoriented, almost unsteady on his feet. "There's some business I have to attend to. I'll find you later."

He stumbled away, leaving Norman alone on Main Street, baffled, with the pigeon's shadow bobbing on the cobbles beside him.

*

By that evening, preparations for the End Day feast were in full swing.

Not a word had been said about cancellation, even after the other scavenging parties had returned, and their own stories of death and destitution had spread to every ear. With the city's sullen mood finally on the verge of breaking, Norman didn't have the heart to speak up.

Despite searching for the remainder of the day, he didn't see Alexander again until the following evening. Nor, in fact, did anybody else.

VIII

The rowboat hit sand with a shuddering jolt, neatly sliding from the sea onto the windswept beach. There, it slumped onto its side, and its three occupants fell with it, rolling into the surf.

All was still for some minutes while the breeze kicked up the shifting dunes and a flock of gulls screeched above, wheeling around to circle the wonder from across the sea.

Then, one of the limp, dehydrated figures stirred. A haggard middle-aged man struggled to lift his head and clap eyes on his surroundings, uttering a breathless cry when he saw what lay before him.

Alien land loomed beyond the beach, primordial cliffs, grey skies, and an endless, unbroken forest.

*

Don swam up from unconsciousness towards sunlight. It was tough, tiring work, like throwing off a lead duvet. Shapes loomed from fuzzy oblivion: two bodies, one large and one small, and beyond them a blurred tapestry that could have only been land.

A sound escaped his throat, somewhere between a laugh and a scream. They had made it.

Through heavy-lidded eyes he could only vaguely make out Billy's figure. But he could make out her chest—rising and falling, rising and falling…

She was alive.

Satisfied, he sank back towards blackness for a while, and rested.

At some point he began struggling up the beach on his hands and knees in a series of bursts that he would later only recall in brief flashes. Somehow, he managed to drag Billy with him, and even to return for the old man.

The inevitable happened just after the three of them had passed the tideline. He began coughing. A single throat-clearing jolt was enough to send his lungs into spasm. He hadn't the energy to do anything but ball his hands into fists and try to keep his airway free of sputum until it had passed.

Afterwards, he laid gasping, tasting blood, not daring to move. A steady pain was pulsing through his abdomen and his head felt fuzzy, his thoughts distant and diffuse. Between the pain and the disorientating roar of the surf, he lost track of time. Staring down at the sand, he was content to remain there for as long as the day lasted.

On several occasions he oscillated between waking thoughts and vacant darkness. The world would settle into focus for a few moments before darkening, pulling away and vanishing.

After an amount of time that could have been anywhere between a few seconds and several hours, he was strong enough to sit up and look around. The boat was where he had left it down by the water, lying on its side. Their things, however, had been unloaded and set in the dry sand, such that they cast a long shadow over his body.

Billy was beside him, cross-legged in the sand, gazing at the land spread out before her and surveying the coast from end to end. When Don moved into a more dignified position, she started. "You were asleep," she said.

"What? No, no, I was just tired. You know I get tired a lot at the moment."

She shook her head, smiling. "You were snoring."

"I was?" Don looked down at his spread-eagled impression in the sand, firmly set and comically accurate, a strict mould of the contours of his face. "How long?"

Billy looked stricken, and glanced at the pocket watch dangling from his belt. "I don't know time, Daddy," she said.

"You can tell time." Despite his exhaustion, he kept his voice firm and pointed to the sky.

Billy glanced at the sun and hunched her shoulders, shying away from it. "I can't," she said.

"Of course you can."

"I don't like to. You can do it better with your watch. The sun isn't as good, you said."

Don sighed and used their piled supplies to haul himself to his feet. He took a deep breath as a pang of land sickness nauseated him. "Roughly," he said, rubbing his eyes. "How long, roughly?"

Billy scrunched up her face. After a few hesitant stutters and false starts, she shrugged. "I don't know."

Don leaned against the boxes and rested his head in his hands. "Billy, I know that you can tell time. You've been able to do it since you could talk."

She looked unsettled. "I don't like to," she said. "I like your watch. I like you to tell time."

Don caught her glancing at the pocket watch; an intrigued, but distantly frightened look, as though she suspected that it contained untold powers, which only adults had the wisdom to wield.

Don nodded. "Alright," he said.

She looked pleased to be rid of the conversation, and resumed scanning the coast.

Don attempted to gauge how long had passed himself. There was no question that the shadows had shifted, but the sun was still high in the sky. He decided that it couldn't have been longer than an hour.

He approached the tideline and craned his neck, trying to peer around a distant peninsula blocking their view to the south. Besides the boat and themselves, there was nothing distinctive about the landscape at all. They alone seemed to break the landscape's perfect symmetry, caught between the four elements of sky, sea, sand and forest.

"Where are we?" he said.

"New land," Billy said. "It is New Land, isn't it, Daddy?"

"I don't know. Wherever it is, it definitely isn't home."

She made a noise of bemusement. "It has a name. Enger Land?"

"England."

"That's a funny name. I think Enger Land is better."

Don straightened when a shadow appeared from the forest and made its way towards them. His momentary shock gave way to recognition as the old man's unmistakable figure emerged from the shade of the treetops, stumbling and cursing his way across the sand. After what seemed like an age, he reached them. Dropping an armful of dried wood in front of them, he dusted his hands and gestured to it with a cry of satisfaction.

"What's this?" Don said, inspecting a twisted lump of dried root.

"Fuel, dear boy."

"Good."

"We'll stay here for the night. There's no sense in wandering now. We'll only get lost."

Don looked around at the barren dunes. "We'll be seen," he said. "The beach is too open. We should move inland."

The old man gestured to the trees. "There's nobody there."

"You don't know that."

"Past the trees, there are more trees. That forest is thick…it looks like it goes on for miles. There isn't a break in sight."

"So?"

"So? No water, no room, no animals. There's no reason for anybody to be anywhere near here. So we'll stay the night."

Don thought of arguing—wanted to argue—but the old man had already set about constructing a plateau in the sand upon which to build their fire. He avoided Billy's eye and started helping the old man without another word.

Once a nest of flames was crackling in the sand, the three of them stretched out beside it in silence, listening to the surf as the sun began its long descent. After a while, the old man brought out a small pile of bruised fruit. They cut it into slices, perhaps too thin in an effort to make it last, but it was still far from a satisfying meal.

The old man threw a spare stick into the flames and let loose a high-pitched titter. "We were aiming for Bristol, but I climbed a hill on the other side of the trees… I don't see anything.

"I think we must have overshot. The winds were against us. They must've won, pulled us around the head of Cornwall and into the Channel." He lapsed into silence, but still looked troubled.

Don waited a few moments before prompting him. "Where are we, then?"

The old man thrust out his bottom lip and shook his head. "I don't recognise this coastline. We were drifting for a whole day." He laughed again, but there was no humour in it. "Portsmouth? Brighton? Maybe even Hastings… I don't know."

He looked unsettled for a moment longer, then his face cleared, and a thin smile touched his lips. "Still, spilt milk and all that—"

Whatever that meant, Don thought.

"We're here. That's all that matters. We should just get some sleep and see what we find tomorrow." He lay down and closed his eyes.

They lapsed into silence.

Don lay with his back to the sea and kept watch over the trees, unable to shake the creeping sensation that had settled along the back of his neck.

Billy sat beside him, twiddling the remains of the matchstick they had used between her fingers as her eyelids grew heavier. She inspected the charred tip, her brow furrowed, and said, "How do you make matches?"

Don smiled. "Will you ever stop asking questions?" he said.

"I don't know. Maybe when I know everything, like you and Grandpa."

Don settled into the sand and gazed at the sky. "I have no idea how to make matches," he said.

Billy recoiled. Her face contorted, as though she'd tasted something bitter. "What?"

"I don't know."

"But you know everything."

"No."

Billy looked at the match, offended by its existence. She turned it over in her hands and threw occasional glances in his direction. "If you don't know how to make matches, then how do we have them?"

"We found them."

"Who made them?"

"Others."

Billy looked about. "Where are they?"

"Gone."

"Where did they go?"

"I don't know."

Billy seemed confused by the concept of there being knowledge that Don didn't have immediate access to.

"You need phosphorus and potassium chlorate to make matches," the old man said without warning. His eyes were closed, but his voice was strong and awake. He sounded amused by the turn of events.

Billy looked at the old man and then back to Don. "You lied?"

Don blinked, taken aback. "No."

"You *do* know everything."

"No."

"Grandpa knows how to make matches."

Don leaned over and pulled her towards him. "Grandpa's older than I am, and so he knows more than I do."

"How does he know more?"

"He asked his father questions, like I asked him questions and like you ask me questions. But I never asked him how to make matches."

What Don failed to mention was that his father had survived the end of the Old World. Billy knew nothing of it. To her, their lives were merely the latest in an eternal struggle for survival in a world full of inanimate knickknacks.

It was better that way, and Don had done his best to safeguard her ignorance.

"Oh." She looked at the old man, who now looked as though he could be asleep. "How old is Grandpa?"

She looked fascinated. Don suspected that, so far as she was concerned, her grandfather had been present at the creation of the world.

"Almost seventy, so far as I know."

Billy looked horrified that the old man had been forced to live for such an inordinate length of time. "Does *he* know everything?"

"No, nobody knows everything."

"But he knows a lot?"

"He's a gifted man."

"Who gave him his gift?"

Don's patience was waning, and he was beginning to slip away towards sleep. "Nobody, he was born that way."

Billy seemed to be following suit, yet her mouth continued to work, as though independent of her mind. Just when he thought she might have drifted off, she turned towards the fire and sighed. "New Land looks like home," she said.

Don grunted, on the edge of sleep. "What were you expecting?" he said.

"I don't know. Something different, maybe."

A few minutes later, the pace of her breathing relaxed. She was out.

Don hauled himself into a seated position to stoke the fire, barely suppressing a coughing fit. Once certain the flames would burn for a while longer, he curled around Billy, smelling traces of lemon in her hair—her mother's scent—as sleep overtook him.

He dreamed of better times.

THIRD INTERLUDE

The storm had descended within moments. Alex lost his footing upon the crest of the largest hill for miles and crashed to the bottom of a steep ravine. While his face was smeared with thick, stinking mud, thunder clapped above. He clung to his bag, toppling end over end, until flung face first against waterlogged rock. Gasping, he stared up at the blackened clouds as his battered body sang with fresh agony.

The dog was beside him moments later, yelping in distress, but her cries were barely audible over the roar of the heavens. She tugged at the hem of his trousers until he waved her away.

He groaned and turned over, staring along the ravine and out over the surrounding moorland. Naked granite boulders set in boggy fields of windswept heath were already drowned under an inch of water.

The hills were now skewed by perspective such that they bore down on him on either side, rendered monstrous cliffs.

Beneath a flash of lightning he blundered along the ravine, following the cascading rainwater. His clothes were heavy rags, clinging to his skin. His bag, having been carefully protected, was the only thing that hadn't been ruined.

After ten minutes, through the enshrouding haze he saw the cottage. Perched atop a distant rise, visible in silhouette only, the oasis seemed to beckon him, welcoming him with open arms.

As he drew closer, the storm grew fiercer, tearing at his clothes, trying to rip him from the side of the hill. After what seemed like an eternity he left the ravine and reached the hilltop upon which the cottage rested. He approached, uncertain.

Uneven whitewashed walls, crooked beams and windows cut into diamond lites by diagonal muntins sat beneath a low, thatched roof. An encircling picket fence guarded a garden of hardy plants against the moorland, failing to quite disguise the crumbling remains of an outdoor privy. The gate flapped in the wind, dragging against a skeletal patch of feather grass, and the door had been left slightly ajar.

Alex paused. It was a stark contrast to its formerly pleasant silhouette. Up close it was decrepit, creaking, unsettled.

The dog seemed to sense his hesitation. She had ceased her yelping and stood beside him, low on her haunches, eyeing the cottage with suspicion.

He stood beyond the gate with the rain crashing down upon him and called out to the storm, "Hello!"

Only a rolling thunderclap answered.

He took a last glance around at the barren moor before pushing his way through the gate and across the threshold.

Inside, all was damp and cold and darkness. An unpleasant, musty smell filled his nose. He faced a fireplace, set against a far wall, nestled within a ring of threadbare furniture. Edging inside, he closed the door against the storm. It snapped shut with a reverberating rattle, an ugly sound that hung in the air, taunting him, jangling in the recesses of distant rooms.

Alex remained still as he acclimatised, his senses overloaded from fighting the storm. His skin danced with the ghosts of raindrops and his cheeks throbbed as blood began to return to them.

The dog, having tired of his reservations, scrambled forwards, spinning in tight circles by the fireplace, spraying the walls with rainwater. Once dry, she set about prowling the periphery of the room, sniffing each object in turn.

Alex staggered after her, leaving long streaks of mud on bowed hardwood floorboards. Besides the squelch of his footsteps and the hum of the rain against the thatch, the cottage was noiseless. He had grown used to quiet homes, but here the silence still sat awkwardly, draped like a blanket over every surface.

"Hello?" he called again. Only a cracked, uneven echo returned from the farthest rooms.

He lingered a moment longer before advancing into the living room and, satisfied that he was alone, tore his dripping jacket from his shoulders. He cast it away into the kitchen, along with his boots and pullover, and then dropped into the nearest armchair.

Exhaustion swept over him immediately. His eyes drooped despite the cold, and he sank low into the cushions. A blissful sensation swept through him, drawing him towards sleep.

He decided he would stay in the chair for a little while, rest for a minute—just a minute—and then get himself dry…

Had a scream not cut through the silence like a lance, he would have fallen asleep without another thought. But it did come, with such suddenness that he was on his feet and standing before the door of the nearest bedroom before he'd had time to do anything but utter a wordless cry.

When his weary mind caught up with his body, however, his blood ran cold. Broken and riddled with a low-pitched gargle, the cry was unmistakably that of a baby.

Panic, raw and primal, surged in his gut. His bones suddenly felt brittle, and bile was rising into his throat. He looked at the closed door before him, listening to the choked, screeching wail, aghast.

His hand reached for the handle of its own accord and pushed the door open. He was left looking in at a darkened room, sweat pouring from his forehead and mingling with the rainwater upon his crown.

The room was as dim and dull as the fireside, but the air was drier, and had a foul odour about it, one that tickled the back of his throat.

Panic was on the verge of overcoming him, and his legs had tensed, preparing to send him running. But then the wailing reached a new crescendo, plastering him to the spot.

Lying beside an unmade bed—upon the pillows of which rested a pair of sleeping masks and the collars of empty pyjamas—was a pine cot, smothered in a nest of blankets, from which rose a pudgy fist.

Alex approached on shaking legs. He was desperate to escape—to hurl himself back into the storm and take his chances with hypothermia—but still he approached on shaking knees, staring open-mouthed at the cot's occupant.

A pair of green eyes, insectivorous in proportion, gazed up at him. The infant clasped its hands together with a blank expression on its face, blinking. Alex felt a thud deep within his chest, unable to break its gaze. Neither of them moved again for what seemed like an age, growing accustomed to each other's presence.

The infant must have been in the cot for days, and during that time clearly hadn't been fed, changed, or had anything to drink. On closer inspection, he saw that it was closer to a toddler than a baby. It had appeared so small at first due to dehydration; it was almost pruned, with colourless lips and sunken eye sockets. He was certain that it would be unable to move to save its life, let alone stand.

He bounded from the room in search of water. His mind was still too shocked to offer up thoughts of any clarity, but his limbs were content to operate under their own power, marching him into the kitchen to remove any containers from the cupboards. He then carried an armful out to the garden to fill in the rain.

By the time he fled back inside, he was shivering, and could do no more until he had hunted for replacement clothing. Also draping a thick duvet from the spare room over his shoulders, he proceeded to carry out his tasks with at least some semblance of comfort.

Having grown bored with exploring, the dog had slumped down on the floor beside the armchair, and watched him with faint curiosity.

In the study he found thick piles of tax returns that would be of little use to their owner now, ideal fuel. He hauled them to the living room fireplace and dumped them into the sooty grate. By the time he'd fished his matches from the depths of his bag and the flames had caught hold, the toddler's cries had begun to weaken. The sound of its slurring, half-uttered whimpers was far worse than the previous wailing.

He stoked the flames for just long enough to be sure that they wouldn't go out, and rushed back to the bedroom. At the sight of him, the infant's wailing resumed. Desperation now filled its eyes, and it proceeded to work itself into a state of giddiness, crying with such force that its face turned a shade of puce.

Alex reached down and wrapped his arms around it, retching at the stench. He was shocked by how cold it was to the touch, how rubbery its skin felt against his, how feebly it held its head—how very close it was to death.

He hurried to the fireplace, where he set the child down, throwing off the duvet hanging around his shoulders and building a kind of nest in which to settle the wriggling creature. Sliding the nest along the floor until he was certain that the child wasn't in danger of rolling into the grate, he coaxed the fire to full life and stood back.

The warmth stemmed the child's cries, but only for a moment, during which time it glanced into the flickering flames, its eyes bulging with wonder. But then a strange expression crossed its face—perhaps as it had remembered it had a good deal more crying to do—and then resumed its wailing.

Shivering once again—the time taken to light the fire had been enough for the chill of the storm to have eaten its way to his bones—and now also cursing, Alex dashed back out into the rain. He collected as many of the filled containers as he could manage, returning with a gust of wind at his heels.

Searching the kitchen until he came across a suitable bottle complete with a plastic teat, he filled it with rainwater. He set it beside the fire to warm and took the infant into his arms, swaying it experimentally. It had no effect. The wailing continued.

It was some minutes—minutes full of mind-withering screams and hacking cries—before the water was fit to drink. When he finally pressed the bottle against its mouth, it latched onto the teat with astonishing zeal and began to squelch away, its eyes fixed upon his in an eternal stare.

He laid it back into its nest with the bottle, knowing that the peace would only last until the water ran out, and filled another from the containers, setting it beside the fire.

He changed his clothes once more and searched the bedroom until he found the child's compartment in the wardrobe. Picking out whichever items he thought suitable, he took a pile to the living room.

He returned just as the child drained the bottle, and the wet squelching sound shifted to a dry whistle. Before the wailing could resume, he replaced the empty bottle with the new one. The squelching began in earnest once more.

Leaving the pile of clothes beside the fire, he wandered away to assess the cottage. He tried the telephone and heard nothing, no dial tone or noise of any kind, just as with every other he'd tried since…since that day.

How long had it been now? Three days? A week? More?

A laptop left on the coffee table was unresponsive to every attempt he made to bring it to life. When he shook it, he heard only a rolling hiss, and was at once certain that the innards had disintegrated into dust.

The lights, however, still worked. He wondered how long the power grid could operate on its own, without anybody to maintain it. He guessed they had a few days, maybe less.

He'd have to find some candles; it was going to get dark at night.

In the study he rifled through cheque books, utility bills and bank statements addressed to William and Martha Chadwick—who he supposed had been the ones wearing the sleep masks and pyjamas in bed before vanishing, leaving their child to wilt in its crib, alone. On the desk he found a book containing the child's birth certificate, first handprints and suchlike. He took it into the living room and sat down in the armchair to read while the toddler rolled in the blankets, drinking in great gulps. Already, he noticed, colour had returned to its lips, and it looked a good deal stronger.

The birth certificate named the child as James William Chadwick. He flipped through the baby book to find a large, colour photograph of the toddler bundled into the arms of a beaming couple in their forties. Together, they all smiled giddily out at him.

James Chadwick spat the empty bottle from his lips and belched explosively. He smacked his lips for a while and then, after some reflection, began wailing once more. His skin regained its vile puce colour within moments.

The dog seemed as annoyed by the noise as Alex. Groaning, it rose to its feet and slumped away to the bedroom in search of quiet.

Alex steeled himself and approached James, kneeling down beside the fire. Taking a gulp of air, he unfastened the boy's rotten nappy, praying that his shaking fingers wouldn't slip. James refused to help his chances, and wriggled in his grip, screaming all the while.

After being changed, dressed in fresh clothes and given yet another bottle of water, James promptly urinated. Hydrated and warmed, he now screamed only louder and seemed on the verge of struggling from the nest of duvets to run rampant.

Alex dashed away to the refrigerator, and was pushing his way through its contents, throwing aside pieces of pungent cheese and curdled yoghurt, before he realised that the box was at room temperature. It was just as broken as the phone and computer.

He cursed and began opening cupboards at random, staring at tins of corned beef and bottles of ketchup with a sinking heart.

There didn't seem to be any baby food. Of course there would be, somewhere. But how long would it take to find?

"Do you eat food?" he shouted over the roar of the rain.

The toddler glared at him and then returned to its busy schedule of rolling and screaming.

"Food," Alex repeated, dragging out the syllable until the consonants were lost in a sea of supplementary vowels. *"Foooood?"*

Again, James appeared nonplussed by the sound of his voice. This time he didn't even stop crying to listen.

A banana eventually became the most serviceable meal to Alex's eyes, mashed viciously with the back of a spoon and spilled into a bowl. After having the pap placed before him, James wasted no time in placing his hand into the bowl and smearing its innards across his cheeks and past his gums.

The screaming, it seemed, had ceased for the time being. Alex collapsed onto the floorboards beside him and let loose a long sigh. With his hands extended out towards the fire, he slowly warmed himself on the living room floor. Once the chill had left his bones, he sat forwards to observe James finish the banana paste.

James smacked his lips together and sucked on his fingers with glazed, satisfied eyes.

Alex couldn't help but smile at the clumsy and yet deliberate way in which he conducted himself, as though great intelligence was concealed behind the blankness of his features.

Overcome by sudden and all-consuming affection, he leaned towards the boy and muttered into his ear, "Hello, James. I'm Alex."

IX

Billy stared into the light of the fire. Grandpa was singing to her. Her eyes lolled, half-closed, and her heart seemed to beat to the rhythm of his voice:

"Oranges and lemons, Say the bells of St. Clement's…"

She sank further towards sleep. Her lips formed the silent words, 'You owe me three farthings' in perfect unison with those he sang aloud. The blankets enveloped her, and within moments she was barely aware of anything else. She was on the verge of sleep when her stomach rumbled explosively.

"I'm hungry," she said.

Daddy's tired sigh rang out from somewhere nearby. "I know, we're all hungry, Billy. We have to save our food. We don't know when we'll be able to get more."

Billy nodded, but her stomach kept grumbling nonetheless. "We need to get more soon," she said.

"I know. There isn't any here."

She didn't understand. Food had grown all over the place back at home. She had collected her own breakfast from the berry bushes behind their house since she had been able to walk.

Not this year, though. This year there had been none. They had gone hungry—so hungry that there hadn't been enough to go around for the four of them, not enough by half. Billy had been scared, not just by how Daddy and Grandpa would leave home for days to find them a meal, but by Ma.

Ma had started sneaking her food away at mealtimes. After dark, she'd come to Billy's room and force her to eat it. Eat it all.

Billy had begged her to stop, to take it back—to eat just a spoonful herself.

But she hadn't stopped. She had forced Billy to eat every bite, day after day. When Daddy had asked why she was getting so thin, she had lied—lied to his face. Billy knew that had hurt her bad. She had seen her crying after telling a lie one morning. As the winter had worn on, and the forests had turned black, she had forked over her share again and again, wasting away before Billy's eyes.

When she had finally gotten sick, she had been too weak to put up much of a fight.

Billy's heart ached, just as it had done each day since they had buried Ma in the barley fields behind their house. But tonight her rumbling stomach hurt just as much as the heartache. Maybe more.

New Land seemed to have even less food than home. In fact, she had seen none at all. She, Daddy and Grandpa had been walking since dawn, having left the beach and headed inland, and seen nothing but abandoned towns, rotten crops, and bones.

She no longer dared guess how far they had come.

"Where has it all gone?" she asked.

There was a silence, during which she refused to look away from the fire. The campsite was full of ominous, angular shapes, spread in a recess at the edge of an endless stretch of lifeless meadows.

"I don't know," Daddy said.

Billy hugged her knees closer and sighed, settling back into her bundle of blankets. Grandpa said nothing for a while, and then began to sing once more, quietly at first but then louder, until eventually he was back in full swing, as though nothing had happened:

"When will you pay me? Say the bells of Old Bailey…"

Billy continued to mime the words along with him as she once again sank towards a black abyss, her hunger almost forgotten in the wake of his gentle voice.

After a while, Daddy joined in. At first, he was quiet like Grandpa had been, and his voice was rough—his coughing had made his voice hoarse as the day had worn on—but after only a few moments he too sang merrily, and Billy smiled.

She soon stopped miming and sang along with them, watching the blood-red ghosts of dancing flames through her closed eyelids. Together, the three of them overwhelmed the crackling of the fire, the singing of the insects, and the barren whistle of New Land's winds; they could have been back at home, where they belonged.

There were no meadows, no foreign skyline, and no hunger. Just the three of them, and their singing.

After all their tunes had run their course, their voices petered out until, once again, Grandpa sang alone. His tone, however, was undiminished. Billy wondered for how long he could go on before even he tired of it, but then remembered that Grandpa was so old that, to him, years were probably like minutes.

She hoped that it wouldn't be years before Oranges and Lemons stopped filling her ears.

Sleep still eluded her. Occasionally she fell towards it in great swooping dives, but would return to wakefulness at the last moment. Something other than her empty stomach was keeping her awake, but she couldn't figure out what it was.

After a while she turned onto her back and looked up at the night sky.

The stars twinkled and fizzed above like fireflies. She wondered how many people had looked upon them in times past, and how many were doing so at that very moment.

There was a rustling in the grass nearby, and then a shadow crept up and lay down in the grass beside her. Daddy's distinctive cheekbones were cast in silhouette against the sky. She snuggled against his chest and looked back at the heavens while Grandpa continued to sing.

"What are they?" she whispered.

"Stars?"

"Yes."

He uttered a formless grunt, and cleared his throat. "I couldn't tell you," he said.

"Why not?"

"It means that I don't know."

"Oh."

On the other side of the fire, Grandpa stopped singing Oranges and Lemons, and began to mutter the words of Twinkle, twinkle, little star.

"Is he drunk?" Billy asked.

"No, he's just old."

"Does he know what stars are?"

"Up above the world so high, like a diamond in the sky…"

Daddy shuffled in the grass—Billy suspected that he was looking at Grandpa over the fire—and then settled beside her again. "Probably," he said.

"Should we ask him?"

"I think we should just let him sing. We'll ask him another time."

"Okay." As Billy stared at the stars, she began to see the outlines of bunnies and dragons in their midst. Then a thought occurred to her. She turned to Daddy, whose face was a black mask against the glow of the fire, and said, "Where does Grandpa get his songs?"

Even though it was dark, she knew he was laughing at her. "I'll eat my hat on the day you stop asking questions," he said.

"Why would you eat your hat?"

Instead of answering, Daddy only laughed harder. He didn't stop until he was wheezing. "It's a figure of speech," he said finally.

"Where did it come from? I've never heard that one before."

Daddy sniffed and raised his hands. "Where does anything come from? What you know, you got from me, and what I know I got from Grandpa, and so on."

Billy leaned back, dissatisfied. From the words 'so on', all she could surmise was that Grandpa had simply been gifted with every shred of knowledge at the beginning of time. It was the only way that made sense.

"Twinkle, twinkle, little star, how I wonder what you are...," Grandpa muttered, and grew silent.

Daddy looped an arm over her, and the two of them enjoyed a brief lull, during which only the sound of their breathing and the crackling of the fire reached their ears.

And then Grandpa started over with *Oranges and Lemons*, apparently resigned to go on until dawn—or until they gagged him.

"Are we going to find some food soon?" Billy asked.

Daddy was quiet for a long time, allowing Grandpa's singing to fill the silence.

"Daddy?"

"We'll be fine," he said. "I promise."

"We'll find food?"

He ruffled her hair. "Of course we will!"

"Tomorrow?"

"Tomorrow."

Billy nodded. A weight had lifted from her chest. She now thought only of Grandpa's words, and how firmly Daddy's arm was coiled around her. As she finally fell towards the depths of sleep, the faintest cosy warmth burned in her belly.

Then the attack came. Had it not been for Grandpa's abrupt silence, she would have had no warning. So close to black oblivion, she had very little sense of it. In one moment she was curled up on the floor, the next she was flung into the air. Then she was running and screaming. In a single moment, from peaceful silence to the deafening score of battle.

"DONALD!" Grandpa roared.

In the darkness, Billy waved her arms wildly, blinded. The fire was the only source of light, flickering somewhere in her peripheral vision, its embers having spilled into the grass. Figures darted before it, black profiles outlined against the dying conflagration. Somewhere in the darkness, people were fighting for their lives.

Amidst the din, Billy stumbled and screamed, "Daddy!" Her sobbing voice fell short in the cacophony, a mere overtone to the chaos.

A towering body rushed by, so close that a gust of air whistled against her ears. A moment later there was a thump somewhere in the dark as it impacted something unseen. She could hear Daddy shouting, but couldn't tell what he was saying.

She wandered into the darkness with her hands stretched out before her, blinded further by tears that sprung from her eyes in torrential rivers. She managed only a few steps before another body passed close by, this time colliding with her and sending her flying through the air. She crashed into the grass while a horrible smell filled her nostrils: unwashed skin and rotten breath.

She was standing again almost immediately, groping thin air once more. She skirted the edge of the fire, which was by now dying in the dirt, blinking as her night vision began to develop.

The scuffling had grown quieter, but she could sense that she was in no less danger. As the night came into focus, she began to see the outlines of half a dozen figures, struggling on the ground. There was no way to tell one from another.

"Daddy!" she screamed.

At the sound of her voice, one of the figures looked up. A moment later it was struck across the head by the figure beneath it and toppled into the grass. The victor stumbled to his feet and dashed towards her, arms outstretched.

Billy recoiled and flailed before the figure's shadowed mask resolved into the angular profile of Daddy's face. A wordless cry escaped her mouth as she flung herself into his arms. "Where's Grandpa?" she stammered.

Two people lay unmoving in the grass, but three more still struggled and thrashed some distance away. Grandpa was in there somewhere, but there was no telling which figure was his. Daddy took hold of her shoulders and turned her head so that she stared into his eyes.

"You stay here," he said.

"But—"

"You stay!"

She nodded, and he dived headlong into the fray. From then on any distinguishing features blurred into nothing more than a stifled struggle between shadows.

"Daddy! Grandpa!" she wailed.

But this time her cries didn't bring Daddy running back. After half a minute, somebody else toppled into the grass, but by that time one of the fallen figures had regained its footing. The fight continued with equal ferocity.

From her left came Grandpa's voice, "Donald!"

From her right, Daddy's choked reply, "Dad!"

In the darkness, a woman shrieked, momentarily visible as she flew over the fire's remains. She crashed into the grass and moved no more.

The odds had turned, and the fight broke. Four of the figures had bunched together, flailing on the ground. Two others remained in the grass, unmoving.

Two further shadows dragged each other to their feet and dashed to the side. Once clear, they paused and turned to her. "Billy!"

She ran to them, skirting the fallen menaces. Strong arms gripped her, Daddy's face flashed somewhere above, and then she was being dragged through the grass.

Grandpa puffed alongside—a single bag slung over his shoulder—but he soon fell behind, limping badly. He stopped and started, faltering, and could then only take a few steps at a time.

Daddy let go of Billy and ran back to him, looping an arm over his shoulder and hauling him along. Billy ran alongside them, crying, and Daddy hushed her as they crashed into the forest at the meadow's edge.

At the very same moment the moon crested the horizon, and the first of its silver beams thrust through the canopy, throwing their cover of darkness to the wind. Billy tripped over the roots of trees and ducked beneath overhanging branches, struggling to keep pace. The forest, now dressed in a steely veil, was dark and yet blinding, gnarled and terrifying.

Behind them, their attackers plunged into the trees' midst and gave chase, taking far less care with how much noise they made, breaking fronds and branches in great swathes. It sounded as though a great, grumbling monster was in pursuit.

With Grandpa's limp slowing them down, they would be caught in moments. Already Billy could feel a creeping along the back of her neck.

Daddy jabbed her chest and pointed towards a rocky outcrop, silver-white in the glare of a dense patch of moonbeams. It was cragged and riddled with fissures, in such a way that its shadowed crevices would make ideal hiding places. He gripped her arm and plucked her into the air, planting her feet atop the nearest rock. She leapt out upon the archipelago of boulders and bluffs, painfully aware that one slip would break her ankle, and headed towards the deepest cleft in sight.

Grandpa scrambled after her while Daddy glanced over his shoulder at the approaching shadows. "Hurry up!" he whispered.

The three of them bounded towards the cleft, which turned out to be at least six feet deep, and wedged themselves in place. In the sudden stillness their exhalations were deafening.

Billy tried to slow her thundering heart and wiped cold rivers of tears from her cheeks. "Daddy!" she whimpered. He hushed her, but she couldn't help it. Terror was rising in her chest in waves. "*Daddy!*"

He took hold of her arm and held it tight. The fear burned lower—just enough to let her take control of herself.

The heady stink of rotting mulch and mildew swam around her, clawing at the delicate flesh at the top of her nose, and something that moved too fast and had too many legs was crawling along her thigh.

But now she scarcely noticed. All her attention was focused on the darkness beyond their hiding place.

Less than a minute later, their pursuers arrived at the outcrop. The group of shadows skidded to a halt at the lip of a sharp decline—which lay just beyond the rocks, leading some fifty feet down to an empty streambed—and bent double, catching their breath and cursing.

Billy made not a sound. Her lungs burned, begging for air, but she resisted the urge to gasp—though that did nothing to stop her heart pounding in her chest. Beside her, she sensed Daddy and Grandpa holding their breath.

Together, they peered at the steaming shadows as kittens would spy a prowling fox.

As their attackers regained their composure, they began to scan the streambed and the forest beyond. But they didn't throw a single glance in the direction of the outcrop.

There was a moment when Billy thought they had escaped, a moment in which elation and relief dared to flare up amidst the terror.

But then Daddy's grip upon her arm became vice-like, hard enough to make her wince. In the moonlight, his darkened features were furrowed and his eyes were wide with horror. Billy nudged him to get his attention, but he had begun to shake.

And then, to Billy's disbelief, he coughed explosively. His grip upon her arm paralysed her. During the ensuing seconds she could only watch while he bent double and set about great bellowing gargles.

"Don!" Grandpa hissed.

Billy watched as Daddy clamped his hands over his mouth to stifle the sound, but it was far too late. The attackers had turned towards the outcrop and dropped into feline stances, half-crouched amidst the chrome-plated woodland.

"Come out!" sang a high, feminine voice, almost sweet, and yet chilling, without a trace of feeling. Another bout of Daddy's coughing answered.

The shadows began to creep forwards, as though sensing weakness. The manner in which they moved pulled a string deep in Billy's mind, one that sensed something unmistakably predatory.

"We know you're there." The woman again, her voice a chilling jeer.

Daddy was holding his chest, groaning. His grip on Billy's arm had redoubled, and Billy was forced to bite her lip to stop herself crying out. He bent low and gasped while the shadows grew closer.

"Donald, run," Grandpa said. His voice was no longer a whisper. He swung the bag down from his shoulder and pressed it into Daddy's lap, patting him on the shoulder.

"We can't," Daddy gasped. "Your leg."

But as he spoke, Grandpa was climbing out from the fissure, onto the cragged bluffs. Before Daddy or Billy could utter a word of protest, he gave a huge roar and surged towards the looming pursuers, who merely stood in his path, stunned. He spread his arms and caught them all in his reach. Colliding with them at chest level, he sent them all hurtling over the lip of the hill.

"Dad!" Daddy cried. He was on his feet and had climbed to the other side of the rocks before Billy had had time to react at all. He skidded to a halt at the precipitous edge and bellowed down at the streambed.

From below came Grandpa's voice, weak and stifled, "Run!"

Billy now stood beside Daddy, but had no memory of having moved from the outcrop; everything was being blurred by instinct and terror. Together, the two of them searched for Grandpa amongst the darkness.

As they watched, the shadows materialised below and proceeded to race over the moonlit streambed. They converged on a huddled figure, and seconds later Grandpa's voice filled the air once more. This time, however, he yelled only in pain.

"DA—!" Daddy bellowed, but his voice caught in his throat and he doubled over, wheezing as another coughing fit overtook him.

"We have to help him!" Billy shrieked, and leapt over the lip of the hill. For a moment she felt wind on her face as she fell into blackness, but then she ground to a halt in midair, held aloft by Daddy's arms. She thrashed and kicked in his grasp, squealing in protest as she was lifted back to even ground.

"Donald!" Grandpa wailed. By now he was crying out every other moment, and his voice was slurred. "Run! Take Billy! Run!"

After a further moment of crying out, Daddy stopped.

Billy continued to thrash, shouting for him to help her save Grandpa from the shadows. But instead he slowly stepped back from the decline, and whispered in her ear, "We have to go."

Billy saw silver tears glowing on his cheeks.

"No! No, we go down. We have to get Grandpa!"

He didn't answer. He only looked at her, and in that moment Billy realised that there would be no saving anyone.

She flailed in his grasp, but could do nothing against his iron grip. He was lifting their bag from the crevice and heading back towards the campsite. All the while, she twisted and kicked beneath him, hauled backwards through the dirt by her collar.

She wailed at the sound of Grandpa crying out in the night as monstrous shadows stamped at his body. "Daddy, what are you doing? We have to go back! Grandpa—Daddy, no, wait, please—GRANDPA!"

Her screams echoed in the forest for a long time.

*

The old man awoke in the dirt, shuddering. His vision was blurred, and his arm lay stretched out before him. What had once been his hand was now only a misshapen mass of flesh. He tried to breathe, but his chest only fluttered, delivering a dribble of air to his burning lungs.

Behind him, somewhere in the woodland, voices chattered. Slumped against the silt of the streambed, he could only lie still and listen. Each breath was sacred now, as satisfying as water in a desert.

"Idiots!" said a new voice—a sighing, sibilant hiss that struck a chord deep behind the old man's eyes, sending his heart pounding and his balls shrinking. A moment's pause followed. "I think I'm a reasonable man. I've a fair heart, I do. So I'll give you a chance to explain yourselves… What did you *think* you were doing?"

The female voice—the one that had spoken before—stuttered, "We were just looking for some food, is all. We've been watching that fucking city for days, and we haven't heard a peep out of anybody else. How were we supposed to know when we'd get supplies?" She grew bolder, "They was alone, nobody else around. Easy pickings, we thought. But they went and tried to fight, didn't they?"

The woman's voice gave way to a metallic clatter. Her short scream was cut short by a solid thump.

The first voice had grown quieter, but still the old man's gut squirmed at the sound of it. He'd travelled far and fought hard in his time to make a life after the End, and he'd met enough maniacs along the way to know one when he heard one. "Well, there wasn't any food, now, was there? Not a grain. And you could've ruined everything before we've even got started. You risked it all… You risked His plan."

The woman's voice, wet and snivelling, "Please, Jason…"

"*Shut up!* Stupid bitch." A pair of footsteps and a change in tone. The old man guessed he was addressing the others, "Where've his friends gone?"

A third voice, wavering, said, "They ran a while ago. We can't find them."

"You pathetic piss stains!" A tense pause. "Where's your weapons? Give them to me, you're not worthy to carry them."

Even from the ground, the old man sensed the uncomfortable silence. The woman spoke again, slurred—perhaps by a mouthful of blood—and hesitant. "We don't have any." A moment later she cried out again—a cry that quickly became a choked whine.

"So what you've done is run off in the middle of the night—no lights, no weapons—and raid a troop of fucking bumblers for breadcrumbs? And then you let them get away!"

"We weren't looking for trouble. We just come across them, like." A pause. "We was hungry."

"So you thought you'd try risking it all?" A dark laugh echoed beneath the forest canopy. "Pathetic. You couldn't even slit an old man's throat."

The third voice, still quivering, "What's the problem? We kill people all the time, right next to you."

"It's not the killing, you dopey shit. It's you being stupid is what's wrong. You know how careful we have to be right now. What if they were from the city?"

"They weren't, we were sure," the woman wheezed. "I swear." She whimpered at the sound of a pistol hammer being cocked.

"I should kill you," the sibilant voice whispered. "Only reason I'm not going to is because I don't want your mangy fur all over my shoes. But if you slip up again, I'll eat your brains for breakfast. That goes for all of you. You hear?"

"Y-Y—"

"*Do you hear?*"

"Yes!"

Another silence, the sound of the pistol's hammer being relaxed, and then, "Get up."

The old man, with great effort, turned onto his back just in time to see a slight figure scramble to its feet, surrounded by almost half a dozen others. Apart from them was the maniac, there was no mistaking that; his outline was just as feral as his voice.

Once he'd moved, the strangers paused, considering him afresh, and then began to approach. It was as though blood had been dropped into shark-infested waters.

The maniacal, sighing voice cut through the air once more, "What happened to this one?"

"Pushed us down the bloody hill, didn't he?" the woman said venomously.

"A little tumble wouldn't do that to someone."

"We might've helped him along a bit." Now that she no longer had a gun to her head, she sounded amused. An unstable giggle as unsettling as the man's voice escaped her lips. "Looks miserable, don't he? Making me feel a bit sick, just looking at him."

The old man, sensing the end, peered through the silver haze of moonlight to the rocky outcrop high above. Where Don and Billy had been, there was only the bare lip of the hill.

Shuddering and breathless, he managed a bloodied smile. He was sure that most of his teeth were missing, but to smile up at them felt like enough. Felt like a *victory*.

The approaching footsteps gradually wiped it from his face, until finally a shadow fell across the length of his body. The sibilant-voiced man was crouching beside him.

Up close, he was lean-faced and unshaven, with china-doll eyes and a lupine maw. From his direction came a disgusting aroma, one that made the old man suspect that he hadn't washed in his entire life. Held in his hands was a long, curved knife, which he twirled in his grip with frightening dexterity. He observed the old man almost curiously, with his head tilted to the side. Behind the childlike stare, however, there was not a man, nor a soul, but a monster. "What's your name?" he said.

The old man was quiet. Under their cold stares, he continued to stare at the moon, again smiling despite the agony growing steadily in his bowels. Even if they walked away into the woods right now, he didn't have long.

"I won't waste any more of your time." The man beside him was smiling, revealing a set of putrid, pus-yellow teeth. "I know a strong man when I see one." He touched the old man's shoulder, a gesture that, instead of bringing comfort, sent a wave of nausea coursing through his chest. "My apologies for my associates'…error." Then he stood. "Get rid of him, quietly if you can. Here, think you can handle one of these without another fuck-up?"

The woman, out of sight, giggled—yet her voice was laced with fear. "I knew you couldn't stay mad at me."

"Just get it done."

The old man shuddered when the sensation of a cold ring—unmistakably the profile of a gun barrel—was pressed against the nape of his neck. He closed his eyes and waited for darkness.

The woman muttered above him, "Tough luck, mate—"

"Who's there?" yelled a distant voice.

Despite only being privy to a view of the sky, the old man sensed the strangers start and drop lower to the ground. A palpable tension condensed from the ether. The half-dozen shadows melted into the forest. He couldn't even hear them breathing.

From somewhere nearby—though he had no idea which direction—the woman's voice whispered, "What was that?"

The monster's hiss answered, no more than a sigh on the wind, "Shut up."

For a moment all was still.

Then the old man frowned. Something light and crinkled had alighted on the back of his hand. The unmistakable texture of paper kissed his skin.

Had they dropped something in their haste? A note? Something important?

The forest's shadows flickered, its silver tint having been infected by a streak of pale orange. Through the distant trees, a sphere of fire bobbed: lantern light. Accompanying it was a new voice. "Who goes? Show yourselves!"

Without knowing why, driven only by the vague goal of in some way striking back at his attackers, the old man hauled his hand towards his trousers, clutching at the unseen scrap of paper. Shaking and gasping, he had just managed to poke it into the ragged remains of his pocket when the silence broke.

"We can't be seen!" the woman hissed. "What do we do?"

The sibilant voice, "Let's go."

"It's that gorilla from the mill. He's always alone. We can take him."

"Later."

A pause.

"What about the old goat?"

The old man felt cold steel against his neck once more.

"Leave him."

"*What?*"

"He's finished either way. Let's go. Now."

As the old man began to tremble from the effort of drawing the merest of breaths, the strangers fled into the woods. Defeated, he could only listen to their retreating footsteps, and then to those of the lone newcomer as he made his way through the forest.

"Who goes?" he would roar occasionally.

The old man tried to answer, but all that he could manage was a feeble whisper. As his lungs gave out and drawing breath became too much, the moon seemed to grow dimmer. After a while he could hear nothing but a dull mumble.

The night continued to blur until only the stars remained, and somewhere beyond the shadow of the newcomer—who now stood over him, shouting something inaudible—he thought of Donald and Billy.

While he stared up at the heavens, he choked out the words of a lullaby he had sung into both their cribs, once upon a time:

> "Then the traveller in the dark,
> thanks you for your tiny spark,
> he could not see which way to go,
> if you did not twinkle so."

X

"Forty years."

Alexander's reverberating voice thrummed in every crevice beneath the cathedral's roof. White stone scintillated and shadows danced, bathed in the amber glow of a thousand candles. Carvings of every kind stood sentinel in the gloom, and the sound of whispering trickled in myriad forgotten corners.

Canterbury Cathedral, though long stripped of its ancient treasures, had lost none of its glory. The walls were bare and pallid, its deeper recesses were sheathed in cobwebs, and the transept floors were carpeted with over an inch of dust—yet the eight hundred people gathered beneath the nave's great pillars never ceased to gawp in wonder.

Save for the occasional appreciative murmur and the whining of small children, there was absolute silence. Every head was turned towards Alexander, raised above them in the wood-carved pulpit. He could feel the pressure of each pair of eyes pressing against his skin.

He took a deep breath. "Forty years of struggle, hard work, and loss."

The silence deepened until it bore down on his shoulders with physical force. Yet, amongst the crowd, not a gaze flickered, not a single brow creased.

"While we may never know what happened to our world, where our friends and families have gone, or whether the terrible event that shaped all our lives will strike again, we have done our best to rebuild. With what little was left to us, we have made this place as close as possible to a real home—our home."

There was a short chorus of cheering, accompanied by a few roars of approval. Alex felt a swell of pride in his chest at the sight of brimming eyes and pumping fists. He raised his hand and waited for quiet before continuing, "For a long time this day just marked another year gone by, full of nothing but despair, fighting. They were desperate times, times that most of us lived through, grew up with, and have tried to forget. But in recent years we have finally found some peace, and can now recognise this day for what it should be. This day, in part, defines us. It has shaped our way of life, and the fate of the entire world. To this day we owe our thanks…thanks for being given a second chance."

At this, there was a strained, deeper silence, punctuated by only the rumblings of empty stomachs.

"We continue to bring children into the world, children who ask questions we can never answer. But the fact is that people have forever been plagued by those very same questions."

He planted his hands abreast the pulpit banister and leaned over the rail. "Who are we? Where do we come from? Why are we here?

"I admit that the list of questions has some…new additions. But we face the same problems as our forebears, we make the same daily struggle, we fight the same fight."

He paused to pick out Norman and Lucian from the crowd. They sat with the elders up front—the thickness of their hair and the colour in their cheeks set them in sharp contrast to the shrivelled relics of the Old World around them, but nobody questioned their presence there.

Only Norman looked uncomfortable.

Alex suppressed a pang of annoyance. The Anniversary was no time for stage fright or self-doubt. But no matter. Norman would find his feet, in time. Alex was certain of it. He pressed on, "This year, we've fought for more than just ideals or politics. This year, without doubt, we have struggled with every breath merely to feed ourselves. Even now, we are yet to leave the darkness behind, and the harvest has only served to remind us of just how far we have to go."

The crowd shifted restlessly, but Alex kept his hand raised until they settled, determined to finish. "The road ahead looks daunting, even for those of us who built this place. But remembering why we're here, and what we're trying to do, is more important than ever.

"Leadership is…difficult. It's not a duty that any of us envy. But we have to face the fact that our elders are," he allowed himself a wry smile, "getting old. Soon, our children will have to fight our fight without us. They'll be carrying the torch for a world they've never seen with their own eyes." He raised a finger. "But there is hope. There are those among us whom I believe in—whom we can all believe in. Now, before I bore the lot of you into the dirt—"

A ripple of laughter trickled through the cathedral.

"—if I may, I'd like to call a toast." Alexander stopped pacing and faced Norman. "To our champion," he said, and raised a glass of precious cider.

The room gave a single, raucous cheer. Norman's shoulders constricted, but nobody seemed to notice, and his grimace went unnoticed by the crowd. Alexander nodded to him, flashed his most encouraging smile, and addressed the crowd a final time, "If this is our second chance, we can't wallow in mourning for what we've lost, we have to celebrate what we have. Now eat up!"

A last cheer filled the nave with an echoing rumble. The smell of food was thick in the air, and every face twisted with hunger. The congregation fragmented as Alex backed away from the railing, and the droves about-faced with ravenous eyes.

Piles of steaming food lay at the rear of the room: venison, pork and chicken; a mountain of roast potatoes; eggs and loaves of bread—which were even free of sawdust; a pile of ancient pre-End food tins; mushrooms and seeds of every kind; fruit and vegetables; bowls of stuffing; a table of heaving pies; and, most sacred of all, several barrels of golden cider.

Plates and chairs enough for everyone were laid out across the nave. Before each seat was the best china and crystal the ruins of England had to offer. The crowd blustered past the rich appointments in passing, oblivious to the luxury. The promise of the first full meal they'd eaten in almost a year occupied the entirety of their attention. They each swept up a plate and hurried off towards the food. Some were close to breaking into a run.

Alex blinked in surprise when he saw that a few had remained sitting beneath the pulpit, their eyes still fixed on him. Among them were the same founding elders who lingered every year—Lucian and vacant-eyed Agatha at their heart—but this year youth peppered their ranks.

Norman, John DeGray, Richard Maxwell, Robert Strong, Sarah Clarke and even Allison Rutherford stood together in the aisle. They watched and waited beside one another, without impatience or any sense of grudging duty.

Alexander felt his chest flutter at the sight of their unity. They reminded him of another group of young people, who had stood together and faced a broken world just as they did now, long ago.

Perhaps there wasn't so far to go after all, he thought.

He walked towards the pulpit steps.

*

"Nice speech," Norman said. His cheeks still burned from being toasted by the crowd.

Alex, sitting across from him, smiled. "Not too much?"

They sat at the end of one of the central tables, eating amidst the heart of the celebration. They had drawn a short distance from their neighbours, almost yelling to be heard over the raucous, echoing din.

"Wouldn't have mattered. If you told these people you could walk on water, they'd believe it."

A strange expression crossed Alexander's face, but before he could respond they were both being clapped on the back by a passing group of men upon whom the cider had done its work. A chorus of slurred sentiments—*We'll have your speech yet, Mr Creek! I'll sleep safe another night with you both at the helm. Three cheers for the Chosen ones!*—made Norman's stomach shrivel. He bowed his head until they had staggered back to their tables, resisting the urge to hide his face in his hands.

"How do you do it?" he muttered.

"Do what?"

"Handle all the attention. Look so...so...in control all the time."

Alex took a bite of pie, furrowing his brow in sweet satisfaction. "Practise. *Years* of practise. A lot of them."

Norman sighed. "I know you're relying on me to step up just as much as they are..." He hesitated, shook his head, and blurted the rest, "But I'll never be like you. Most treat you like a god. There are people who live in caves a hundred miles from here who know your name. I'll never have that…command, over people."

Alexander steepled his fingers. "Don't be fooled by pomp and circumstance. It's all smoke, all fluff, all part of the fiction. The stories, they're just that: stories. They have been even since before you came along, and everybody knows it—they know I'm nothing special. I'm just another man. But people need a figurehead, somebody to pin their hopes on. And I got the short straw." He leant forwards. "I know it must look like you drew the same straw, but *I* believe you can do it, and so does everybody else. And"—he crammed the rest of the pie into his mouth—"at the end of the day, that's all that matters."

Norman traced his finger along the pristine china before him. "That's just what I mean. If everybody's following you, it's all on your head when you fail." He gestured to the joyful, satiated faces around them. "If it had been down to me, I'd have called tonight off. Our stores can't take the hit, and we all know it. But…look at them. Look at how much stronger they all look." He shook his head. "If I'd been in charge, they'd have had just another hungry night."

To his surprise, Alexander's face brightened. "The very fact that you'd think of everyone else, even now, when you're surrounded by all this, means that you're exactly the man they need."

Norman drummed his fingers on the tabletop a few moments longer, trying to think of a better way to articulate his disquiet. Failing, he reached for the nearest pie, frowning against a strange feeling—a not-quite-unpleasant one—welling up from his stomach. "Screw it. You win. For now." With enormous effort, he forced a smile. "Let's eat."

Alexander beamed and sat back to observe his rejoicing flock.

Most were laughing exuberantly. Some were dancing, parading about their tables as they ate to the tunes of old Mr Hadley's band, which had taken to the pulpit for its acoustics. Others silently played cards, with mountains of coloured chips laid out beside their empty plates, their food having been demolished in minutes.

A few lined the nave's shadows, leaning against the walls, eating spiced meat and watching the celebrations as though from above, basking in the laughter and good cheer.

All were smiling.

Elders danced, children giggled and frolicked between the columns. Some were disappearing into the cloister through the iron gates at the back, while others slipped through rusted side doors to laugh and be foolish outside.

Light, humid summer breezes whistled in through the main entrance, rustling the hair of a group of men gathered around the cider barrels, chugging the amber liquid with zeal and cheering each other on. One of them lay on the floor at the others' feet, clutching a chair leg and staring up at the ceiling with inebriated glee.

Lucian sat beside Norman, leaning over Agatha with a tenderness that he'd always reserved for the likes of her, for she had been among the city's founders—though Norman suspected it was more than that. He treated her almost as a mother, spooning her morsels of pastry.

Across from them, Sarah lay in Robert's arms with a book open in her lap, tracing her fingers along the defined contours of his bulging arms. He, in turn, remained motionless, gazing down at her in an eternal stare.

Richard and John had taken the adjacent table, bent over their chessboard. Their faces were set and emotionless, but about them was a static that betrayed their underlying joy—even as John lifted Richard's king from the board. "Checkmate."

"Son of a bitch," Richard muttered.

John turned to his foot-high mound of stuffing with the smallest of smiles upon his face, pausing to grip Richard's shoulder. "You'll get it," he said.

Richard muttered under his breath and got to work on his own plate, but Norman couldn't help but notice the smirk playing upon his own lips, all too similar to the Master's.

Amidst flickering candlelight, Norman ate and watched the celebrations. He was glad that the foraging had been worth it, but still his stomach churned at the sight of their glee. For each face that he saw before him, smiling and satiated, he saw a skull in his mind's eye, half-buried in the wilted grasslands beyond the city.

At some point he heard Alexander's voice, far away. "Are you alright?"

He didn't respond immediately. "Yes."

The potato was delicious, the best he had tasted for what seemed like decades. He hadn't seen butter since November, and there had been no chance of churning any even for the feast, but something had been mixed into the mash to make it creamy and smooth. The pork had been braised with a sauce rich in notes of apple and cinnamon—the latter of which he suspected had been acquired through many hours of sifting through buried Old World spice racks.

Though his taste buds squirmed with delight and his distended stomach throbbed with bliss, he found it ever more difficult to swallow. He was finding the celebration harder and harder to watch.

It was too much, too absurd. To be so indulgent was almost an act of bravado. Those around him would forget their worries for a few hours, but the cost of such a reprieve was surely that of many lives. Dozens, perhaps hundreds, had most probably seen their last day and faded from hunger so that they could dance, drink and be merry.

He was on the verge of finally rounding on Alexander when Heather appeared in their midst, a tall woman in her early forties, sporting an equine face and waist-length, wispy hair. She was the closest thing the city had to a real doctor, the disciple of Clara Fields, a legendary oncologist who had survived the End and travelled the land treating the sick in exchange for bed and board, known across southern England during the Early Years, until she'd met her own end at the hands of squabbling highway bandits.

Instead of recreational attire, Heather was clad in a long white coat and medical gloves, both of which had been marked by streaks of red. Beneath them blue scrubs were visible, stained by perspiration at the collar.

She stopped in the middle of the hall, her eyes darting among the partygoers. A few people stopped dancing to stare, and a couple of wizened old men looked up from their cards, frowning.

Then Heather spotted Norman, Alexander and Lucian sitting at the table and made a beeline for them, taking long strides that betrayed great urgency.

Alexander turned to her, whirling from his seat. "What is it?" he said.

She didn't speak until she was upon them, leaning close. "Come with me," she murmured.

XI

The sun had long since set. The noise of the feast dissipated as they trudged away from the cathedral onto the deserted cobbles of Main Street. Their footsteps boomed in echo, and sodium-vapour streetlights threw an amber glow over their shoulders, draping tall shadows out ahead of them.

Heather's face was drawn tight over her skull. She'd refused to explain until they got to wherever they were going, and led the way at a near run.

Norman quickened his pace until he was beside her. "What's going on?" he asked.

"I need you to see this. I'm out of my depth." She said no more.

Norman frowned, but remained quiet thereon. Alex and Lucian showed no sign of confusion, but he wasn't sure whether that meant they shared his bemusement or not.

They walked in silence for almost five minutes before they came to the infirmary. It was a squat building, nestled between an accountant's office and the boarded-up ruins of a gastropub, all whitewashed walls and wilted public-health notices.

Through the reception window Norman could see piles of machines, instruments and medical journals jammed against the walls. Most of it had long ago been pillaged—or rescued, as Alexander would have said—from hospitals, and hadn't seen a flicker of life for decades. But there it sat nonetheless, waiting.

They pushed their way into the darkened reception. Most of the diverging hallways were littered with pamphlets on hygiene and textbooks on biology, browning and decayed, their pages bloated.

Without pausing, they passed from the reception into one of the few clear corridors. Open doors led off into the ghosts of GP offices on all sides. Boxes lay within, some piled on the desks and others obscuring curled posters of human anatomy on the walls.

They raced along until they came to a much larger space at the rear of the building, what had once been the clinic's storage room. It was now their infirmary.

Polka-dot cubical curtains hung from rails upon wheels, each surrounding one of a dozen beds lining the far wall. Each curtain was open, each bed empty and neatly made—with the exception of the one directly before them. A liberal splattering of thick mud lay on the floor around it, overlaid by a pile of discarded clothing, torn and bloodied.

Lying upon the bed, groaning and gasping, was an ashen-faced old man. His eyes were shrunken and wary in his skull, giving him the appearance of a ghost clad in a paper gown. Only his eyes moved as they approached, swivelling in black-blue sockets to watch them approach.

A nurse tended to him in the gloom. She kept a small sponge moving over his head, such that small trickles of water constantly ran across his cheeks. He didn't seem to notice.

They gathered around him in subdued silence as Heather crouched beside him. "How are you?" she whispered.

The man only stared back at her, slack-jawed and broken. Even when she repeated herself, he didn't seem to hear her. His gnarled fingers clung to the tops of the sheets, trying to shield his withered body. His face was caked with the same thick mud as the clothes on the floor, beneath which lay a mask of crusted blood, faded and rustic in hue. It didn't look like it had come from any particular injury. Instead, it seemed as though he'd merely been basted in it.

"He's been beaten very badly," the nurse said, mousy and nervous in Alexander's presence and, Norman thought, perhaps, his as well.

"We can see that," Lucian said.

She shook her head. "It's not just that, Mr McKay, sir. He has lacerations all over his abdomen, like he was attacked by an animal."

"Have you stopped the bleeding?"

"For the most part, but we can't guarantee that he hasn't got an internal bleed. His stomach is blotchy, but it's hard to see past the bruising."

Heather waved for her to be quiet and turned to the old man. "Are you in pain? We can give you some more medication to help," she said.

The man only sighed. His shoulders slumped by a fraction.

Heather tried again, "Were you alone? If you have family, we can try to find them for you." She waited a moment and then added, "We won't hurt you."

Again, the old man lay still. After several moments he turned his head away from her. "Not now," he whispered, his breath rasping in his throat. "Leave me, please."

His accent was odd. Lilted in a way that Norman had never heard.

Alex and Lucian started.

Norman turned to them. "What?"

"He's Irish," Alex muttered. He blinked, his mouth slightly ajar.

"You came across the sea?" Lucian cried, taking a step forwards. "There are still people there? Are there others?" His breath whistled in his throat. "Is the world still out there?"

Heather reached forward to catch Lucian's arm. "In time," she said.

"But he's—"

"In time. Let him rest." She turned to Alex. "This isn't the kind of injury we see from a squabble over food," she muttered. "His injuries are too severe, too widespread. Somebody tried to beat him to death."

As she spoke, the nurse reached across the old man and removed his blanket, soothing him when he struggled.

Norman almost uttered a gasp as a mottled, skeletal body was revealed, blemished with scurvy sores, misaligned bones and a thousand purpling bruises. Without a trace of muscular tone, striated with tracts of dried blood, the man's body was enough to unsettle his stomach—and to dredge up memories of Margate's starving locals, reaching for him.

Reaching…

He shivered and cleared his throat.

"We've no idea who he is. He won't tell us his name or where he's from. He hasn't said much of anything, for that matter," Heather said.

"What *has* he said?" Lucian asked.

Heather looked away as the old man groaned in pain, and then turned back to them. "When he was brought in he was shouting for someone—Billy, I think—but he stopped talking as soon as we got him to the bed."

"Billy?" said Alex.

Heather shrugged. "He was alone. He might have been hallucinating, because he's taken a good few blows to the head."

Lucian went to the window. His face had contorted into a mask that failed to hide a boiling tumult behind his eyes. His brows had creased into the jagged crevasse between his eyes. "How did you find him?"

"Hubble found him in the woods when he was out on patrol. He says he found him face down in a streambed…that there were footprints everywhere."

Lucian stormed towards the corridor before she'd finished.

"Where are you going?" Alex said.

Lucian's bellowed reply echoed throughout the clinic, "To find Ray!"

Alex and Norman shared a look, and then headed after him, stepping over the pile of stiffening clothes as they went. As they were about to pass the threshold, the old man cried out, "*Stop!*"

They both froze, turning to each other and then to him.

He had struggled onto an elbow, propped up by Heather, who hurried to place a supporting pillow behind his back. As soon as he was settled, he beckoned them, his spider-like fingers waggling, drawing them forth.

Lucian's retreating footsteps, however, seemed to clutch at Alexander's attention greedily. He appeared to size up the old man, shook his head, and turned after Lucian, disappearing into the hallway's shadows.

Norman hesitated, cursing. He expected to follow at Alex's heel but, before he knew it, found himself about-facing to approach the bed. Heather backed away a step to allow him access.

Norman crouched beside the old man. Up close, he was a pitiful semblance of life.

Despite the images of gnarled fingers and putrefying bodies floating in his mind's eye, he leant closer to the bloodied ruin.

Erupting from the sheets, the old man surged forwards and grabbed him by the collar with a bony fist, wrenching him forwards until they were face to face. His strength was incredible, frightening. A burgeoning fury flickered behind his eyes, and his voice carried a fire that it probably hadn't known for a long time. "They didn't want you see them," he breathed.

Norman's voice caught in his throat, "W—What?"

"There's someone out there."

"Who?"

The old man's eyes twitched. "They didn't want you to see," he said. He glanced around the ward, as though expecting to see ghouls awaiting him in the shadows.

"Who didn't?"

"They're watching you, out there."

"Who?"

"*Watching you!*"

Wild-eyed and gasping, he released Norman and collapsed back onto his pillow, still throwing glances around at the room's corners.

Norman lost his balance and fell back onto the floor, aghast. He stared about the clinic in bewildered fright until his gaze fell on the doorway.

Alex stood upon the threshold. Norman hadn't heard him return. The hollows of his eyes were naught but shadows in the semidarkness of the corridor.

*

The racket of the distant feast played upon the edge of audibility as Norman and Alex hurried from the infirmary. Far away they could see Lucian's silhouette as he ran towards the mill, near the edge of the city, far away from Main Street. They changed course to intercept him, scurrying from the streetlights' glow and onto darkened cobbles.

"Did you hear what he said?" Norman said.

Alex nodded with a grimace. "I heard him."

"Why would anybody be watching us?"

Alexander took some moments to reply, "I don't know."

Norman thought he might have seen a flicker in his eyes, but then they'd both broken into a run, and he had to turn his attention to navigating the cobbles without breaking his ankles.

They caught up with Lucian as he approached the mill's iron-gated garden, beside which was Rayford Hubble's adjoining stone cottage. In the day, its thatched roof and lichen-strewn walls were made beautiful by an encircling row of lavender.

At night, however, it was very different—almost foreboding, perched upon its foundations in profile only, crooked and cold, with only the river at its rear to lend it a sense of life. A single light was filtering out through the ground-floor window, but besides that lonely glow the mill was still and quiet.

"Ray!" Lucian yelled, hammering on the door.

They waited for an answer, but none came. The only sound emanating from within was the echoing creak of the water wheel, which jostled in the Stour's current.

"Maybe he's asleep," said Norman.

"No, he's up," Lucian said. "Hubble never sleeps a wink after nightfall. The bastard's been convinced people are sneaking into the city for years." He hammered on the door once more, shaking it upon its hinges.

Again, there was no answer.

"Wasn't he at the feast?"

"Just his family," Alex said, standing back to check the darkened upper windows. "He went on one of his patrols. I tried to talk him out of it, but he wouldn't hear me."

Lucian hammered on the door yet again.

This time, he was answered: the clinking of glass came from somewhere inside.

Norman's gaze jerked to the door. There was something unsettling about that sound and the strained silence that followed.

"Ray?" Lucian bellowed. "Are you alright?"

No response.

"Ray?" Lucian listened a moment further, then waved them back and threw his body against the door, shattering the wood at the handle and slamming it against the interior wall.

Norman glimpsed a blackened hallway lined with flour sacks. Then sudden movement over by the staircase revealed a figure that had been hidden in shadow, rushing into the bowels of the house.

Lucian surged forwards with a wordless howl, racing past the flour sacks and shards of wooden shrapnel, with Alexander following close behind.

Norman froze for a moment, caught off guard, rooted to the spot. It was only with great effort that he surged after them, while the sound of smashing glass and overturning tables rattled out from within.

"Ray, are you in here?" Lucian called, his voice overwhelmed by the rumble of boots on hard floors.

Norman fought his way past toppled sacks, stumbling over spilt flour. As he did so, he caught a glance through the tiny kitchen to the back door, which blew in the wind, with only a single hinge anchoring it to the door frame. Dimly, he registered the heaps of mud that had been traipsed across the floor.

The light filtering through the living-room doorway flickered as bodies passed between it and its source. By the time Norman staggered free, Lucian's voice once again seemed loud amidst fresh silence. "Norman."

Norman whirled past the threshold, cracking glass underfoot. He stepped over a toppled chair, the legs of which lay splintered on the floor. He came to a stop just behind Alex and Lucian, laying eyes on what lay below.

A heavy silence fell over the room and its shredded furnishings. The light they had seen through the window had come from an old oil lantern, which hung from a high peg near the ceiling. It was still alight, throwing the horror upon the rug into sharp relief.

Ray was a huge man, with a head the size of Norman's torso and arms like slabs of ham. Bald and bearded, he was dressed in a checked lumberjack shirt, covered by a moleskin jacket that would have reached his ankles if he'd been standing.

Spread-eagled on the floor, his eyes were fixed on the crumbled ceiling, unseeing. He had come to rest wrapped around the edge of his tattered dining table, his legs bent and his skin white as snow. His throat had been slit from ear to ear, and a pool of his blood had stained the carpet scarlet.

Norman stared at the fallen giant, open-mouthed, as Lucian struck the doorframe with his fist and hurried back into the street. The sound of his footsteps dissipated into the night, accompanied by a feral growl gurgling from deep in his throat.

Norman and Alexander were left standing over the corpse. Alex crouched down beside Ray's body and reached for his eyes. Under his fingers' guidance, the lids rolled limply to a close, and Ray's eyes were veiled from view forevermore.

*

"What are you doing?" Norman said.

They stood in the armoury. A small building that appeared to be little more than a shed from the outside, it was in fact heavily fortified and surrounded at all times by half a dozen armed men. Breezeblocks formed an additional inner wall to that of the red brick exterior, while the ceiling was lined with steel and edged by rings of razor wire.

Four men and three women, pulled from sentry duty throughout the city, were now gathered in the cramped space, grabbing rifles. They each bore masks of studied focus, and worked with efficient and nimble gestures, asking questions without pause—*How many are there? Are they armed? Which way did they go?*

Lucian answered each with, "I don't know."

Norman grabbed him by the arm, taking him aside. "Do you really think that this is a good idea?" he whispered.

Lucian blinked. "What? Are we supposed to let them get away, Norman? What kind of message does that send?"

Norman felt incredulity rear up in his stomach. "What kind of message will it send? That's not important right now. What's important is *assessing the situation.*"

Lucian cast a hasty wave of his hand. "We don't have time to assess anything."

"You're going to go out there into the middle of nowhere at night? You don't know what could be waiting for you, and you don't know where they went." He paused. "In fact, we don't even know who did this. We know nothing!"

Lucian scowled, tucking a pistol into the seat of his trousers. He then lifted an assault rifle from a rack beside the door, picked up a pair of magazines, and pushed Norman aside. "Norman," he grated. "Those people in the cathedral may have the luxury of being ignorant enough to believe that we're safe here, but not you and me. You've seen what happens to people out there, I know you have. We're no different." He pointed to the door. "There was somebody here who we didn't so much as catch a glimpse of. They've killed an innocent man in his home, and beat another half to death. If we don't go right now then they're going to get away with murder."

He made to push past, but Norman held firm, gripping Lucian's wrist. "Everybody's looking to me to make a decision. But when I try to make one, it falls on deaf ears. If I can't convince you of this one thing, who can I convince of anything?"

Lucian looked at him searchingly for a moment. "Not this, not now," he said.

He tried to pull away, but Norman only gripped harder despite himself, feeling desperation crawl up his spine. "Lucian—"

"Listen, boy! I don't have time for your crisis of confidence tonight," Lucian spat, his eyes alight and his brow furrowed into its deep crevasse. With a jerk he pulled himself free and stalked off down the street, followed by the procession of guards, leaving the city defenceless.

Norman remained in the doorway for some time, trying to quell the lump in his throat.

He thought of going to Alexander, but quickly cast the notion aside; if Lucian wanted to go, then there was nobody who could stop him. Besides, Alex had already left for the cathedral to warn everybody.

And, said a voice deep in his head, *what good are you ever going to be if you need him to fix every little thing? Just this once, do something yourself.* He stepped out into the street and looked away towards the mill.

Ray's murder had been stealthy and quiet, far removed from an outright attack. It was more akin to something that Norman had only read of, something that belonged to the history pages of the Old World: an assassination.

There couldn't have been more than a handful of intruders if they'd gotten in unobserved. Such limited numbers made for good odds in a showdown.

But Lucian's hunting party was still in danger. There was no plan. They had set off at random into the night. Lucian had given chase without a single thought for what they would do when they caught up with their quarry.

Sighing, Norman ducked back inside, grabbing a pistol and shutting off the lights. Locking the door and throwing the keys to the nearest armoury guard, he took one last look back towards the cathedral and then hurried after Lucian.

XII

Don ran through the night. He was sure the crunch of his footsteps in the leaf litter was loud, too loud, but all he could hear was the roar of the blood rushing in his ears. Billy was clinging to his back, sobbing into his coat. He hushed her with a shaking voice as he struggled uphill, his legs burning with each stride.

Clawing for purchase, he slipped and staggered his way uphill. The trees were wreathed in darkness, and the underbrush was disorienting, undulated in the moonlight. From every direction he sensed eyes upon him.

But whenever he blinked, expecting to be set upon by a dozen shadows and beaten into oblivion, he instead found himself an inch higher up the incline, still struggling—still alive.

Billy's sobs showed no signs of stopping, and soon Don was fighting back tears of his own, pawing like a dog at unseen leaf litter. Detritus clung to his hands and caked the ragged soles of his shoes, slowing him further and threatening to send them both crashing back to the floor of the ravine below.

But he couldn't stop. Instead, he pushed on at the same headlong pace.

He hadn't the slightest inkling of where he was going, or what he was going to do. Without any of their things, and with no shelter in sight, there wasn't much he could do. Their situation was looking more hopeless by the moment.

But he wanted to live.

He had to, for Billy.

XIII

Norman crouched low to the ground, inspecting a displaced arc of dirt. Leading away from it, the grass was bent at an odd angle at regular intervals. From then on the ground was softer, and a trail of footprints almost seemed to glow in the twilight.

Canterbury was now far behind them. They had scaled hills and traversed ravines, following the river. They now stood at a farm gate between two hedges, leading to a winding country road.

The gate hung ajar, swinging in the wind; someone had passed through recently.

He stood up and signed to Lucian: Close.

Lucian nodded and waved the others forwards. They passed through the gate one by one, instinctively drawing closer to the ground and picking up their pace.

*

The cathedral had grown quieter. Old Hadley's band still played in the pulpit, but the mood seemed dampened by the muttering that had erupted from all directions. The fizz of the celebration had been extinguished, as though water had been thrown over a roaring fire. Hundreds were milling around the chapel, casting worried glances in the direction of the doorways.

Most had stopped eating or drinking. The food and cider lay scattered across the tabletops, growing stiff and flat, forgotten.

"Why Ray?" Allie said.

She stood at the head of a group that had surrounded Alexander, asking myriad questions over the top of one another. Alex held up his hands, doing his best to calm them, but his voice was drowned out by the sheer volume of enquiries. "I don't know," was his constant reply. "I don't know. I don't know."

Eventually, somebody at the back called a question he was able to answer. "Where did you find him?"

"The mill." He was so pleased at being able to offer a reply that he failed to consider its implications until it had passed his lips. By then, it was too late. Each face had grown slack.

"*In his home?*"

At that, their voices grew frantic. Some whirled and rushed for the door, muttering about family who had remained at home. The rest stood fast, now yelling—*We're not even safe in our own homes? How'd they get in? How could you let this happen?*

The news spread throughout the cathedral within moments. A gaggle of children playing between the cloister's pillars were besieged by guardians who swooped down to claim them, gabbling like startled hens.

Alexander watched the growing unrest with bated breath and sighed. There would be no calming them anytime soon.

He turned to Agatha, who sat close by, ancient and decrepit, watching the pandemonium. Despite her misty grey eyes and slack-jawed senility, an air of indignation at their uncouth panic seemed to seep from her pores. She turned to him and offered a throaty chuckle. "Don't make 'em like they used to, my boy," she croaked.

"I suppose not," he said, bending down and taking her hand. "I have to go and check on something. Could you watch them for me?"

She met his eyes, and the ghost of a great woman winked somewhere behind the cataracts and fog of dementia. "Of course," she whispered. Her cheeks stirred, her eyelids narrowed, and she touched his face. "Alex...."

He nodded, waiting.

Her brows furrowed, and for the briefest of moments Alex was looking into the face of an old friend—and a mother. "You look so old," she whispered.

He squeezed her palm gently, nodding. "I know," he said. Then he headed for the door, keeping his head low.

*

Norman's eyes took some time to adjust to the light of the campfire. Only after minutes of squinting did the silhouettes of three men become visible. Until then, all he had to go by was a ghostly muttering, carried on the wind.

Camped in the depths of a steep depression, backed against a screening of foliage provided by the boughs of an aged sessile oak, they could only have been seen from above. Unfortunately for them, it was from just such a position that the hunting party from Canterbury now watched them.

Lucian was still agitated and restless, in constant danger of sending a cascade of pebbles over the edge.

The others were balanced on their heels, crouched low to the ground, perched like vultures atop the ridge. Their long cloaks hung around their shoulders and pooled on the floor, turning their bodies into only so many amorphous bulges in the dark.

Norman knew they would be invisible if the men looked up. There wasn't enough light to reveal their profiles against the sky, for the stars were veiled and the moon had retreated behind a silver spattering of cirrus.

Through his binoculars, he observed their unsuspecting quarry.

One of the three men—the youngest, judging by his slimmer, gawkier outline—was tending to the fire. His hunched shoulders and violent stokes suggested that he was irked, perhaps angry.

The other two argued in hushed voices, gesticulating without pause.

A few pre-End tin cans lay discarded nearby, their contents warming over the flames. Two rifles were propped up against a nearby rock, their barrels glinting.

Their attire was ragged and haphazard: overcoats muddied and basted top to tail with grime; footwear that looked to be patchwork-sewn walking boots; and packs that appeared limp and empty, sparse for light travel.

They had paused often over the last few minutes to look over their shoulders, but the argument the two elders were having had dulled their senses.

"Who are they?" whispered Richard. He and John had caught up with them after Alexander had delivered his announcement at the cathedral.

Norman had groaned when they'd materialised from the night at the edge of the city. Neither of them had much in the ways of field experience. The fact that Lucian had, in his haste, neglected to send them packing was just another misgiving to add to the pile.

Norman shrugged. "They don't look like any of our people. I haven't seen them before. Do you recognise them?"

Richard shook his head.

"There was nobody from the city out tonight," Lucian said. "Just Ray."

John murmured so close to Norman's head that he started. "We can't rule that out," he said. "They could be lost." He sighed, brushing his hair back from his portly face, centimetres from Norman's. "Or they could be emissaries from London. They could have missed us. It's not hard to walk right past us if you don't follow the roads properly."

All theory, Norman thought, watching him. *All classroom wisdom.*

John hadn't been out of the city—or his classroom, even—for over a year. All he knew came to him from the mouths of others, rather than his own eyes.

But it seemed that he had been told about the amber halo that lit up the city like a monstrous firefly at night, suspended in the eternal dark of the wilds, courtesy of the streetlights.

Nobody answered him, but Norman could see exasperation reflected in several pairs of eyes.

He turned his attention back to the men below. By now they had let their argument rest and retired to the fireside, a sullen silence heavy over their shoulders. The youngest passed each of the other two a bowl. Even up on the ridge, Norman could smell tinned beans.

He would have known that decades-old stench anywhere. At winter's peak they'd subsisted almost entirely on the last of the tinned food. Now he feared he'd never clear his nose of it.

The gawky youth then sat in a heap on the grass, his head dipped.

"They're not ours," Lucian muttered. "Look at them. Their clothes are rags."

"That doesn't mean a thing," said Norman. "Look at how run down we got at the coast."

Lucian was unperturbed. "No, there's something about them. It's too much of a coincidence to find them here—right here."

John uttered a nasal note of disquiet. "Lucian, don't—"

"Be quiet."

"But—"

"I said *shut it*, DeGray. Save it for the blackboard."

John looked to Norman for help, almost as though he expected him to reprimand Lucian for his indecency.

Norman could only stare back at him, biting back shame, until John's shoulders slumped almost imperceptibly.

That hurt worse than the pleading stare—the disappointment. It stung at his flesh.

Spurred into life, surprised by his own actions, Norman gripped Lucian's arm. "We're not killing them," he said. He wasn't sure what had awoken in him, but suddenly he felt a force driving him forward, an unseen will, acting through him, one that applied a pressure that wasn't only physical to Lucian's arm. He swallowed, and muttered, "We'll approach on foot."

Lucian almost smiled—as though, somewhere deep behind his bloodlust, he was relieved—but then his face twisted into an angry sneer. "By foot? And do what?" he hissed.

Norman took his pistol from the seat of his trousers and deposited it behind his hip, where it wouldn't be seen, but could be easily reached. He then lifted his trousers higher and buckled his belt one notch tighter so that his footfalls would be deadened.

What the hell am I doing? he thought.

Pushing himself into a crouch, he made for the forest. "We're just going to have a talk," he said. "That's all."

*

Alexander strode into the infirmary and made a beeline for the old man.

"What's going on?" Heather said, poking her head from her back-room office.

"I need to talk to him," he said, settling down beside their bloodied guest.

Heather shook her head. "He's deep under. I wouldn't bother. Didn't Ray tell you what you needed to know?"

Alex glanced at her and then back to the old man. "Ray's dead," he muttered.

Her face fell. "He's what?" She hurried into the room. "What do you mean?"

"I mean he's dead. We found him up at the mill. Murdered."

"B—wha—by who?"

Alex shrugged and shook the old man's arm. "I don't know. Creek and McKay have gone after them." His jaw tightened at that. He'd almost cried out in anguish when he'd heard from the armoury guards that Lucian had headed off into the wilds—and that he'd taken Norman with him.

Heather sighed and held her head in her hands. She then began to shake, silently weeping. Alex watched her clutch at one of the beds, ready to catch her if she fainted. With the colour disappearing from her face, she had to suck in deep breaths to regain her composure. "How could somebody get into the city without us knowing?" she said, hiccoughing.

Alexander nudged the old man once more. "If somebody wants to get in, they can. There aren't enough of us to cover all the streets, all the fences. The city's built too tight." He paused, and fought back the urge to swallow. "Besides, I'm sure they've been here before."

"What do you mean by that?" She lurched forwards and took Alex's hands away from the old man's frail body. "I've drugged him. He won't be awake for hours—Alexander, what do you *mean*, they've been here before?"

Alex took to searching the man's clothes. "Whoever killed Ray knew where he lived, and they knew how to get out again without being seen."

He paused with his hands immersed in the remains of a tattered trouser pocket. When he withdrew his fingers, they were wrapped around a folded piece of paper.

"What's that?" Heather said.

Alex shook his head and slipped it into his pocket. "I don't know. I'll look at it later."

Without another word, he nodded to her and left the room.

*

Norman had descended into the depression without breaking a single branch, and was now secure behind the trunk of the enormous oak. John had somehow shifted his bulk with equal success, and was stooped beside him. Crouched behind neighbouring trees were the others.

They signed to each other in the shadows, with the three strangers only twenty feet away.

Norman pointed to the flanks of the clearing: Go around.

Lucian nodded and led the others off into the darkness. John left the oak's trunk without protest, stumbling once too often to excuse his presence. Norman tracked their silhouettes until their weapons appeared to be nothing more than extensions of their bodies. By the time they were settled, their outlines blended seamlessly with the blackened underbrush.

A single ghostly shadow, however, remained pressed against the trunk closest to Norman.

It was Richard. The whites of his eyes pleaded to be allowed to stay.

Norman signed for him to go and join the others, but he didn't move an inch. His eyes flashed with defiance, and then he ambled towards the oak despite Norman's shooing waves.

"What are you *doing?*"

"Maybe Lucian's right: maybe my Master—DeGray— is out of touch. I'm tired of being useless. I need to be out here, in the thick of it. I need this."

"You've never even been—"

"You need somebody else to go with you. They might attack on sight if it's just you."

Norman made to protest, but instead sighed. This was no time to argue. They were on the clock.

"Fine," he said. "On three." He ran a hushed three-count, and then they stepped out, hands raised.

*

As Norman and Richard moved into the firelight, there was a moment in which the three men looked up from their food and only stared, too dumbstruck to respond.

And then they burst into action. Norman froze as they leapt to their feet and grabbed their weapons, raising them to shoulder height as they stalked forwards. He couldn't help glancing to the trees, afraid that the men would be dead in seconds, before he could ask a single question. He would need to act quickly, before Lucian felled them.

"Who are you?" the youth bawled. His pencil-thin face was dominated by his bared teeth.

"We're from the city," Norman said. "We're looking for somebody."

The eldest of the men, hollow-cheeked and loose-skinned from severe malnourishment, frowned and gripped his rifle tighter. "What city?"

"Canterbury," Richard grated.

The older man spoke again, lacking the hostility of his younger companion. "Who are you looking for?"

Norman lowered his hands. "A murderer."

The friendlier man blinked. Now that Norman observed him in detail, he could see that he stood apart from his peers, dressed differently. "Canterbury…" He turned to his companions. "Isn't that where Jason was… But you said…you promised that you—"

"Shut up! If you ever want to see your boy again, *shut it right now!*" the younger man screeched.

The older man fell silent. Suddenly he looked frightened.

Norman hesitated, taking further stock of the other two men's clothes, which were grimed by putrid plant matter. A pungent odour was coming from each of them. "We're not here for revenge." He did his best to emphasise those words, for Lucian's sake. "We're looking for answers. Now…lower your weapons. I'm sure we can work out some kind of deal."

The younger man sneered. "Answers? You mean you're looking for a neck to tie a noose around. You expect us to put our guns down so you can drag us off to the wicker man?"

"Like I said, somebody was murdered."

As he spoke, Norman's attention was drawn to the final man, whose eyes alone unsettled his gut. A neckerchief had been pulled up around his nose and mouth, and long hair hung about his cheeks. Only his eyes were visible—eyes that Norman thought, for just a moment, he might have recognised.

The thought was fleeting, but enough to make him start.

"Why should we tell you anything?" the younger man jeered, raising his rifle to eye level. "What made you think that you could just follow us and expect to walk away? You people are all the same. You think that you own the country, trespassing on other people's property, snooping around places you have no business with."

His hands were shaking with anger. The barrel of the rifle wandered from Norman's head to his chest. "You're the reason that nobody's got anything to eat. You're the reason that nobody has the balls to go within a hundred miles of London. You've stripped the place bare!"

At that, he cocked his weapon and took aim. "I don't think that we'll be letting you run back to rustle up a posse."

"Peter, wait," the older, emaciated man whispered.

The youngest flinched at the use of his name. "Shut up!" he whispered.

"Just wait. I knew you were up to something, but…not killing people!"

"One more word and I'll shoot your boy myself when we get back."

"Just wait. Think about it."

The man with the neckerchief kept still, his eyes darting back and forth between the other two. He'd lowered his rifle to his side, and showed no sign of interfering. In fact, he took a step back, away from them, towards the shadows.

"You can't just kill them," the older man muttered.

"I said SHUT UP!" the young man screamed. He licked his lips and took a step towards Norman. His finger crawled towards his rifle's trigger, and began to depress it. "I'm gonna enjoy thi—"

Norman closed his eyes as a high whine rang through the air, accompanied by an explosion of splintering wood. For a moment he thought he'd been shot, and waited for the pain to come, but none did. Instead, he felt a gush of air soar over his head, towards the three men.

Movement erupted from the surrounding forest as dark shapes emerged from the gloom, surging into the clearing.

Peter yelled in shock, whirling in circles and spraying bullets into the trees. His companions wasted no time. They threw themselves behind bushes, tall grass, and any other cover they could find.

Another bullet whizzed past Norman's ear and he flinched instinctively. And yet, he felt stupefied by the silent man's gaze. The two of them had locked eyes across the clearing, even amidst the storm of gunfire.

Those eyes burned into him, hypnotising him. Everything had slowed to a crawl.

He was glued in place, unable to move. In a moment he'd be shot dead—he had to move!

But those eyes. He recognised them.

A tickling under his skin, behind the scar above his ear—

A rough fist grabbed him by the collar and wrenched him to the ground. Over the gunfire he heard Richard shout something incoherent as he landed on top of him.

Norman drew his face from the dirt just in time to watch Lucian pass the campfire, his body cast in brilliant crimson tones that caught the wild whites of his eyes. In a fraction of a second he had drawn his automatic and fired.

A wet splatter and a scream of pain answered the shot, followed by the dull thud of a body hitting the floor. Norman turned to see one of the men topple out of sight with a bloody hole in his chest: the emaciated man. The one that had tried to save them. His limp body rolled over the ground, coming to rest upon the gnarled roots of the giant oak.

Six shapes swooped in from the right, sending bullets snapping and bouncing around in the clearing. The tooth-rattling din threatened to burst Norman's eardrums. He struggled to his feet, slipping in the mud and passing the scattered remains of the fire. He raised his pistol to the man with the neckerchief, now fleeing. "Stop," he bellowed. His voice was barely audible over the hail of bullets. "I said stop!"

The man paused for only a moment, at the edge of the clearing, and stared back at him.

Norman caught a glimpse of his eyes once more: a rich, shimmering green.

Emerald eyes. Eyes he'd seen before…

Norman jerked as something stirred deep in his mind, something buried in the fog that obscured his youth, something he'd long forgotten.

Then the man turned and melted into the dark.

*

The night was well past its zenith when Alexander finally forced himself to look at the scrap of paper from the old man's pocket. As starlight splashed across it, it seemed to exude a malevolence of its own, one that threatened to taint his skin.

He only hesitated once before his patience waned and he unfolded it with a curse.

There was no reason to suspect anything of it, anyway. In all likelihood it was nothing more than a sentimental keepsake that the old man had picked up on his travels, or perhaps a cherished letter from before the End—

But it was neither. Before he had even finished unfolding the sheet, he recognised the handwriting upon the page.

He stared, open-mouthed, while a pigeon hooted outside the open window.

What he saw made his blood run cold.

*

"Did you find anything?" Richard said as Lucian and three others returned to the clearing.

Lucian kicked a charred log in two. "Nothing," he panted. "They just disappeared."

Norman was crouched over the body of the emaciated stranger, patting his pockets. The rank odour of perspiration and urine rose from the body in waves.

"They didn't leave any tracks?" Norman asked.

Lucian shook his head again. "Nothing from that quiet one," he said, "he's just gone." He gripped Norman's shoulder. "I couldn't see from back there. Did you get a good look at him?"

Norman shuddered at the memory of the silent man's emerald peepers. Unsure of why he was doing it, he shook his head. "What about the other one?" he said.

Lucian cursed. "There's blood everywhere. He made a right mess when he ran off. I don't think he'll last long by himself."

Norman looked out at the darkness. Then he sat down on a log beside the dead man, rubbing his eyes with the palm of his hand. "He wasn't like them," he said. "He was trying to help us."

"He hung out with the wrong crowd." Lucian's expression flickered. "We can't save everyone, Norman."

Richard crouched beside Norman. "I'm sorry," he whispered. "I know I messed up." His face had fallen, his expression sorrowful, repentant. "I just got in the way. Maybe if I'd just done what I was told... I just wanted to help."

Norman heard him as though from far away. But despite his weariness, he forced his hand to Richard's shoulder. "No," he said, "you saved my life. Thank you."

Richard still looked ashamed, but a glimmer of a smile played on his lips. "All the same, maybe I'll stick to the classroom from now on."

Norman managed a smile. "Don't count yourself out just yet."

"At least we scared them off," John said, tying a haphazard bandage around the arm of one of the guards. The bullet wound was already bleeding through. He was eyeing Richard carefully, a slight frown upon his brow.

Lucian scowled. "What good is that?" he said. "Two got away, and one of them is perfectly capable of bringing others right to us. They already know they can waltz right onto our streets and slit our throats."

"But why?" Richard said. "We didn't get an answer… Why would somebody do this?"

A silence fell over them as they stared about themselves. A concentrated sense of isolation had crystallised from the ether, making the short distance that separated them from home seem far greater. The trees seemed suddenly sinister, as though their darkened bark concealed untold evils.

Norman thought he sensed something change about Lucian—he seemed to stiffen and avert his gaze. But he said nothing. Norman sighed. "That doesn't matter now." He stood up. "We need to get back. We're going to be missed."

He made the comment in passing, without thinking. He was therefore surprised when everybody, including Lucian, froze mid-action and set about gathering their things, preparing to leave.

He watched them, disbelieving, and felt his gut squirm with distant unease. They were looking to him.

They left the emaciated man's body in the clearing beside the dying fire. At the tree line, Norman looked back at his sprawled profile, slumped against the oak. The pity he'd felt moments before was now overshadowed by fear of retribution.

*

The night was a long one. Many people were too frightened to return home in the dark and opted instead to remain in the cathedral. Dozens of guards were posted all over the city until sunrise, which brought with it only a tenuous sense of safety.

When Norman and those following him—following *him*, not Lucian—returned, they learned that the old man had died, having slipped away in his sleep. After talking to Norman, he'd never said another word.

While Norman and the rest of the hunting party made for bed, Lucian refused to check his weapons back into the armoury, and stood on sentry duty until midday. By that time he had sagging bags under his eyes, and his head would droop to his chest without warning.

After several complaints from harried guards, Heather convinced him to take an anxiety pill of her own making, after which he finally slouched into a clinic bed and dropped into a deep sleep.

Once he'd rested, Norman went north-west with him and Robert to look for any sign of the young man from the fireside. Lucian was still convinced that the sneering youth had been too severely wounded, and would not have survived.

They found him as sunset neared, face up in a patch of bluebells.

His mouth and eyes were already crawling with insects, and his skin had drained to a sickly marble pallor. A wound in his abdomen had been bound with makeshift bandages, torn from the hems of his trousers. The blood upon them had long since coagulated, and had spread into sticky pools on the forest floor.

They buried his body without a marker, beneath a pile of stones amidst the bluebells. They spoke sparingly while they worked, and afterwards there was a moment's silence before they returned to the city.

They continued to search from then on for the man with the neckerchief—but, for reasons Norman couldn't explain even to himself, he never spoke of those green, hypnotic eyes.

They found nothing. No sign of him, none at all. He had simply vanished.

FOURTH INTERLUDE

Morning.

Alex held up a hand to shield his eyes from the sun's rays and groaned from the depths of his duvet. He rolled over, and for the briefest of times enjoyed the sun's warmth, along with the sound of dying embers crackling in the grate.

Then there was a thump, and the crying began.

Beside him the dog groaned, rose to her feet and slumped away to the recesses of the cottage once more. He wished he could have gone with her. He stumbled to his feet, taking James in his arms and walking him around the periphery of the room.

The previous night, the two of them had eaten a meal together by the fire. After dusk the rain had continued well into the evening, and its patter upon the roof had been almost peaceful. The abundance of tinned food and a few pieces of unspoiled fruit had allowed them to take their fill, and then some. Alex was sure he'd burnt, maimed and spoiled every last bite, but the two of them had eaten ravenously nonetheless.

However, before and afterwards, all that James had been content to do was cry. He cried when he was talked to, sang to, left alone, held, swayed and rocked, for so long and with such force that Alex was at times entertained by the notion of him wailing himself unconscious.

He had cried overnight too. It had only been in the early hours of the morning, when the storm had lost its voice and the rain had abated, that he had finally succumbed to sleep.

Now, it seemed he had been rejuvenated by his short bout of rest. He ignored Alex's pleas, wriggling and screaming, his face scrunched into a puckered maze of puppy fat.

After an hour, Alex found that the noise had lost its edge. He abandoned his attempts and sat with James in the armchair, watching the embers fizzle until he felt enough strength to stand.

He then left James to cry on the floor beside the grate's residual warmth, heading for the shower. There was still some hot water. Apparently the water system had yet to fail, along with the power grid—for now.

Grime sloughed from his skin and tangled hair in great mudslides, basting the bath in a layer of jet-black sludge. The water splashing against his face was blissful, ruined entirely by the fact that he was obliged to keep the door open, lest the child fling himself onto the ash pile in his unattended state.

Afterwards, wrapped in a towel, he brought a bowl of lukewarm water to the fireside. Dipping the struggling child into its depths, he did his best to clean James's stinking, soiled body. Lathered with soap and sporting tufts of hair that stuck out at wild angles, the boy's screaming quietened. Once or twice, a gap-toothed smile broke out onto his face—one that seemed to light up the world.

Alex changed into another set of clothes from his bag, along with a waterproof coat, and set about shuttling in the last of the containers he'd put outside to fill in the rain, all of which were by now full to the brim.

The chill of the air outside was bracing, even more refreshing than the shower. With his arms full, he paused in the doorway and looked out over the land surrounding the cottage, which was no longer obscured by the storm's cloak of mist and rain.

It was another moor, stretching away in all directions towards the horizon. Heather, moss, tall grasses and dense forests were dotted here and there, painted onto the surface of the land as though by an artist's brush. Far away, blurred by extreme distance, was a small chain of mountains, their peaks capped with a fine smattering of snow.

Radden Moor was now far away indeed, as was every other town that had lain along the road. Even the peak of Porter's Pass—the tallest in all of Radden County—had fallen out of sight. Not a single human construction was visible. The only thing apart from the cottage hinting at habitation was a dirt road leading away down the hill. He suspected that, eventually, it would lead back to the motorway he'd left the previous evening, before the storm had taken hold.

"Where am I?" he said.

The wind answered, whistling in his ears. It snatched his voice from the air and carried it away down the hill until it bled away into nothing, leaving only another gust in its place.

It seemed impossible that he could have wandered so far into the middle of nowhere, and in so short a time. It also seemed impossible that the trance he'd been under—an emotionless pall that had been marbling his mind—had passed. He knew that it still encapsulated him, shielded him from the shock, yet he was unable to lift it. He was merely privy to a dim knowledge of it, along with the knowledge that at some point it would lift, and leave him exposed to the harshness of reality.

He turned and stepped back into the warmth, and to the wailing. Returning to James, he crouched and sighed. "What am I going to do with you?" he said.

James was whimpering, having cried himself into a state of exhaustion. He watched Alex's every move and beat at the air feebly with his tiny fists, but still seemed unable to stand, talk, or move much at all. However, the unhealthy tinge remained absent from his lips, and his skin was far less pruned.

"Why you?" Alex said. Looking down at the child, tiny and pathetic upon the blankets, he was suddenly at a loss to explain why, of all of the people in the world, it had survived.

He backed into the armchair and huffed. "Why *me?* I'm nothing special."

James merely rolled around and gurgled, oblivious.

After a while, Alex found himself speaking again, "We can't stay here."

He was all at once certain that he'd spoken the truth. He was ill equipped to deal with a child by himself, dangerously so. The only decent chance the boy had of survival was if they found others—if there *were* others.

He spent the day searching the cottage for anything of value, adding it to a small pile beside the fireplace, before repacking. Most of the clutter he'd taken from his bedroom ended up being replaced by water bottles, canned food, lighters, maps and bedding.

By the time he had done even this, the sun had passed its zenith and he was forced to accept that he would have to spend at least another night in the cottage. He cooked them another meal, faring no better than he had the previous day. Together, the two of them once again ate a burnt dinner.

James still cried often, stopping only occasionally to regain his breath before continuing. Irrespective of whether Alex held him, watched him from afar or ignored him entirely, he blubbered. It was only at dusk that he stopped, and dropped into a slumber from which there was no waking him. Alex took his duvet and spread out on the floor beside the snoring infant, watching his splayed body rise and fall with each breath until he drifted off himself, still helplessly caught in his emotionless trance.

The next morning, just after dawn, the three of them left the cottage. Alex marched along the dirt path, James swaddled close to his chest, held tight by a loop of cloth that ran across his back. In one hand he held a strong stick, and with it he propelled himself towards whatever lay ahead.

The air was cool, and the morning dew still clung to the grass at his feet. Refreshed, he made good progress. The cottage had become a mere speck on the horizon within the hour.

The mountains grew steadily closer, and by midday he had left the path in favour of open grassland. The path would only lead back to the motorway. There was nothing for him there, only the crushed remains of thousands of vehicles, housing as many piles of empty clothing.

The chill and dew had disappeared without grace as the sun took its place directly overhead, replaced by a heat that Alex, with his fair complexion, found intolerable. In the open fields he grew hotter by the moment, until a sticky layer of perspiration soon coated his skin, and the dog panted without pause.

All the while, James cried in protest.

The wailing and the heat took their toll. He could only bear the sun for a further hour before retreating under cover. Once beneath the canopy of a nearby forest, however, seeing green spots and stumbling over roots, he realised that shade would come at the price of speed.

As he struggled through the underbrush, the first bird he had seen since the Great Flocks landed upon a high branch and cooed as though in greeting, cocking its head.

James gurgled at the sight of it, uttering an unmistakable cry of joy. His chubby, stunted fingers reached for the canopy, wriggling.

"You like him?" Alex said. He looked up at the bird, recognising it as a homing pigeon. As he watched it, he saw that it was swaying from side to side, as though dazed.

The dog sat low on her haunches and yipped, staring up at the bird with distrust in her eyes. A low whine thrummed in her throat. She glanced to Alex, as though pleading with him to get rid of it.

There was definitely something odd about the birds.

"You got turned around by whatever killed the microchips, huh?" he muttered. "Some magnetic storm?"

The pigeon cooed in reply, and took to following them for a while, swaying less each time it landed on a new branch. Sometime later it departed, taking a route that at first seemed uncoordinated, but soon settled into a more defined flight path.

It seemed that, at the very least, the birds were recovering.

They spent the rest of the day wandering on a loose diagonal through the forest, during which time Alex's map-reading skills were shown to be as abysmal as he'd feared. When the trees finally cleared, the moor was nowhere in sight. They were now at the edge of an industrial district.

James had seemed comforted by the constant movement throughout the day and had cried somewhat less, but now with the grinding stop he resumed his wailing. The sun was falling again and they had only an hour to get settled before the light began to fade. Alex had no intention of being caught out in the dark.

Spying a vast warehouse close to the perimeter fence, he approached with trepidation, dwarfed by the structure. He passed through the doorway—four storeys tall, left ajar like a gaping maw—and found endless aisles of boxes before him: tens of thousands of Clingfilm-wrapped packages, waiting for customers that would never come. He opened a few, and found auto parts, mostly spark plugs and ignition coils.

To one side were a series of offices, sealed off by plasterboard walls, cluttered with computers, desks, and mountains of unfiled paperwork. He coaxed the dog inside the largest, though she was mistrustful of the strange smells and industrial surfaces, and settled them on the floor. He then built a small enclosure for James out of bulging ring binders, hoping that it would contain him.

"Don't die," he commanded as he set him within it. After propping open the window and setting a desk fan beside him—it seemed the power grid was more resilient and automated than he could have hoped—he set about making them a fire in the waste bin. Once the flames had caught and he was sure the smoke would be blown outside instead of choking them, he set enough paper aside for fuel, and unpacked their blankets.

The two of them were wrapped up and set to sleep in a mere handful of minutes, both utterly defeated by the day's travelling. Alex kept close watch over James as night fell. The child was only visible in silhouette as darkness set in, as the fire threw out meagre light, but neither of them would sleep if he turned on the harsh fluorescents overhead.

They had both started to grow groggy when a stray thought crossed his mind: to lock the door.

At once the idea struck him as ridiculous. There was no point in sealing a door against nobody. Yet the niggling urge refused to fade. Eventually, cursing, he scrambled from his blanket and flipped the latch, stepping away from the door with an added sense of security.

As darkness cloaked the land in earnest, things of the night—things that had once been pedestrian, but now seemed primal and threatening—came to life and prowled the woodlands. The twilight symphony of hooting owls and yipping foxes was now complemented by the barks and meows of a great many cats and dogs, wandering across the land in search of absent owners.

The dog's ears flipped and turned with each of their cries. At first she paced by the window to ward away any that strayed too close to the warehouse, but she was soon overwhelmed by the sheer number of trespassers, and curled against Alex's leg for the night, whining.

Alex reached over the wall of James's pen and rested his hand on the boy's shoulder, feeling it rise and fall, taking comfort from its warmth. At some point, he saw the fire's licking flames no more, and slept. All the while, the dog continued to whine at the endless droves of abandoned pets.

236

XIV

Alexander was in a hurry. There were many problems to deal with today. The most notable: recovering their exhausted supplies. The End Day celebrations had fallen flat and short, but what hadn't been consumed had already spoiled.

And then there was Ray's murder, the unknown assailants, the old man's note…

But that would have to wait. They had to eat first.

He was so preoccupied that he didn't notice the pigeon on his doorstep until it hooted underfoot. He looked down, lifting his leg. The slightest of gasps escaped his lips when he saw the bobbing, silver form before him.

Numbness stole along his arms as he pressed himself against the doorframe. He blinked fiercely, hoping that it would disappear—would vanish as any hallucination should.

Instead, it cooed and bobbed a moment further before taking flight, riding the breeze, as real as the ground beneath his feet.

He cast a glance around at Main Street, but saw only the usual sights: the cathedral doors being swept open for morning prayer, children flocking to the school building, and those on the early shift dragging themselves towards the fields or a quick breakfast. Nothing untoward met his gaze. Apart from the dozen guards posted at Main Street's edge, and the nervous glances every second person aimed at the hills above the city, it was a perfect summer morning.

Nevertheless, venturing any farther from his door now seemed impossible. It seemed as though a vast chasm had formed between him and the rest of the world.

He slunk inside without taking his eyes from the street, and slammed the door.

XV

"Wait, wait," Don wheezed, sinking against the trunk of a sapling yew. The soft bark bent under his weight, sending him sprawling on the ground. There he lay gasping, staring up at the sky, which had grown far away and dim.

He and Billy had spent the last hour trudging through boggy wetlands, braving stinking pits of tar-like mud in lieu of skirting a precipitous ravine. But now that the way was finally clear—a gently sloping meadow lay before them, cropped short by a milling herd of distant goats—he was spent. Taking another step was beyond him.

Each breath seared his lungs. It was as though the air contained not oxygen, but instead thousands of tiny, red-hot knives.

Billy shuffled up beside him and fell to the dirt with a thump, her eyes dead to the world. He'd kept them moving since the attack, and they'd stopped for no more than three hours a night to sleep. During that time they had eaten only what they could snatch from the deepest reaches of the forests, where the trees hadn't been picked clean: overripe berries, shrivelled fruits and half-rotten tubers.

In all that time, he'd been too busy keeping watch to take a good look at her—at what was happening to her. Now that they both sat a mere foot apart, slumped and panting, tears welled up in his eyes.

She was filthy. Her eyes were glowing masses of sclera amidst her mud-spattered face, surrounded by a maze of tear tracks that converged at her chin. Her hair reached for the sky in a matted tangle, thatched with dried leaves, and her eyelids drooped almost to a close.

"I'm sorry… I'm so, so sorry," he wheezed, reaching to cup her chin. Then he shook his head and fell back in the grass. "I can't…"

He wanted to tell her to go on without him, to find food, shelter, people, and to never look back. But before he could say a word, the numbness festering in his limbs rushed along his spine and into his head, consuming all thought. He fell towards thoughtless nothing. Threads of darkness invaded the meadow from his peripheral vision, and the sky receded along a tunnel of blackness.

But then his arm jerked in its socket, tugged by insistent fingers. He opened his eyes and fixated on Billy. Her face was set, her eyes alight with fiery intensity. She was pulling with shocking strength—strength that seemed to defy common sense.

Despite his disbelief, she hauled him from the ground and scrambled into the nook beneath his shoulder, draping his arm over her back. "Come on, Daddy," she said. "Take a step."

He complied without thinking, staggering a few feet forward. Their motion was unsteady, and brought tears back to his eyes, but it was a step nonetheless.

Together, they proceeded from the midst of the sapling grove, teetering every step of the way.

XVI

Norman grimaced, ankle-deep in putrescent sludge. The remains of corn, beans, potatoes, and entire orchards—the result of over two decades of toil—lay in an unbroken layer across the land, having rotted down to pureed compost. The elements had seen the green-black carpet shrink and contract into a desiccated paste, but beneath the surface laid a preserved soup that exuded noxious fumes.

When the crops had failed the previous year, it had been clear from the outset that it would be a complete loss. The only option had been to save their strength, and try again as early as they dared the next season.

But the countrywide decay hadn't ended, not even by the time they had come to sow the wheat in early spring. After a lacklustre and last-ditch bout of effort, they had watched the hesitant growths wilt along with the last of their optimism.

They had resorted to scouring the wilds soon after. Now, even the ruins of all of southern England had been exhausted. Things were too desperate not to try turning the fields again.

The odds of raising a crop worth harvesting by summer's height were slim, but there was a chance of scraping enough to tide them over until the land recovered, so long as they moved fast enough.

In any case, it was a distraction. Not only from hunger—for the End Day feast had been but a thimble in a caloric deficit of tens of thousands—but from the thought of Ray's murder.

His loss had been made only more noticeable by the bakery's loaves of late. Somebody else had ground the daily flour in his stead, but the bread was now almost inedible; he had apparently been adding something to temper the taste of sawdust, a secret he'd neglected to share with anyone.

Yet another shred of knowledge lost to the world forever.

Norman stooped and took a handful of sludge into his hands. He cast it into the waiting mouth of the sack that Allison held open for him. She looked as disgusted as he felt.

Close by, Lucian stooped beside John—who, to their surprise, had once again elected to stray from the classroom, though he and Lucian still seemed to share a certain animosity—and farther away loomed Robert's sloping, muscular shoulders. Barely visible behind him was Sarah, who held the neck of another sack open with an expression all too similar to Allie's.

Beyond their close-knit group, hundreds of others worked in resigned silence.

To clear the way for the turning of the soil, those on field duty had insisted that all hands were needed. For now, at least, things like Ray's burial plans would have to wait. Even school had been called off. The children had been mustered into a conveyer belt, one that ran bulging sacks out to the distant tree line, and returned them empty.

As Norman paused to flex, a pigeon landed atop the rusted skeleton of a nearby grain silo and cocked its head to look at him—to look at all of them. When it cooed, another answered from afar. Moments later, a third warbling rained down from atop a listing telephone post, directly overhead.

He turned to set eyes on it and frowned.

"We tried everything," Robert said, registering his glance. "They just keep coming back."

"Where did they come from?"

Robert shrugged. "Just appeared out of nowhere."

Sarah shielded her eyes to stare up at its bobbing profile. "Funny, we've never had them before," she said.

"I think they're cute," Allie said. "They make a nice change from the crows."

John grumbled, mopping his portly brow, leaning on the shovel in his hands. "In fact, it's just more bad news," he said. "They must have been forced to migrate. No food for them elsewhere. We had the same problem in the Early Years, when the perishables started rotting. You couldn't go anywhere near the cities, couldn't lay eyes on concrete for all the vermin. Right, Lucian? Lucian?"

Lucian didn't answer. He stood stock-still, gloved hands by his sides, staring over Norman's shoulder.

"Ooo, shoo!" cried a broken voice behind him.

Norman followed Lucian's gaze to see Agatha seated in the shade of a tarpaulin awning. A straw hat shielded her ash-white face from the sun as she handed out drinks to passing children from a hamper. She was flapping a hand at one of the pigeons, which had alighted nearby.

She leaned forwards, addressing Lucian, her hands on her knees and her mouth creased into a maternal grin. She spoke to him as though he were no more than a child. "Lucian, be a dear and lock away your brother's birdies, would you? They're gettin' on Auntie Aggie's nerves again somethin' fierce."

Lucian stiffened, and Norman caught a glance being cast in his direction. Then he cleared his throat and said, "I will, Agatha. I promise."

She scanned the bird mistrustfully a moment longer, then sat back and closed her eyes, pulling the hat's brim down over her brow. "Thank you, dear," she sighed. "I think I'll have a little nap now... Recharge the ol' batteries."

A moment later, she was snoring quietly.

Norman glanced from her to Lucian. "What was that?" he said.

Lucian shrugged. "She's just confused," he muttered.

"Doesn't look that way to me."

"She's getting on, Norm. Forget it."

They each glanced to him in turn as he stood unmoving. "They're just birds," he grumbled, then set back to the sludge with renewed vigour, not looking up.

Norman looked to Robert, who merely shrugged, eyebrows raised. They were on the verge of returning to the sludge when a series of wet, slapping footsteps rushed towards them.

Richard appeared in their midst with a wordless cry, breathless. From even a glance it was clear that he had just sprinted quite some distance. "You're not going to believe it!" he cried.

They all froze mid-action, wide-eyed.

"What is it?" Lucian said, straightening. "Did something happen?"

"No—I mean, yeah! We just got word from London. They've found something." He splashed through the rotting treacle and gripped John's shoulder. "They've found a radio!"

All activity for some distance in every direction ceased. All eyes had turned to Richard, leaving frozen hands to drip great clods of sludge onto their trousers. A few seconds of distilled silence followed, during which Richard looked to each of them in turn, his face creased into an expression of beaming satisfaction. "It works," he breathed.

They had all heard of radios, seen their carcasses wherever they went, lying behind every door, infesting entire towns and cities with their useless bulks. Just like the rest of mankind's machines, none of them had worked for forty years.

Countless people had tried to fix them, one of the first things that had been tried after the End, when people had been scattered across the country, clueless and alone. When they'd still been looking for rescue crews that had never come. When they'd still had hope that all hadn't been lost.

But a working radio in their world could do only one thing: blare an ear-splitting shriek of static, one that blanketed every frequency. No transmissions, no voices, nothing.

It was just another unanswerable mystery.

Therefore, the first word spoken after Richard's announcement was not unexpected.

"Bullshit," said Lucian.

Richard shrugged. "They're saying it works." He seemed to scintillate with excitement. "They're saying they've got a signal."

The silence deepened. Richard was now staring at Norman.

"They want to call the council's summit early," he said. "They say two weeks. Runners from the Wharf are waiting for an answer. We need somebody to sign off on it."

Norman glanced over his shoulder, expecting to see somebody of authority behind him, but there was only more black-green slime. He turned back to Richard. "Me?" he said.

Richard frowned. "Why not you?"

"Where's Alexander?"

At that, Richard looked slightly uncomfortable. "Nobody's seen him today. He's been acting a bit…funny, don't you think?"

"He's fine," Lucian muttered, gesturing to the fields. "Just the stress of this mess."

"No, he has seemed a little…off," Sarah said, nodding.

"I'm sure he's fine," John blustered. "He's got us through worse than this."

Norman was still looking at Richard. "I can't," he said. He looked to Lucian for help, but found that he only stared back at him, unmoving.

Since Norman had overruled him with the hunting party, they'd said little to one another. He sensed that Lucian's protection had come to an end. He was on his own from now on.

But it wasn't just Lucian. They were all staring at him. He swept a glance around at them, and saw the same expression upon each of their faces: expectant, awaiting his verdict.

He mouthed wordlessly until a sigh escaped his throat, and he shook his head. "Fine," he said. "Two weeks."

Before he could look to the others for their agreement, they'd all turned away, accepting his words without comment. They returned to work, leaving him to stand and watch Richard race away to inform the Runners. The others were gabbling about the news, excitement threading their voices, but Norman heard not a word of it.

His head was reeling. Was this how it was going to be from now on? Alexander would abandon him to make decisions in his stead? When he was so sure that he wasn't ready?

While his thoughts swirled in knots, he couldn't resist the urge to look up at the pigeon atop the post once more. It was still watching them work, cocking its head. For a moment he thought that, perhaps, it had eyes only for him.

*

Alexander didn't appear at all that day. Only once the sun had set and the evening meal on Main Street was afoot did he emerge. But he wasn't himself, didn't say a single word to anyone. His head was ducked, and he blanked the welcoming cries of the city folk. He spoke only once, to Norman, in passing. "Keep them in the fields."

Then he retreated to the rear of the kitchen, beside the inglenook, to eat alone.

The hall was soon buzzing with muttered chatter, and fleeting glances leapt in his direction every other moment. But nobody dared approach him. His eyes were too staring, too empty—elsewhere. His gaze didn't leave the flames.

For a while, his sullen puss weighed heavily over everyone. But the excitement stirred up by the radio was too great to be tempered. The news had sent the city into a storm of heated discussion and debate. Norman's decision to convene the council in London was mentioned just as often.

Many already claimed that he'd ordered it himself—had demanded that representatives from settlements across the country be brought together.

At first, Richard tried to correct them. But when those many became most, he surrendered, and even began conjecturing along with them. Within an hour, it was common knowledge that Norman had had a hand in the radio's discovery, and had ordered the Runners away himself, part of a brilliant plan between him and Alexander.

What was that plan? Everyone was sure they'd be told in time.

Norman was beginning to understand how the elders' stories had started, and grown into the legends they were today—even the legend of Alexander Cain.

Opinions flew every which way, well into the night. The debates were fierce.

But it was all only so much smoke, obscuring the naked truth that now tortured their empty stomachs: This was the last full dinner they could expect to eat for some time.

They could from now on only afford one meal per day, itself composed of mere meagre rations, leftovers dredged from beneath crates and hauled from the weeds in the wilder parts of the city.

In addition, Ray's murder had choked any plans for further foraging expeditions. During the day, few had dared to go beyond the fields, the streets, or even their own homes. Most were convinced that the wolves were at their door.

*

The End Day cheer and the buzz kicked up by the radio died quick and quiet deaths. The mood became sour and disgruntled in a matter of days, kept from falling into a senseless, hungry stupor only by the continued labour in the fields.

People began to come to Norman, to single him out from the crowd and demand to know what they were going to do, what the Big Plan was, and from where they'd be getting their next meal.

Each time an angry face appeared in front of him, his patience would wane all the more rapidly. While he spent most of his time at the school in search of privacy, people still made their way into the building, usually under transparent pretences—delivering lunchboxes to children who'd already eaten, or 'homework' that Norman hadn't set—to question him. Their expectant, pleading—yet almost hostile, demanding—stares ate at his nerves like acid.

He suspected that even if he'd wanted to, he couldn't have helped much—not without Alexander. With their prophet shut away, the people were aimless, their efforts impotent.

Soon, he too stopped leaving home unless it was necessary, withdrawing from a city that was beginning to wilt.

252

XVII

New Canterbury looked as haggard as its drooping populace under an ugly sky. The sun had disappeared behind black clouds hours before. Now, as it dropped below the horizon, the bulging thunderclouds overhead looked fit to burst.

Jason crouched low to the ground atop the hill, tapping his fingers to the beat of the timepiece in his palm. He glanced to the ticking second hand and nodded.

9:30: lights on, then shift change for the guards.

The lazy bastards he'd been charged with babysitting these long weeks better be right. If they were off by so much as ten seconds, he'd skin every last one of them.

But maybe they weren't as useless as he'd thought.

He smiled as a thousand twinkling lights cast the city's heart alight. A moment later, he sensed movement about the shadowed rooftops as the sentries were relieved. His sneer grew only wider as the first dainty drops of rain began to patter down around him.

Showtime, he thought. If tonight was the night, then it had to be now, before the new guards' night vision could settle. Under the cover of the storm, it would be a cakewalk.

"Are we ready?" said a voice beside him; flat, quiet, almost a sigh.

Jason turned to Him, and for a moment dared to look into the shards of emerald that were his eyes, suspended between flowing locks of auburn hair and a face obscured by black cloth. "We're ready."

The pigeons were cooing in the forest nearby. He hated that fucking racket.

As Jason grimaced, one of the damned rats with wings fluttered over and alighted upon His palm, bobbing and pecking. He uncurled his fingers to unveil a small pile of seeds, which the bird set to without hesitation. He stroked its head and looked back to the city. "You have a way in that won't cause any problems this time?"

Jason wasted no time with boasting or jesting. Last time, they'd almost gotten Him killed. The others had all paid for that—paid for it dearly. Jason had delivered the lashings himself. "We have," he said.

"Then let's get to it."

"Yes, sir."

Jason was left alone on the hilltop as He stalked towards the tree line, the pigeon still perched aloft upon his raised index finger, muttering to it all the while.

Jason turned back to the city as the others stepped up around him. A few of them were slaves from the coast, and eyed their waiting prey with forlorn reluctance. But none of them would lift a finger against Him. Jason had made sure of that. If they ever wanted to see their wives and kiddies again—with their skin still *on*, that was—they would do whatever He told them.

He felt a delicious stirring in his limbs—one that stole all the way down to his groin—as he unsheathed his knife and sang, "*Oh, little pigs, little pigs, let me come in...*"

*

Norman's eyes flitted across the yellowed pages of the old paperback in his grasp. Turning the leaves with measured care, he shifted restlessly in his living room armchair and tried to maintain focus on the story. But his mind wandered, adrift.

Now that the storm was in full swing, the rain hammered the windows and competed with the crackling of the flames in the grate. Upon the water-stained walls, the furnishings of the elderly Old World couple hung in their respective places, untouched by his hand: silver-framed family photographs, an ancient mahogany-finished piano near the sofa, and innumerable ornaments upon the mantelpiece and windowsill, most of which had been carved out of precious stones and crystals.

He'd never been one for collecting furnishings of his own, with the exception of his extensive personal library, made up of the rejects from Sarah's warehouse. He had started small at first, but over time had built up quite a collection. Now he was running out of places to store them, and had resorted to precariously stacking them in the hallway.

His eyes began to drift further from the page. Soon he put the book down and simply sat staring into the fire. In moments he was lost in the flames, turning over possibility, consequence, and nightmare.

Ray's burial had been put off again. But they were determined to give him a proper funeral. He and Robert had scoured funeral homes for the embalming fluid Heather had needed. It would give them enough time to make the necessary preparations.

But now that it approached, it seemed like only another hurdle to brave. With Alexander shut away, Norman was sure that he'd be expected to say a few words.

But try as he might, he could think of none.

A flash of lightning drew him back to the living room some time later—how long, he couldn't tell. The windowsills were now creaking under the rain's bombardment and the howling wind. The entire house was filled with the storm's whistling scream. Outside, he could see bushes, trees and fences churning in the gale.

He stood up and glanced at his half-eaten dinner: a morsel of the new miller's inedible bread and a handful of browning berries, which he had taken from the kitchen on Main Street to eat at home, desperate to escape the diners' prying stares. He thought of forcing himself to eat the rest—he was going to need the strength—but couldn't bring himself to take another bite.

Grunting with dissatisfaction, he picked up the plate and headed for the kitchen. In passing, his gaze settled on the gritty window—

There was a man standing on the other side of the glass, staring in at him.

Norman had time to observe his hooded face, the mouth and nose obscured by a neckerchief of mud-stained cloth. It was unmistakably the man who had escaped them: the silent man.

Norman jerked in shock. Panic pinched his heart. As every muscle in his body seized, the armchair took his feet out from under him, and he fell against the lamp stand. Once he had regained his balance, he blinked furiously, letting loose a wordless cry. Struggling over to the window, he slammed his hands flat against the glass and stared out into the night.

Each raindrop glittered as it fell past the window, catching the light of the fire. Wilted hedges fluttered in the wind. The paved drive was submerged beneath a deep puddle that stretched across the house's width. The streets beyond were cloaked in blackness, on occasion thrown into sharp relief by distant cracks of lightning.

But there was no face to be seen on the other side of the glass.

He backed away, numb from head to toe. A tight knot had formed in his gut, tugging at his spine.

Had his mind been playing tricks on him?

It was possible. He was tired, and two days into a strict new diet. The rain could easily have caused him to take an amorphous collection of raindrops for a face.

But as the moments passed, his mind's eye threw that fleeting glance back at him. The neckerchief, complete with spots of grime. The tendrils of dripping hair caught in the wind. Those wide, piercing eyes…

No, the man had been there. He was sure of it.

He shivered. Suddenly, he felt alone, trapped in his own home. The image behind his eyes was replaced by that of Ray's dead body, bled out on the ground, open-mouthed and chalk-white.

His pulse quickened, thumping against his ribs and throbbing in his neck. He began panting as he backed away from the window, his mind reeling—

He yelled in fright as something solid met the front door with a resounding clatter.

A branch caught in the wind? he thought.

Not likely, answered a more primal part of his mind.

He looked from the window to the hallway, breathless. For a moment he considered running for the back door, but instead his feet began to carry him towards the source of the noise, as though independent of him.

His heart was now rattling at a feverish pace, and he could hear blood rushing in his ears. A surge of adrenaline sent his extremities trembling until, though they carried him towards the door, his legs yearned to run—to escape.

Hijacked by his own instincts, he shuffled past a pile of hardbacks, stepped over a stack of *In Search of Lost Time*—

Who the hell ever found time to read that *shit, anyway?* cried a stray, half-hysterical voice in his head.

—and peered through the frosted glass panes set into the door. He could see two dark shapes looming from the night. When his hand was mere inches from the doorknob, he froze, gripped by apprehension.

What was he going to do? Confront a horde of murderous barbarians in his dressing gown?

He glanced around the darkened hallway for something to put between him and an attacker. Shadows danced under his gaze, throwing everything out of focus, but after long moments of frantic searching he spied a small collection of sawed-off sections of drainpipe nestled amongst the books. They had planned to restore central heating the previous year, but plans for that had been cut short when the crops had started to wilt.

He tore one up from the ground, bringing it to head height and bouncing it in his palm, testing its weight. There was silver insulation foam wrapped around most of its length, but the tip was exposed copper pipe, the rim sawn in a ragged line, almost like a maw full of serrated teeth.

The clatter rattled from the door again, and he saw the looming figures on the other side move closer to the glass, as though trying to peer in.

Now armed, Norman approached the handle once more, holding the pipe ready at shoulder height. "For God's sake," he muttered, steeling himself and tearing the door open, ready to strike.

"Jesus Christ!" a voice yelled, followed by a high-pitched shriek of terror.

Norman opened his eyes while the wind tore into the hallway and kicked up his hair. Allison and Richard's shocked faces were staring back at him, half-cringed in the doorway. Norman blinked, then glanced at the piping held over his head, still ready to battle his imaginary foe.

He dropped his arm hurriedly to his side and threw the pipe back into the hallway. "Sorry," he said. The two were alone, and by now their shock was being replaced by anger. "I thought I saw something."

"So you try to kill us?" Allie shrieked, brushing past him and into the hallway. "My God, I'm soaked."

Richard eyed Norman for a moment, still on the doorstep. "What was it?"

Norman glanced over Richard's shoulder, seeing nothing but the overflowing puddle on his lawn. "Nothing," he muttered, standing aside and gesturing him inside.

Richard shrugged and followed Allie, moving gingerly around the stacks of books and disappearing into the living room.

Norman took a last look around before closing the door. Though he saw nothing, the hairs on his neck stood to attention as he turned his back on the frosted glass. Despite his relief at seeing them, already his overriding sense was one of being intruded upon. It was as though a spell of the macabre had been prematurely interrupted, and was barely being kept at bay by the presence of his visitors.

He followed them into the living room and cleared a pile of Richard Matheson paperbacks from the tattered sofa, dusting it off for them. "Sorry about the mess," he muttered, gathering his dressing gown tighter around his waist. "I wasn't expecting anybody."

"When do you ever?" Allie said, dropping down with an exhausted sigh and wringing out her dripping hair.

Norman watched them until they'd settled, then cleared his throat. "So, what is it?" he said.

They exchanged a glance. "We were just with Lucian," Richard said. "He's still pretty pissed."

"Try obsessed," Allie muttered.

Richard shrugged. "It's not like him. He's pushing for more sentries again. He'll have half the city up on the rooftops before long."

Norman nodded, forcing himself to chew on a few mottled berries. He sighed, looking at his hands. "I know."

"We thought maybe you could talk to him…"

"So, what? I'm the new babysitter?" Norman shifted, trying to keep his eyes from the window. "I'm supposed to go and fix him up?"

Allie started, uncomfortable. "We just thought, since you've known each other so long…"

"Lucian's always been that way. He's a fighter. Maybe this one's got the better of him, but…it's been a tough year." He waited for them to say more, but they merely stared back at him. "Was there something else?" he said.

"We just wanted to check on you. You haven't been at your best the last few days," Allie said.

Norman patted his book. He tried to smile, but his cheeks had been tightened by fright. "I'm fine. Nothing that *I Am Legend* can't fix."

She shook her head. "You're not talking to anybody. You've been cooped up in here on your own."

"I'm *fine*. Really. I just needed a change of scenery."

"What about Ray's funeral?" Richard gabbled. He was eyeing the tension between them with mounting concern in his eyes. "People are starting to get worried about what's decent, keeping him out of the ground so long. But we still can't spare the manpower from the fields…"

Norman barely heard him, his attention still on the window. The hairs on the back of his neck hadn't fallen flat since leaving the doorway. He did his best to nod along, but still their faces became only more concerned.

Richard looked to Allie—whose tentative smile had faltered without grace—and then back to him. "Are you sure you're alright?" he said.

"I'm just tired." Norman wasn't sure he sounded convincing.

They lapsed into silence until Richard and Allie slid to their feet.

"We'll be off then," Allie said.

Norman nodded once more. He heard himself speak, but his voice sounded far away. "Alright."

He followed them back out into the hallway, where they stood for a few moments longer.

Looking at them in the half-darkness, dripping and unsettled, he saw them afresh: young, at odds with one another, but drawn together and to him in search of comfort—of direction.

Yet he couldn't bring himself to say a single word.

A long silence stretched out between them, forcing all eyes to the ground. Norman edged past them to open the door. A gale screamed in, rustling the millions of pages around them. He squinted into the night, seeing naught but swirling rain, and turned to bid them farewell.

Allison scowled as she ducked out into the storm, covering her head with her arms.

Richard made to follow, but turned back at the last moment. "Listen, I know it's not pretty, taking all this crap from everybody," he said, "but they need you. We all do."

And then he was gone into the night. In a few moments he and Allie had been consumed by darkness. Another crack of lightning revealed their retreating forms, sprinting beneath the gushing torrent.

Norman sighed and looked around. Once again, there was nothing. No stragglers from Main Street tonight. But that wasn't only on account of the storm. Only the sentries walked the streets after dark now.

He shut the door. It took considerable effort to turn his back on it yet again.

Though Richard and Allison were gone, he still felt a definite presence. A tingle ran across his skin, heralding the unmistakable sense of being watched.

He returned to the living room and looked down at his chair. Suddenly, sitting down didn't seem very attractive at all. Adrenaline still coursed his veins. Tired as he was, he felt like running a mile.

Absentminded, he bit into a knob of bread and grimaced. No matter how many times he swallowed, he couldn't shift the gummy paste coating the inside of his mouth. He made to wash it down with a mouthful of water, but the jug was empty.

Cursing, he picked it up and stomped across the room, pulling the curtains shut against the storm. The sound of the rain slashing against the glass was still loud in his ears, but at least he didn't have to deal with the nagging worry of somebody staring in at him. Heading into the hallway, he cursed when the tingle at the nape of his neck failed to abate.

I'm being skittish, he thought.

Nobody would have a chance of getting back into the city with the increased security. The previous night he had taken a shift himself, and had seen firsthand how much the attack on the mill had affected people.

His kitchen was large, but cluttered with a thousand unnameable utensils. He suspected that the old lady who had once lived here had loved to cook. He slouched between myriad hanging pots and pans, heading towards the sink, the empty jug trailing from his hand.

Before he had taken two steps, he knew that something was wrong. Freezing in place, he had just enough time to register a shadow behind the kitchen door slither in his peripheral vision—purposeful movement, unquestionably human.

He had only just begun to bellow for help when the form enveloped him and covered his mouth with a filthy hand, crushing his lips against his teeth. Tasting blood, he flailed for all he was worth, grasping for the assailant as he tried to yell around the muffling hand.

A pair of strong arms gripped his and forced his elbows back until his clenched fists were touching. Hot, rotten breath billowed across his right ear. The assailant's mouth opened and a slight, snakelike voice murmured into his ear, "It would've been so easy to stick you, nice and quiet, and let you bleed here on the floor." The sound of gummy lips working. "Pathetic, just like that gorilla from the mill…complacent, blind to everything going on around you—"

Norman bucked his head back and made contact with the man's jaw with a sickening crack. A single grunt rang out, and for a moment his grip on Norman's arms slackened. But then the constricting arms flipped him bodily through the air and slammed him against the kitchen floor.

He collided with the tiles with enough force to send his breath sailing from his lungs and the back of his head throbbing. He gagged as the walls of his throat glued together.

For a horrific moment he tried to inhale, but nothing happened.

The world swirled as pain ripped through his head. In this moment of panic, during which he was powerless to do anything but fixate on his own burgeoning suffocation, the assailant brought a booted foot down on his chest.

A dull crunch announced contact between it and his sternum. Upon trying to scream, Norman found his torso filled not with air, but instead white-hot, stabbing iron rods, squeezing tears from his eyes.

His vision began to blur almost immediately. He made to grab at the man's boot, but his grip was loose, his arm limp. Dizziness struck with shocking force as the world overturned, and his stomach gurgled as he fought the urge to vomit. Through a blaze of flashing lights he tried to follow the dark figure—which was now walking around him, out of sight—but lifting his head proved impossible.

As his chest fluttered, drawing only the tiniest of breaths, the world became dark and blank.

*

A sting erupted from the gloom.

Norman yelled. Fresh pain seared his cheek. He tried to wrench backwards, but his lower half was only so much numb flesh. Vaguely, he sensed that he'd been hoisted into a seated position. After a bout of extreme effort, he managed to open his eyes by a fraction of an inch. Blurred colours gnawed at his retinas.

Pain erupted across his other cheek. Something solid and sharp—perhaps a ring—split his lip. A voice spoke far away, strung out by the fog clogging his mind. "Wake up."

Norman grunted as his vision resolved and the world morphed into definite form.

He was still in the kitchen. The hallway lights had been extinguished. His attacker was seated directly before him, having pulled up a stool from the stove. He expected it to be the man with the neckerchief, the one he was now certain had been staring in through the window. But it wasn't.

Norman had never seen this man before. He was surprisingly small for the strength he had wrought. Dressed in a ragged shirt and a tattered pair of jeans, wrapped in a floor-length black overcoat, he had an unassuming, ugly face, peaky and sallow.

He waved his hand through the air. "Can you understand me?" he said. His voice was an unsettling sigh, lisped and snakelike.

Norman nodded, something he regretted as stars flashed before his eyes and nausea revolved the ground beneath him. He tried to answer, but his lips were still numb. "Wh-Who are you?"

The man smiled, but the expression was disturbing, almost horrific. The teeth were rotten, patched with brown decay, the canines stunted. His grin, closer to a sneer, made him look almost like a wolf. "My name is Jason," he said.

Norman glanced around, but saw nobody else in the room with them. Looking down, he saw that he was slumped in a dining room chair, bound to its armrests with handmade twine. "What do you want?"

"To talk to you, just like you wanted to talk to us."

"And what's to stop me calling for help?"

Jason's lupine sneer grew wider as he looked through the window at the storm raging outside. "I wouldn't waste your time."

"You never know until you try." Norman jerked his shoulders, trying to shift towards the doorway. But the chair didn't tilt a single degree.

Jason produced a wicked, curved knife from behind his back. In the highly polished blade Norman saw his own reflection, slumped and bleary-eyed. "How's this? Make a sound and I'll open up your jugular," he said, pointing the tip of the blade towards him. "It'll take but a second."

"Like you did to Ray?"

His eyes twinkled. Sickly delight lurked amidst their inky, lifeless depths. "That's right."

Norman wriggled his wrists, testing the knots holding them to the chair. Flawless. No fool's knots. It'd take hours to worm free. He sighed. "What do you *want?*"

"I'm here to deliver a message."

"So send a letter to the office."

Jason gave a full-throated belly laugh that sent his head flying back. "Sorry, postman's got a day off," he said once he'd recovered.

"Why me?"

Jason shrugged. "Word on the street is you're next in line for the Chair, that the Big Cheese is on the way out, that he's got his knickers all in a bunch over a few birdies." He tittered at that. "Also," he raised an eyebrow, "you make an easy target. Been alone in the dark for days."

"Just like the old man, eh? You had a message to give him, too?"

"He saw us. We reacted," Jason's face had fallen slack. "You weren't supposed to see us. Not yet. The old man wasn't part of the plan. I was just clearing up a stupid mistake of some…associates of mine. Same goes for the boulder head at the mill." He took a step forward, twirling the blade in his grasp, observing Norman with frank curiosity. "But then you had to step in, didn't you? You couldn't just let things rest. You had to come after us, had to rock the boat."

"You killed two innocent men. Who's rocking the boat?"

Anger flashed behind those onyx shark eyes. Yet Jason's face creased into another smile. Somehow, seeing his cheeks upturn was so much worse. "After all that you and yours have done—after all the lives you've ended—I can't imagine where you could find the gall to say something like that."

"That we've ended!" Norman surged forwards, straining against his bindings. "We've done nothing!"

Jason's grin widened, such that it almost reached the lobes of his ears. "You have no idea what you've done, do you?" he whispered.

Norman swallowed. The slight, hissing voice reverberated deep in his chest, sending a vat of liquid fear boiling in his guts. "What are you going to do, finish me off as well?"

"What would be the point in telling you a titbit of jack shit if I was here to kill you?"

Norman licked his bleeding lip. "A message, huh? You want to get me a pen?"

Jason's smile lost its strength—died a slow and sickly death. He took yet another step forwards and dropped to his haunches. The two of them were now at eye level. "You took everything," he hissed.

The intensity of his stare felt as though it would set Norman's flesh ablaze. He swallowed. "What?"

"All of it. Every scrap, every weed, all of it. You took it all. You just wandered into people's homes and took what you wanted like it was yours, not a care in the world. All those people's work—all the sweat and blood they put into growing enough to scrape by… you took it all."

Norman looked at the ground. "What do you want?" he murmured.

Jason's face became uglier. "Do you know how many people you killed? How many children died in their parents' arms, shrivelled up like rotting prunes?"

Norman grimaced. As the words washed over him, pangs of pain danced across his heart. His mind's eye spat out images of the begging, emaciated creatures at Margate once more, reaching for him…

He shook his head and glared at Jason. Despite his own guilt, he saw nothing stir in his captor's eyes. He couldn't have been more certain that the man cared little, if at all, for the troubles of others. "What do you want?" he repeated.

"I'll bet you haven't even seen it with your own eyes, have you? The hundreds of starving skeletons, crawling around like worms?"

Norman started, gritting his teeth. "I've seen it."

"Yet still you took. And now everybody's gone, moved away, left everything that they had, because of you."

Norman felt his guilt putrefy into shame, dripping along his spine and festering in his bowels.

Still, Jason stared back at him without a flicker of emotion. He'd spoken with intent, but there had been nothing to the words, no glimmer of genuine feeling. They had merely escaped his mouth mechanically, as though rehearsed.

"What do you want?" Norman breathed.

"We're not going to tolerate your greed anymore."

"Who?"

"Survivors. Those of us who managed to hold out long enough. People who've lost everything. People who want to see justice done… People who want revenge."

Again, not a trace of sincerity touched his eyes. Some other voice was speaking through this monster; another greater will, far more sinister than Jason's feral wickedness.

It was enough to send Norman's skin crawling. He leant forwards against his restraints. "What do you want?" he yelled.

Jason bore his scream without even a twitch. Then he inched forwards. "We want you to run," he whispered. "Disband, scatter—all of you. Run to the corners of the earth, along with everyone like you. We'll give you this one chance to atone for what you did." His voice slowed to a halting shudder. "Then we will descend upon you, and we will show no mercy."

Norman leant back against the chair. "You're crazy," he muttered. "You kill innocent men, crawl into our homes like rats, and you think you're in a position to make demands?"

Jason leapt forwards, anger flaring in the depths of his eyes as he brought the blade up to Norman's throat. There, the blade hovered a millimetre from the skin of his trachea, shaking as Jason's eyes searched his own. Norman remained as still as possible, desperate to hold the snarling beast's gaze despite his racing pulse.

After almost ten seconds, seconds that seemed to stretch into an age, Jason let the knife fall to his side. "We're the rats?" His lip curled. "If most had their way— if *I* had *my* way—you'd all be dead already. The only reason you're still breathing is because He—"

"Norman!"

A deathly silence stole over the two of them as a voice rang out from the front door, accompanied by a rapid succession of hammering knocks.

Jason's expression had contorted, a small distance removed from surprise, more intrigued than angry. Norman realised that he was taken aback, almost impressed. "What's this?" he said, bringing the knife back to Norman's throat.

"How should I know?"

"Why'd they come back?" Jason looked out through the back window, cursing. His eyes darted in their sockets, considering.

The pounding at the door came again, accompanied by another yell. "Norman!"

It was Allison. Minutes before, Norman would have wished for nothing but for her to leave him alone. Now, hearing her babbling voice made him almost delirious with joy.

Jason appeared to have weighed his choices. Norman was sure that he could have put an end to her in a trice, but something seemed to be holding him back—perhaps that same greater will that had been speaking through him all this time. "Well, Norman, I hate to cut it short," he said.

"Oh, hush." The pain in Norman's chest was growing sharper, driving his peripheral vision towards darkness. "No need to apologise."

Jason grunted. He was pacing closer to Norman's side, prowling close enough to fill his nose with the nauseating, raw pang of sewage, so intense that it made his eyes water.

The knocking at the door was louder now, more emphatic.

Norman blinked his vision clear, and struggled to speak through rubbery lips. "We were desperate. We did what we had to." He swallowed with difficulty. The floor was falling away. "I can believe that people want revenge. Even justice—even now, after all that's happened." He locked his gaze on the feral man's wild eyes, desperate to keep the darkness at bay. "But I bet you didn't lose a thing. Men like you get blown towards trouble like tumbleweed in the wind. So what are *you* doing here?"

When Jason answered, his maw constricted into a half-grin, half-grimace—a step away from mania. "Every wasteland needs a devil," he said, bringing the curved blade's handle above his head. "We're done waiting. Your time's up, so think about what I said."

Norman saw the blade flash before his eyes for only a split second before the handle came down, and a thousand bells erupted in his head. Then all was black, and Allison's cries were muted.

XVIII

"You have to go," Don muttered. His sentence's end was followed by a great, wracking wheeze that sent him sliding down the face of the rock upon which he rested.

Billy, cross-legged on the floor with her arms clamped over her shins, started. Her head, ducked into her lap, shook violently. "No!" she whined.

Don was powerless to stop himself sliding until a mere inch above the dirt. Even moving his arms was now beyond him; breathing itself occupied the entirety of his attention. He had reached the point of no return days ago. He wasn't at all sure how he'd kept going since then. Even staying alive for Billy's sake wouldn't have been enough to sustain him, had it not been for her incredible tenacity.

She had shown him no mercy, had marched him day and night.

Every village, town or hole in the ground along the way had been unapproachable. It seemed that people here had fared even worse than back home. The wreckage of entire communities, built on top of the Old World's wonders, lay in growing ruin, blowing in the wind. Overgrown motorways had been dotted by the shrivelled bodies of the recently deceased.

In some towns, life had held on. But these places had been barricaded or road-blocked by stacked Old World motorcars. Enormous painted signs had hung from the tallest buildings, declaring: '*NO FOOD HERE*', '*STEAL AND DIE*', and '*WANDERERS SHOT ON SIGHT*'. Beside a few of these signs had been the bloodied bodies of those who had ignored them, nailed to walls or hanging by the neck from nearby tree branches.

Even the merest scraps of food had disappeared. They had once again reached the coast, but Don hadn't a clue which it was, or to which sea the waves belonged. He'd lost all sense of direction in the forest days ago. In his exhaustion, he hadn't even been able to make sense of the stars.

"You've been a very good girl," he said, managing a single word per exhalation. "You've been strong. I'm so proud of you." He swallowed, and dragged another ragged breath. "But Daddy's not getting any better. I'm just going to get sicker, so you have to go now. Find someone who'll help you."

Billy unfolded her body into a sitting position. Her eyes were wild, aflame with a light that Miranda had once commanded. "No! You said that there would be food here. When we find it, you'll be better."

Don shook his head. "I was wrong, Billy."

"No!" she cried. She leapt up and marched over to him, tugging at his sleeve.

His body bent to her will without resistance, and he felt his back lifting away from the rock behind him.

She had pulled him to his feet many times now, and on each occasion had managed it with a little less effort. At first he had thought such ease had come with her growing strength, but now a sickening truth seemed obvious: he had withered to the point that an eight-year-old girl could lift him without trouble.

The thought stirred a pang of fear in his gut as she righted him and looped his arm over her shoulder. She began to haul him from the rock, silent tears spilling from her eyes.

"Stop it," he muttered.

She wiped her eyes with a jerk and shook her head. "No," she sobbed.

"You have to—"

"No."

"Billy, you have to go. I want you to leave me!"

"No, Daddy! No. I'm never leaving you."

"Let go, Billy. Run."

"No, Daddy."

"Let me go and run!"

"No!"

"BILLY, YOU HAVE TO—"

The rest of Don's roar died in his throat. Something had caught his eye, nestled in the foliage ahead. Recognition blared behind his eyes, but he contained his surge of relief with enormous effort, suspicious of any good fortune after all they had lost.

Billy was staring up at him, open-mouthed, tugging at his sleeve. She looked frightened by his sudden pause. "Daddy, what is it? What's wrong? Is it the Bad Men?"

Ahead, through the foliage, he could see a break in the trees, and a cliff edge beyond. Nestled beside it, he discerned a rectangular mass of slate tiles, capped by the unmistakable profile of a chimney. Beneath it were four walls of shoddy brick and plaster.

"It's a cabin," he whispered.

Billy whirled, fixed her gaze in the direction of the structure, and then turned back to him. Her eyes were wide. "Safe?" she whispered.

There was no time for caution. Either they got under shelter now, or there would be no chance for either of them.

He nodded. "It's empty. It'll be fine." He sent a silent prayer and nudged her. "Come on, let's go."

Billy began to haul him towards it immediately, moving faster than ever.

Don couldn't quite keep himself from indulging in the same beginnings of hope that now seemed to infest her every move.

FIFTH INTERLUDE

"Find anything?"

"Nah! There's nothing here!"

"Keep looking!"

Alex was drawn from a nightmare—one of fog, fire, and a pair of leering, darkened eyes—by the voices, which at first he assumed had hailed from the tail end of a better dream. When he opened his eyes, however, he still heard them yelling from afar.

"What about these ones?"

There was a reverberating series of metallic clatters and a spate of cursing, and then Alex was fully awake and upon his haunches. The dog stood nearby, emitting a steady whine.

He checked on James. The noise had failed to rouse the boy, and he showed no sign of waking any time soon.

Good, he thought. *God, please let it stay that way.*

Satisfied, he rose to his feet, pressed himself against the wall, and listened.

"What are you doing?" one of the voices bawled.

"What does it look like? I'm trying to reach," said another.

"If you're going to help then do it properly. Those things are no good to us if they're broken."

People. Survivors.

Alex almost yelped. He whirled back to James and took the boy into his arms, hushing him as he whimpered and stretched. He ruffled the dog's fur and nudged her aside, turning the doorknob with the utmost care.

He took a steeling breath and stepped out of the office.

Out in the warehouse, the aisles still lay in every direction, and the behemoth door was still ajar, but there was a stark difference about the place. The floor was littered with gutted boxes and mechanical parts of all kinds and of various sizes.

Between them, bickering and reaching for a set of high shelves, was a group of people. Not military, not aliens, not demons. Just regular folk, dressed in work denims and the remains of business suits, sporting boring haircuts and budget Seikos, their pockets bulging with the profiles of wallets and keys.

Alex stood in the doorway of the office and watched them, stunned. James gurgled as he woke in his arms, and the dog continued to whine by his side, but the people continued in their search, none the wiser. He stared without a single thought for a long time, his duvet still hanging from his shoulders, unmoving. Slowly, he began to believe that they were really there, right in front of his eyes, arguing and talking.

His frozen stupor stretched on until the dog gave a somewhat louder whine. The noise whistled along the aisles, echoing under the warehouse's vast roof.

The people froze and glanced over their shoulders, some with heavy boxes held precariously in their arms. Upon spotting the three of them, crammed into the office doorway, their mouths fell open, and they stared just as Alex had stared at them.

A tense moment of silence stretched out between them.

Then James began to cry. A moment later, the warehouse was ablaze with noise.

They burst into motion, leaping down from the shelves and sprinting forwards. Alex surged from the doorway at an equal pace. They met at a fork in a wide aisle and skidded to a halt, still some distance apart, each group uncertain of the other. Alex hefted James's struggling body in his arms and hushed the dog, which still whined at his side.

The group was composed of a young couple barely older than himself, a powerful-looking woman in her forties, a young child, and two middle-aged men. All of them observed him with calculated stares. Their numbers and obvious unity automatically leant them authority over the motley crew of teenager, baby and household dog.

Alex waited for them to make the first move.

Eventually, one of the men cleared his throat. "You choose strange company, lad," he said. His face was striking: far longer than it was wide, marred on the right side by a lazy eye that bulged almost free of its socket.

Alex opened his mouth to answer, but only a shuddering gasp passed his lips. He suddenly wanted to withdraw into himself, to shield James from their combined stares. He had almost accepted that he would never see another person again. To have that certainty falter now, and then have this turn out to be part of some torturous dream—or another intrusion of the macabre into the real world—would drive him to insanity.

But he was saved by the mature woman's instincts. Smiling with such sincerity that his heart almost melted, she stepped forwards with her hands held out for the wailing child.

Alex placed James against her bosom without protest, and looked to her for guidance.

She smiled with such warmth that he could have sworn she had reached up and caressed his face. She held the child with an expert, soothing ease that no man could ever achieve, and began to rock him. "Beautiful, so he is," she said.

"Y-Yes," Alex stammered.

James, within the blankets, continued to cry, unheeding of the momentous occasion. Despite the great tenderness with which he was held, he cried only louder.

Yet the other members of the group seemed encouraged by the exchange and stepped forwards. The young couple stayed back a little farther, grasping each other for support and regarding Alex with a shadow of suspicion, but the others surrounded him with excited mutterings.

"What's your name?" the woman said.

Alex hesitated, but under their expectant stares he managed to speak, "Alex… Alexander Cain."

"Alexander," she said, "it's an honour." She swept a hand towards her chest. "I'm Agatha. Auntie Aggie to the young'uns—ain't that right, sugar?" She tickled James, unbothered by his continued wailing, and flicked her head to indicate the others beside her.

They were introduced in sequence. Their names broke against Alex like waves against a pier, but he nodded nonetheless to each of them.

The man with the bulging lazy eye was Oliver Farringdon. "*Sir* Farringdon, no less," he cried. "Officer of the late British Empire!" He shook Alex's hand with sound enthusiasm, clapping him on the back. His fingers were rough and calloused, yet tapered and dextrous: intelligent, practical hands.

An engineer? Alex thought.

The young couple were Helen and Hector Creek. They nodded politely, yet stayed some distance away. Hector seemed warm enough, tall and wiry, with a mop of thick, unkempt hair. Helen, small and wispy, held back, swaddled close to her husband's chest, still wary.

The remaining man was Paul. Agatha seemed eager to skip him, perhaps owing to his hostile stance and his refusal to shake hands. Sporting a meaty paunch covered by a vest only, with a shaved head and red face, he looked like somebody Alex would usually have avoided at all costs.

He did his best to keep his greeting neutral, but was sure a slight waver had crept into his voice.

The young child, meanwhile, ignored Agatha's attempts to get his attention. Sitting on the concrete floor, he faced resolutely away from them all with his spindly arms wrapped around his knees. But she didn't seem put out in the slightest, sending a soft, affectionate reprimand his way before turning back to Alex. "What you doin' out here?" she said.

"Sleeping," Alex said. "Searching for…I don't know. Somebody. Something."

They all nodded without further question. At that, the remnants of their reservations dissolved, and even the Creeks relaxed. Oliver and Paul marched away and began to filter their way along the aisles once more, looking at the boxes high above.

"Don't go frettin'," she said. "We're not looting. Just ganderin' for engine parts," Agatha said.

"What for?"

She seemed to find some difficulty explaining. "The cars don't work," she said eventually. "Just don't."

"Not much seems to," Alex replied.

"Televisions, phones, computers…"

"Yes."

"It's the circuit boards," Oliver called, hefting a box into his grasp. "They're dust now."

"We've been trying to get a motor goin'. Maybe then we'll find what the Beelzebub is goin' on. Though I don't rightly think there's a soul else around for miles. Have you seen anyone?"

Alex's throat grew tighter as a memory of Paul Towers flashed before his eyes, with his bare, seared flesh. Flashes of the conflagration amidst the pile-up followed, then the figure he'd seen, standing across the street—all dark-ringed eyes and leering maw. He swallowed with difficulty. "No," he said.

Though he could see she made a valiant effort to keep her features warm and motherly, he saw the disappointment in her eyes, and the almost imperceptible slump in her shoulders. "Neither did we," she said.

She gazed down into James's screaming face and seemed immediately brightened by his chubby, wriggling body. "And what about this'un?" she said. Her voice changed to one of interest and delight. "Wasn't your big brother 'n angel to bring you so far?" she cooed. "Yes, he was."

"James," Alex said. "His name is James. I don't know who he belongs to. He's not my brother," he said.

Agatha's smile only widened. "You're brothers now," she said simply. And then, as though she had been privy to a hidden secret all along, she placed James back into his clumsy grasp.

The crying came to an abrupt end. James looked up at him, grasping his toes, and a partially toothed smile broke out upon his face. Alex blinked, and looked back to Agatha.

Her eyes twinkled. "You're welcome to stay with us," she said. "'Less, o' course, you got an appointment to keep."

Alex laughed. But as soon as his chuckling began, sobs welled up from the pit of his stomach, and his vision clouded with tears. He hung his head as his shoulders began to heave. Without a break in her stride, Agatha took his arm and led him into the aisle, soothing him all the while.

Once she'd brought him to a run-down Land Rover parked askew in the warehouse doorway and seated him with James against a nearby wall, he felt better. While his sobs abated, he watched the strangers work.

Paul revealed his true nature soon after: a garage mechanic turned God-fearing zealot, judging by how he held a greasy wrench in one hand and a tattered bible in the other, one from which he had yet to remove the library sticker. When not speaking, he busied himself with muttering scripture under his breath. To everybody else's bemusement, he seemed under the impression that they now inhabited a world on the verge of Tribulation—after the Rapture of the New Testament.

Agatha and the Creeks seemed equally at odds with him as Alex, but for the time being nobody bothered to speak against him.

On several occasions Alex rose to his feet to help, but each time was forced back to the wall, for James would now grow increasingly distressed at his absence. He was from then on relegated to watching over the child while the others worked.

The group bickered and debated on how best to deal with the choking engine, which stalled and whined and crunched whenever the ignition was turned. They worked away on the gutted engine for hours, growing ever more irate and slimed with grease. Spent or mismatched parts littered the floor in every direction. They reached a point in which Alex was sure every component had been replaced, but they kept experimenting, regardless.

After some time, Agatha came away for water, sipping regally from a flask. She then filled the lid and took it to the small boy, who still sat in the aisle with his hands over his knees. She returned stiffly, backing away from him as a hiker backs away from a riled bear.

The skeletal child looked after her until she was at least twenty feet away, his mouth twisted into a feral sneer. His eyes twitched to each of them in turn, watchful orbs set within a face rendered filthy with grime and hair knotted beyond recognition. He then tipped the lid and gulped, leaving streams of water to pour across muddied clothes.

"What about him?" Alex whispered.

Agatha glanced at the boy and somehow managed to draw another motherly smile from within. "We found that little darlin' yesterday," she said. "He was comin' down from Glasgow, from what we could get outta him."

"Where was he?"

She frowned at the boy and spoke slowly. "The woods... fightin' off a pack of Rottweilers, with a stick."

Alex looked at the tiny child. "Him?"

The boy, as though he'd heard every word, glanced to the both of them and fixed Alex with a narrow stare.

Agatha nodded. "A fighter."

"Did you get his name?"

The boy continued to stare at him with wild eyes and drew his arms even tighter over his legs.

Agatha nodded once more. "Lucian. Lil' Lucian McKay."

She returned to work without another word, leaving him to watch over James.

Once alone, he looked from her to Lucian, then to the timid Creeks and the spluttering men working themselves to distraction. They were all there, a mere step away. Real people.

He was not alone.

"I didn't think we'd find anybody," he said to James and the dog.

They both stared back, blank as slate. He ruffled the dog's fur as the Land Rover was reduced to a collection of rivets and pipes, rocking James in his arms. Soon, the reality of his situation began to bear down heavily on his shoulders.

In a sudden rush, the unshakable conclusion that the abandoned baby in his arms was no subconscious fabrication solidified in his mind. The feverish workings of the people before him were part of no dream. It was all really happening.

He began to shake. The world blurred and his breathing became ragged. It lasted for only a few minutes, but in that time Alex was sure that anything could have happened. He could very well have disappeared himself, leaving behind only a neat pile of clothing.

When the shaking finally stopped, the trance—the one that had shielded him from the truth for the long days since the End (that was how he thought of it now: the End, a black mark on the world's timeline between now and Before)—had lifted.

At last, a hand on Alex's shoulder drew him back into his body again. He jerked and gazed into a pair of kind, feminine eyes, standing over him.

Agatha's soft voice murmured, "Alex… We're goin' now."

He nodded and stood on legs that had grown numb, following her towards the Land Rover, which now purred nearby. Somehow they'd got it started. "Where are we going?" he said.

Agatha responded in a tone just hesitant enough to convince him that she scarcely believed the words herself, "We're goin' to find answers."

They all piled in after Alex had collected his things from the office and stowed the dog in the boot. Backing away from the industrial park, they left the warehouse behind and began to weave their way through the great burned-out wrecks upon the roadways.

As they moved onto the motorway, heading south, Alex turned to Agatha. "What happened?" he whispered. "Please, tell me. Tell me you know *something*."

She laid her hand over his, and he knew that there were no answers to be had, not from her, not from the others, and not from anyone else.

Nevertheless, Paul saw that moment as ideal to pipe up. "The End of Days," he bawled. "Mark my words, it is. And we've been left behind, because we're the damned."

Alex looked down, cupping protective hands over James's ears, staring into his emerald eyes. There, contained within the child's bulging cheeks and fixed gaze was everything that he would ever need to carry on. He was certain of it.

James never cried in his arms again.

2

DESTINY CALLS

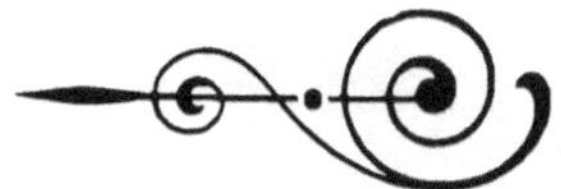

The destiny of man is in his own soul.
— **Herodotus**

Norman drifted. A medley of smeared images—or maybe memories—flashed in the dark: rain, falling white stone, and a sharp pain upon the side of his head. But instead of falling into focus, they flickered and jumped, taunting him from afar.

"Got your head knocked around pretty good, didn't you?" said a disembodied voice. It spoke with something akin to good cheer. "Not the first time, huh?"

Norman rolled end over end in a blackened void.

What are you talking about?

The voice came again, this time less cheerful, more jeering, "What's the matter? Don't you remember?"

Norman grunted as the stream of images flickering before him quickened, shifting between light and dark; faces and buildings; a great tempest surging above a city of towering skyscrapers; and he, horizontal, staring up at a collection of drenched, worried faces. They yelled down at him, exacerbating the throbbing pain above his ear— coursing the jagged contours of his scar—until it was almost unbearable, the urge to vomit all-encompassing.

One of the faces was clearly Alexander's, though much younger, perhaps no older than Norman was himself. Moments later, he glimpsed Lucian among the sea of dripping faces. His brow bore no sign of the signature crevasse that Norman knew so well, half-obscured by a shock of long, brown hair—luscious, vital locks of which there were now only silver, patchy remnants.

The others were a blur—except for a single figure that clearly did not belong in the picture. Didn't belong at all. It stood off to one side, some distance behind the others, crouching over him without a trace of rain upon its body—almost as though the rain passed right through it. As though it were not really there. Its face was young and angular, carved with fine detail. Norman sensed an overbearing strength and sinister intent; the eyes staring out from the pale features seemed to see right through him—no, directly into him. Surrounding each eye was a dark streak, a halo of darkness around the glowing, white sclera.

He nodded to Alex and Lucian (their faces still younger, not yet buckled by time and strife), who still called out above Norman, bent close, shouting his name— though he could only tell from the movement of their lips, as their voices were no more than smeared, incoherent warbles.

Norman's own voice spoke from the ether, as though he'd spoken aloud, voicing his thoughts. What is this?

The figure merely smiled. "*Remember, Norman,*" he said. "*Remember. You were all there. You* all *watched it happen.*"

And then he was gone.

The city's palette of colours liquefied and reformed, swirling back into focus until the face of the man with the neckerchief was upon him, staring through the glass of his living-room window. For a moment, Norman felt a twinge of recognition, one tenfold stronger than the one he'd felt several nights before, by the campfire.

And then nothing.

Darkness.

He drifted.

Then he felt his body once more—his real body. He was being moved. Distantly, a twinge registered in the crook of his elbow, which built to a sharp pain, and something cold ran up his arm. Then nothing again.

"How is he?" said an addled voice, warped and inhuman. It hung in the ether, faint and undulating.

"I just gave him a shot. He should stop struggling soon," another voice answered.

"Will he be okay?"

"I'm not sure. We'll have to wait and see."

Norman slid further into nothingness, and the voices became silent.

*

"Here," Lucian said.

Allie started as a blanket enveloped her from behind. His rough fingers brushed her cheek and she sighed, running a hand over his wrist, blinking eyelids that felt like they were made of concrete. "Thanks," she muttered.

She glanced over her shoulder and took in the sight of his grizzled silhouette. He looked terrible. "You've been up there again, haven't you? In the hills. People are worried about you." She hesitated. "I'm worried about you."

He grunted. "Any change?"

She let it pass, returning her gaze to Norman's bedside. "It's like he's never going to wake up."

"He will. Give him time." Lucian staggered over to the other side of the bed and looked down at Norman's lax face. He glanced at her, then around at the darkened clinic. "You need to get out of here, let someone else watch him."

"I'm fine."

"You haven't slept."

She couldn't help smiling at the sacks under his eyes and the wild angle of his unwashed hair. "Look who's talking."

His eyes bored into hers until she shifted and straightened. "I can't help but feel responsible," she said. "I was there not a minute before. There must have been some sign, something I missed."

"Bullshit. You were the one who found him. If anything, everyone should be parading in here to thank you." He grew quiet for a while, and gripped Norman's forearm. "It's me who's responsible. I failed him."

"What are you talking about?"

"It's my job to keep us all safe."

"There's nothing you could have done."

"There's always something you can do."

She pulled the blanket tighter over her shoulders, hoping some words of comfort she could offer would fall into her lap. They didn't.

She settled for companionable silence. It was a strange thing, knowing that the two men before her had become her closest friends. When she had arrived in New Canterbury, coming up on two years before, she hadn't expected to stay long. She had just been passing through.

Funny how things had turned out.

"What are you doing in here?" Lucian muttered.

She blinked. "What?"

"You heard me."

She swallowed despite herself. "He's hurt."

"So let Heather patch him up. What do you care?" Despite the coarseness of his words, his tone was flat, probing, without edge.

She looked at Norman and found that her voice had abandoned her. What *did* she care?

Not long ago she had been taken in by the legend of the Champion just like everyone. He had been the paragon to which the masses could rally. Then she had been assigned to scavenging duty with him, and for a while thought him a bobblehead on which the city hung its hopes and dreams.

And now? Now that had changed again. He wasn't the hero from the stories. How could anyone really be such a person?

But there was *something* about him. It was buried somewhere deep, so deep that maybe it was just her imagination playing tricks. He was no Champion, but he was no fool, no everyman. Lost, maybe, and frightened, like a deer staring down the barrel of a gun. Yet, though she tried to deny it, he plagued her thoughts.

"He's my friend," she said finally.

The slight curve of a faint smile touched Lucian's lips. "Sure."

"What's that supposed to mean?"

He didn't reply. His eyes had grown unfixed, glassy. For a while his knuckles whitened, gripping Norman's sheets, and an ugly snarl flickered over his face. When he finally stepped back, his lips were twisted into a sour slant. "Get some sleep." He stalked away into the gloom.

"Where are you going?"

"To keep watch. Nobody's getting in here again. Not ever."

Alexander watched Lucian carefully as he dropped a yellowed package before him.

His expression was quizzical for a moment, the wind blowing his hair until horizontal. A week's stubble glittered on his chin. His hunched form was nothing but a shadow atop the hill, overlooking the darkening city. He opened the package with care, revealing its contents with a grunt. "Another?"

Alex sighed, looking down at the cathedral, and nodded.

Lucian sat silently beside his rifle as the pressed silver feather dropped into his hands, the grass lapping at his bare shins in the wind. It had been a hot day, and only now was the temperature beginning to drop. The tree line sat a hundred metres away, hidden by an evening heat wave that shimmered without pause.

Lucian's face contorted into a grave mask: his eyes steely and his mouth a set, hard line.

Alex walked a small distance away and looked towards the sun as it began to dip below the horizon. He waited for a while, unmoving, his mind blank.

"Where did you get this?"

"My doorstep. Just like all the others."

"When?"

Alex shook his head. "It could've been left any time."

"How many is that now?"

"I've lost count."

Lucian scowled. "What are we going to do about this?"

"I don't know."

"We can't just sit around and do nothing."

Alex rubbed the bridge of his nose, shielding his eyes from the glare of the sun. "You need to stop coming out here." He turned to face him.

Lucian scowled. "And *you* need to stop shutting yourself away. People are looking to the kid, and he isn't ready to say 'Boo' to a goose. So they look to me, and I—I can't stop thinking that if I see anyone within a mile of this city, I'll kill them. And it won't matter who it is. I'll pull the trigger all the same."

Alex swallowed to loosen the lump forming in his throat. "I mean it," he said. "You can't be out here."

Lucian looked taken aback. "Why?"

For a brief moment, Alex considered showing him the scrap of paper he'd found in the old man's pocket, the one with so many of the city's secrets scrawled across it: where their sniper nests were hidden, the guards' shift-change times, where the entrances to the catacombs lay—even the elders' names.

He hadn't told a soul about that. It had taken a great deal of wile and patience to reposition each nest and change the sentry shifts without piquing anyone's attention.

But, right now, Lucian looked on the verge of breakdown. He'd have to keep it to himself at least a while longer. His fingers, straying close to his back pocket, dropped back to his side.

He gestured to the darkening forest. "We've been attacked twice in as many weeks, two people are dead, and Norman is unconscious."

Lucian only shrugged, looking away towards the forest. "I know that they come from the east," he said. "They wouldn't have come across the river, and the land to the North is too flat." He looked back to Alex. "I know they're out there."

"You've seen them?"

"No… But I know they're there. I can feel their eyes on me sometimes."

Alex couldn't quite keep his own gaze from flitting to the tree line. The forest suddenly seemed daunting, malicious. "All the more reason to stay back in the city," he said.

Lucian ignored him. "How's Norman?" he said.

"Heather says he'll be fine."

Lucian nodded. He turned slowly, squinting as the sun set in earnest. "Why him? He was too young to be responsible…he doesn't even remember what happened. What could He want with him?"

"I don't know."

Alex pulled his coat tighter over his shoulders as a sudden gust of wind tore at his flank. It was cooling fast. The sun had dipped to a crescent of fire, slowly being consumed by the earth. He turned away and headed down the hill.

"You never get used to it, do you?" Lucian called.

Alex halted, looking out over the barren wasteland, where crops and vineyards had once been. His eyes swept past the blackened fields, towards Canterbury, broken and collapsing as the forest overtook the land, year upon year.

Lucian continued, "The silence. Sometimes I wonder whether there was ever anybody else here at all."

Alex didn't answer.

"We still have to figure out what to do about this."

Alex nodded before continuing on towards the city.

Norman heard his breath whistle through his teeth long before he opened his eyes. The world, having been a blur for days, finally materialised. A harsh light bore down upon him from a fluorescent strip light fixed to the ceiling, clawing at his retinas.

He groaned, trying to turn his head away, but the weight of his chest seemed incredible, crushing. A stabbing ache in his intercostal muscles was rendered unbearable with each breath. He opened his mouth, felt stale air stir in his throat, and his cheeks move sluggishly against his teeth.

"Hello?" he called. His voice emerged clipped and broken.

The small effort brought such pain that he subsided, closing his eyes. He listened hard, trying to hear something—anything—over the rasp of his breath against his parched throat.

A bustling caught his attention: building footsteps from afar.

"You're awake," Heather said, appearing above him.

Norman ran his tongue around the inside of his mouth, trying to free his jaw from its concrete-like set. "What happened?" he croaked.

"You were attacked."

"No, no, I remember that. What happened to Jason?"

"Who's Jason?" Heather asked, absentminded as she bent over his bed and pushed two fingers against his wrist.

"The man who was in my house. He did this to me."

She scribbled on a chart at the foot of his bed. "Yes, I know. We looked all over, but we couldn't find anybody. But we did find out how they've been getting into the city. Lucian found a maintenance door to the sewer system, up on the hill. They've been going right underneath our guards and popping up wherever they please."

Norman blinked against the fluorescent glare. "That's very clever… Shut that light off, will you?"

"Sensitive to the light?" Heather crossed the room and flicked the switch. "Does your head hurt?"

Norman sighed with relief in the sudden gloom. "I'm fine," he lied. "How long?"

"Two days." She sounded unperturbed by his denial, shining a penlight into his left eye. "You'll want to be careful. I suspect you've cracked a few ribs, and your head's taken a nasty hit. Take it easy for the next few days, at the least. Probably weeks. No work in the fields for at least two."

Norman cowered away as pain ripped through his head. Heather clicked the light off and put it away, her eyes stern.

He lay back, frowning. "What have I missed?"

She maintained her stare for a moment longer before replying, "Not much, just a lot of panic and moping. We've sealed all the manholes that we could find and doubled the guard again."

"You sure that'll stop them? They've been getting in just fine so far."

"Half the city's volunteered to keep watch. The place is as loud at night as during the day. Almost everyone else is sleeping in the cathedral. Nobody feels safe. Lucian is having trouble keeping people working in the fields without Alex around, and now that you're in here…he's not coping very well."

Norman sat up, wincing as his limbs protested. "What's he been doing?"

"He's been out on the hill since we found you. We're worried about him. Robert found him sitting on a rock with a gun, talking to himself." She paused. "I'm afraid he might do something stupid."

Norman braced himself against the headboard, gasping. The clinic swam before him as nausea took its course. He lowered his head until his vision cleared.

Heather moved away, her footsteps dissipating.

With his isolation came memories of Jason looming over him, the chilling stare of the man with the neckerchief, and the marble-faced leering figure who had plagued his semi-conscious daze since dreaming of the city and the storm.

Despite the infirmary's stifling heat, he shivered.

Heather appeared at his side, bearing a pile of clothes that he recognised as his own, from his bedroom.

"Thanks," he said, trembling as he sat up. "Would you mind giving me some privacy?"

Heather nodded. "I'll tell Alex that you're awake. He'll want to speak with you."

"I thought you said nobody's seen him."

"We haven't. But I know he's been coming here. I think sometime during the night."

"How can you tell?"

The smallest of smiles played on her lips. "Somebody's smoothed your sheets by the time I clock in every morning."

She made for the door, blocking the light filtering in from the hall. She stopped at the threshold and turned to face him. "We're burying Ray and the old man tonight," she said. She looked down. "We decided that night. We just couldn't take the injustice of leaving them any longer. Allison was coming to tell you...that's how she found you."

"Allie found me?"

The memory of her voice was a blur, but now that he thought of it, he did remember it, and the banging at his door.

Heather shrugged. "She woke the whole city, hollering like she did. She's been in here nonstop since. More than anyone else."

"She has?"

Heather considered him for a moment, smiled minutely, and nodded. "Sundown," she said, tapping her watch.

"I'll be there."

She turned and left.

Norman was left alone to sit and stare. The other beds were empty, for the most part. The two rows of identical frames, covered with neatly folded sheets, sat unused and dusty in the gloom.

Only two stood out from the rest. The first was the bed in which the old man had been stretched out. The sheets had been made up, but traces of blood and dirt still stained the floor at its base. On the second sat Agatha, staring into space, so still and absent-faced that she blended almost seamlessly into the background.

After a while, footsteps from the corridor signalled Heather's return. Alexander and Allison followed her into the room, and the trio gathered around his bed.

Alexander stopped a few steps away. He looked haggard, unlike himself. His lips were pale. Yet he smiled, standing at the foot of his bed. "How are you?" he said.

"Can't complain." Norman tried to return the smile, but as Heather helped him into a sitting position, he gasped. The stabbing pain tore across his chest again, and he collapsed back.

"Alright, I think you'll be staying here at least another day," Heather muttered.

"If you insist," Norman managed to speak over a stifled grunt, but only just.

"You'll be fine, you just need to rest up."

Allison sat by his heels. "When did you wake?" she said.

"A minute ago."

"We've been all over the city looking for them… When I found you, I thought you were dead."

Norman leaned forwards, cradling his head in his hands. "I owe you my thanks," he said, pushing the heel of his palm into his brow. The pressure eased the pain, but couldn't mask the stabbing agony.

Alexander had grown closer. He gripped his shoulder. "You scared me for a while there," he said.

Norman nodded.

"I'm glad you're okay, James, dear," Agatha sang, rocking to and fro upon her mattress. Her eyes drifted across the room and settled on Alex, and for a moment her face grew tighter. "Alex…you look so old."

Then her cheeks fell slack, and her eyes grew distant once more. She stared at the wall, her lips forming unspoken words. They watched her for a while and then Norman looked to Alex.

"James?" he said.

Alex shrugged. Perhaps his eyes flickered, and his lips grew a shade whiter, but the pain in Norman's chest was too great for him to care.

Heather handed him a walking stick, one that had obviously seen many years of service in the hands of previous owners. He palmed it with a curse and sidled to the side of the bed.

"She has good days and bad days," she whispered, her eyes on Agatha.

Norman hauled himself onto shaking legs. When pain erupted in his chest once more, he collapsed onto the cane. He balanced atop it momentarily, staggered, and fell back onto the bed. There, he lay gasping, until he and Alex shared a look.

He cursed, and muttered, "That man, in my house…he was a messenger. They're out there. They want us gone. All of us."

IV

Norman could stand resting in the clinic for a mere half an hour before escaping Heather's clutches. Despite being surrounded by a safety net of aides and nurses on the clinic floor, a great many people found their way to his bedside within minutes, and refused to give him a moment's peace.

The news of his awakening had spread fast. In times gone by, he would have suspected that Allison's legendary ability to disseminate information to all ears within the city single-handedly was responsible. Now, however, he was at a loss to explain it. She had been by his side since before the droves stormed into the clinic.

His visitors ranged from grey-haired discontents—though none were old enough to be elders—to children young enough to be recognisable from his own martial-arts classes. But the resounding impression they left was identical: people were no longer only disgruntled, nor only hungry. They were angry.

In fact, having been left for days to toil in the fields without a single word from Alexander or Norman, led only by Lucian's blustering placations—who had in the interim spent most of his time alone in the hills—they were quite beyond that. After Ray's murder, the attack on Norman, and the still-increasing scarcity of food, it was unsurprising that the entire city had been driven to the point of a tumultuous, feckless rage.

Before he could escape, they were still marching up to him with fire in their eyes and ugly grimaces plastered over their cheeks, demanding to know what he planned to do, and when more scavenging parties would be sent out to gather fresh supplies.

He was only able to stare back at them, dumbstruck. These were the very same people who had greeted him in the streets each morning, worked beside him in the fields, laughed with him over countless meals.

All of that seemed forgotten. Now they looked to him for comfort, for his divine guidance, as though he and the city's elders had been holding secret meetings amidst darkened dungeons.

If Allison hadn't been by his side, he was certain that he would have burst into a tirade. His head throbbed, and the burning in his chest was still as fierce. Patience was in short supply. But she had been there and, to his utter surprise, had allowed the visitors to speak for only moments before shepherding them away. As soon as he'd showed the first signs of wanting to escape, she had ducked beneath his arm and guided him from the clinic, heedless of the nurses' cries for them to return.

She was different. She had grown in some slight and yet unmistakable way that had changed the essence of her presence. It was almost as though a spell had broken, and maturity had fallen over her like a blanket draped over her shoulders.

Now, as they left the clinic, she all but carried him into the streets, and he felt the faintest of flutters in his chest as he glanced down at her determined face. For a moment he thought that the flutter was brought on by the look she in turn gave him—one that had ceased to be expectant and become watchful, almost enraptured—but then the nature of it sharpened, and he was then sure that it was something quite different.

She was wearing her sandy-blonde hair up today, and her clothes were neater, closer in style to the practical, simple robes worn by the elders. She was, he saw, without her pall of adolescent affectations, quite beautiful, all rosy cheeks and soft lips.

"Where to, then?" she said.

Norman blinked. The flicker had gone. He thought of going home to sleep, where he wouldn't be disturbed, but cast the notion aside. Not only was Jason's intrusion still too raw, but the last thing the city needed now was for yet another person to shut themselves away. Instead, he pointed along the street, and guided her towards the school building.

He planned to drop in on Sarah's class of eight-year-olds, intending to take Sarah up on her offer to act as a guest for the daily English lesson. Maybe there he'd find some peace.

He didn't even get close. He was accosted at the door by a crowd of over half a dozen parents, all of who outwardly appeared to be waiting to pick up their children, but all had eyes for him.

It took all of his resolve not to explode.

Once again, Allie saved him, guiding him through the sea of angry faces, parting them with fierce glares. By then, he was gasping for breath. The journey, although a distance of only a few hundred yards, had been more than enough to make the pain in his chest unbearable. His ribs didn't feel just cracked, but shattered. It was as though an entire window's worth of glassy shards had been woven into his skin.

"I need to rest," he said.

"Where?" Allie said, breathless from the effort of dragging him.

"DeGray's classroom," he slurred. "Alex said he and Richard are in the fields."

She led him along the darkened hallway, leaving the lingering crowd muttering bitterly. They rounded a corner and stepped into the dim hovel usually occupied by the Master and his disciple.

"Over there." He pointed to the desk upon which the chessboard lay, and the Master's chair before it—a tattered leather wingback that seemed to exude the distilled essence of its owner.

They ambled closer awkwardly, and Norman kicked the door shut as they went.

"There we are," Allie said, easing him down.

He wheezed his thanks and set to rubbing his chest, which felt as though it glowed white-hot, and almost brought tears to his eyes. But once he had settled his breathing and sat still for a few moments, it began to ebb, descending to a dull and persistent nagging.

"Any news on the radio?" he said.

Allie looked taken aback. "No," she said, eyebrows raised. She tittered without humour. "To be honest, I think everyone forgot all about it after you…well, you know."

"The summit's still planned, though?"

"So far as I know. The elders' council. All of them." She looked sheepish. "But we still can't get a word from Alexander."

Silence settled over the room, and they turned their gazes to the chessboard, set up and ready for a new game to begin.

"Do they always play?" she said.

He smiled. "Every day."

"Why?"

"Old habits…keeping them alive, along with everything else."

She picked up Richard's king piece, squinted at its fine ivory detail, and set it back down. "Does Richard ever win?"

"Not once. John says that he'll be in this room until he does."

They shared a chuckle, one that persisted for several long moments and left in its wake a more relaxed atmosphere. Eventually, however, the nagging doubt of Allison's change of heart became too great for him to resist any longer, and he looked at her until he caught her gaze. "Why are you helping me?" he said. "Everybody else is lining up to bite my head off, and you're here…picking me up off the floor."

"All the best gossip, right from the horse's mouth," she quipped. "You're hot news right now." She offered him a wry grin, as though to cement his certainty that her words were in jest.

He smiled, and felt the first genuine semblance of good humour that he'd felt for a long time boil away in his bowels. "No, really," he said.

She took a while to reply, in the meantime straightening Richard's king unnecessarily, tightening her lips. "I'm here because I see something in you." She swallowed with an audible crack, averting her eyes. She swayed from side to side, running her finger along the desk. "I don't know what it is, but it's there. I know that you don't believe in destiny, Norman, but I'm starting to think that you might be the one to save us after all."

V

Lucian pulled his coat up against the burgeoning shock of hair upon his chin, shivering in the evening chill. He was beginning to squint in the growing darkness as the sky turned from a rich pink to duller orange, and had laid his rifle horizontally across his lap. His eyes were set hard upon the tree line a hundred yards away.

Behind him, distant booms and whirs echoed across the landscape as their handful of biofuel generators—which were currently enjoying a new lease of life thanks to the composted waste from the fields, aiding the struggling wind turbines—chugged to life, flooding the city with white light.

A great yawn forced his mouth ajar, drawing a tired growl from his throat. Fatigue was hitting hard now, and he was finding it difficult to keep the trees in focus. He would have to leave soon and make his way home. Even within sight of the city, it was unwise to remain after dark.

For the last few days he'd only left the hill to stand guard at night near the clinic. From what he could remember of it, he hadn't slept for more than three consecutive hours since they'd found Norman.

But there was a good reason for his self-imposed isolation. A very good one.

Two days before, when Allie had sounded the alarm, he had been so infuriated that he had mistaken an elderly man for the attacker. Lucian had tackled him to the ground in the street. It had transpired that he hadn't felt safe in his own home and had been walking to the cathedral in the rain when Lucian had leapt upon him. The elder, a man of great wisdom and kindness, had been Rayford Hubble's father. He would need crutches for a month. The guilt and embarrassment were still raw and fresh in Lucian's mind, like a splinter.

He rubbed his hands together against the cold and looked up at the sky. The orange tinge was now long gone, and only a glimmer of indigo remained, clinging to the treetops, imbuing the forest with a shimmering aura.

He stood with some difficulty, his knees stiff from lack of use. He stretched, holding his rifle at arm's length.

Then, a sound: wailing. Wailing carried on the wind.

He dropped into a crouch, trigger finger ready. Only his eyes moved, scanning for a sign of movement. The same meadow met his gaze. The same tree line. The same silence. But the growing darkness had taken on a more menacing tone. Besides the moths and bats swooping and diving amongst the treetops in the distance, the floor beneath the canopy was still. Yet still the hairs on the back of his neck stood on end.

Then the sound came again: a reverberating howl, coming from the maintenance gate that led to the sewers. Somebody was down there.

FIRST INTERLUDE

Candles flickered in the gloom. The group of survivors sat back from the table, belching, satisfied by their meal. They had dined well tonight on the bounty of tinned foods the Old World's ruins had to offer. Conversation was sparse, low-pitched, and trivial. The night was passing lethargically. Alex watched the proceedings unfold, for the most part contributing little.

Seven years having passed, with all things considered, he still hadn't managed to shake the numbness that had plagued him since the End.

The first years had been the hardest. The power grid had soldiered on for almost a week before trundling to a stop. From then on, what was left of the world was plunged into darkness whenever the sun set.

After a near eternity of searching, it turned out that there had been others, individuals at first, lost or halfway suicidal. Then there had been couples, partners exploring the New World together. Eventually, groups had emerged, with leaders and followers—shepherds leading flocks of bewildered IT managers, stockbrokers, farmers, and TV stars alike.

But they had been so far flung that an encounter had never ceased to be exceedingly rare. Whenever paths crossed, a universal and mutual suspicion had been exchanged, preventing them from adhering together. People had feared large groups—feared each other. It was almost as though they'd been afraid that, if they ever tried to rebuild their lives, they too might disappear. Instead, they locked themselves away, found safe corners to sequester, and waited—though for what, nobody had known. And so it had gone. People had stewed, days had become months, and months years. During that time, almost all had been content to remain in isolated clans, gradually helping themselves to the vast stores of resources amongst their fallen civilisation's great cities.

However, those stores were now becoming thin on the ground. Tea, coffee, fuel, cigarettes and alcohol had very nearly ceased to exist. These commodities now held worth far exceeding that of anything else, and were in many cases viciously fought over, within and between groups.

The End's survivors were now rushing headlong towards a situation they'd all foreseen, yet lacked the will to prepare for. There had been no crops farmed, to their knowledge, at all, anywhere in the country.

So far as Alex could tell, the End had struck randomly, indiscriminately, with no rhyme or reason as to who vanished or who was left behind. The likelihood of seasoned farmers having survived in large numbers was tiny. Even if any *had* survived, they would have been left alone, helpless to stop their crops falling into ruin without a single helping hand for dozens of miles.

Even the group Alexander had come to think of as his family were painfully aware of their ignorance. Lighting fires, navigating, sterilising water, storing food and performing basic maintenance work were things still largely beyond them. Endless hours researching in eerie public libraries had taken them only so far. Even now, they would get lost, sick, or hurt and be unable to do anything about it. When something broke, it would forever remain broken, or be replaced by a scavenged double. When they came across the injured or sickly, as they occasionally did, they could do nothing to help.

As close as he'd grown to the others, Alex sometimes couldn't help but feel that he *was* alone after all. The others seemed almost content in their ignorance, and lacked drive, as though merely waiting for the next disaster to sweep them away. When they looked out the window, all they saw were ruins. Only Oliver and Agatha seemed truly *present* in the slightest, but even they seemed ready to sit and watch time deal mortal decay to the world.

He, however, saw dormant homes, schools, hospitals, and factories. He saw what had once been, and what could be again. He never failed to hope that perhaps the world had been restored when he awoke each morning.

He'd devoted every spare moment to reading everything he could find, along with saving as many books as he could manage. He also saved whatever else he came across: paintings, instruments, electronics and mechanical parts, storing it all away where it wouldn't rot or be buried in rubble.

Even if everybody else had given up, he would fight their decline to his dying breath.

"As soon as this winter ends, we can finally get some seed in the ground," Oliver said.

Paul huffed. "What's the point of that?" he said. He hiccoughed and took another swig of merlot from the bottle in his grasp, which was smeared with a layer of dust so thick that the vintage was most likely older than any of them.

Turning to God hadn't been enough for Paul, and so he had also turned to the bottle. His habit had been a persistent thorn in their side, forcing them to make weekly forays in search of untapped cellars.

"It'd be nice to eat a meal," Oliver said, his lazy eye bulging. "The canned food isn't going to last forever. At the rate that we're using it, we have months, not years, and then we're on our own."

Agatha nodded. "Won't be enough to grow our own. We're goin' to have to strike up some kinda deal with others…some kinda trade, if we're going to get everythin' we need."

Paul sneered. "There's no sense in it," he said.

"There's sense in eating," Oliver said.

"There aren't enough people left for us to go knocking on their doors. Folks want to be left alone."

"We have to do something, Paul. We have to start anew, or make the first steps, at any rate. Somebody will come along eventually and we'll work towards something."

"Too few!" Paul roared, and slammed his fist against the table for good measure. "I tell you, there are too few of us left to form anything of the kind. It's ridiculous, Aggie. You know it is!"

Agatha sat stiffly and observed Paul along her lengthy nose as though from a great distance. The two of them glared at each other. "What'd you have us do?" she said.

"There is nothing *to* do," Paul said. "Look out the window. The world is gone. None of it is ever coming back. All this talk of starting over is just wishful thinking."

"Why does it have to be wishful thinking?" Alex said, leaning forwards. A pang of anger leapt in his chest.

Paul rounded on him. "I'll tell you why," he spat. "The only reason we're here at this table is because we're damned. We've been left, because of the lives we've led. It may not look it, but this world is soon to be Hell. Mark my words."

Alex shook his head, his chest convulsing. "What about the boy?" he said. "A baby? He's done evil worthy of being left to...the fires of Hell?"

Paul didn't answer, but instead proceeded to let fly a great spiel of scripture, eyeing him with unfathomable contempt. He stood up, wandered from the table, and stumbled outside, where he grumbled even louder to the wind.

The table was left in silence. Alex collected his thoughts, while the others stirred with visible discomfort. The Creeks stood from the table, Helen casting a contemptuous glance about at them all. "I don't want to hear this," she said. "Goodnight."

They all murmured a farewell as the Creeks disappeared into their bedroom.

They were trying for a baby. Alex was gripped by panic at the thought of a child. After the food had run out, what would they feed it? Wasn't anybody thinking about that but him? If they were going to bring a child into the world, there was no sense in it being raised by a bunch of folks interested in nothing but waiting for their own end.

At least he had Agatha and Oliver in his ballpark. That was something.

"He's crazy," Agatha said at last.

Oliver wheezed, his lazy eye bulging. "Of course he is. But he has a point."

Alex paused midway through an appreciative smile, and his jaw fell ajar. "*What?*"

Oliver sighed. "There's not going to be any starting over."

Alex looked to Agatha for help. But at the sight of her face—downcast, guilty, yet sincere—he realised that he was indeed alone, more alone than ever. He collapsed back into his chair and raised his arms.

Maybe his ballpark was empty after all.

"You can't be taking his side," he said helplessly.

Oliver leaned over. "There's no side to take. Paul's right. There are just too few of us left to do anything but try and stay alive for as long as we can. The End decimated the population of the entire world, as far as we can tell. The Old World is gone. There's no coming back from this."

Alex raised a pointed, accusing finger before he could stop himself. He could feel his heart yearning to burst free from his ribs and was sure that his eyes were ablaze. "You've given up."

"There's nothing to give up on! I'm not saying that starting over isn't an admirable idea, but it's a pipe dream, Alex. Leave it at that, lad. There's a good boy."

Alex looked to Agatha for help, but she, too, seemed unable to quite meet his gaze.

"You're a visionary, Alexander, so you are," she said. She was quiet, but her voice reached his ears without hindrance. "You're the greatest of all'a us, there'll be no denying that. But you're young, so it ends righ' there. Paul's right. We're not ready." She paused. "Might never be ready."

Paul ambled back into the room and settled into his seat, still grumbling minutely. His derisive stare added to the lingering sting of Agatha's words, amplifying Alex's sense of isolation. Acknowledging that he'd been defeated, he leaned back. "I have to check on the boys," he said.

He stood amidst awkward silence and shuffled away towards the corridor, passing beyond the candlelight's reach. At the mention of children, the conversation had grown embarrassed and diminished, hushed and somehow more sober, more lucid.

Alex walked beyond their line of sight and paused, waiting for them to continue in his absence. Perfectly still, he pricked his ears and held his breath.

"There's something to that lad, I'll admit," Paul said. "But he's still the devil's work, I tell you now."

There was uproar at the remark.

"Can't be callin' Vision the devil's work, you daft ol' goat!" Agatha said. "That boy's the one thing keeping us goin'. Without him, there wouldn't be any hope, and hope is the only thing tha' makes me get outta bed in the morning. Wha' else is there?"

"Hope?" Paul blustered. "What place has hope got here? Everybody that we ever loved, gone, and whoever's left is scrabbling for purchase. All the while, the world takes a nosedive towards fucking Armageddon. And you're clinging to *hope*?"

"S'all we got left. S'all that matters so close to such a thing."

"Ah!" Paul grumbled dismissively. "The words of the devil!"

"Paul, we talked 'bout that word," Agatha said. "Ain't God's will, an' you'd do well not to test him in times like these."

Paul sighed. "I know, Aggie," he said. His voice had grown a touch sheepish.

"You'll see it, so you will. One day tha' boy's hope will change the world, and there won't be a word 'bout the devil that'll change anybody's mind 'bout it!"

Paul grumbled something incomprehensible. In reply, Agatha gave her final word on the matter, in a voice that pulled at strings within Alex's gut, "Not everythin' boils down to the End of Days. There's more to life than tha'. Folks live on, and they'll do whatever they got to do to survive. I tells you now: We're not gonna give up. Wha' we've been left with ain't enough, so we're gonna take back what we had."

"Unite under the boy's banner, then?" Paul huffed. "I suppose that makes us his gang, running around and singing Kumbaya? That's your idea, is it? We're Alexander's Pals now? The Kin of Cain?"

A moment of silence. Then, "You're bloody well righ' we are."

Paul grunted. The conversation died at that. Reverting to idle grumblings and comments upon the meal and weather, talk from then on was stinted and overly polite.

Alex, smiling, continued along the corridor until he came to the last bedroom. He knocked and received an invitation to enter. He found James already tucked in, pyjamas and all, propped up against the headboard, waiting.

He seemed somewhat disquieted by the raised voices, but at the same time he smiled and welcomed Alex inside. As soon as the door was closed he bounded up and down beneath the sheets, brimming with glee. "Story!" he cried.

Alex couldn't help laughing. Already dinner's troubles seemed far away and inconsequential. He stooped into the child's stool beside the bed and glanced about the room.

Lucian snored amidst the other bed's sheets, against the far wall. He had little interest in stories at his age. Over the past year he'd taken to disappearing for hours at a time into the wilds. Nobody knew where he went—except Alexander.

He'd followed him once, through expanding forests, along roadways lined with rusting cars, across fields littered with charred airliners. Eventually they'd come to a bluff amidst dense burdock, one overlooking miles of barren wilderness.

Hidden amidst foliage, Alexander had watched him stretch his arms towards it, embrace it, breathe it in, relish it in a way that he'd never relished any wonder of the Old World.

The others were talking about keeping him home before he got hurt, but Alex knew they couldn't if their lives depended on it. Lucian needed the wilds; needed to *be* wild.

He loved the boy—even dared to say he loved him more than he'd loved his own family, before the End—but knew that they would never understand one another. They were too different.

Lucian didn't lament what the world had lost, but accepted it as it was. He slept soundly.

Alex turned from him to assess the rest of the room. He had perhaps become carried away with furnishings.

Apart from Lucian's drab, adolescent décor in the corner, the room was alive with vivid colours, painted patterns, models hanging from strings, and myriad toys of every description. It was filled to the very brim with stuffed animals, picture books, enormous reams of paper, colouring pencils, paints and board games. For each item, there was a replacement underneath, and another beneath that.

"Story," James repeated, his emerald eyes brimming.

"You're getting a little bit too old for bedtime stories," Alex said.

James looked shocked and horrified. "Why?" he said.

"You can read."

"I like you to read."

Alex laughed again. "Looks like you've got a book right there," he said. "What is it?"

James turned the leaves of the hardback in his grasp, revealing its title: *Birds of England.*

"Birds again?"

James merely smiled.

Alex sat on his bed and flicked through the pages. "You've always liked birds, ever since you were a baby."

"I was reading about pigeons," James said. "People used to send them to their friends with letters tied to their legs." He hesitated, but met Alex's gaze. "We could do that, one day."

Alex's cheeks were already aching from the strain of smiling. "Maybe," he said. "Maybe we can." He closed the book and put it aside. "What story would you like to hear tonight?"

"I don't know," James said without embarrassment. "You pick."

"Most people have favourites," Alex said, standing and perusing James's generous collection.

"I like all stories."

Alex felt a flutter of glee. James had been more like him than the others since he'd been able to walk and talk. Something of Alex's own reverence of the past seemed to have been infused within the boy's mind. Now he yearned for knowledge, yarns and discovery.

"All stories?"

"I like to know that there's more."

Alex frowned and glanced over his shoulder. "More?"

"More," James affirmed, then looked ashamed. "I like to know that it isn't just…this."

The hairs upon Alex's arms stood on end. He fumbled with the books upon the shelf, trying to hide a giddy grin.

The boy was the key to starting over. Alex might never live long enough himself to realise his dreams—dreams of bringing it all back from the brink, of saving what was left of the Old World—but James could carry on even after he was gone. James could unite people, bring them from the gutter and claw back some civility in the world. For him, there would be time, time to fix it all.

Alex had had the same thoughts a thousand times, lying in bed at night, but never before had they seemed more obvious. The others could never be counted on to make the first step or carry the torch. If anything—or anyone—was ever going to be saved, it was down to the two of them.

At the realisation, he stood bolt upright and hurried to his own bedroom. He returned a few seconds later, holding a bundle wrapped in old cloth. He met James's quizzical gaze, settled into the stool, and unravelled the package with nervous, shaking hands, revealing the mottled green cover of his father's copy of *Alice in Wonderland*.

James fixed his eyes on it. "What is it?" he said.

Alex said nothing, just pressed the book into James's hands and sat back. He followed James's gaze as he looked over every inch of it, turning it over in his hands with great care by the candlelight, somehow sensing that the book deserved special attention. He read the cover and looked up at Alex, a frown upon his face. "*Alice in Wonderland?*"

"It was mine, when I was a boy. Before that, my father's."

"It was yours? Before?" James looked at the book with fresh reverence. He glanced up ruefully and held it out for Alex to take back.

Alex shook his head. "It's yours now."

"I can't," James stuttered. Not a glimmer of childishness remained about him now. His manner of honour, of polite refusal, was crushingly adult.

"Of course you can," Alex said.

"It's your book."

"It's a gift." He knelt beside the bed, holding James's hands, gesturing to the cover. "It's important," he said. "You have to promise that you'll take it."

In the flickering light, James's enormous eyes glittered. He nodded slowly, and took the book into a tender embrace. He opened it with great care and looked down at the illustration on the cover's reverse side: the White Rabbit, dashing through the grass, pocket watch aloft, waistcoat trailing. Not once did he ask to be read to. After a long time, a frown crossed his face and he looked up. "Why is it important?"

Alex leaned forwards, gripping James's hands, and cleared his throat. "Because I have a very important job for you. One that only a special boy like you can do."

"Special?"

"That's right. Other boys aren't like you, because they see what's there. Not like you. You see what could be."

"Are there other special people?"

"Many, once. Now…" He shook his head. "Not anymore. Just you, and me."

James's frown had only deepened. He replied as carefully as Alex had spoken himself, "What job?"

Alex swallowed.

Could he really just come out and say it? Surely it would only frighten him—something that big would frighten anyone. But, looking into those piercing eyes, full of life and ambition, he knew that James could handle it. He leaned forward and spoke in a voice so hushed that

James was forced to turn his head. "Can I tell you a secret?"

James leaned close, glassy-eyed. His mouth had fallen ajar, and his pupils had dilated.

"One day you'll save the world," Alex whispered.

James blinked. Only a moment's pause stretched out before he said, "The whole world?"

Alex smiled. There was no fear in the boy's eyes, nor incredulity. "The whole wide world."

James's expression didn't change in the slightest, but behind his eyes Alex saw a million thoughts erupt into existence. "How do we do that?"

Alex sat back. "I don't know. But I promise you—I *promise*—that we will."

James didn't move for a long time. Only his eyes gave away his feverish internal reaction, darting left and right. Eventually, he said, "How do you know?"

"Know what?"

"That we can do it. If that's what we're...supposed to do."

Alex smiled and stood, leaning over and placing a kiss on his forehead. "Because some men have a destiny." He took James into his arms. "And you've got that in spades."

Holding back tears, he looked down into James's adoring face, and felt his conviction grow tenfold. He placed the candle beside the bed and backed away towards the door, pulling it half-closed behind him before pausing to glance back in. "I love you, brother," he said.

James smiled, the book tight in his grasp. "I love you, Alex," he whispered.

Alex closed the door and crept away to his room. He froze at the sight of a figure, stock-still and wreathed in the kitchen's shadows, staring back at him.

Agatha's smile was not only friendly, but maternal. It always had been, to all of them. She had taken Alex and James, broken and helpless, kept them alive, and warded away the worst of the pain. Even gruff Paul had found comfort in her embrace when gut-rot had been in short supply.

Right now, her eyes twinkled. She held her diary in her hands, laden with their only records of after the End, the only thing that might remain of them if they didn't get their house in order. He smiled back at her, and that was enough for them both. They went back to their business without a word to one another.

Alex snapped the door shut behind him and sighed. White walls, bare and lifeless, met his gaze. His uncarpeted, unfurnished, cluttered room sat unsaturated and beige in the candlelight.

He'd never decorated. Never cleared the Old World relics from the cupboards or cabinets. Never changed a thing.

What did he need wallpaper for? When he lay here at night, he didn't see these walls anyway. His dreams took him far away, dreams of what mankind had once been, and could be again.

He lay on the bed and looked across at the ancient fireplace, which lay dormant, unusable, and littered with mouse droppings. But the mantelpiece remained, and upon it were the purple and orange tattered packages that had been his parents' last gifts to him. Beside them sat a framed photograph of the dog, long since buried.

She had died saving his life. A dark voice in his head sometimes plagued him with promises that she was the first of many casualties, if he was ever going to save anything.

He stared across at the gifts for a long time, having settled beneath the sheets, listening to the sound of Oliver and Paul singing merrily to an incomprehensible tune. Their argument had apparently become lost to a mellow rhythm and drink-addled giggling. At some point, his eyes ceased to look upon the packages. But still he saw them in his dreams. The faintest of smiles remained upon his lips even when he woke the next morning.

VI

The screaming carried for hundreds of yards in every direction. It permeated every wall, struck every ear, and echoed in the Old World's darkest ruins. The rancid figure in Lucian's grip had long since curled itself into a ball, desperate to prevent further injury. But that didn't stop him dragging it along the street like a dog.

Each time its broken body impacted a stray cobble or scratched against the road, it would issue a groan or whimper. Its awful clothes, hanging in tatters, barely covered its body. None were recognisable as trousers, coat, or shirt, having been reduced to a single pall of filthy cloth.

Lucian grunted as he hauled the creature down Main Street, his fist closed around its neck. His short stature didn't for a moment hinder his stride. His anger made up for lost height many times over.

Muted whispering passed between onlookers, but only for a few moments. With shocking rapidity their voices became louder, and then they began to yell with uncontained fury. The city's bottled fury, which had for so many weeks boiled away in suppressed silence, burst from them like floodwaters through a broken dam. They yelled for family members to come quickly, hurling insults at the cowering figure, congratulating Lucian. Some simply released amorphous screams of raw anguish.

When each newcomer arrived and saw what Lucian held in his grasp, none questioned its origin. The conclusion that this creature was responsible for their woes and strife was reached unanimously. They had been waiting for a donkey on which to pin such a tail for countless weeks. This pile of rags was ripe for the pinning.

Dozens poured from nearby buildings, forming a mass in the middle of the street as Lucian approached. Their faces bore no sympathy for the creature's unending screams. Yells soon became angry roars that reverberated amongst the backstreets, filling them with a ghostly, riotous din. People stepped forward, their arms outstretched, hands formed into tight fists. Some spat. Others sought to trample.

Lucian swept a glance around at them all and dropped the creature at their feet. He then walked away into the crowd without looking back, abandoning it to its fate. He didn't take his gaze from the floor again until he'd reached the porch of a nearby cottage, from where he watched the scene unfold on the cobbled streets.

He was beyond feeling now. Beyond anger. He felt nothing but the dimmest satisfaction at the sight of the creature being swarmed by fists of fury.

The gathering was by now a hundred strong, and the rancorous racket was drawing more from across the city, even from the fields. The creature whimpered in the dying light, its cries now drowned out by the encroaching mob. It huddled against its knees, rocking back and forth on the ground.

But it was shown no mercy. A single kick from Sid Robeck—a stocky guardsman whom Lucian had sat beside on many an overnight watch; a quiet, amiable man, slow to anger—brought its head back with a snap. Blood spurted from a cracked lip. The back of its head made contact with the concrete with a sickening crack.

The crowd grew bolder at the sign of weakness, and approached the creature—which, now spread-eagled on the ground, no longer obscured by the pall of cloth, had taken the shape of a young man. Blurred limbs flew from every direction, swiping, kicking, and punching. A sharp scream rattled above the roar of their voices, but the crowd was heedless. The people had found their culprit—

"STOP!"

The new voice was no louder than any other, almost lost to the cacophonous ocean of furious bleating. However, those nearest to its owner froze, and immediately became quiet, their eyes growing wide and their bodies still. They regained their composure as what they were doing seemed to suddenly dawn upon them.

The silence spread exponentially. The crowd's noise went from a deafening roar to an uneven hum in mere seconds.

Then, nothing. A hundred embarrassed pairs of eyes observed as many pairs of feet but, as though drawn by an irresistible, mysterious force, each gaze eventually settled on the voice's owner: Alexander Cain, gaunt-faced, eyes ablaze, filling the town hall's doorway.

*

The silence in the aftermath of the riotous outburst was deafening. People appeared unsure of what to do, or where to look.

Alexander stepped out into the street and walked towards the cowering young man, who shook as Alex approached, while his wild and bloodied eyes bulged in their sockets. Several of his teeth lay on the floor beside him in a pool of his own bodily fluids, and his left cheek was badly torn.

Alex crouched down beside him. He suspected that he was the first of the city folk to make eye contact.

The young man raised an arm to his face, ready to shield himself, but Alex took hold of his shuddering hand and slowly pushed it to the floor. Then he stood and looked around at the hundreds of furious faces.

A solid lump had settled in his throat. He sighed and forced a nod. "I haven't been here," he said. "I wasn't here when you needed me." He paused. "I can only beg your forgiveness. I've been…troubled. I know that all of you have been patient, that you've worked hard, that you've gone hungry. I know that I've failed you."

He pointed down at the young man, and to his bleeding wounds. "But we are BETTER THAN THIS!" he bellowed. "We can never let this happen. We can never allow ourselves to fall this far. We can never BE this!"

Shame infected every face in sight. A thousand feet shuffled.

A faraway pigeon cooed. He gritted his teeth, determined to stay the course, but couldn't help searching the rooftops for a bobbing silhouette. He pushed on despite himself. "We're going to stay strong. We can get through this. I know that I haven't been here when I should have. But from now on, I will be. I promise."

Silence filled Main Street.

He swallowed. "We're going to talk with this man. *Talk* with him. I want everybody back to the fields. We can be ready to reseed by the week's end if we keep at it. We *can* get through this, but only together."

He drew a long, calming breath, then crouched down once more and addressed the young man. "Who are you?"

The young man hesitated, his eyes darting from Alex to the mob. He seemed to weigh the danger of talking against that of being torn apart if he stayed quiet, and mumbled, "Charlie." His missing teeth addled his words, but Alex could still make them out. "My name is Charlie."

"Okay, Charlie. I need you to tell me where you came from."

Charlie stiffened, clocked the crowd once more, and then sank back. "Manchester."

"Who was with you?"

"Nobody. I—"

Alex cut him off with a sigh. "Charlie, don't lie to me. If you spin a tale then the people behind me will kill you right here on this floor. But if you tell the truth, I promise that nobody will hurt you."

Charlie looked horrified, his eyes darting into the crowd once more. He seemed to find no comfort amongst their faces, and swallowed audibly. "There were three of us. We were here to send a message."

Alex nodded. "We've heard. This…Jason, he was with you?"

Charlie blinked. "Yes."

Alex stood up, looking around at the others. He suspected that the crowd now consisted of over two-thirds of the city's population, and more were still coming.

"Who brought him here?" he called.

There was a moment's silence in which people looked around at each other, shrugging.

Then a call rang out. "I did."

Alexander turned with the rest to see Lucian standing beneath a nearby doorway. His face was set and harsh, but his eyes remained placid. "I found him in the sewers. Leg was broken."

Alex felt anger burn in his gut, but forced his expression to remain neutral.

Lucian came forwards without a word, parting the crowd in his wake, and crouched beside the young man. "Can you stand?"

Charlie shook his head. "Not a chance."

Lucian and Alex grabbed him by the arms and lifted him to shoulder height. He groaned, making no effort to stand under his own power, and was half-dragged down the street. The crowd parted like the Red Sea, furious yet forlorn, as Charlie was taken away to the clinic.

*

"The sewers?" Norman said, frowning. He was ambling, but walking under his own power. Alexander's emergence from hiding had been enough to get him standing.

Alexander nodded as they proceeded into the clinic with Allison in tow. "Lucian dragged him into the street and let the others tear at him for a while."

Norman cursed. "Why would he do that?"

"To punish him. And me."

Norman glanced to Allison, arching an eyebrow.

She merely shrugged.

He couldn't help but notice that she no longer looked to him in the same way; no longer were her eyes expectant, but instead comfortable, almost complacent.

They entered the clinic's back room and laid eyes on a filthy young man lying in the nearest bed.

Norman felt something stir in his gut at the sight of him, something unexplainable that tugged at his attention, but he couldn't quite place it. He shook his head, and kept in step with Allie.

"Keep still, Charlie," Heather said.

The young man screamed as she applied her fingers to his leg, squeezing hard. He tried to claw at her, to get away, but Lucian grabbed him by the shoulders and held him down.

"Stop moving." Despite being no louder than a whisper, Lucian's voice shook.

Charlie looked furious, his eyes red and his throat emitting a deep hum, but he lay back nevertheless and set his arms down on the mattress.

Norman limped to the bed, weary of being back in the clinic so soon. He looked over to his own bed in the corner, still unmade. The sheets were probably still warm. By the time he'd turned back to Charlie, a palpable tension filled the room.

Charlie was barely into his twenties, with a small torso and spindly arms. His eyes were deep-set in his ruined face, and his bloodstained neck was filthy with slicks of grime. Just like the men they'd hunted down after Ray's murder.

Again, he felt a tingling at the back of his mind. But he couldn't quite place it.

"How's the leg?" Lucian muttered.

Charlie spat a tendril of saliva that landed upon the bridge of his nose.

Lucian hardly reacted. His arms remained crossed over his chest, and his eyes remained set. All that moved was in his mouth, which formed a strict, paper-white line. Several moments passed. Then, slowly, he took his left arm from its locked position and wiped away the spittle. A stifled sound rumbled in his throat, and he shifted slightly so that Charlie could see the rifle slung over his back.

Charlie turned away, his face strained and emotionless. Norman thought he saw a glimmer of fear in his eyes.

"There's no way for me to be sure. But if I had to guess, I'd say he has a closed fracture on his left tibia," Heather said. She locked eyes with Charlie. "Try to lie still. Don't move until I can get you something for the pain."

She moved up to the remains of Charlie's face, turning his head left, then right. "Move your head in a circle."

Charlie jerked his head in a haphazard, jagged motion, wincing. "It feels fine," he grated. "My mouth hurts."

Heather yanked his jaw down and stared into his mouth, clicking on a penlight. "You have a gash on your tongue and a few missing teeth."

Charlie pushed her away, massaging his chin. "How many?"

"Four." Her voice was cold.

She'll treat him, Norman thought. *He's her patient. But she's not happy about it.*

He knew that she was strong enough to keep her urges at bay, above mindless spite. Yet he couldn't help wondering whether she'd have been part of the mob on Main Street if she'd never taken the Hippocratic oath— whether any of them could have been, if they hadn't had so many people looking to them.

It was frightening to think so. But he'd seen good people do things of late he would have thought beyond them a year ago, Lucian chief among them. It was almost as though he hadn't really known some of them at all.

Alex sat down on the bed. The springs creaked under his weight. "We'll take care of you," he said, "but you're going to tell us what we need to know."

Charlie's eyes grew as he bolted upright. He winced momentarily before speaking, slurred, "No!"

"You'll talk or we'll throw you into the streets," Lucian breathed.

"I can't!"

Lucian's face became an image of untainted fury. He ripped the rifle from his back and pushed the barrel against Charlie's temple, his teeth bared and his eyes searing.

Norman and Heather moved to stop him, their wild cries blurred into a wordless groan.

Lucian ignored them. "Better yet," he said slowly. "Instead of waiting for you to die of your own accord, I'll tell everybody exactly who you are, and why you're here. They'll blow your brains right into the gutter."

Charlie jerked. Tears burst from the corners of his eyes and his mouth fell ajar. His bleeding gums shone under the fluorescents. "Please!" he yelled, "I can't tell you anything! I don't know them!"

He raised his hands, pleading. "Please," he whispered, "please. I met them just over a week ago. I was with my dad. He and I had been on the road for a few days, just looking for some food, like everybody else."

He paused, staring around at them, his eyes darting from one to the other. Lastly, he turned to Lucian, and paused.

Norman held himself at the ready, ignoring the shooting ache in his chest, determined to lunge for the rifle if it came to that.

A muscle jumped in Lucian's jaw. The crevasse on his brow brimmed with sweat, but after a final grunt he took the barrel of his rifle away from Charlie's temple.

Charlie hesitated, but, under their watchful gaze, continued, "They came during the night. Put guns to our heads. Told us that we'd do whatever they told us, or we'd die right there…"

He looked to Lucian. "You people are just the same."

"We're not like them," Alexander said, giving Lucian a stern glance. "Just continue, please."

Charlie sighed. "One of them," he muttered. "He didn't speak all that much at first, but later—when he'd sent the others away—he gave us some kind of…recruitment pitch. He said he was gathering an army."

"Who was he?" Norman said. He blinked, surprised that he'd spoken. He'd been caught in Charlie's words. His breathing had grown shallow.

"I don't know," Charlie said. "I didn't see his face. He wore a cloth over his head the whole time, like a mask."

Norman felt a chill run up his spine as the man with the neckerchief appeared in his mind's eye. He could feel Alexander and Lucian's eyes move over him, but tried to ignore them.

"They took my dad," Charlie was saying. "They didn't want me, said I was too weak, or wasn't motivated…or something. I don't remember. But they took Dad. While he was away with them I was kept with the others."

"Others?"

"Women and children, mostly. They kept us under guard and made sure that we didn't leave."

"Where?"

"A building, not far from here."

"*Where?*"

"Never saw it before then. I think it had been a tower block once, but the top half had fallen away."

Heather turned to him with a pan of water, a dripping sponge in hand. "Why would they guard you?" she said, dabbing at his face, smearing blood across his chin.

"Insurance. To make sure nobody who went with them ran away." He swallowed. "They were making people do some pretty bad things. Sick things."

They exchanged looks.

"Who are they, really?" Norman said.

Charlie shrugged. "It's like I said: They just found us and took my dad for some mission."

"Mission?"

"That's what they called it."

"What kind of mission?"

"They wouldn't tell me, but they've got it in for you. Everything that they said was about you." Charlie looked around. "What did you do to them?"

"Nothing," Lucian said. "We did nothing." Then, almost too abruptly, "How many of them are there?"

Heather finished wiping away the blood and set the bowl aside, observing Charlie's face critically. After a few moments of poking and prodding, she disappeared from the room.

"From what I saw, two dozen or so."

"From what you saw?"

Charlie nodded darkly. "I don't think they were on their own."

Heather returned to the bedside holding a small black box in her hands. She thumbed the lid open and took out a long silver needle. "You'll need stitches," she said.

Charlie looked revolted. "You're going to knit my face closed?"

Heather paused, her brow set. "If you'd prefer, I could just leave it to rot from infection."

"Why don't you?"

"I'm a doctor." Her lip had curled. "But don't tempt me."

"Charlie, focus," Alex said. "How do you know that there are more?"

"It was the way they talked. That man—the one with the mask—spoke with too much…what's the word? Conviction?"

He grimaced, his face bunching up as Heather applied the needle to his face. He gave a stifled whine of discomfort as the needle punctured his cheek.

"What happened to your father?" Norman said.

Charlie took longer to answer than before, growing pale. He spoke stiffly, keeping his cheeks and jaw still as Heather worked, moving only his lips. "I don't know. That's why I was here. I convinced them to let me on one of their missions. I was hoping that maybe I'd run into him."

"Why would you do that?"

"I didn't know where he was! He hadn't shown up for three days."

Norman stiffened. "And you came into the city through the sewers?"

Charlie nodded.

"To attack me? You were with Jason?"

There was a pause.

"They didn't tell me that they were going to hurt you," Charlie muttered, his eyes downcast. "They were just talking about sending a message."

"But like you said: They've made people do some pretty bad things," said Lucian. "So you knew it wasn't going to be pretty."

Charlie said nothing.

Norman felt a surge of nausea at the thought of Jason. Yet, behind the churning in his gut, that prickling sensation was still pulling at his attention. The way in which Charlie angled his head, and the manner of his speech, were somehow familiar.

"If all you wanted was to find your father, then why did I find you crawling in our sewers two days later?" Lucian asked, leaning close to his face.

Charlie cowered, clutching the sheets, apparently having forgotten about the needle imbedded in his face. "I fell," he squeaked, his eyes pleading.

Norman released a breath he hadn't been aware of holding. The longer he watched Lucian, the more certain he became of an impending breaking point. The bloodlust in his eyes was unmistakable, but at the last moment Lucian seemed to regain control and straightened back into a standing position, folding his arms once more. "You fell?"

Charlie nodded, grunting as Heather cut into his cheek once more. "I was supposed to guard the manhole: our escape route. I was at the top of the ladder, and I heard somebody shouting from the other side of the street."

Norman looked to Allie, who nodded.

"Just after I found you," she said.

Charlie waved his hands in embarrassment. "I panicked, and it was raining. The ladder was wet. I fell down the chute, landed on top of my leg."

Lucian cleared his throat. "And what did they do when they found you?" he said.

Charlie lowered his head, his eyes growing red and his voice weak. "They left me. I begged them. I begged. But that man," he said, looking up at Norman, "the one with the mask. He took one look at me and led the others away." He swallowed, lowered himself onto his pillow, and closed his eyes.

Heather pulled the thread taut, closing the wound on his cheek. Crafting a neat knot, she cut the line deftly.

Alexander stood amidst fresh silence, his eyes glazed. "I believe you," he said. "We'll fix your leg. Then you can decide where you want to go."

Charlie barely responded, his face red as a plum and swelling.

Alexander turned to the others. "Does anybody else have anything to say?"

Silence stretched out as they looked around at each other.

Heather excused herself. "I'll check on you in an hour or so," she said over her shoulder.

Charlie nodded glumly.

"You too, Norman," she called as she left the room.

Norman barely heard her. The odd sensation that had been tugging at his bowels had finally sharpened into focus. It took him by such surprise that he swore aloud.

Charlie bore a striking resemblance to one of the men they'd hunted down after Ray's murder: the emaciated man who had been so unwilling to fire on them, whom Lucian had shot dead, whose body they had left to decay in the forest, unmarked.

They had killed Charlie's father. Not a misguided fool who'd taken the wrong men for company, but a hostage. An innocent man.

VII

Norman straightened gingerly, and fresh pain tore across his chest. His legs throbbed. He let the hoe in his hands fall to the ground and sucked a deep breath, turning away from the half-dug furrow at his feet.

The film of putrescent slush in the fields had finally been cleared away. Their pace had slackened of late, but at Alexander's return, people had been all too ready to burst into action. With startling vigour, people had leapt to work, filled with new life.

Norman stood a small distance apart from the main body of activity, working in small bursts whenever he could manage it. Heather had repeatedly insisted that he stay in the clinic, but merely being near Charlie had been enough to unsettle his stomach.

The sun was half-obscured by the distant forest, but it was still sweltering out in the open. Any stray breeze was lacklustre, claggy.

The others on shift didn't seem bothered. Their bodies arched amidst shortening shadows, turning the soil with shovels or tearing at remaining weed stalks with blunted scythes, fervent, possessed by common will.

A guard patrolled fifty yards away, an automatic rifle slung over his back. Farther away, another figure paced amidst the spreading furrows. Though he saw no others, Norman sensed that a great many more surrounded him.

He couldn't get used to all the guns being thrown around. They'd kept the armoury locked up tight for years, guarded at all times. Now, it seemed that every second person brandished a rifle.

He bent over with a grunt and struck at the ground. He looked at the pitiful track that he'd dug in the ground and sighed. He wiped away the band of sweat on his brow after a further minute, cursing under his breath. His arms felt like blocks of lead. His chest was on fire.

"You should go back," Robert said, brushing past. His huge arms were making light work of the weed-ridden ground, carving vast furrows with each stroke. Sweat glistened on his dark skin, accentuating his bulging biceps.

Norman felt a pang of jealousy at the sight of his powerful movements, wishing that he could just take a breath without feeling as though he were at death's door. "I'm fine," he said.

Robert straightened, towering over him. "You look like the Reaper," he said. "It could take you a while to get back to being yourself, so don't push it."

"I'm fine," Norman repeated, stabbing ineffectively at the ground. "How's Sarah?"

Robert nodded. His clipped hair sprayed droplets of sweat onto the newly exposed earth. "She's good." He wiped his top lip with a free hand, not quite hiding a frown.

Norman waited for him to elaborate, allowing a courteous silence to stretch out.

"I mean, she's not doing too well with the siege," Robert blurted, his eyes slanting as he turned away. "She's a trooper, though."

"You're getting along well?"

"Sure. She usually spends her time with her books in the warehouse, but she stays at home with me now." He paused for a moment, looking skywards. "It's nice," he said. "A nice change. So long as I've got her, all this is just a bump on the road."

Norman tried to smile, to congratulate, but in the next moment he found himself doubled over, gagging and spitting in the dirt.

"Go back," Robert said firmly, hacking away. "I think I can cover your load." He cast a wry grin at the thin tract at Norman's feet.

Norman sighed, trying to hold onto his lunch. "Alright," he gasped. "You win." He dragged the hoe in his wake, retreating to the city. "I can hear my brain frying."

Robert called after him, "Rest up. Just make sure you're ready by nightfall."

VIII

"You just have to give it time," said Heather, prodding Norman's bare chest.

"You're sure?" He tried to keep the pain from showing on his face. "I've been walking around nonstop and it's exactly the same."

Heather snapped off her gloves. "It's not going to heal in a day, and definitely not in a few hours. I told you: broken ribs take weeks, sometimes months. And I can't be sure that you don't have other injuries. Especially your head. You need to watch it, and make sure you tell me if you notice anything out of the ordinary."

She swung the overhead lamp out of the way and stood, heading towards her desk on the other side of the room. She rifled through the various detritus upon it, returning a short time later with a small plastic bag containing shrunken bark.

"White willow?"

She nodded. "Painkiller. It's all we've got. Don't overdo it. It can cause gastric problems if you take too much, but you're not going to be much use to anybody like this." She handed him the bag. "Chew it up, one piece at a time, every six hours or so. Too much and it'll kill you."

"Comforting." He took the bag and peered at its desiccated contents. It didn't look inviting, more like dried mouse droppings. He didn't relish the thought of putting the stringy, dried pulp anywhere near his mouth, but thanked her nonetheless.

She gave a loose salute. "I have to get back to work," she said. "I have to have the caskets ready before…" She left with a sigh.

Only a moment of silence endured before a voice rang out from the gloom.

"I'm a dead man," Charlie said. He was sitting up in his bunk, his cheek knitted closed by Heather's stitches, and his injured leg stuck out at an odd angle. His face was catatonic, unblinking.

Norman pulled a string of dried willow into the light, grimacing. "You don't look dead to me," he said.

The lights flickered overhead, momentarily casting Charlie's face in dull shadow. He looked to Norman. "I'm going to die, and you're making jokes?" he said, his voice quivering.

Norman looked over his shoulder, checking that they were alone. All was quiet, save for the distant footsteps emanating from Heather's office. "Who says that you're going to die?"

He watched Charlie's face grow pained and sorrowful. "Nobody has to say it," he said. "I'm not an idiot. I know a murderer when I see one."

"You're talking about Lucian?"

"Who else?"

Norman shook his head and popped the string of pulp into his mouth. He tried to shift it to the back of his mouth as quickly as possible, but still the sour taste made him cringe. "We promised that we wouldn't hurt you, and you've been just fine so far," he said. "Your leg looks better already."

"Don't do that," Charlie cried. "Don't pretend that you're all not just waiting for him to come in here and strangle me."

"He's not going to kill you."

"Oh yeah?" Charlie said. "How could you know that?"

Norman picked up a nearby bedpan and spat a milky slick of saliva into it. "I just know," he muttered. In truth, he wasn't so sure at all. The look in Lucian's eyes had been unlike him—consumed, almost feral. Just like the night of Ray's murder. It had looked almost as though Charlie had wronged him personally, or reminded him of someone who had.

Norman hadn't seen him since setting out for the fields.

Charlie snorted, turning away. He remained silent for a long time.

Norman was halfway to his feet when Charlie surprised him by speaking again. His voice filled the room, muffled by his missing teeth, but was clear enough. "He came to me. Your man: Lucian. He told me that you chased a bunch of folks into the woods, that they must have been the same folks that took me. That you hunted them down like animals. Is that true?"

Norman swallowed, hoping that he was far away enough from the lights for the shadows to be hiding his face. "They murdered one of ours."

"So you killed them?" Charlie's lip quivered. "You killed my dad?"

Norman scratched his head. Suddenly, the willow's taste didn't seem so bad at all. "I'm sorry," he said. "I really am."

Charlie didn't respond. He sat from then on, staring ahead, while tears burst forth onto his cheeks and fell to the sheets below.

IX

Lucian caught Norman on his front doorstep, fumbling with his keys. The cane made everything difficult, awkward.

"Norman," he said, throwing furtive glances over his shoulder as he approached.

Norman tried not to turn his body too much. The willow dulled the pain, but not as much as he'd have liked. "What?"

Lucian was still looking about himself as he crossed the drive, his face set. He didn't speak until he was only inches away. For the first time in Norman's memory, he looked afraid.

"Can we talk?"

Norman felt his eyes widening as shock bounced around inside his head. He frowned, but after several moments could only nod. "Of course," he said, opening the front door and gesturing inside.

Lucian stepped into the hallway, moving past the piles of books that lay within.

Norman stared in after him. He thought that he'd never want to come back here again. He'd expected that he'd have to move. But by the time Robert had sent him away from the fields, he'd known that he was coming back.

The attack had come and gone. Something told him that he was in no danger of a repeat event. The damage had been done, and the message delivered.

After a moment, he followed. The base of his cane thudded against the floor every second step. He ambled, winced, cursed. It was humiliating to rely on the stick, but he couldn't get around without it. Heather said he'd need it for a few weeks, even with the white willow numbing him up.

He pushed the door shut with his elbow, sending a red-hot bolt into his abdomen. It almost brought tears to his eyes, but he barely noticed, so focused was he on Lucian's hunched shoulders. Once he'd regained his breath, he made for the living room.

Lucian was already seated, his head bent low and his hands clutched together between his knees.

Norman ambled over to his chair and sat over a period of several seconds, easing himself down. His lamp stand was still askew where he'd fallen over it. He blinked until flashes of the neckerchief man standing at the window had passed.

"How's the pain?" Lucian said. He looked miserable. His voice was flat, hollow.

Norman shrugged. "I'll live."

Lucian looked up. His face had become a mask, his features drooping, a grotesque caricature of his usual firm expression. He seemed locked in a fierce internal struggle. His eyes darted in their sockets, focused on nothing in particular. A line of sweat rested on his upper lip. It was clear that he meant to speak, but he seemed reluctant to utter another syllable.

Norman opted to wait, lest he push him away through unnecessary coaxing.

Lucian was rocking slightly, though he seemed unaware of it. His breathing was heavy. "Do you trust me, Norman?" he said.

Norman straightened in surprise. "Of course."

"Still? After how I've behaved?"

Norman sighed. "You had every right to be angry about what they did to us. Nobody blames you for being…out of the ordinary."

"When I saw that boy's face out on that hill, I felt myself break." Lucian spoke slowly, as though only to himself. "It felt like I'd left my body, and I was just watching my fist beat his face. I could see it happening, but I couldn't stop." He paused. "I think I'm losing my mind."

Norman's subconscious proffered up an image from his dream: the storm above the city, the younger faces of Lucian and Alex yelling down at him, the pain in the side of his head, the leering figure that didn't belong. Just like the memory of the neckerchief man, it flashed before his eyes for only a moment, and then it was gone. He shook his head, clearing his throat.

Which of them was really in danger of losing their mind?

It might have been the drugs, but he didn't think so.

"People who are crazy don't know it," he said, clearing his throat to cover his slow response.

"Of course they do. They just don't think about it. They're too busy being crazy."

Norman smiled, banging his cane softly against the floor. "Since I can remember, I've seen you rushing off to save the day. Nobody thinks you're losing your mind. You're just doing what you've always done: taking care of us."

Lucian looked annoyed. "Every time I think about…that kid…my blood boils."

Norman frowned. "You have to remember," he said. "Charlie hasn't done anything wrong."

"That's my point," Lucian shouted, leaping to his feet. "He's just a boy, and all I can think about is ripping him limb from limb."

"Why?"

Lucian stiffened and began pacing. That single word appeared to have a resounding effect on him. "Our past isn't all roses, Norman," he said.

"Well, I can't remember most of it."

"I know."

Norman frowned. "Since Ray was killed, you've been after blood. Something's got you riled. So if these people are really as bad as you think they are, why don't you tell me? Why don't you just *tell* me what happened?"

Lucian shook his head and sighed. He faced resolutely away. "It doesn't matter anymore," he said. "What's done is done."

Norman pointed the tip of his cane in his direction. He was doing that more often. The stick was already becoming a part of him. He hid a grimace and pressed on, "Fine, but you need to stay away from Charlie if you feel that way. We may still need him."

Lucian gripped the sofa's arm, as though for support. "I need to step away from all of it. Everything," he said. "I need some time to myself."

Norman shook his head. "Everybody needs you. You're a strong face. You just need to get some help. Talk to somebody."

Lucian looked stricken. He waved his hand. "No," he cried. "No, nobody else can know. I can't have people thinking that I can't take a walk without a gun in my hands."

Norman stared. His chest ached from the strain of sitting, and his head was throbbing from all the white willow. The volume of Lucian's voice was doing his building migraine no favours.

He took a deep breath. "I'm tired. And I need to get some sleep."

Lucian's eyes grew wide. "You're kicking me out?"

"No," Norman said, standing. "You can stay if you want." He pointed with his cane—*Already a part of you,* a voice jeered in his head—to a stack of paperbacks on a nearby table. "I took those from Sarah a few days ago. You should have a look at them for me. It'll keep you busy."

Lucian sighed. "What should I do?"

Norman moved towards the hallway. "I don't know," he called as he ascended the stairs.

He had to wait for some time before he heard Lucian leave. He spent a quarter of an hour lying in bed, wishing that sleep would come. But his efforts proved fruitless. A sea of thoughts waged an unending war behind his eyes. If he didn't do something, Lucian was apt to snap.

Whatever that meant for Charlie, it wasn't good.

He needed help.

X

Alexander's house was within direct sight of the cathedral. It was no simple abode. Spread upon a street corner, it rose some forty feet from the ground, tapering to an ornate carved roof. Atop it, angelic figures and gargoyles were set within glistening white stone, glowing in the afternoon light.

To have called it a home would have been wrong, almost as wrong as it would've been to have called Alexander its owner. It was a museum—or mausoleum, some said—of the Old World, and he was its custodian. Within, the spirit of mankind had been captured in miniature. Thousands of years of history, culture and memories lay nested within its walls.

Upon it, their entire way of life had been based. The principles by which the city's hundreds of citizens—as well as the many thousands in the wilds who had heard its legend—now lived had been laid down here.

After the End, the holy sanctity of places like the cathedral meant little to most. This was their temple. This was hallowed ground. This place was never unprotected.

Guards had patrolled the neighbouring rooftops in twos and threes since long before the first attack on the city.

The garden spoke volumes of the dedication it had been shown. A tiny stream ran through its centre, spanned by an arched bridge, the wood ancient and hard as diamond, having been trod upon by a million soles. The grass was cut short and neat. Stripes of exuberant flowers ran in a grand hexagonal pattern, bright purples and pinks, blues and reds; the only flourishing plants for many miles.

Before the famine, some had even made pilgrimage to this spot, to look upon the house, hoping for a glimpse of the living legend within.

Norman walked the garden path, taking his time. The pleasant glow of the midafternoon sun eased his aching chest, but his head still throbbed. In time he arrived at the front door, which towered over him, all brass and rich mahogany. Two fifteen-foot totem poles stood on either side of the door, resembling creatures Norman had never seen beyond the pages of books, eerily stretched beyond accurate proportion: the snarling head of a wolf, the serene stare of an owl, and the powerful bulge of a brown bear's maw.

He took the heavy knocker in his hand, slammed it once against the brass plate, and waited. From afar he heard calls of people returning from the fields after a hard day's work. Alexander's return from self-exile had inspired new hope, enough for most to have almost forgotten their problems. Amongst the voices was a hum of merriment— even contented laughter.

The door went unanswered. He knocked once more and waited for over a minute further, hearing nothing but the distant trickle of the stream and the continued ruckus from the fields. After a moment of hesitation he grabbed the handle. With a *clunk*, the heavy latch released and the door opened. He was surprised to find it unlocked, but proceeded nonetheless.

Once he was over the threshold, he peered around at the atrium. Polished wooden floors ran underfoot, and a wide staircase led up to the second floor, out of sight.

High ceilings. Freshly dusted walls. But no host.

"Hello?" Norman called.

His voice penetrated deep into the belly of the house, echoing in dark corners and forgotten crannies. Once, dozens of visiting emissaries had provided a steady hubbub here, exchanging ideas and gathering knowledge to be relayed to lands afar, part of a network Alexander had painstakingly built up since the End. Now it all sat gathering dust.

The atrium gave way to a long corridor. Of all the mahogany doors lining either side—of which there were at least two dozen—only one lay open. He left the staircase behind, his mind turning back to years past.

He'd been raised in this house, schooled by Alexander himself, trained to be the one he said they all needed. The saviour of mankind. How many would have given anything for that chance?

Countless.

And how many times, sitting at his desk in Alexander's study, had he wished to be somewhere else—anywhere else?

Again: countless.

He passed into that same study now, and shivered as a flood of memories leapt forward from the back of his mind. It occupied more than two thirds of the ground floor. He paused in the doorway and stared inside. He'd seen it every day in his youth, year after year. But he'd never grown used to it. It always sent a lump forming in his throat.

Destiny aside, this place took his breath away.

Nearest to him was a forest of spindly stands, their polished steel frames glittering. Upon them were more musical instruments than he could have possibly named. Each shone with fresh polish, set with loving care upon handcrafted bespoke cradles.

Beyond them stood an enormous bookcase, easily fifty feet long and fifteen high. It was stuffed several layers deep with books that teetered on the shelves, the collective wisdom of the ages: from Shakespeare to Steinbeck; Calculus to Haematology; Ancient Egyptian mythology to Lycanthropy.

On the opposite wall, every inch had been filled by the frames of a hundred painted canvases, great sunsets, harbours, hills, mountains, and figures walking the streets of forgotten Old World cities.

Here and there were glass trestle tables, covered with trinkets and souvenirs from all over the country. A pitted brass Sextant, a tall golden globe, the ceramic body of a white rabbit, the long ears broken and the paint long faded. Others were covered with writings and figures, tiny statues of Greek and Egyptian gods, pieces of jewellery, Chinese and Arabic scrolls, pendants and pocket watches.

Yet this was only the cap of a mile-high peak. Beneath the manor—amidst a vast web of catacombs that had once been wine cellars, pumping stations, sewers and air-raid bunkers—were miles of Old World treasures.

Only Alexander and Sarah had the keys to that place. Even Norman had only glimpsed its innards a few times. In fact, most of the city folk didn't even know it existed.

Within, libraries that dwarfed even the mountains in Sarah's warehouse were filled to capacity with leather-bound first editions, ancient manuscripts rescued from hallowed shelves, pocket paperbacks, and picture books. All meticulously treated, seal-wrapped, tagged and logged. Great stores of vinyl records, CDs, cassette tapes and DVDs diverged from a kilometre-long hall of canvas masterpieces, drawn from all the land's galleries.

Alexander and his ilk had been collecting mankind's discarded trinkets for a long time.

The farthest depths of the study were dotted with leather furniture, arranged in a parabola around a central fireplace. The grate was aglow, with the aid of disparate gas lamps casting the room in a rich, warm light.

Finally, upon the fireplace, was an arrangement of packages. Despite being rotted and old, they retained their bright colouration: oranges and purples, covered with cheery patterns. Some were wrapped in bright bows, and had cards taped to their sides.

All was still, waiting for the absent master to return. Uncertain, Norman idled near the trestle tables and looked around at the rescued remnants of endless dead. As hard as he might have tried to in some way emulate this temple, he would never know what he was trying to reproduce. He had never seen the Old World, never heard its din. These relics, while breathtaking, could never truly overcome that kind of estrangement.

In some ways, the Old World was truly dead, and would forever remain so.

"You look terrible," said Alexander's disembodied voice, echoing off the walls.

Norman started, and turned to the door. "I feel terrible," he agreed.

Alexander's eyes narrowed as he advanced into the room. He looked grizzled, his face peaky and drawn, his robes tussled and creased. He clearly hadn't slept for some time. Yet still he smiled, and gestured to the leather chairs by the grate. "You should have Heather take another look at you. Make sure you're really all there." He tapped a finger to his temple.

Norman shrugged, easing himself into the seat opposite him. They both took a moment to lounge, staring into the crackling fire before Alexander continued, "Surely you won't begrudge me for worrying. You're too important to go unchecked."

"I hate that." Norman looked down at his hands. "I'm no more important than anyone else."

"You're the only one who can carry on our work after we're gone, Norman. It's your—"

"Destiny. Yeah, I know."

He'd heard those words a million times, but never before had they seemed so absurd, so irrelevant. Never before had he felt so lost.

Alexander's brow twitched. "You should rest up—where Heather can keep an eye on you."

Norman sighed. "I can't sit in there. Not with him."

"Charlie?"

Norman nodded.

Alex clicked his tongue and stared into the fire for a while, motionless. "You've come to ask me something?" he said eventually.

Norman paused for a moment, unsure of how to proceed. He thought of asking why anybody would ever attack them, why Jason—and those he claimed to represent—would want them gone, or why Lucian, a man he had thought he'd known as well as Alexander himself, was on the verge of strangling a wounded slave boy.

But the look in Alexander's eye—distracted, distant—made him hesitate. Perhaps this wasn't the time. He suspected that if he asked now, he might do more harm than good.

Judging by how Lucian had reacted when he'd asked—*Our past isn't all roses, Norman*—maybe it wasn't a good idea to start pulling skeletons out of cupboards. Right now, he wasn't sure he'd like what he might find.

He began to speak slowly, glancing at the door as he did so. "I'm worried about Lucian."

Alex didn't respond for a while, his eyes still on the fire. He raised a hand to his chin, rubbing at the stubble on his neck absentmindedly—Norman was surprised to see the two-day growth. Alexander had been clean-shaven every day in living memory. "I have every confidence in him," he said after a long silence.

Norman splayed his arms. "I'd like to say that I do too, but after what I just saw, I can't say that I do."

A bizarre twinkle scintillated in the deep-blue halo around Alexander's pupils. "He was always the first to jump, always the first to respond, always the first to lash out...never thinking before doing. But it was never vicious, it was never...cruel."

Norman averted his eyes. "I'm not sure where you're going with this."

Alex rubbed his temple. "For all his ill temperaments, his intentions are what make Lucian who he is. For all of the years that I've known him, he's never done anything to harm any friend of his."

"Maybe not," Norman said, leaning forwards. "But if he continues like this, he's going to get us in trouble. He's going to kill that boy anytime now."

Alexander nodded. "Yes," he said. "I suppose."

Norman flailed. "What? That's it?"

"He's gone too far for us to restrain him through reason."

"Maybe we could restrain him physically? Knock him out or lock him up until this blows over?"

Alexander gave him an odd look. "I doubt that will help. Anyway, I'm almost certain that this situation will not simply blow over anytime soon. Having him around is vital for morale."

Norman looked over towards the door again, his voice dropping to a whisper. "If he gets worse…," he said. "If he gets out of control, what do we do?"

Alexander sighed. "I don't know," he said. "I suppose we'll have to simply hope that he doesn't. We can't afford for him to. With the hunger, the attacks, this news of the radio, and the funeral, the city needs him. Needs us all."

Norman swallowed.

The funeral. It was now only two hours away. Already, the ruckus of returning field hands had given way to respectful silence outside.

If they could get through the burial without incident, a weight would be lifted from their shoulders. Perhaps things would step down a gear.

But could Lucian wait that long?

XI

Alexander threw yet another feather at Lucian's feet. "What in God's name is wrong with you?" he spat.

Lucian had once again retreated to his post upon the crest of the hill above the city. He barely moved as Alex set to pacing around him, his features unmoving. After a while he leant forwards and picked up the feather, turning it over. His face grew even grimmer. "Where did you get this?" he murmured.

"My doorstep, again," Alex said. He fiddled with the book in his hands—green and battered, adorned by an intricate golden title. "And this, too."

He hadn't seen it for years. Not since…

But there it had been, lying atop the feather, upon his doorstep. Waiting for him, looking just as it had when he'd first picked it from his bedroom clutter all those years ago.

Yet Norman apparently hadn't seen it when he'd left. That meant that it must have been placed there only moments before he'd found it.

He shivered.

Lucian was quiet for a while. The wind whistled around them. When he spoke, his voice was low and broken. "Why is He doing this?"

Alex swallowed. "I don't know."

"Just to torture us? See us dance?"

"I don't know."

"Remind us of what we've done?"

"I don't know."

"What do we do about it?"

"I don't know!"

Norman had left for home minutes before Alexander had raced for the hillside, but he was still visible in the city below, ambling down the street. Alex watched until he had passed out of sight before rounding on Lucian. "You're getting out of control," he said. "You could ruin everything."

"Ruin what?"

"Everything. All of it. People need somebody to look up to."

"Like you?"

"Like you. People look to you. You have to control yourself."

Lucian looked up sharply. His eyes were grave. "You don't want them to look to me, you want them to look to Norman."

Alex frowned. "It's his job to lead them. Maybe not now, or tomorrow, but someday."

"You made it his job."

Alex bent closer, dropping his voice. "He just came to me, worried about you, fretting over you harassing that boy!" he hissed. "He's got enough to worry about without you making it worse for him. If he starts doubting what we're doing then everything we've ever done, all we've sacrificed—it'll all have been for nothing."

Lucian snarled, "That boy never wanted any of this."

Alex stopped. "What?"

"Oh, come on: you've forced this on him since he was a child. Just like you did the first time."

"I've never forced him to do anything."

"You force everybody to do everything. You've already destroyed one life, and now you're doing it all over again with Norman," Lucian yelled, rising to his feet. "Even now, here you are, grilling me like it's the Inquisition!"

"I just want to know what's gotten into you."

Lucian waved the feather before Alexander's eyes. "*This* is what's gotten into me." He pointed to the book. "And *that!* This has nothing to do with starvation or survival. This is all happening because of what we've done."

Alex said nothing.

"We have to tell them."

Alex felt his jaw tighten. "We're not telling them anything."

"They have a right to know."

"If anybody finds out then they'll leave, and we'll be back to where we started. We'll lose society, civilisation, everything. If they go then they'll just become more of what's already out there."

"I can't do this anymore. I can't keep lying."

A silence swept over them, interrupted only by the howl of the wind and the rustle of distant leaf litter.

"We have to," Alex said finally. "It's our destiny."

XII

The soil was dark and the grass a dappled blue under the overcast evening sky. Stray rays of light streamed from the distant streetlights. A light wind ran through the graveyard, rustling the trouser cuffs of those gathered amongst the thousands of weathered headstones.

Behind the five dozen mourners lay the remains of the uninhabited parts of the city, its crumbling walls made only greyer by the sombre procession. Two dark slabs of rock had been carved into an approximation of the surrounding ancient stones, courtesy of Robert's hard labour.

Upon the first was carved 'Rayford Hubble—Loved Son and Husband—2004-2048', before which crouched Ray's wife and father, who both bawled without reserve. Several others wept with them, while many more stood close by, tight-lipped, heads bowed.

The other stone simply read 'Friend', a title decided on after much deliberation, marking the grave of the old Irishman.

Norman stood at the rear of the congregation, leaning on his cane at the summit of a slight rise. From his position, he could see over the heads of the others.

Norman hadn't known Ray well—had only talked to him on a few occasions, and known his family even less—but the heaving shoulders of his prostrate father made his gut shrivel.

He started when a sniffle sounded beside him. He looked down into Allison's tear-stained face and felt a distant flutter stir in his gut, one of many he'd felt when close to her lately. He laid a hand on her shoulder, and she gripped it, giving a strained smile.

Alexander stood with Agatha, Sarah and Robert a short distance away, silent and bowed. Agatha appeared to be muttering a silent prayer. Opposite them, on the other side of the congregation, stood Richard and John. Lucian stood behind them, his face pallid and tense. His hands were bunched into tight fists, such that the knuckles had been stretched until pure white. The crevasse between his brows had furrowed into a perfect V shape, and his eyes almost seemed to be shaking in their sockets.

Norman kept his head angled towards the graves, but kept watch in his peripheral vision. Lucian's face seemed to grow redder by the second, his jaw drawing closer and closer to his skull, until Norman was sure he must have been crushing his own teeth.

He sighed, focusing on the graves.

Alexander had stepped forwards, standing between the two gravestones, facing the crowd. He began a slow and careful speech, monotonous but sincere. Yet he seemed distracted, glancing frequently towards a small flock of pigeons perched atop a few nearby gravestones.

Ray's wife continued to sob, and many eyes traced the wilted lawn. Norman managed to discern a few words of the speech, each of which hinted at a fond farewell to both men. Half-listening, he swept a look around at them all once more.

He jerked. Lucian was gone. Sudden panic reared up as he looked wildly about, scouring the surrounding area.

But Lucian was no longer a member of the crowd. He'd simply vanished. Nobody else seemed to have registered movement. The crowd's unanimous attention was being devoted to Alex.

He cursed, turning full circle, scanning the distant buildings, looking for a silhouette, but nearby grass swayed gently, giving no indication of having been disturbed.

He grunted when he eventually spotted him trudging his way along a narrow gravel path, running along the edge of a group of crumbling cottages. He was moving fast, low, light on his feet. A definite sense of purpose hung about him.

Norman felt a deep and genuine fear spread in his bowels. He backed away from Allie one inch at a time, rubbing his chest, feigning a spell of pain. She didn't appear to notice his muttered complaints.

As soon as he had slipped away, he strode after Lucian.

The pain was almost unbearable. Within moments his chest was heaving and his legs screaming. Lucian was at least a hundred metres ahead of him, and continued to accelerate away. Norman was powerless to stop him. Tears were forming in the corners of his eyes as he tried desperately to keep pace, and razor-sharp bursts of air lashed against his lungs.

The funeral was behind him now, and Alex's voice was nothing but a dim echo. Norman tried to call out, but Lucian had by now cleared the farthest of the outlying buildings. He'd hoped that there would have been somebody else around to signal to, but the streets were empty. Everybody was either at the funeral or had retreated inside to sleep off the day's work.

Ahead, Lucian disappeared from sight, entering the clinic.

Norman was by now seeing spots. The pain in his chest was so severe that he'd half-forgotten why he was moving in the first place. He was nearing the cottages, but a thick span of mud lay directly underfoot, adhering to the tip of his cane and further hindering his progress.

Lucian had been out of sight for over a minute before he could clear the field and make his way onto tarmac. He began to dread reaching the clinic, afraid of what he might find. He fought a bout of nausea, both the sound of his heavy breathing and the roar of the blood in his ears turning his stomach. He stopped in his tracks when Lucian stepped back into the street.

He stood stiffly, his mouth stretched into a tight line.

"What have you done?" Norman wheezed, his heart racing.

Lucian didn't respond, nor did he even acknowledge Norman's presence. He about-faced, and the dark nose of an ancient service revolver glinted in the light.

Norman took a step back as a scream of fury rang out from within the clinic. "What do you think you're doing?" Heather roared.

Lucian waved the revolver. "Stay where you are," he called in reply. Then his voice changed and became quieter, addressing someone closer, "Get out here."

There was a shuffling, coupled with a shuddering moan. Several seconds passed before a figure appeared in the doorway, stooped and snivelling. Charlie stepped into the light, dragging his broken leg. Most of his smaller wounds were still inflamed beneath Heather's stitching. Tears ran down his face as he stepped forwards, his hands clasped before him. "Please," he whimpered. "Please don't. I'll do anything, I swear."

Lucian didn't respond, instead only waving the revolver, signalling for him to keep moving.

At first Charlie froze, his eyes wild and his mouth drawn into a gape of silent terror. So focused was he on Lucian that he'd entirely missed Norman. "Please," he said. "You said you would help me."

Lucian shook his head. "I promised you nothing."

Charlie uttered a high-pitched, childlike cry as he stumbled out into the street, his chest heaving. Norman could see his eyes darting in their sockets as he hyperventilated. "I haven't done anything," he whispered.

Lucian put the barrel of the revolver to the back of his head, pushing him farther into the street. "You think that matters?" he said, a grimace appearing on his lips. "You think you can just sign up with whoever takes your fancy? That you can kill one of us and not pay the price?"

Charlie whimpered. "I didn't mean any harm. I just wanted to find my dad."

Lucian frog-marched Charlie away from the clinic. With the revolver coupling them together, an odd, slow dance played out in the street as they advanced. Charlie was dragging himself forwards, having adopted a pathetic, hopping gait.

Norman gave chase as fast as his broken body would allow, but to what end he was unsure. Lucian was armed, and on the brink of murder; any attempt at negotiation could very well provoke the act all the sooner. He could only follow and look on, aghast.

Lucian led the boy off Main Street and any semblance of safety, into the quiet parts of the city. Charlie's pleas became ever more desperate, until his mouth worked fruitlessly and only strangled groans worked their way past his lips.

The buildings became more dilapidated with each passing second. Walls of untouched white stone soon became splashed with ancient graffiti.

The trio waddled forth until they reached a place devoid of all activity. Weeds grew thick here, bursting through the tarmac, reaching for the light. The wind was dead, blocked by tall buildings and a narrow street. Every shuffle and footfall was amplified in the unstable silence, intermittently interrupted by Charlie's shuddering cries.

Lucian prodded Charlie's neck. "Stop."

With visible reluctance, Charlie complied. He no longer spoke. His arms had fallen to his sides, his hands bunched into sweaty fists.

Norman paused a short distance behind them, his mind racing. The notion of rushing Lucian in his weakened state was absurd, and yet it remained in his mind's eye, plaguing him. He was helpless to do a single thing.

"Get down on your knees."

Charlie drew himself up to his full height, for a brief moment topping Lucian's stature. "I will not," he said. His voice wavered, but was laced with defiance.

Lucian pushed the revolver hard against the base of his skull, forcing a groan of pain from his lips. "I said," he spat, "kneel."

Charlie appeared to burst, or break—Norman couldn't tell which. His arms took flight as he fell onto one knee, moving awkwardly around his broken limb, yelling in a broken squeal, "You're going to kill me? Shoot me right here like an animal?"

Lucian raised his thumb to the revolver's hammer, pulling it back with sinister sluggishness. He was panting, and his hand was shaking. "That's right."

Charlie gave a burst of laughter, full-throated and hysterical. "Just like you did to my dad? You're a murderer. *Spineless*. What have I done that you haven't?

All I've done is what I've needed to do to survive. Can you say the same?"

Lucian fumed, and with a swipe of his arm struck him across the back of the head. The wound drew blood and sent Charlie sprawling, but he surged back to his knelt position with shocking resilience.

"You're one of them," Lucian said. "You killed Ray. That defenceless old man. Attacked my friend and left him half-dead. Innocent people. Good people. Why do you deserve to live?"

Charlie growled, a deep and hateful sound. "And you?" he said. "You hunted down and slaughtered two men. You gave them no quarter."

"At the camp? It was self-defence. They would have killed Norman and Richard."

Charlie turned his head fractionally. "Would they?" he said, his voice lower, almost inquisitive.

Lucian recoiled for a moment, and the revolver dropped somewhat. His hands shook so much that he required the strength of both to keep the barrel steady. "You can't live," he said, his eyes wild. "You're one of them."

Norman remained completely still. His eyes darted between them, as though the scene was a deadly tennis match.

"I just wanted to find him," Charlie said, his arms dropping to his sides. His body seemed to deflate, as though he'd now accepted impending doom.

Lucian's hand stopped shaking. His knuckles became bone-white, and the face of the Reaper overtook his features. His index finger squeezed the trigger. "Goodbye," he said.

Norman rushed forwards, pain exploding in his chest as Charlie leapt to his feet, screaming for his life.

For the briefest of moments, time itself appeared to undulate, to flow and whorl like churning floodwaters. Norman felt his voice build deep in his throat over what felt like years, but must have only been microseconds. He had time to watch Charlie launch into the air with his mouth open in a piercing yell, time to watch the revolver's trigger slam against the cartridge.

Then, in a blurred flurry of motion, time snapped back into place:

"NO!" Charlie howled.

"Lucian, don't!"

Click.

…

Norman blinked.

His mind was blank. His eyes surely fooled him, for Charlie's head remained intact.

Lucian lowered the revolver to his side, his eyes calm and dim. The revolver's barrel was free of smoke.

Charlie was absolutely still. He remained so for several moments before lowering his arms. However, he didn't dare turn around. "What…?" he managed.

Lucian took a step forwards and leaned close. "Close your eyes and walk a thousand steps, and then you can open them again. I'll be watching."

"What?"

"Go. Get out of here. Never come back."

Charlie remained frozen, his mouth working. "But…you…," he gasped. "You're not going to kill me?"

Lucian stepped away. "Go."

Charlie remained for a moment more before turning his head. His eyes softened as he finally met Norman's gaze. He looked from his face to his wobbling cane, and his mouth formed a thin white line.

He nodded, and then closed his eyes.

Norman ambled towards Lucian as the young man began his solitary journey down the street, towards the horizon. Together, they stood for a long time, watching as Charlie hobbled away in silence, until his body was no more than a distant speck.

"The gun wasn't loaded, was it?" Norman said after a while, not looking away.

Lucian glanced at the revolver in his hand. "I couldn't. I just wanted him gone."

"Then why the theatrics?"

Lucian glanced at him. His eyes were bloodshot. "In the end, we all have to pay for our mistakes. All of us." He lowered his head and muttered, almost to himself, "In the end…"

Norman nodded slowly.

Would he ever know what that meant?

Maybe. But something told him that this was only the first thread of a vast web of secrets, one so tangled that he might never reach its end.

They watched until Charlie was gone from sight. "You know that he's probably going to be picked up again?" Norman said.

Lucian nodded. "I know."

XIII

Charlie crawled. His leg dragged behind him as he scaled the hill on his stomach, tearing at the soil. The wind ripped at his clothes, drying the tears on his cheek as he inched closer to the tree line.

The streets of that cursed city were behind him, but he still felt eyes upon him, watching.

He'd counted each of those thousand steps he'd taken away from the barrel of that revolver, expecting a bullet to find its way into his back at any moment. But no shot had come.

Instead, he'd been left to the elements. No quick death, no mercy. Instead, condemnation to a long, savage decline. A boiling hatred rose in his gut at the thought of the grey-haired monster. His fingers curled into the mud, and a gurgling snarl rose in his throat as he hauled his broken body skyward.

By the time he reached the shadows of the forest canopy, the wind had kicked up, icy and vicious. Shivering, he pushed on into the cool, wet mud beyond the tree line, whimpering, ashamed, lost.

There was nowhere to go. Nobody would find him, nor help him. There was no food, no water, and no shelter—nothing.

There was nothing for him out here but death.

He stopped, propped himself against a tree, and wept.

When he finally stopped, the wind was alive with the sound of footsteps. Charlie opened his eyes and tried to stifle his sniffling, turning this way and that, searching for the source of the noise. With a grunt of fright he fixated on a shadow as it emerged from the depths of the forest.

The figure drew closer and resolved into focus. Charlie had time to take in the sight of long, tattered clothes, eyes of searing intent, and a face obscured by a dark balaclava.

"What do you want?" Charlie breathed.

The figure grew closer still. Emerald eyes stared down at him, piercing, hypnotising. Charlie pressed himself against the trunk at his back as the figure crouched down beside him and reached out a hand invitingly.

SECOND INTERLUDE

James looked out over the London skyline in awe. In the midday sun the city was ablaze with light, glass glittering and steel shining.

The waters of the Thames had risen since the End. The city's great Barrier, broken and useless, sat unused and drowned downriver, helpless to impede the progress of the floodwaters. The banks had long since burst, and so now waves lapped against the edges of street curbs, traffic lights, and skyscrapers.

These new shores rendered the great bridges useless, having flooded the low-lying roads that fed them. They were now only so many vast and ungainly islands, jutting from green tidal waters, stretching for land that could never be reached.

"I don't see it," James said, squinting.

They were high up upon the rooftop of a crumbling block of flats—so high that buildings he knew to be enormous appeared tiny.

Alex pointed into the sea of concrete and steel, drawing out an area far away, low and antiquated. James followed his finger, past the wreckage of the Great Wheel, and laid eyes on a series of oblongs, pillars and a grand central dome, centred in a swathe of glass.

"I see it!" James said. "It looks big."

"It is."

"There must be a lot inside."

"There is."

James frowned. "How do we save it all?"

Alex laughed. "We can't. Even if we could, there would be nowhere to put it. It's safest to just leave it all there for the time being."

"Won't it all rot?"

"It's been stored better than we could manage."

James nodded. His legs began to quiver with excitement as he drank in the enormity, and grandiosity, of the great city. He thought of all of the pictures he'd seen of the treasures that lay waiting in that distant dome, of all the things that waited to be seen, the wonders that waited to be rediscovered.

"Can we go inside?" he said.

Alex smiled. "That's why we're here."

They descended to the streets and walked in silence, too sensitive to the echo of their own voices to strike up conversation. The capital's streets had a habit of amplifying even idle chitchat to a ghoulish, disembodied rumble.

Instead, they were content to merely let the scenery pass by, fascinated by the monstrous scale of it all and the desolate stillness.

To most, it was disturbing. For all the land's emptiness, the countryside at least carried on unhindered; grass and branches danced in the wind, birds flocked in the sky, and great herds of sheep trampled the land. In the country, there was life.

London, however, had been stone dead since the End. It almost appeared vacuum-sealed, wrapped in protective sheeting and stored away for a distant future. All debris had been swept away by the wind and waves, and the food waste had been consumed by giant bird flocks and swarms of vermin in the Early Years. Perfectly sanitised and lifeless, the streets sat dormant, waiting to be traversed by bustling crowds that would never come.

Underfoot, clothing still smothered the pavement. James weaved around blouses, work shirts, square-shouldered black jackets and denim jeans, stepped over necklaces, rucksacks, and briefcases emblazoned with strange words: '*Prada*', '*Levi's*', '*Armani*' and '*Louis Vuitton*'. He wondered for the millionth time whether the stories the others told were really true: that these things had once belonged to people—real, breathing people. Millions of them.

It was almost too absurd. It boggled his mind.

Though the great city had to have come from somewhere, James was sure that it could only have been crafted by departed gods. The perfect geometric shapes and gargantuan heights could only have been forged by creatures of unimaginable power.

The people he knew, as great and kind as they had been to him, were not omnipotent, and they were certainly not gods. And yet, supposedly, they were descended from those who had built every crevice that he saw before him.

He looked to Alex, frowning. "Did people *really* build all this?" His voice boomed back at him a hundred times in echo, filling every alley and room for hundreds of metres. But he ignored the racket. His eyes were fixed on Alex.

He needed to know.

A strange expression crossed Alex's face as he met James's gaze. "What?"

"People?"

"Yes."

"And there was nothing here before them?"

"Just the land, like where we live."

"And they built it all from nothing?"

"Of course they did. Who else could have built it all?"

"Others."

Alex's face contorted into a confused smile. They walked for a while as he mused, tilting his head. "You don't think that people can build these things?"

"How could they?"

"Builders built, architects designed, electricians wired. People spent their entire lives mastering a single thing."

"And where are they all now?"

"Gone."

"I don't think that's it," James said. "I don't think that people can do those things anymore."

"Books can teach you anything."

James shook his head. "A book can't teach you how to ride a bike," he said.

Alex stopped and looked down at James. His frown had grown deep and his eyes forlorn, troubled.

"I read that in a book," James said. He felt that he might have said the wrong thing, but wasn't about to apologise. In their classes, Alex had always said it was more important than anything to speak his own mind.

Alex started walking again, but this time he looked away, across the river, and didn't speak for some time. James trudged alongside, staring at the floor, waiting for his reticence to wane.

They passed a set of black gates and arrived at the steps of the great building they had seen from the rooftop. James took in the sight of its marble pillars and the entrance beyond, and any thoughts of his indiscretion were forgotten in an instant. The two of them exchanged a glance. Alexander's eyes were alight, and reflected in them James could see his own giddy smile.

They hurried up past the pillars and took their first hesitant steps inside. Within, it was cool, dusty, and dark. They walked past the unattended reception and stepped into a cavernous space. There, they both stopped, agape.

The court of the British Museum lay before them, bathed in amber light that struck down through a roof of tessellated glass panels. Portland Stone surfaces sat gleaming, untouched by time's hand. To James's eyes, Olympus itself would have paled in comparison.

"You were right," Alex said. In the vast space his voice was rendered an endless echo, louder than cannon fire. "We can't do this anymore."

James saw something grow hollow in his gaze.

But the sadness was brief. Within moments it had passed, and an infectious smile played upon his lips. The two of them dashed into the building's depths, feverish with excitement, marvelling at passing wonders, unwilling to leave any individual piece for fear of neglecting it, making countless oaths to return to ornate ancient statues, tablets, tombs and sarcophagi. Dashing from exhibit to exhibit, and from room to room, they spent the rest of the day hopelessly wrapped up in their own thoughts, often on opposite sides of the museum. On several occasions they lost each other completely and were forced to make their way back to the entrance to rendezvous.

James's mind had all but ground to a halt at the sight of such richness. He did his best to absorb all he could, but knew that he could only take in a thimble's worth—at least on this visit—and hoped to high heaven that the day would never end.

Eventually, they made their way into a large room close to the great court. They looked at the unusual objects in the same manner as they had looked at everything over the past hours: with a burning desire to allocate a week to each exhibit.

Their fascination, however, was nothing compared to what they felt when they laid eyes on the isolated glass capsule and the broken tablet that sat within.

They approached slowly, unspeaking, unflinching, lured inexorably forwards. In the glass's reflection their eyes were round as saucers, bulging from their heads. Side by side, they spent the longest time looking at the stone, and the three passages of mysterious, unintelligible writings inscribed upon it.

The top was smeared with the most striking of the three, the letters in fact tiny drawings of birds, eyes, staffs and ankhs; the middle scrawled in strange, complicated glyphs; and the bottom a more geometric, aesthetic script.

James had seen all three passages before in his reading, just as he had seen the stone. He and Alex had studied it for many weeks. "Is this it?" he said.

"This is it."

James grinned, wide enough to make his cheeks ache. "It's beautiful."

Alex smiled along with him. "It is."

"We're going to save this?"

"One day."

Alex gestured towards it with a grand sweep of his arm. His eyes were alive, his body in constant motion. "This is the key," he said, hushed. "All of these things are. These are the things we have to rescue, the things that are going to teach us the future."

James leaned forward, instinctively reaching out to balance himself by pressing against the glass. Before he could complete his ascent onto tiptoes, Alex had caught his wrist in an iron grip and squeezed hard.

"Don't touch it!" he hissed.

James gasped and collapsed back, catching a fleeting and sudden fury in Alex's eyes. He backed away, seeing for the first time a monster, born of obsession, lurking under his brother's skin.

The look was gone before James could blink. Now Alex's eyes were wide, and his mouth was ajar. "I'm sorry," he said, blinking.

James cradled his crushed wrist, taking a step back.

"Did I hurt you?"

James swallowed and stopped. The pain in his arm dulled at the sight of such sincere shock. "I'm fine," he said.

Alex rushed forwards and took him into a crushing embrace. James stood uncomfortably between his arms. Alex was shaking his head. "I shouldn't have done that," he said. "I shouldn't have." He pulled James to arm's length and sighed. "You know I'd never hurt you."

James nodded. "I know."

"It was instinct. These things are just too old and delicate for us to be putting our fingers all over them. They're too important." Alex's face took on that odd glaze yet again. His voice grew hazy, distant. "They're too important, even more important than you or me."

XIV

Norman sat with a sigh, back in Alexander's study. A strange medley of sensations was at war within him: exhaustion, burgeoning guilt, and a distant throbbing emanating from his extremities.

The fire still roared in the grate. Warmth permeated the darkened room, and a gentle wind whispered at the windows.

He looked down at the faded green book that Alex had laid in his hands, taking note of the title's delicate golden lettering. "Alice in Wonderland?" he said.

Alex smiled, thin-lipped. He looked more drawn than Norman had ever seen him. Speaking at the funeral must have taken its toll. "Give it a try," he said. "You might like it."

"Why are you giving me this?"

Alex looked still more distant. "Tradition."

Norman frowned, but let it pass, resting the book in his lap.

"The boy is gone, then?" Alexander's slouched position made his figure hard to distinguish in the flickering light, his face hard to read.

"Yes. He just let him leave."

A light smile wandered over Alexander's features. "Where's Lucian now?"

"Guard duty, with Robert."

Alex nodded, and said no more for some time. When he finally spoke, he sounded no more present. "How's your chest?"

"It hurts."

"Heather told me to watch you for any strange behaviour. I thought I'd just come right out and ask."

"Ask if I'm seeing pink elephants?"

Alex glanced at him. "Are you?"

Norman smiled, but felt it grow tight on his face as the memory of his dream flashed before his eyes yet again—

The storm. The city. The yelling faces. The leering stranger.

Each time he remembered it, the details seemed that much clearer, that much more forceful.

And yet, it had been just a dream. Hadn't it?

It was probably nothing. Yet, despite himself, he cleared his throat and caught Alexander's gaze. For a moment he merely sat and listened to the crackling in the grate, and then he spoke. "When I was out, I had a dream…only I don't think it was a dream. I think that I was remembering something. From before you took me in."

Alex's silhouette was deathly still amidst the shadows. He said nothing, just waited for Norman to continue.

"I remembered a storm. It was raining hard. Everything was flooded. It was a city—I think London. I was lying on the ground. You and Lucian were leaning over me, yelling… I'd hurt my head. I'd hurt my head badly." He paused and shivered as the image in his mind's eye sharpened once more, so much so that he could almost taste something awful, something stagnant. He thought of mentioning the marble-faced, leering figure—

"Remember, Norman. Remember. You were all there. You all watched it happen."

—but, perhaps because Alexander had mentioned watching him for strange behaviour, he thought better of it. Instead, he grunted to fill the brief silence that followed. "Is that why I can't remember?" he said. "Was that the night of the accident?"

Alex stared at him for over a minute. Something stirred behind his eyes. "That was the night that your parents died," he said. "And yes, it was also the night of the accident, and the night that I first told you about…"

"About my destiny?"

Alex nodded.

Norman waited, but he said no more. He itched to know the rest—to pry further into this mystery—but Alexander's expression, along with the fresh memory of Lucian's blood-curdling near miss, made him think twice.

He was tired of the questions, of the secrets, of not knowing. But perhaps this was something best saved for another night.

Norman shook his head. "Why me?" he muttered. "I've always wondered. Of all of these people, any of a hundred of them would have been a better choice. Why did you choose me?"

Alex looked away into the flames. "Because some men have—" He paused, and drew a deep sigh. Then he shook his head. "I didn't choose anything. It was always going to be you." He cleared his throat and shifted, as though uncomfortable, and fell silent.

After that, the night took hold in earnest. The din of Ray's wake, which spanned the breadth of the city, fizzled and petered out. While the city grew peaceful and the sleepy rhythm of the night set in, Norman rubbed his chest and broke the silence. "What's the news on the council summit?"

Alexander grunted. "It's going ahead as planned. I'm very interested to hear about this radio signal. But now that this…trouble has come up, we'll be able to address everyone. Warn them."

"Of what?"

"Of what's coming."

"You think the others are going to be targeted as well?"

Alex didn't need to reply. A glance was enough.

They turned back to the fire, enjoying each other's company as New Canterbury slept. The shadow that had hung over them all for so long now seemed punctured by the faintest glimmer of hope.

"When do we leave?" Norman said.

XV

Don coughed. His breath wheezed deep in his throat and he shivered without pause beneath the bedcovers despite the thick, greasy sweat coating his chest and brow. Through bloated eyes he could barely make out Billy's form, sitting upon a wooden chair beside the bed.

The cabin had become their new home. Dilapidated and ancient, it had appeared to be little more than a shack from outside. But there were beds, a small living space, and even a miniature kitchen. More than he could have hoped for.

In truth, he'd been utterly defeated before finding it. Now, there was a chance.

"You mustn't cry," he said.

A small candle burned in a dish on the bedside table, casting a meek light upon Billy's tearstained face.

"I'm scared," she whispered, wrapping her arms tighter around her knees.

"You mustn't be. You have to be strong."

Billy whimpered, hiding her head.

"Stop crying!" Don coughed, and lay back, groaning.

Billy hiccoughed, and her sobs died under his tenuous glare.

"I'm sorry," said Don. "We'll be alright."

She nodded.

"You don't believe me?"

"You're sick, Daddy." She grumbled for a moment, lowering her head towards her knees, until her eyes peeked just above her arms.

"I know. But I'll get better. Everything will be fine."

"Alright."

"You're still worried."

"It's dark outside."

Don sat up, glancing at the grimed window. It was almost opaque, but still he could tell it was pitch-black outside. "You've never been afraid of the dark before," he said.

"Now I know they're out there. The Bad Men."

"They're not here right now."

Billy's gaze remained trained on the window. "How do you know?"

"I just know. Trust me."

She nodded, and began to rock once more upon the chair. Its joints creaked even louder.

Don sighed, turning to their bag at the foot of the bed. Dragging it towards him, he pulled it open and rummaged inside. Billy's head lifted as he produced a torch from its depths, thin and stunted.

He'd been saving it for an emergency. Once the candles burned down, it would be their last stopgap before having to rub sticks together. Their supply of lighters and matches had long since run dry.

He clicked the power switch, and a harsh beam of white light lanced across the room, pooling against the far wall. Once satisfied that it wouldn't falter, he handed it to Billy and sat back, gasping from the exertion. He had the sudden urge to sleep. "There you go," he said between ragged breaths. "Now you'll know if they're near."

Billy took it with extreme care, unravelling her limbs and staring with wonder at the magic of the black bottle. Waving it to and fro, she smiled—a true smile, one he hadn't seen in a long time.

"How did they get all of this light in here?" she breathed.

Don laughed, holding his ribs. "That's not how it works."

"Then how does it work?"

He coughed, sinking lower into the pillows' folds. "I'll tell you another time, I promise. Now get some sleep."

He needed to rest. His eyes pulsed with a steady, dull pain, the lids heavy. They rolled to a close, and he immediately began to drift.

A bump jerked him awake some time later. After opening his eyes once more—a task that required extreme effort—he saw that Billy had moved across the room and climbed onto a stool to shine the torch through the window.

She turned to him, smiling. "Magic."

Don laughed, and then began to drift once more. "That's right," he said. "Magic."

XVI

Birdsong filled the summer air, accompanied by the trickling of the Stour. Dragonflies flitted across open water, racing parallel to the glassy surface. The sky was bright, the morning fresh, and the mist of dawn was evaporating to be replaced by a pleasant golden glow. There was no cloud cover other than a distant spattering of cirrus, many miles away.

The riverside was alive. Milling droves hauled luggage along the bank, loading it into a small fleet of rowboats. Almost half the city had gathered to help load supplies, and to bid farewell to family and friends. The air was thick with excitement, saturating every crevice.

On the far shore, a convoy of horses, wagons and other supplies was being assembled. The ant-like figures of two dozen men and women scurried without pause, moving between animals and boxes.

The earth had been turned. The fields sown. No more attacks had come.

In the fortnight since Ray's funeral, without the presence of the unwelcome prisoner hanging in the air like a foul stink, things had improved. The first signs of life were returning to the forests. The grass on the hills was growing green again. Tensions had lessened just enough to allow the radio signal to have become the subject of conversation once more. Rumours were spreading, whispers filled every street corner, and debate at the dinner table was rife.

For many, the reality of it had finally struck home: they might not be alone.

Somewhere out there, there might be others, others for whom the candle of civilisation still burned. Just maybe, after all this time, they might be saved.

Norman watched, sitting on a decrepit bench a small distance from the main body of activity. His cane was propped beside him, a painful reminder that, after two weeks, he was only just beginning to feel better. Since his visit from Jason he'd started to feel trapped, imprisoned behind a broken body.

Yet, despite his frustration, he *was* recovering, and his strength was returning.

Heather crouched beside him, checking his collarbone and chest, where the pain was greatest. "You're sure it hasn't gotten any better?" she said, frowning as she massaged his shoulder.

He shook his head, wincing, then hesitated. "Slowly," he said.

"How bad?"

Norman looked at her, trying to keep a straight face. "I can't think," he said. "It feels like I have glass under my skin."

She nodded absently. "You should be mending by now. You might just need longer to recover. There's no way to be sure how bad the injury was."

"You're sure that I'm okay to go?"

She wobbled her head. "As long as you don't walk too much, you should be alright. Make sure you take a few deep breaths every hour, or you'll get pneumonia." She paused for emphasis. "If you get any worse, get help from somebody. I still don't know if you're punctured internally."

"I'd feel a lot better if you were coming along," he said.

She laughed and touched him on the shoulder. "I wouldn't mind going either, but with so many people in and out of the clinic, the city would go crazy." She sighed, brushing her prematurely greying hair from her face. "People are acting…odd."

"This is new for all of us," Norman said, struggling to his feet.

She nodded, standing with him for a time, watching the proceedings.

Not long after, Sarah appeared, walking hand in hand with Robert. Her face was more alive than Norman had ever seen it, its soft curves strikingly feminine, bearing a smile so intense it outshone the sun.

Robert, meanwhile, looked beside himself. A goofy, childish grin appeared out of place upon his enormous head.

A gaggle of children surrounded them, giggling as they jumped to and fro, their shoes clattering on the cobbles. They chattered for a moment, and some of the older boys attempted to strike up conversation with Robert, their heads turned skywards in search of his face.

It was only moments before a girl gave a cry of delight, holding Sarah's outstretched hand. The children swarmed the two of them, circling and laughing in a gibbering frenzy, calling for parents and guardians to come quick.

The activity stirred a sudden interest among others, who milled for a while before approaching. Some stretched their necks to see over the sea of children, while others instead rushed forwards. Boxes of supplies lay abandoned on the ground, and the boats were left lifeless.

On the far shore, the workers looked nonplussed. Some scratched their heads, while others called out, waving their arms. They were met by silence.

The excitement grew to staggering proportions in a very short time, until Norman himself was drawn closer. The couple were now invisible beyond the bodies of others. All attention had turned to them.

Norman skirted the edge of the crowd, careful not to snag his cane on flailing limbs or the faces of small children. Before long he could see Sarah and Robert, overrun by ecstatic women and jovial men. "What is it?" he asked.

His voice was barely audible over the squeals and merriment. Moving around to the side a little more, Heather split from his side and attempted to burrow into the sea of bodies, but to no avail.

Sarah stood in her partner's shadow, her hand held up beside her. A thick golden band of metal adorned her fourth finger. As he watched, the joy of a middle-aged woman beside him spilled into physicality, and she pulled him into an awkward hug. He struggled free and fought his way to the front of the crowd. In the corner of his eye he saw Heather forging her own path, parallel to his.

"Congratulations," he said as he reached Robert, stepping forwards to grasp his hand.

Sarah was pulled by Heather into a crushing embrace, and both women propelled their voices to a high-pitched, incomprehensible babble.

"How did this happen?" Heather cried.

Robert shrugged, his face frozen in a foolish smile. "It was a spur-of-the-moment thing."

"Where did you get the ring?"

Robert looked at Sarah and then to the ring upon her finger. "It was my grandmother's," he said.

"We just thought that we should do *something*," Sarah said. "Just in case."

A stray voice, young and curious, arose from the incoherent rumble of the crowd, and a figure stepped into view. "What's going on?"

Allison froze when she saw the betrothed, her eyes bulging. The muscles of her forearms began to twitch as her mouth worked. Norman had only a moment to prepare for the forthcoming racket.

She sprinted for Sarah and Heather, and the three of them entered a frenzy of heightened, even louder screeching, hugging and leaping on the spot.

Norman squinted at the pain in his ears, sharing an uncomfortable look with Robert, with whom he was still shaking hands. Those around them threw glances of equal discomfort, some holding their palms over the sides of their heads.

"When are you planning on holding the ceremony?" Heather asked.

Robert and Sarah exchanged glances, their expressions blank.

"The autumn?" Robert suggested.

After a moment of thought, Sarah's face brightened. "What do you think?" she said.

Robert thought for a while—or, Norman suspected, pretended to—before nodding.

Norman groaned as the three women enjoyed another bout of squealing, embracing each other once more.

The crowd began to break up, and returned to work. The fleet of boats became more active. A number of women remained to hug and harass Sarah for a short while longer.

"I suppose you're not coming then?" Norman said.

Robert shook his head, holding Sarah around the waist, his bulging arms dwarfing her body. "Alexander wants me to sit this one out and take care of things here." He shrugged. "You'll be fine without me."

Norman wasn't quite as certain after looking over his shoulder. Only a select few were to make the journey to London. It had been decided that a larger convoy would express undue risk.

The city elders were being helped into the farthest boats—Agatha sitting in the prow of the closest, dazed and starry-eyed. Only members of the council, their families, and a security detail were to go—with a particular emphasis on security.

Nevertheless, he forced a smile. "I'm sure we will."

Robert sagged with relief, finally releasing Norman's hand. He steered Sarah from the riverside, retreating into the streets, disappearing from sight.

Heather and Allison watched them leave with simultaneous sighs of feminine passion. Their bodies remained motionless, staring after the retreating couple.

Norman stood and waited for a while, looking for something on which to focus his attention. In the aftermath of the excitement, the pain was returning.

"I wish somebody would come and take me like that," Allison said. Her swoon became masked by a sudden and uncharacteristic depression. Heather uttered a longing sigh of agreement, her hands wedged deep in her pockets.

Norman cleared his throat, leaning on his cane, awaiting their return to reality. They turned to him slowly, their faces downturned and reserved, spawning an unwelcome pity in the pit of his stomach.

"Come on," he said to Allison, beckoning to the rowboats. "We have to be going."

Her eyes were glazed as she nodded, bidding Heather farewell and then joining his side.

"You'll be careful, won't you?" Heather said.

Norman patted his cane. "I'll be fine."

"That's not what I meant."

He almost smiled, but didn't quite manage. Instead, he pulled her into a weak one-armed hug. "Take care," he said.

She returned the sentiment before stepping away to join the rest of those who were to stay behind. The crowd now waved and called to the occupants of the retreating boats.

Allison fell into step beside him as they wheeled towards the last of the boats still docked. They were beckoned forwards by John, whose face was adamant as he pointed to the sun, which was already nearing its zenith.

"This should be interesting," Allison said.

Norman glanced at her. "You've been to London plenty of times."

She grunted hollowly. "Maybe," she said. "But I've never had to be escorted by a small army." Her voice wavered. "Maybe I should stay behind."

She looked over her shoulder. Her eyes had softened, and the corners of her mouth were twitching.

"No," he said. He hesitated, but pressed on. "I want you to come."

He had at first been thinking of whatever disaster could be averted by leaving the city with Allison in tow, removing the city's primary source of gossip. But after mere moments he realised that he genuinely wanted her company.

An odd fluttering sensation was once again prowling his bowels.

"I could use a hand with getting about," he added hastily.

She stood motionless for a moment, her eyes darting between the boats and Main Street. "You're sure it'll be safe?" she muttered.

Norman offered a hand, attempting a smile. "Trust me," he said.

XVII

Heather smiled as Robert and Sarah drifted into the kitchen. They walked hand in hand, still plastered with numb expressions of giddy joy. Sarah had changed into a long, billowing dress, adorned by sunflowers and abstract swirls that complemented her fiery locks.

She observed the couple at length, her head falling sideways as she cupped her chin in her palms. A pang of jealousy rose in her gut, an ugly mixture of longing and deep-seated, instinctual hatred for a woman who had found happiness, one whom she considered her closest friend.

She scorned her thoughts. Her own love life had been lacking of late, but there was still time for her. So long as the stray grey hairs on her crown kept at bay. In the meantime, what better sight was there amidst so much loss than untainted devotion?

She watched them walk towards the counter, which had been abandoned when people had volunteered to aid the travelling party with supplies. They disappeared for a short while, and the sound of clinking and interested grunts filled the air.

She busied herself with a sudden interest in the tabletop, using a fork to deepen an excavated crevice. Exhaustion reared its head. She'd eaten little, like everyone else. They'd ploughed the fields and reseeded for the summer months, but it would still be weeks before they saw anything worth harvesting. Rations were now meagre handfuls, mainly roots and berries, maybe with a slice of hard bread.

She wanted nothing more than to stay at the bench for the remainder of the day, but the hypochondriacs that infested the city needed her.

The couple reappeared with a single plate of leftovers, no less a maddening picture of happiness. They looked around and spotted her. Sarah's face brightened and she dragged her new fiancé in Heather's direction.

"I can't believe it," she said as she sat down. Her mouth worked as she stared dumbly at the far wall, her eyes glazed and her free hand caressing the worn golden band upon her finger.

Heather looked to Robert, who seemed amused by Sarah's absence. He jerked his shoulder, nudging her from her reverie.

She stirred. Her glasses briefly magnified her eyes to enormous proportions as she turned to face them, her usual analytical, intense mannerisms gone. What Heather saw before her was a child whose greatest fantasy had come true.

"What?" Sarah mumbled, blinking.

"Are you alright?" asked Robert.

Her eyes remained cloudy for a moment before she nodded. "Yes," she said, "of course." She looked at the ring, holding it up to the light before speaking again, "I just can't *believe* it."

"Believe what?" Heather put down her fork as jealousy sparked red-hot behind her eyes. She cleared her throat, bowing her head.

What was wrong with her? She made a mental note to rest up properly.

Sarah didn't seem to have noticed her tone. Her voice was hollow and slow, far removed from her usual clipped and excited tongue. "I just can't come to terms with the fact that I'm actually going to get married." She looked to Robert. "I never thought that I'd get to experience it for real."

Robert took a cube of diced turnip and fed it to her, his face aglow. "Lucky you," he said.

Heather leaned forwards, overcome by the intoxicating miasma surrounding them. "I'm really happy for you both," she said. She managed a smile. "What did you have in mind?"

Sarah thought for a while, a critical frown momentarily punching through her mask of glee. "I'm not sure yet," she said. "As we said: this just came out of the blue. But a white wedding, I think—"

An extraordinary rumble ran through the ground. Plates jangled, glasses overturned, and tables leapt a foot into the air. An almighty roar—akin to the bellow of an enraged dragon—blasted through the open door and tore at their ears. The table jumped beneath them again as another shockwave reached the hall, sending any remaining cutlery clattering to the floor.

The three of them surged to their feet. Heather's heart was in her throat. Looking around wildly, she stumbled, trying to make sense of the blur of rushing diners as they clambered for the door.

Robert's immense shadow passed by as he bolted into the street, with Sarah following close behind. Passing through the crowded doorway, Heather squinted, blinded by sunlight. Dozens of gabbling people surrounded her, and the rumble of rushing footsteps sounded from all directions.

"What happened?" Robert bellowed above the racket.

Through half-closed eyes, Heather could see that some were still returning from the riverside, rushing forwards with astonishment written over their faces.

Skywards was an orange glow, distant and obscured by the houses opposite; the horizon was ablaze. Smaller shockwaves still thrummed up from the cobbles, rattling her bones.

Sarah was standing before her, jumping up and down on the spot, screeching in a blind panic, calling for Robert as he parted the crowd with his bulk, still calling, "What happened?"

Those in the crowd shrugged unanimously. Some women had taken their children in their arms, eyes wild as they struggled to keep pace.

Heather grabbed Sarah, shaking her by the shoulders. "What is going on?" she yelled.

Scared and tearing eyes met her gaze. "I don't know," Sarah squeaked. She threw herself into Robert's arms.

He pulled her close, looking up to Heather. "I think it's another attack," he said.

Heather glanced down the street, almost expecting to spy an angry mob advancing towards them. "What do we do?" she said.

"I don't know. I have to go." He turned to Sarah, leaning at almost forty-five degrees to stare into her eyes. "I need you to stay with Heather," he said. His mouth was set, his tone firm, yet his eyes were wide with desperation.

Sarah protested, but, under his gaze, relented, and kissed him fiercely.

He remained for a moment afterwards, his hardened gaze broken. Then he released her, and Sarah shrank away, her cheeks streaked with fresh tears.

Heather guided her back towards Main Street as the people arriving from the riverside began to race past. "We'll be in the clinic," she called.

Robert nodded, and ran for the armoury.

XVIII

The grey stallion galloped across the meadow amidst sweltering heat, breathing hard and leaving a trail of wispy vapour in its wake. Lucian sat erect upon the saddle, glad for the gentle wind being generated by the movement. The air was otherwise still, and stagnant.

The grass here had grown tall and the peripheral hedges of the meadow wild. A sea of rapeseed had erupted across the surrounding hillside, filling the air with a heady aroma. Dotted here and there were a few archipelagos of flowers; stars studding a carpet of yellow as uniform as the dark of space.

The lease of life was slight—any other year would have seen the grass waist-high and ablaze with colour—but it still set something resembling a smile on his lips.

He swung his gaze in a wide arc as he rode, his eyes trained first on the horizon and then the middle distance, studying every crevice for a sign of activity.

Seeing none, he focused instead upon ascending the slight rise that lay before him: an embankment of dark soil and patched grass. He encouraged his steed with precise nudges, being careful to avoid the many rabbit holes that pockmarked the incline. As he reached the summit, he pulled on the reins and ordered a halt, surveying the ground below.

A convoy of wagons, horses and city folk trudged along a small valley road nestled between the embankment and another on the far side.

Previous summits in London had seen Canterbury emptied. Today, only a few dozen lined the roadway. Some rode, the rest walked, while the elderly or tired sat atop the wagons, surrounded on all sides by piles of supplies.

Looking up from them, Lucian observed the members of the security detail lining the embankments. Half a dozen dotted the crest of either rise, standing sentinel, strung out over a mile, each on horseback. Their stillness made them invisible, unless one knew to look for them.

His attention was so focused on the convoy that he didn't notice Norman approach until his hand touched his shoulder, at which point he jerked, cursing.

Norman was seated stiffly, with a pained squint splashed across his face, holding his side.

"You shouldn't be up here," Lucian said, still scanning the landscape.

Norman coughed, leaning forwards, wincing. "I'm fine," he gasped.

Lucian scowled, pointing down to the nearest wagon. "Just go and sit down, will you?"

"I didn't come along to sit down there with my thumb up my arse."

Lucian looked to him. "What if something happens right now?" he said. "What are you going to do?"

Norman grunted. "Everybody expects me to be the one to step up, but when I finally try to do it, I'm told to go and sit at the kid's table." His eyes flashed with defiance. "I'm not going down there. I'm *fine*."

Lucian shook his head, looking back to the convoy. Many people looked sullen and frightened as they proceeded along the road. The mood was stark in contrast to the cheer that had hung over their heads not an hour before. It seemed they all sensed that something wasn't quite right.

They had refrained from taking the dual-carriageway route as usual, fearing that if they were ambushed in the open terrain, they'd have nowhere to hide. With so many old and frail among them, they would have been defenceless, and had instead opted to take the smallest and most secluded of paths. It was safer, but would take far longer.

At the time, it had seemed the obvious choice. Now, Lucian wasn't so sure.

In the distance, Lucian could see the distant profiles of the tallest of Canterbury's buildings. They were still close to home. Close enough to turn back.

But if someone was watching, turning tail now would only trigger an attack.

"Think we'll make it?" Norman said.

Lucian huffed, looking down at the decrepit elders upon the wagons. "If they were out there, we'd know it by now." He looked out at the silent expanse, but saw only a flock of swifts swooping overhead. The meadows were barren, and the sky clear. "We're alone out here."

Only a further moment of silence ensued before he was proven wrong—very wrong.

A blast of brilliant orange light blinded them, sending their mounts rearing and bucking, very nearly throwing them both off. They both ducked as a deafening rumble reverberated along the valley towards them. A solid wave of heat followed soon after, striking them on the broadside and forcing their hands up to their faces.

The screams of those below reached them a moment later, tiny beneath the continued rumble, which rattled through the air in concussive blasts, surging and ebbing like great ocean waves.

Lucian yanked on his reins, red and green spots appearing before his eyes, trying to regain control. But his mount was spooked, and bucked to the very edge of the embankment before he could wrestle it back to sense.

Norman grabbed his shirt, his face invisible behind a wall of dancing spots. "What was that?" he yelled.

Lucian struck himself on the temple with the heel of his palm, trying to clear his head. "I don't know!"

"Was it the turbines?"

Lucian rubbed his eyes as the spots dissipated. The grass of the embankment had been tinged deep red, and the sky a fierce orange. Beyond the far embankment was a monstrous fireball, reaching into the sky, as though the heavens had been set alight. A single plume of black smoke was billowing skywards, already beginning to block out the sunlight.

As the sky darkened, several more explosions erupted beside the first, forging vertical bands of fire from the ether. Ground zero was out of sight, but the rising fire itself was indicative enough of the location: the wind farm was being destroyed. If it was left to burn, their power-generating capacity would be halved. Perhaps worse. At the very least, New Canterbury could be without electricity during the night, leaving them exposed.

"Come on!" Lucian barked, yanking his reins and urging his mount forwards. Charging down the hill, he weaved between the floundering bodies of the fleeing members of the convoy, who clambered up the embankment on their hands and knees.

The security detail had gathered along the valley floor, surrounding the wagons and supplies, yelling for the others to rally to them instead of scattering.

Looking back for a moment, Lucian saw that Norman was barely past the precipice of the embankment. His face was creased into a grimace of pain, yet he too called down to the others all the same, as though he were as able-bodied as the rest.

Another blistering explosion rang out in the distance, eliciting another bout of screams from those fleeing in terror.

Through the mass of writhing bodies Lucian spotted Alexander, riding atop his white steed, bellowing over the din of the explosions and roaring fires, "Everybody to me! *TO ME!*"

His voice brought some back from the brink of panic. Stopping in their tracks, they about-faced, the gravitas of the situation hitting home. They wheeled to their leader, infected with sudden purpose.

"We're under attack," John DeGray cried from the back of the farthest wagon. "We have to get out of the valley. We're trapped down here—trapped on lower ground."

"It's the turbines!" Norman called from afar, still twenty feet from the main body of the convoy.

Alex looked pained. "It very well may be," he said. "But if it is, they may not know that we're here."

Lucian felt incredulity blossom on his face. "They decide to take out our power just as we leave?"

"It doesn't matter," Alex said. "Either way, we have to leave now."

Lucian wheeled to the far embankment. "Okay, everybody," he called. "We have to get back home as soon as possible."

Alex jumped in before he could say any more, cutting across him, "No! We can't go back."

Lucian whined, "*What?*"

"It'd be dark by the time we could get back, and then what would we do? We can't get across the river without the lights."

"So what then? Just keep going?"

Alex looked at the angry faces surrounding him. All members of the convoy had now gathered around the wagons. "We need to press on to London, and go from there. If we go back then we'll be vulnerable."

Norman finally reached them, his face pale and perspiring. "What about the city?" he gasped.

"They'll be fine for one night," Alex said. "They have plenty of people standing guard—to mount a defence, if need be. There aren't enough of us to warrant turning around. We'd probably do more harm than good."

Lucian shook his head, adamant. "No. I'm going back."

Alex started in distress, but Lucian turned away before he could utter a word. "Who's coming with me?" he called.

There was a brief silence, and then a dozen calls of affirmation rang out.

"I'm coming too," Norman said.

Lucian turned to him, shaking his head. "No." He looked around at the cowering members of the convoy, to Alexander's fuming face, and then back to him. "They need you here."

"What about everybody else?"

Lucian pulled his reins and steered his mount towards the far embankment. "Like you said: They may not even know we're here."

He gave his stallion a vicious kick, and together they charged up the hill, followed by a dozen members of the security detail, leaving the others behind. He looked over his shoulder as they neared the summit, and yelled, "We'll catch up to you."

XIX

Not far from the site of the blast, Charlie stood atop the hillside above New Canterbury, beneath the shadow of the tree line, silent beside two stoic companions. High above the convoy that had been snaking away from the city for the last few hours, they each looked out across the meadow at the distant embankments, watching the pandemonium.

They had waited here for days. By now their supplies were low, and their water all but exhausted. A small camp lay behind them in the undergrowth, but the fire had been stamped out hours ago to keep them hidden.

Despite his companions' assurances, he'd begun to suspect that the rats would never leave their hole.

But now, at last, their quarry had arrived. And he could watch his very own private light show without fear of being spotted.

He turned to the pair beside him. "I'm sorry I doubted you," he said.

As he spoke, yet another explosion ripped across the hillside complex that housed the Old World Power Mills.

The older of the two grunted, His face obscured by a balaclava. He only offered his eyes to the outside world, diamond-hard and unblinking. He was focused on the group of distant specks upon the horizon, which now moved away along the valley, disappearing from view.

Charlie stepped forward. He still had a heavy limp, but had grown numb to the pain. In any case, he wasn't going to miss this on account of a gammy leg. "What do we do now?" he said.

The masked man stood for a while in silence before answering. "We do nothing. Just follow them. For now."

Charlie growled. "But they're defenceless!" he cried. Sudden panic set in, sending his pulse racing. He couldn't have his prize snatched from under his nose now. They were so close. It wasn't *fair*.

The remaining man, short in stature, wielding a huge knife, struck Charlie across the back of the head. "Watch your tongue," Jason muttered, picking the underside of his fingernails with the tip of the monstrous blade. "That's not part of the plan."

Charlie started forward. "You said they'd bleed. You promised!" he cried.

The masked man observed them both coldly. "Patience," he said.

XX

The skyscrapers rose like sheer cliffs above the superstructure of London, imposing and darkened, for the most part as abandoned and dead as the surrounding city. Save for one.

One Canada Square, a pyramid-capped obelisk of stainless steel and glass, rose fifty storeys into the sky, reaching for the heavens. On some days it even punctured the clouds. Visible for thirty miles, its walls remained strong, and after forty years of neglect and punishment it sported only a vague weathering. The perfect beacon with which to draw wandering traders, intrepid explorers, and lonely travellers.

The tower was aglow with blue artificial light, throwing a ghostly shadow upon the crumbling remains of the surrounding capital. The blackened waters of the Thames were painted with reflections of the glittering spire and the decks of wizened ships lining the quays.

The sight brought Norman ultimate relief. The darkness of London had been a harrowing gauntlet; the tall buildings had blocked out the starlight, leaving him near blind, save for the convoy's few scattered lamps. The sound of hooves upon broken tarmac filled his ears as the light of the tower drew the procession from the darkness.

He rubbed his chest, desperate to keep straight upon his saddle. Glancing around warily, he scanned the kerbs and alleyways, his flesh crawling. Alexander rode alongside him, his gaze locked fast upon the tower. He had spoken little since Lucian had broken off with the majority of the security detail.

The convoy was quiet, calmed by the twinkling jewel ahead, now no more than a quarter of a mile away. The surrounding streets were blackened voids, with only the very outlines of town houses, corner shops and office buildings identifiable. All other detail was lost in a black haze. Anything beyond the dim glow of their lamps would have been invisible.

The light emanating from the tower's base was cut off by an intervening object as they approached: a black wall running perpendicular to their course.

Norman flinched as the convoy was engulfed by an intense beam of light. The halogen glare pooled upon the tarmac and sent them all scrambling for shade.

A deafening voice boomed in the night, amplified by a loudspeaker, commanding and agitated. "*Stop!*"

Norman groaned, squinting. His eyes were met only by brilliant whiteness, excluding all objects from view, rendering him blind and half-deaf for the second time in a day. He sensed Alex stir beside him, then the clatter of his white horse's hooves upon tarmac, moving ahead of the cowering travellers.

"The convoy," Alex called, "the convoy from Canterbury."

For a short time there was no reaction, and then the light vanished with a reverberating clatter, revealing the compound before them. The black wall was relatively new, solid concrete, fifteen feet high and at least three feet thick. Atop it, a hundred pairs of eyes watched them, brimming with suspicion.

They had reached the outer perimeter of the London camp, the central trading hub and seat of political might for all that remained of the land's civilised peoples.

The wall marked the edge of their territory, running the length of a sizeable chunk of the Isle of Dogs, enclosing an area of over half a square mile. Upon a raised metallic catwalk, stationed guards held steady, all wielding deadly looking automatic rifles.

As his vision adjusted, he saw their suspicion wane. They lowered their weapons, calling out to one other. The floodlight that had been shut off was replaced by small secondary lights mounted along the wall's edge.

The convoy stood silent in the night, waiting to be granted access.

"I knew I shouldn't have come," said a voice in the gloom.

Norman turned and squinted until Allison's figure resolved from the shadows. The whites of her eyes were aglow, wide and afraid. Several smaller pairs of eyes hovered close to her side—children's eyes. "I knew something bad would happen. It's my fault. I jinxed us."

She paused, and her voice grew thinner. "Do you think they'll let us in?"

Norman glanced at the wall, and then back to her. "They'll let us in. And no, you didn't jinx us."

"You're sure?"

"You should know."

"I've only lived in New Canterbury two years." She tittered. "Country girl, through and through. I'm just useless… I shouldn't have come."

Norman looked to the young, wide eyes around her. He now saw that she held them all close, bundled against her waist. Even a few elderly folk had crowded close around her. They were *looking* to her, just as they had looked to Alexander. Just as they had looked to *him*.

While her voice wavered and her eyes flickered, she stood strong, braced against the night.

"You're not useless," he said—

Not anymore, uttered a stray voice in his head.

—and looked to the wall once more. "They'll let us in. No question about it."

Here, the name Canterbury was as revered as Alexander's. Here, they were all prophets.

The loudspeaker boomed again, and the same deep voice rang out. "Open the gate."

An electronic buzzer sounded, followed by a resounding *clunk*. Norman perceived movement beneath the catwalk, and a brilliant halogen light filtered through a central crack that appeared in the wall. Its width slowly increased until the iron doors of a twenty-foot gate became visible.

Above the gateway, the armed men beckoned them, now docile as lambs, almost ignoring their presence. Their eyes were trained back on the surrounding darkness, braced to strike, as though hawks perched upon a cliff edge.

Alexander rode onwards as a man appeared at the gate's threshold, walking out to meet them. After a moment's uncertainty, reins cracked, horses snuffled, wagon wheels creaked, and the streets were once again filled with the sound of footsteps.

The convoy was waved to the left, stretching through the gate and around a tight corner. Norman lagged behind a short distance, ensuring that everybody had passed through before he did so himself.

Then the gate was behind him, and he'd entered the camp. With the imposing wall now gone from view, Canary Wharf was revealed in full. Many behemoth towers stood stoic amidst the blackness, but only theirs flickered with so many thousands of twinkling lights.

Halogen lamps had been erected across the courtyard beyond the gate, set atop the tips of long poles trailing thick, ugly cables. The light they cast was white and unflattering, yet clean and comforting.

Around fifty people milled in the courtyard at the foot of the tower. At the sight of the convoy, they all rushed forwards with enthusiasm, smiling and greeting the newcomers with open arms.

Yet the smile burgeoning on Norman's face and the warmth buzzing around his heart were quelled almost as soon as they'd arrived by another noise, one altogether more unpleasant.

"What do you mean you've lost power?" said a voice, high-pitched with outrage.

Norman turned to see Alexander and a man who stood upon the gate's threshold, locked in conversation. He peeled away from the wagons and paused a few feet from them, waiting in silence.

"There was some kind of explosion," Alexander said. "McKay took most of our security detail to see what it was about."

The man stepped into the light, his arm flung in the air, fists bunched with rage. His wizened face creased into an angry grimace and he cursed profusely. Norman cringed when he recognised him: Marek Johnson.

Marek was, to Norman's knowledge, the only person to supersede Lucian in the arts of being stubborn, short-tempered, and uncouth.

"You mean to tell me that you brought all these people here without security?" he bellowed. "We told you to stay together at all costs, Alexander."

Norman found himself, as usual, disturbed by Marek's lack of respect. Most didn't dare even meet Alexander's gaze. Raising one's voice to him was unthinkable to all but a precious handful.

But Marek knew no bounds. His ruthlessness was his saving grace—instilling a steady peace in even the most skittish of men—yet such blatant disregard had never sat right with Norman.

However, he kept quiet, merely listening.

"I remember," Alex answered in a clipped, testy voice. "But I thought it best to think."

"*Don't…talk…like…that…to me,*" Marek growled, his face growing puce. "You should have kept them with you until you got here."

"So far as he could see it, leaving eight hundred people in the dark was more of a risk than the forty of us chancing it in full daylight. And, judging by your remarks, I assume you've discovered some way by which Lucian can be made to *listen* to anybody other than himself?"

Marek didn't answer, stalking forwards, teeth bared.

"Canterbury is going to be in dire need of assistance without the turbines," Alexander said. "We need to send help as soon as possible."

Marek nodded, flapping his hands. "Of course they will." He fumed. "This shouldn't have happened. We can't afford to lose you." He glanced to Alexander, then Norman. "Especially you."

Then his eyes softened. He blinked and took a deep breath, as though for strength. Then his shoulders dipped and, with evident difficulty, he said, "Truth is you're lucky to be alive."

"What do you mean?"

"I mean they're here, Alexander. Here, in the city. They've been going around the outer settlements, burning them to the ground, absorbing anyone who'll bow down. We tried to send word not to come, but our scouting parties were gunned down before they made it a mile past the wall. I don't know what's going on, but there's no way in hell you should have made it here." He looked around at them all. "You should be dead."

"What about the radio transmission you intercepted?"

"I haven't heard anything. To be honest, I haven't given it a thought. This summit isn't about that anymore. It's about how we're going to survive, because right now, we're being exterminated."

Alex scratched his head, his eyes darted to and fro. "Have the other council members arrived?"

"You're the first. And I wouldn't hold your breath for any more. Even if some smell a rat and hole up, it could be days before they get here. The rest…"

"We don't have days! We're on the clock, Marek."

"Tell it to Evie. I'm up to my eyeballs with security." He paused. "It's good to see you."

Then his gruff barrier shot up once more, and his mouth drew into its signature crooked line. He pointed towards a large group of shacks, lean-to shelters and storage tents. "We'll wait for your security detail first. We'll chance making it back to Canterbury, but there's no way I'm going anywhere in the dark. The new stables are over there."

Alex said no more, and led his horse away. Frightened glances lanced in all directions, then one by one people filed away into the night.

Norman remained alone in the gloom for some time before following.

XXI

It was quiet.

Norman had tried to sleep, but had given up fast. While most—including Alexander—had bedded down immediately to be ready at first light, John and Richard had insisted on a midnight game of chess, desperate to retreat into abstraction. So many real-world dangers had been too much for them.

Norman had only been able to bear so many of Richard's frustrated grunts and John's bored utterances of "Checkmate."

It had been minutes before he'd crawled from his bunk, donned his coat, and set to prowling the catwalk outside. At so late an hour, even the perimeter guards had thinned in number. Only a few heavyset veterans still patrolled the floodlit catwalk.

He drew his coat closer around his body in the midnight chill. The journey had taken its toll. His tired eyes worked with difficulty, as though old machinery in need of oiling. His body had been worn ragged. It felt sluggish, abound with aches and pains.

From here he looked directly across the Thames. The ghostly ripples of the black water reflected the tower's pale blue halo, cut into which was the undulating profile of his own body. The buildings on the far side were long ruined, their roofs fallen, and their walls crumbled. Some of the older and sturdier specimens were still standing, but they had nevertheless failed to escape extreme dilapidation. The streets were buried beneath lank vegetation, which snaked around millions of rotted briefcases, handbags, earrings, and rusted smartphones. The carpet of clothing that had blanketed London during the Early Years had decomposed, leaving behind a dark crust that stained the tarmac.

No signs of habitation were visible in any direction.

He started as a series of voices rang out from afar, accompanied by the clanking of boots upon metal. He turned to see the blinding searchlights flicker to life above the main gate.

A trio of guards had congregated there, their weapons trained on the ground beyond the wall. They turned and called to others upon the far-side catwalk.

Norman made for the nearest staircase. As he reached the ground he saw Marek's silhouette appear from an outbuilding not far from the gate. He ran with a loping gait, his shirt hanging from his shoulders as he tried to pull it on mid-stride.

Norman jerked when the buzzer sounded, immediately followed by the deep, metallic clanking of the gates. As they swung open, the guards overhead relaxed.

"What's going on?" he asked as he came to a standstill beside Marek.

Marek turned to him, looking him up and down. He pulled his shirt on fully, ruffling his collar and averting his eyes. "They're here," he said. Then, reluctantly, but firmly, he added, "Sir."

Norman eyed the gate as the searchlight's beam filtered in through the opening doors.

Thirteen figures on horseback cantered through, stretched out in a V formation, their faces taut and withered. Lucian, leading at the head, nodded to him as they moved into the square.

Norman strode after him. "What happened?"

He didn't answer at first, his eyes downcast. He dropped to the ground, sighing. "Nothing but ash," he said. His face was set, emotionless, but his eyes betrayed a seething rage bubbling beneath the surface. His movements were calculated, smooth, overcompensated.

Norman mouthed silently, lost for words. "All of it?" he managed after some time.

Lucian looked over his shoulder. Norman turned to see Allison, who had just emerged from the tower. She had clearly overheard; her eyes were fawning, her cheeks fallen. She held her head in her hands, groaning.

"It looked like a crater," Lucian said. The crevasse between his brow was deeper than Norman had ever seen it. "There's no chance of salvaging anything." He fumed for a moment, and then turned the others. "Get over to the stables. We need food."

There was no protest, nor a change in the volume of chatter. The small crowd simply milled for a time before dispersing, disappearing into the night.

Only Norman, Marek and Allie remained with Lucian, subdued, yet on the verge of outburst. His grey mount was restless, tugging against Lucian's grip on the reins. But he didn't seem to notice. His eyes had glazed and his mouth was slack as he gazed into the middle distance.

And then Marek rushed forth, growling. He blasted past Norman and collided with Lucian. With a sharp push he launched him back, lifting him from his feet.

There was an endless moment in which Lucian seemed to hang in midair. Then he collided with his mount's thigh, bouncing from it with an utterance of horror. Norman, stunned, watched his face go through a startling transformation: passing through several emotions associated with surprise before settling on dawning fury.

He steadied himself, his eyes wild. "How dare you!" he cried, rushing forwards with teeth bared.

He was almost a foot shorter than Marek, but he looked no less intimidating. A guttural growl escaped his throat, but then he took a deep breath. "After the day I've just had, I would really like to get some sleep. But right now, I wouldn't mind—"

"Shut up," said Marek. "Who do you think you are?"

Lucian struck him hard in the chest, sending the larger man careening back through sheer force. "What are you talking about?" he hissed.

Marek rushed forwards, his muscles taut beneath his shirt. "You and your stunts. They're going to be the end of us if you don't start taking orders, you little runt."

Lucian's eyes popped wide. "Don't you dare," he said.

Marek ignored him. "You think you can just wander off at the first sign of something interesting?" He jabbed Lucian's chest as he spoke, snarling. "You have a responsibility, a job to do! There are people who could have died because of you."

Lucian's face had become a doppelganger of Marek's, his eyes brimming with pent-up anger.

Norman had time to exchange a look with Allison, who seemed strangely unbothered by the sudden hostility. Her eyes were still dazed, and her face slack. He guessed she still hadn't recovered from the news about the wind farm, or the fact that they were probably trapped here.

Lucian's face was millimetres from Marek's, both of them stretched into tight masks of fury. "I had to find out what was happening," he said through gritted teeth.

Marek's finger struck his chest once more. "And what if it had just been a trap to lure you away? Divide and conquer? Did that cross your mind?"

Lucian gave a humourless bark. "Oh yes, that's very insightful. Perhaps if you had been there then everything would have been just fine, except for the fact that anybody back in Canterbury would have been ripe for the slaughter."

Norman watched the argument jump back and forth, his eyes following each aggressor in turn.

"Not everybody needs you to protect them."

"They wouldn't have been ready during the middle of the day. If something had happened, they would have been caught off guard."

"It's too late for 'ifs' and 'buts'."

Norman turned towards the sound of footsteps echoing in the square behind them. A magnificent regal woman was stalking towards them, her face thunderous despite her withered eyes. "Enough!" she roared.

A long pink shawl hung about her, making her torso appear elongated and amorphous. A generous smattering of jewellery hung around her neck and adorned her fingers, twinkling in the blue halo of the Wharf. Her face was heavily scarred down one side, and on the other marred by the kind of leathery wrinkles that only come with extreme age.

Evelyn Fisher was a sight for sore eyes. She held herself rigid as an iron rod, observing Lucian and Marek from the summit of her long, cragged nose.

Lucian didn't seem to notice her deathly stare, his eyes still fixed on Marek.

Marek, however, appeared to deflate. The fire left his eyes, and his shoulders slumped. His breathing remained shallow and ragged, betraying the fire still crackling beneath the surface. But, after a moment's hesitation, he took a step back.

Lucian looked perplexed. Evelyn's draconian stare suddenly seemed to become visible to him. In time, he too slackened and stepped back.

Evelyn didn't seem to derive any satisfaction from the ceasefire. Her stare remained merciless, aglow with scorn. Her body shook under the halogen glare, vibrating with barely contained abhorrence. "What is going on here?" she demanded.

Lucian turned from Marek, pulling open a small satchel hanging from his mount's saddle. There was a clinking as he reached inside, turning back towards them and holding something up to the light.

It was a piece of charred metal, bent, twisted, and blackened. Norman thought he might have been able to discern a sharpened edge skirting its periphery, but couldn't be sure.

"What is this?" Evelyn said.

Lucian turned the shard in his hands, such that the jagged edges threw off a dazzling collection of reflected light beams. "This was all I could find," he said. "Everything else was vaporised, or melted into the ground."

Evelyn stared at the sliver of wreckage, and her eyes softened for a moment. Then the moment passed, and her face tightened back up. She held her head high, throwing her desiccated white locks over her shoulder. "So they've lost power?"

She beckoned Marek with a flick of her wrist. He complied without so much as a blink, reaching her side and stooping to match her stature.

She whispered something incoherent, her words lost in the void between them and Norman's ears. However, he could tell by her tone that they were no words of praise, nor even frank discussion.

Marek answered in high-pitched protest, but apparently the argument wasn't to her taste; she dismissed him with another flick of her wrist.

Marek scowled, his head rearing to one side, his hands gathered into shuddering fists.

Evelyn ignored him, turning to Lucian. "I trust you're unaware of the situation?"

Lucian frowned and looked at Norman and Allie.

"They're here, surrounding us," Norman muttered. "We can't get word out, but they're letting people in."

Lucian paled. "They're gathering us up."

"Like sheep for the slaughter."

Evelyn cut across them. "It's prudent that we move quickly. However, little can be done tonight, and I therefore recommend that each of you rest as best you can." She fixed Marek with a stern look. "Let that be an end to this foolishness. We have few friends left. We can't afford animosity now." She gave a small bow. "Goodnight."

With that, she departed, leaving them amidst an awkward silence. Little moved as she swayed across the square and disappeared.

Marek remained a while longer, his eyes downcast. He moved close to Lucian. "Stay out of my way," he muttered. Then he too wandered away, back towards the hut by the gate. The door slammed behind him, and the light emanating from within winked out soon after.

Lucian didn't move until Norman patted him on the arm and said, "It's good to see you."

He mumbled something in return, and then hurried towards the tower.

Norman watched him go, sighing, and then took Allison under the arm, leading her inside. "Come on," he said, "we need some rest. Evelyn's right: There's nothing more we can do tonight."

She didn't protest, bending freely to his will. "How could this happen?" she whispered. "This isn't how it's supposed to be. Not how it goes in all those stories the elders told. We're supposed to be the strong ones, Norman. We're supposed to be the good guys."

He swallowed, and his throat cracked. "There *are* no good guys. And it's never like it is in the stories."

XXII

Robert crept across his front door's threshold, his face creased into a strained, desperate grimace. He was determined to tread only upon the hallway's edge, but his bulk still sent the floorboards snapping like bullwhips with each step.

His mind buzzed with the day's run of mayhem: flashes of endless thickets, fields and meadows, accompanied by the buzz of a hundred blurred voices; a thousand half-remembered conversations; screams and shouts, anguished and furious alike.

He hadn't returned to the city since the explosion. Working at the turbine site, securing the surrounding area and searching the denser forest beyond the hills had taken until long after dusk.

By then the streets had been pitch-black, and there had been little point in staying out to search the city itself. There had been little else to do but ensure that the guards were at their posts and slink away in the distant hope of a night's rest.

If he was lucky, he'd get a few hours' sleep before sunrise. Then he'd go out to the hills again and see if he could find some trace of a trail. If he could find one, maybe he could find out how those bastards had gotten past the perimeter. Maybe he could set up some kind of defensive strategy.

The house was crooked, misaligned. He and his father had built it themselves, many years before, when Canterbury had been home to just the two of them. That had been long before the others had arrived, before the rebuilding or the restoration.

Before Alexander, even.

The hallway's low roof forced him to bend at a ridiculous angle, but it quickly split off into two perpendicular doorways, forming a T-junction. He made to cut away into the kitchen, but before he could take another step, a rumble built from the living room: the patter of running feet.

Sarah appeared in the doorway, candle in hand. Her hair lay lank and knotted over her glasses, throwing red, puffy eyes into shadow. Her cheeks drooped, pallid, and her mouth quivered, lopsided between dried tear tracks. "Where were you?" she whispered. She strode forwards, and her voice rose to a shriek. "*Where were you?*" She raised her free hand and slammed it against his chest.

He barely felt the impact—her fist rebounded with such a kick that it almost struck her chin—but he recoiled nonetheless. "What's wrong?" he said. He gripped her by the arms, but she struggled, cursing and yelling. The candle wavered to and fro, sending their shadows dancing across the wall. "Wait! What are you doing? What's wrong?"

She ripped herself from his grasp, her mouth working as fresh tears splashed across her cheeks. "What's wrong?" she wailed. "I've been waiting here for hours! You've been out there all this time, and I had no way of knowing whether you were hurt or—or dead!"

Robert gripped her once more, firmly, holding her still, and stared into her eyes. He bent until well below the horizontal, and he reached her head height. "I'm fine," he breathed. "Everything is fine."

He steered her around and walked her slowly to the living room as her sobs began to settle. Once they'd passed inside, he started. Heather was perched on their dusty armchair, a cup and saucer frozen halfway to her face.

She observed them for a moment. "Hello," she said after a brief, taut silence.

"Hello," he replied. "Sorry I'm late." A slab of awkward discomfort landed against the nape of his neck as he sat on the sofa, one that refused to dissipate.

The room was dark. The scant light of a dozen candles, even coupled with glowing embers in the grate, couldn't quite replace that of the dead bulbs hanging overhead.

Sarah sat beside him, straight-backed, her eyes still seeping. There was something within them that made the struggles of the day dim and distant, and yet they inspired a great weakness in his bowels. It was almost as though she expected him to leave her again at any moment.

He put his arm around her and pulled her close.

"What happened?" Heather asked. "We've been waiting all day. But nobody came back. We thought…" She glanced at Sarah and grew quiet.

Robert raised a hand to his forehead and pressed hard. The pressure only somewhat relieved the headache festering behind his brow. He gave Sarah a brief squeeze before speaking, "From what we can tell, they came from the western hills and took out the turbines while we were distracted down by the river. There's nothing left. No power." He cleared his throat. "I'm thinking we might have enough biofuel left to get some lights going by nightfall tomorrow. At least we won't be completely in the dark…for a while."

A brief silence stretched between them.

"Was anybody hurt?" Heather said.

"No. There wasn't anybody up there. I posted the sentries closer to the city to make sure the convoy was safe." He tittered, cradling his aching head in his palms. "Not one of my best calls."

Silence, bar the crackling in the grate.

"Why would somebody do this?" Heather muttered.

Robert shrugged, shaking his head.

More silence, thicker than treacle.

Sarah hadn't said a word, nor moved a muscle. She'd merely kept her head rested on his shoulder, her face masked by matted red curls, which looked like flames licking at her cheeks in the candlelight. Her knuckles were bone-white, locked tight around his forearm.

He caressed her shoulder with his free hand. At his touch, her death-grip loosened slightly, became less desperate. "McKay and a few of the others came back," he said, intent on breaking the lull. He tittered once more, but not a trace of humour stirred in his gut. "He wasn't happy."

"The guard detail? They came back?" Heather asked. "They just left everybody else out there?"

Robert nodded. "I wasn't thrilled either, but there was no convincing him. At the time, I was just glad for the help."

"Are they still here?"

Robert shook his head. "He took off back to London just before nightfall. I suppose he finally came to his senses."

Heather rubbed her head. "I hope they get there alright."

Robert shrugged. "They'll be fine. These people weren't looking for blood today. They were looking to terrorise, weaken. Shock and awe." He paused, catching Heather's alarmed expression. "They'll send help as soon as they can. We'll be fine. We just have to hold out the night."

She nodded slowly, blinked, seemed to take deeper notice of how Sarah was draped over his shoulder, and cleared her throat. "I'll get you a drink," she said, standing with delicacy and hurrying from the room.

Robert and Sarah were left alone amidst fresh silence. Heather seemed to be intent on making a meal of whatever she was doing, crashing pots and pans together. Yet the atmosphere in the living room remained strained until Sarah finally spoke.

"Did you find anything?" she mumbled.

Robert brushed a stray lock behind her ear, looking down at the curtain of hair shielding her face. "Not yet."

She nodded fractionally and resumed her silence. She held up her hand to the candlelight, turning the ring upon her finger until it twinkled and flashed. The two of them looked at it for a long time, not saying a word.

She'd said that she wanted a white autumn wedding.

Did they have that long?

Eventually, she muttered, "I'm glad you're alright."

Robert tried to smile, but the tugging in his gut soon wiped it from his lips. He folded his hand over hers. "Me too."

*

Norman was brought to the gate by the sound of the klaxon like everyone else. He joined the ranks of a growing crowd, aghast, as a ragged group of travellers filed into the courtyard. The sun had barely risen, but there was no mistaking the blood. It lay over everything, every scrap of cloth, every inch of bare skin. Their carts had been purged of goods and loaded up with piles of dead and dying. Their agonised cries filled the air.

Evelyn, Alexander and Lucian raced from the tower. "Mr Rush! What happened?" Alex cried.

A round-shouldered, powerful man stepped forward, visibly shaking, lips trembling. Norman was shocked more by the sight of his fear than the sight of the wounded. Rush had been on the council since its founding with Alexander, representing Southampton. He was a presence to put all others to shame, a commander on par with the messiah himself.

Now he was in tatters, tears streaming down his face. "They came from nowhere. We tried to run, but the way back was blocked. They…they killed…there were over a hundred of us!"

Norman's stomach turned over. No more than a dozen were still standing.

The crowd rushed forward to help unload the wounded and carry the survivors away for treatment. Norman fought his way through to the spot where Rush had collapsed into Alexander's arms. He was whimpering. "Portsmouth and Worthing have been hit," he said. Norman had always known his stare to carry nothing but dignity. Now it was jelly. He shook his head. "There's nothing left."

None of them spoke. There was nothing to say.

As the sun rose, more groups arrived. People poured in, desperate for shelter, some unscathed, some not. None had been hit as bad as those from Southampton. Norman couldn't help but feel they were an example.

Soon the representatives of almost every settlement on the council had arrived. The fact that none of the ambassadors had been harmed, despite reams of fallen aides, friends and family, only fuelled his suspicion. By the time the sun had crested the distant skyscrapers, the courtyard was stained red, and the gates slammed shut a final time. They couldn't risk waiting any longer for stragglers. The council would convene in the coming hours, and their course of action would be decided.

But Norman was no longer sure there was anything to be done. Until now they had been the dominant power in all the land. In a single morning, they had been reduced to rats in a maze.

THIRD INTERLUDE

James stepped out onto the beach and took a breath of rich sea breeze. He surveyed the rough surf and half-buried remains of old yachts, pale in the early morning light, overturned and pitted below the tide line.

The world was moving on. After eleven years, the things mankind had created before the End were beginning to vanish. People were beginning to call everything before that time the Old World.

Lucian appeared alongside him, only a head taller even after his recent growth spurt. Without a word to one another, they ambled along the beach, stabbing their spears into the sand to give them purchase, watchful of the trees. James smiled. His feet felt sure, and his legs strong. The roll of the surf was music to his ears.

Yet, he was more tired than he would have ever shown, especially with Lucian around. They'd spent the morning hunting without success. He didn't relish the thought of keeping it up for much longer, but he'd never complain. If they didn't make a kill, they'd go hungry. The tinned food wasn't as plentiful as it had once been. Now, it was currency in itself. A tin of mackerel could buy you a sack of coal. For corned beef, you could get enough rags to clothe an entire family.

Food had ceased to become a given. If you couldn't hunt, gather, or trade by now, you'd starve. And, from what they'd seen on their travels, many had. The unskilled survivors who'd gorged themselves on the Old World's resources without a thought for how long it would last had followed the rest of humanity into oblivion.

James listened to branches snapping in the forest as the others followed a path parallel to the beach. Sensing that Lucian's gaze was directed towards the trees, he allowed his eyes to droop for a moment. Walking along with half-closed eyes, it almost felt like sleeping.

"Doesn't it bother you, kiddo?" Lucian muttered.

James brushed windswept hair from his eyes and frowned at his brother. "What?"

"You have no time to yourself. You were up all night reading again. You've been out with us since dawn. Soon as we get back, I'll bet my dinner that Alex has a class waiting. Then what? More reading?"

"I like to read," James said, though his gaze fell to the ground. Then he did a double take. "And I can hunt better than the rest of you put together."

Lucian laughed and ruffled his hair, smearing it back over his eyes. "Of course you can."

"I can. You're all too loud. And clumsy."

Lucian appeared to take offence, but at the same time seemed unable to mount any kind of counterargument, so let it pass. "But you've always got to be *doing* something," he said. "If you haven't got your head in a book then you're in the classroom, you're taking care of the birds, you're milking the cows or you're out tending the plants."

"Crops," James corrected.

Lucian was uncomfortable with that word. Like the others, he thought that their field was too small to justify using it. Most of the others merely frowned at its usage. Lucian said it was ridiculous. Paul said things far worse, things James wasn't allowed to hear—Aggie always covered his ears.

But Alex insisted they were raising crops, that their one patch of earth was just the start of something much greater, that one day entire meadows would grow six feet tall with wheat and barley, and they'd be able to feed hundreds of people—maybe a thousand. That was more than enough for James.

"But don't you want to do other things?" Lucian said.

"What things?"

"I don't know…kid things. Don't you want to play?"

James shrugged, frowning. "I play all the time. I love games."

Lucian scowled. James shrank away instinctively, conscious of his bad temper. "Backgammon Night isn't playing," he said.

James shook his head, nonplussed. There was no time for play, no reason for it. Even if he'd wanted to, there was nobody to play with. The nearest people were a few hours' ride away.

No, play wasn't for him. His time was for learning, for collecting the Old World's treasures. For saving the world.

"Don't you sometimes wish that you didn't have to do all those things?" Lucian said. "Don't you wish that you could be free?"

James paused mid-step. His mind had fallen blank. Somewhere, deep down in his gut, anger stirred. "I'm free," he said. His voice was more high-pitched than he'd intended, but he didn't care. He was too busy searching Lucian's face.

Lucian had stopped a few paces ahead. His brow constricted into a deep crease, something he always did when unsettled—James was sure he'd wrinkle early—as though sensing the pain in his voice. "I know," he said.

"I have a job to do. It's important."

"I know, I know, it's your destiny," Lucian muttered under his breath, shaking his head.

James felt his face bunch up as the anger in his gut swelled, but it was quickly overshadowed by sadness—not for the insult, but for Lucian's disbelief. "You don't think so?" His spear had dropped to his side. "You don't think I have a destiny? You don't think… I'm important?"

Lucian's eyes flickered from anger to soft melancholy, and then a diamond-hard look of wonder. "I hope you are," he said.

"You do?"

The look of wonder lingered long enough for Lucian to utter, "If anybody's going to help us—all of us—it's going to be you." Then he cleared his throat, shrugging his shoulders with a gruff jerk. "Who cares what I think? It's your business."

James smiled. The anger's spark fizzled, yet the sadness remained. "Then why ask?"

"I just want to make sure that you're happy doing…whatever it is you're doing."

James thought about all those things over the next few moments: all he did, and all he was meant to do. He could feel it all ahead of him, so close that he was sure he could almost reach out and touch it. "I'm happy," he said finally.

Lucian nodded, looking away, now ensconced in his gruff exterior. "Fine. Sorry I asked."

James didn't miss the flicker lurking behind his eyes, something satisfied, maybe even pleased.

They both turned as a scrabbling issued from the forest, just in time to see Oliver and Alex burst from the trees and sprint along the border between sand and soil, spears held aloft. For a single, dangling second, there was a strained silence. Then, from the forest, came the long and reverberating cry of a stag, followed by an almighty rumble that could only have been made by dozens of hooves.

James watched Alex charge along the beach for a moment, glanced at Lucian, and then gave chase. They passed into the shade thrown down by the canopy and caught up with the others in a few bounding strides.

Alex was swinging his head back and forth, glaring into the trees. He seemed to see things the others could not. They followed his lead, sprinting alongside him until he gave a grunt and veered off from the sand, plummeting back into the forest.

James sprang after him, slipping between the thick brambles without breaking a single twig, leaving the others—heavy-footed and uncoordinated—in his wake. He vaulted deeper into darkness, passing between narrow gaps between trees, bounded shrubbery and rocks without effort, and ducked overhanging branches without a moment's thought. His footfalls made only the lightest of patters. His breathing was deep, calm and unhurried.

He and Alex had spent countless hours in the wilds, honing their senses. But while Alex had grown sharper—his eyes, especially, had become indispensable during a hunt—James had become something else. Over the years, he had felt himself become at home in the forest, one with it.

The Jungle Bookworm, Paul called him. *"Ain't nothing but a dog that can read, that boy,"* he'd once said. *"Look at him, he's more at home swinging from a tree than inside."*

But Alex had shot him down. He'd said that they had to be at home in the libraries as much as in the forests. He'd called it the perfect synergy. James didn't know what that meant, but was sure it was far removed from Paul's comments.

The others, meanwhile, were still much the same as they'd been before the End. Large, bulky, clumsy and loud, they crashed through the underbrush and tripped over the simplest of obstacles, swearing and panting.

The guttural groans of the deer ahead spurred James on. He could hear them struggling to squeeze themselves through the tighter gaps between branches, beating away at the tight-packed foliage blanketing every surface. Slow as the others were, they were all getting closer.

James let his legs navigate for him, taking a backseat and merely enjoying the run, skipping and leaping at leisure beside Alex, keeping pace as a rabbit would with a snail. Testing his agility, he bounced between twisted roots and the trunks of ancient elms.

Then Alex cried, "Through here!"

Ahead, a clearing had appeared in the trees. They wheeled as one and broke out into the open. Unhindered by snagging underbrush, they sprinted through the wild grass, cast into shadow by the surrounding canopy.

On the far side, the deer herd churned to the sound of thunder. The forest beyond was lined by an impenetrable barrier of tangled vines and overlapping tree trunks. Trapped, they kicked and thrashed atop one another, each fighting to gain the herd's centre, crying out.

The men raised their spears over their shoulders. James saw Lucian do the same, and hurried to follow suit. A moment later they were all rushing towards the whorling vortex of flesh.

The herd fragmented. James blinked as they rushed outwards in all directions, disoriented. It took some moments for him to realise that a few were heading right for him. Before he could react, he was immersed in a sea of fur and hooves. Deafening yelps of fright sounded beside him until a dull hum filled his head.

He yelled, throwing his arms up and crouching low to the ground, spear wedged against the dirt. The herd flowed around him as a river parts around a rock, leaping back the way they'd come, crashing through vines into darkness.

Then they were gone, and James was left gazing about the empty clearing. The grass had been churned into a ragged patch of ploughed mud. Standing in the very centre, the others had trapped what could only have been the alpha male.

The stag was enormous, standing six feet at the shoulder, swinging its antlers in a great arc to thwart their advance. Its breath rushed from its nostrils in great plumes and an angry gurgle escaped its mouth, freezing the hunters in place. Oliver's spear protruded from its ribcage, imbedded down to the shaft, more than enough to have already doomed the beast.

Their kill was now a given. All that remained to be decided was how long it would take.

As James approached, blood oozed from the stag's wound, splattering the flattened grass. He looked to the others, trying to gauge their reactions, but their expressions were blank.

"What do we do?" Lucian said.

"It's going to charge," Oliver said. "Get back."

"Just wait," Alex said. His voice, unlike theirs, was flat, calm.

Oliver and Lucian each took a step back regardless.

In turn, the stag advanced, emboldened.

Alex stood his ground, half crouched. James's legs itched to turn tail and join the others, but he kept close to his brother's side, adopting the same stance, watching his every move from the corner of his eye.

The stag's breath had become ragged, and its rippling shoulders were trembling. Yet still it stamped its hooves deep into the earth, advancing on them, a menacing roar rumbling in its throat.

"Get back, lads," Oliver warned.

Neither of them moved, though as James glanced between Alex and the snarling beast, the urge to leap back became near unbearable. The baser nooks of his mind stabbed at his nerve, screaming '*Danger!*', certain that the stag's display would give way to a charge. It was only through Alex's cool, motionless stance that James kept his place.

The charge never came. The stag's breath became ever more ragged, and in a mere handful of moments its antlers had come to a standstill, its eyes drooping. It milled on the spot for a moment, gave a last-ditch buck of its head, and slumped to the ground. There, it seemed to deflate, wheezing as the hunters regrouped and approached.

"Bold," Oliver said. "Bold, but stupid." His face creased into a wry smile. "We don't see enough of that."

Alex cuffed James on the shoulder. James began laughing as mirth boiled up in his cheeks, stemming from a slab of relief amidst those dark corners that had screamed for him to run. They laughed together, looking down upon the stag as it drew its last breaths, bleeding out into the grass.

"It would've been easier to catch a cow," Lucian said. "They're dumb and slow. And they're everywhere."

Oliver gave a wordless cry. "Oh, my boy, there's nothing like a good pound of venison! Besides, plenty of people who'll go hungry tonight would give their left nut to be standing where you are now."

Lucian's face was drawn into a dissatisfied grimace. "I prefer beef."

"Someday soon you'll learn that it's always best to be thankful for a meal." Oliver's face twitched. "There's always tomorrow. Lucky for us, we'll never be low on steak!" He leaned over and made an exact incision across the deer's throat, quelling its last jerks. He patted its head, one hand laid across its eyes, a slow and steady hushing sound whistling between his teeth.

Once the body was still, they set to work.

"Looks like we're eating tonight, lads," Oliver cried, swinging a freshly butchered leg over his shoulder.

They returned home in the early afternoon, laden with meat, parading towards the front door, expecting to be greeted as heroes. Instead, they received an earful of a bone-shaking scream. James surged forth with the rest of them, but even his sprightly legs couldn't keep up with Alexander's headlong charge. He crashed through the door behind the others, spear raised, dumping the meat upon the doorstep.

When he laid eyes on the living room, he froze. The others had done just the same. Together, they took a unanimous step back. Lucian faltered to the side and leaned over in his bloodstained coat, retching at the sight of what lay before them.

"Contractions star'ed this mornin'," Agatha said from the depths of the room. "Gettin' to being fully dilated." Her hair, greying at the temples, had been thrown into a gnarled thatch. "Coulda used you earlier!"

Helen Creek screeched without pause, beet-red and gasping, spread-eagled atop a thick carpet of sweat-soaked blankets. Her dress had been hiked up around her midriff, revealing the tight-stretched skin of her swollen abdomen and the horrors between her thighs. Beside her, Hector sat erect and ashen-faced, grimacing as Helen crushed his hand in an iron grip.

James groaned as his gaze settled upon the blankets and recognised his own bed sheets. Judging by the similar grunts passing the others' lips, they were seeing much the same. They remained frozen in the hallway for some time, blood dripping from their shoulders.

James wanted to turn away, to back out the door and escape, but his feet seemed cemented to the floor. He looked to Alex, hoping for guidance, and was unsettled to see him white-lipped, his eyes darting back and forth.

"I think you'd best take your brother outside," he murmured to Lucian.

"We'll need towels," Oliver said. "And water, hot water—I think." He paused. "*Why* do we need hot water?" he breathed, his lazy eye bulging.

"We'll figure something out," Alex said, piling the meat onto a tarpaulin in the hall.

Lucian took James by the hand and guided him towards the door. As they reached the threshold, James heard Oliver murmur, "I hope Agatha knows what she's doing."

"So do I," Alex replied.

Then the two of them were out in the dank afternoon air, and Helen's screams became muffled.

James tried to clear his throat, but the lump forming there refused to shift, and his knees thrummed with nervous energy. The fresh memory of the awed silence that had fallen over the others kept his mouth dry and his pulse racing.

He'd heard about birth, read about it, wondered about it—sometimes it seemed that all grown-ups spoke about was having babies—but never seen it. It seemed almost otherworldly, akin to reincarnation and the afterlife; something mentioned daily at the breakfast table, but never fully explained.

Lucian was pale. He looked no more at ease than James felt himself. "What happens now?" he grumbled.

James shrugged. He set off around the side of the house.

Patience. Alex's voice echoed in his mind from countless classroom lectures. *Patience is key. Bide your time, and the answers will come.*

Fine, James thought. *I'll wait, and the answers will come—come shooting out of Mrs Creek.*

He skirted the rear side wall and reached the fence leading to their crop field. He could hear Lucian's footfalls close behind, but didn't slow down. He was too busy trying to suppress the images his imagination was conjuring: gory flashes of what might be going on inside.

Without thinking, he made his way to the flimsy cage of scavenged timber that lay nestled near the chimney, crossed by rows of twisted wire such that it formed a coop. He flipped the latch and placed his head at the lip of the entrance, staring into the gloom. His nostrils were filled by the aroma of droppings. Cooing and fluttering emanated from within.

In an instant, the images of blood and guts flickering behind his eyes dissipated. He could almost forget about the others, for they seemed as far away and distant as the crumbling cities upon the horizon. That was how it always was when he came out here. He smiled, and coaxed his friends into view. "Hello," he said, helpless to keep a broad smile from stretching across his cheeks.

The birds hopped from the shadows one by one. Half a dozen pigeons, plump and well kept, wheeled and followed his guiding hand, pecking at his fingertips.

He reached into a small tin beside the cage and brought out a handful of seed. They set to it greedily, pecking away and jostling each other for room. James let them gorge themselves for a few moments, then withdrew his hand. When he'd been younger, he'd overfed them—he hadn't been able to help himself. Now they were always looking for their next meal. "Eat it all and you'll get too fat," he warned. "Then what good will you be?"

Lucian was standing beside him, looking at the birds with an expression of distant disgust, though James suspected that the brunt of it was being held back out of politeness. "Why do you keep them?" he said, frowning. He backed away with an irked cry when one of the pigeons took flight and darted away behind the chimney.

James shooed the rest into the sky before they could besiege his hand in search of more seed. They followed the first bird, wheeling together and disappearing around the smoking chimneystack. "They're clever," he said.

As he spoke, one of the birds fluttered back into sight and alighted upon the roof of the cage, staring at James's hand, as though hoping to be rewarded for its persistence.

"They don't look very smart," Lucian said. The wrinkle between his eyebrows had deepened into a defined crease, and his lip had curled upwards.

James smiled and stroked the bird's head. "They're *very* smart. They were used to carry messages, Before. During the Great War they took mail across whole countries."

"Which war was that?"

James glanced over his shoulder, frowning. "The First World War."

Lucian merely blinked. His face was blank.

James shrugged. Sometimes he forgot how little Lucian—or even the other grown-ups—actually knew of the Old World they were trying to save.

"How do you know that they'll come back?"

"I don't. But they always do."

"How do they find their cage? There's so much land, and it all looks the same. Don't they get lost?"

James shook his head. "They just know." He picked a stray feather from the coup's doorway, twisting it in his hands. "I'm going to use them to send messages too, one day."

Lucian nodded, but James could sense unease in the way he angled his head to the side. "Is *everything* you do for this Great Destiny?" he said.

James dropped the feather and turned to face him. His heart sank as he realised that, even after their talk on the beach, Lucian still didn't believe. "It's my job," he said. "I have to do all I can—have to *be* all I can—for everyone."

"Without any time for yourself? What kind of life is that?"

He held a frustrated retort back with some difficulty. "There are more important things," he said eventually.

"And you're happy to do it? Really happy to give it all up?"

James forced a smile onto his lips, but he spoke with a heavy heart. "Yes."

Lucian nodded once more, but James still saw doubt festering behind his gaze. He would never understand.

Sometime later, the house had grown quiet, and Alex appeared from around its side. His sleeves had been rolled up to the shoulder, and his arms were slicked with something James didn't dare guess at. He paused, locked his sights upon them, and let out a shuddering sigh.

James stammered, "W-What is it?"

Alex's tired face broke into a gentle grin. "You have a new brother," he said. He beckoned, leading the way back to the house, which was now deathly silent.

They were led into the living room, where the others stood in a perfect circle around Helen's grey, exhausted form. They were all whispering to one another, uttering wordless noises of wonderment, enraptured. They parted as James approached, waving him closer.

James looked down on Helen, who lay grey-lipped and sallow-skinned amidst the sodden blankets, and caught sight of the tiny bundle swaddled in her arms. He craned his neck as the Creeks cried and laughed, their faces nuzzled together. Their eyes, swimming with tears, were locked on the tiny pink body between the sheets.

James could only blink as numbness stole along his limbs, and he struggled to take in the new presence, which had been nonexistent only a minute ago.

Then a thump sent them all turning to see Paul in the doorway, hands pressed against either side of the frame, his eyes bloodshot and his face haggard. A near-empty bottle of scotch hung in his grasp. He hiccoughed, staring at the bundle of blankets unsteadily. His eyes softened, then flickered. A long silence stretched out between him and the group, until eventually he grunted. "Devil's work," he slurred. "D-Devil…devil's work."

A moment of tense silence followed before the others whirled back to the Creeks and resumed in their cooing with renewed enthusiasm, turning their backs on him. Not even Agatha spared him this time, leaning over the pink bundle and blowing raspberries right along with them.

James was the last to turn away. As he did so, he caught the glance Paul cast in his direction: subtle and fleeting, yet narrow, intense and deeply unsettling. Though he wasn't quite sure why, his guts twisted with a sudden, raw pang of fear. By the time the sensation had registered and he had turned back to the doorway, Paul had disappeared.

He blinked, unsure of what to make of it, but his attention was soon drawn back to the pink bundle in Helen's arms, and Paul slipped from his mind. Uttering meaningless noises as much as the others, he crouched down beside the Creeks and peered at the newborn baby, grinning helplessly. From a mass of rouge folds of puppy fat, pudgy hands and jerking feet, a pair of watchful brown eyes stared up at him. New eyes, fresh eyes, those of a new brother. "What's his name?" he asked.

Helen, her face aglow with adoration, smiled. "Norman," she said. "His name is Norman."

XXIII

Norman grunted as he opened his eyes. Blinding sunlight bombarded his retinas. His hands rushed to his face as he hauled himself to a seated position, gasping at the pain that erupted in his chest.

He'd been laid flat on a bench. It was warm to the touch despite being in the shade, hinting that he had been upon it for some time. Yet he had no memory of lying down—nor, for that matter, anything after guiding Allie towards the tower.

She stood over him now, with Richard close behind. They wore identical expressions of worry and confusion.

"Are you alright?" Richard said.

Norman shook his head, leaning forwards as the world swirled, off-kilter. His chest was throbbing with a vigour that he hadn't endured since Jason had first stomped down on him. "What happened?" he muttered.

Horses were snuffling nearby. The smell of hay and manure was thick in the air. He guessed that they were somewhere near the stables. As his vision stopped swirling, he glimpsed the tower directly above him. The gate was off to the right, looking bare and lifeless without the compliment of night guards patrolling its catwalks.

"We were going for breakfast," Allie said. "You fainted."

Richard crouched down beside Norman and held up his index finger, moving it first left, and then right.

Norman found himself instinctively tracking it with his eyes, frowning as he did so. "Stop that."

"I'm checking for head injury. I've seen Heather do it."

"Do you know what you're doing?"

"Not really."

Norman brushed his hand away. "I'm fine."

He struggled to his feet, blinking to clear his vision, which had begun swimming again. He held out his hand to keep Allison from taking hold of him, shaking his head. "I'm *fine*."

The courtyard below the gate was filling at a steady trickle as men dressed in dark combat gear emerged from the tower: the security detail from New Canterbury, most of the night guards, and a few who had been part of the convoy. Alexander, Lucian and Marek stood waiting before the gate, giving orders and distributing weapons. Above them, Evelyn watched with narrowed eyes along her crooked nose, perched like a crow atop the catwalk. Behind her, John DeGray studied the wall's defences with detached intrigue, ignoring the proceedings, looking oddly bare without Richard by his side.

The rickety stables rattled as a procession of mounts were led out to be saddled.

"You're not fine," Allison said firmly, laying a hand on Norman's shoulder despite his protests. "You need to stop moving around. You might be hurt bad. You need a doctor."

Richard clicked his tongue. "Abernathy's been treating famine victims north of here the last few weeks. Nobody knows when he'll be back. The best they have here is Anderson, but I wouldn't trust him to fall out of a boat and into water."

"Heather's been teaching him, hasn't she?"

"When she's here during the summer. But he's a ways from being up to scratch."

Allison seethed. "They must have a doctor here. They must have something."

Richard nodded. "Abernathy was Clara Fields's other disciple. He's as good as they come. But he's AWOL."

"Anderson will just have to do."

Norman uttered a wordless yell, holding up his hand to silence them. "Stop it!"

They froze midsentence, bemused, and looked at him.

"What's wrong?" Allison said.

"I'll be just grand, thank you." Norman tried to ignore how slurred his voice had become, ripping himself from Allie's grip and stalking away from the bench. "I don't need you"—he stumbled and had to grab the reins of a passing mount to steady himself—"mollycoddling me all day."

"You've been struggling to even walk since you got up," Allison said. "Maybe Heather was wrong. Maybe you should've stayed home. It looks like you're getting worse."

"She said that...I'll be fine as long as I...rest up," he wheezed. He locked his gaze on Alexander. The distance between them seemed enormous, but he ploughed on nonetheless, determined to reach him. "When are they leaving?"

"Now," Allison said uncertainly.

"They were going to leave me behind?"

"They want to get home by midday. Norman, sit down..."

They *were* going to leave him. Just like Lucian had left him yesterday, just brushed him off.

Was this how it was going to be from now on? After being prodded like a circus animal for so many years, trussed up with responsibility and duty, was he to be left by the wayside, injured, impotent, and useless?

He took a few more steps, almost fell, then cried out and gasped. He needed to chew up some white willow, but couldn't remember where he'd left the bag—or whether he'd already done so.

A few heads turned towards him, owl-eyed and concerned.

But he let loose a guttural groan and staggered onwards, waving people aside as he went. Men twice his size shrank back, bending into polite bows, uttering words of salutation. He ignored the absurd sight of their deference. His chest was white-hot, blinding, nauseating.

"Oh, Norman, don't," Allison moaned.

He carried on regardless, heading for Alexander. Overwhelming fury boiled in his guts, powered by an acute sense of betrayal as he powered towards the gathering. He knew his mind was scrabbling for purchase—that reason was failing him—but he was powerless to stop himself casting the last man between him and Alexander aside, and growling into his mentor's face, "I'm going with you."

Alex blinked, his eyebrows raised. "It's a big risk going at all, Norman. We have to ride hard, and stop for nothing if we're going to break through their lines. If you fall…"

Norman raised a pointed finger, teeth bared. His arm swung wildly, wavering at least a foot from where he had intended. "You can't leave me. Not now."

Allison came rushing through the crowd. "He just passed out," she cried. "He's in no state to go anywhere."

Norman snarled over his shoulder, "I have to go. I have to. You're not leaving me here."

"Norman, you're in pain. You're not seeing things clearly," Alexander said. Worry plastered his face. "Nobody's leaving you behind."

Norman cut across him, spittle flying from his lips. "I'm going with you and you're not going to stop me!" He tore the reins of the nearest mount from its master's hands, gripped the saddle, and made to leap upon the stirrups.

They caught him just in time. He was manhandled back to the ground by half a dozen pairs of hands. A small part of his mind took note that Allison had been the first to leap, the one to stop him truly hurting himself.

Alexander stood over him, his eyes sorrowful and his lips drawn into a tight white line. He reached down and rested a hand on Norman's shoulder.

Norman tried to shrug him off, whimpered, and then slumped, eyes weeping and jaw clenching. His cheeks glowed red-hot, for the pain had peaked, the fog was clearing, and acute embarrassment was coursing his veins. "You can't do this to me," he muttered. "After all you've told me, after all you've demanded of me. It's not fair."

Deep silence erupted in the courtyard. Around them, Norman sensed expectant eyes darting between him and Alexander—between the great messiah and his destined successor—frightened and confused.

Alexander squeezed his shoulder, his eyes on the crowd, wary, and stepped back. "We'll be back," he whispered. "I promise." He turned away, leaving Norman slouched, alone.

Soon after, the klaxon sounded and the gate squealed open. Norman stared at the ground, his head swimming. It was only after the sound of clattering hooves kicked up that he was spurred forth a final time. "Why would you leave us—your friends, your family—to chase a group of thugs?" he cried at Lucian's retreating back. His voice shook. "What's wrong with you—with the both of you?" He rounded on Alexander. "I deserve to know. You'll tell me, or I'll find out. Somehow I'll find out. Someday soon, you'll tell me just what the hell happened!"

Neither of them looked back, yet he thought he saw them stiffen upon their saddles. Then they were racing away along the street to the sound of thundering hooves, turned the corner, and were gone from sight.

Marek led the remainder in their wake. The courtyard emptied within the minute, and the klaxon rang out once more, again followed by the gate's squeal.

Norman stared at where they'd been moments before, open-mouthed. It took him some time to notice Allison's hand clasped around his wrist.

"Come on," she said, "let's get you something to eat. You need to get your strength back."

"You don't want to go with them," Richard said. "They'll be searching the city all day. You can't be doing with that kind of thing. Sit this one out, huh? You need to rest up."

Norman ignored them both, turning back towards the stables. Despite the steady pulse of the mass of nerve endings that his chest had become, he marched from the courtyard at a dogged pace. They shadowed him silently from then on, saying nothing, but remaining by his side nonetheless. He didn't know where he was going. Didn't care. He just had to get away.

Allison's hand was still clutched around his wrist. "Are you going to be alright?" she said.

Norman felt a pang of shame wash over him. "Yes," he said, "I'll be fine."

Her silence indicated that she wasn't convinced, but she didn't contradict him. Richard also seemed to take the message, and remained silent.

Despite Norman's efforts to appear calm, a nigh-unstoppable bubble of all-out panic was rising in his gut. He knew that the pain was addling his mind, but could do nothing to stop it. In moments it would spill over, and he would lose control.

He turned to them both as his throat began to close. "Would you mind bringing breakfast here?" he said. He forced a smile to his lips, barely stifling a scream of hysteria. "You're right: I just need to get my strength back. But I don't know if I can manage the stairs right now."

Their eyes softened; his shame deepened. "Of course," Allison said gently, patting his arm and leading Richard away at great speed. She glanced back sometime later, her eyes warm, yet forlorn.

Norman remained still—though his muscles were breaking out in spasms—until they were out of sight, maintaining the impression of awaiting their return. It was only after they'd passed into the tower lobby that he collapsed against the stable wall, tearing at his shirt, rubbing his chest with desperate jerks. The burning was fierce, enough to knock the wind from his lungs. "I'm fine," he wheezed.

He'd been abandoned. After being hounded for so long to be somebody he wasn't, somebody he would never be, he'd been discarded at the first sign of weakness.

They'd told him every day since the cradle to believe it was his destiny to lead, to continue the elders' work, to lead them all back into the light when the time was right.

But now he saw that he was but a pawn. In the end, they'd all been ready to cast him aside at a moment's notice.

"I'm fine...," he muttered, sliding down the wall until he sat on the grass, wreathed in shadow. "I'm fine. I'm fine..."

XXIV

Robert crouched low to the ground. A bead of sweat hung from his chin, trembling in the breeze. Further rivulets ran the height of his face, following the contours of frown lines and crow's-feet.

He studied the ground, adding minute detail to the mental map of the hillside forming in his mind's eye, taking note of the tiniest landmarks, picking out every bent blade of grass, every broken twig.

The relative cool of the morning was being replaced by humid gales, which caressed the hillside as the sky grew paler. He sensed stifling heat building behind the horizon. Intuition and experience told him that, once the sun had risen in earnest, it would be unbearable in the open.

He would have to move fast. He couldn't afford to miss a sign because of heat fatigue.

At the sound of snuffling, he stood and turned. Canterbury was spread out below. The brilliant white spires of the cathedral undulated behind building heat waves, cast alight in the early dawn light by mobile floodlights—the only lights they'd managed to get going before sunrise.

From here, he could see a few dozen people working away in the fields, tiny ant-like figures scrabbling amidst a sea of youthful wheat stalks. Only those few had dared brave the streets; the rest had barricaded themselves in their homes, joined a guard patrol, or taken flight to the cathedral.

A few metres away, Sarah sat astride her elderly, anserine chestnut mare—the smallest of the Friesian crop in the city's stables, the only mount she'd ever been able to ride with confidence—which looked very much like a Shetland pony beside Robert's mount. Due to his size, he rode one of their precious Shire horses: an obsidian stallion named Zodiac, nineteen hands tall, birthed by his father's hand, a trusted friend since childhood.

Robert kept one eye on her, ready to take her reins at any moment. She'd been unsteady since leaving the stables, and had almost fallen several times. If the horse gathered any momentum up here then the pair of them would go hurtling down the hillside.

It detracted only slightly from his level of concentration, but he feared it might be just enough to make him miss that all-important shred of evidence.

Yet she had insisted. Her bout of rage the night before hadn't dissipated as he'd hoped. After over an hour of fretting and agonising, she had agreed to let him leave the house—so long as she went with him.

There hadn't been time to argue it out. He couldn't leave her feeling abandoned and terrified, yet he had to get to the hills. Against his better judgement, he'd relented.

He scratched the back of his head and peered into the depths of the forest at the hill's summit. His line of sight beyond the tree line was blocked by a thick screening of boughs and branches, beyond which anybody could stand and study them with ease.

Unnerved, trying to ignore the flesh crawling on the back of his neck, he turned his attention back towards the ground. The soil had been moved recently. The disturbance was subtle, scattered, almost undetectable even to his eyes—but it was there.

"Have you found something?" Sarah said.

Robert glanced at her over his shoulder. "I'm not sure." He stood, dusting his knees, and headed back towards Zodiac. Once there, making sure that Sarah's gaze was directed towards the city, he raised a duffel bag from the mount's thigh, revealing the long barrel of a high-calibre rifle—a deadly talisman that warded away some of the prickling upon his neck.

But his talisman hadn't come direct from the lock-up. It had come from under his bed.

According to one of their few enforced laws, nobody was allowed to keep a personal firearm. He himself had suggested it in the first place. In times gone by, he would have put his instincts aside to make a good example.

But Sarah had changed that.

After Norman had been attacked, he'd taken it from the armoury. It had taken a great deal of care to ensure that its absence went unnoticed. Each weapon was engraved with a registration number, and a log was made of acquisitions and returns. Fixing the numbers had been difficult, and only possible because of the increased threat level.

At the time he'd felt as though he was crossing a line—going back on everything he'd worked for over the years—but now he was certain that he'd been wise to do it.

He rested the duffel bag back against Zodiac's leg. "Has anybody been up here recently? Travellers from away? Foraging parties? Kids playing?"

"No," Sarah said. Her eyes were still on the city. "I don't think so."

Robert looked upon the tree line once more as he saddled up, keeping a hand near the duffel bag, ready. "Okay," he said, "let's go."

*

The screech of crickets was deafening, occasionally punctured by the squawk of a passing bird. The clearing's grass towered five feet high, protected from sheep or deer by an encircling shell of beech and oak. The underbrush had grown thick, with nettles and thorns interlacing the ferns and drowning ruined colonies of lavender.

It had taken Robert and Sarah over ten minutes to fight their way through, led only by a sliver of light shining through the canopy, flat on their stomachs. They had advanced by the inch, so that their rustling had been obscured by the din of cricket song.

Now the sun beat down on them from directly overhead, an orange fireball blazing without mercy. The grass was damp, the air between the blades stifling and stale, earthy in taste and lacking in oxygen. Even breathing had become a burden.

Beside him, Sarah's face was creased into a fierce mask of determination, rouge at the cheeks. Curled locks of hair clung to her crown and lay lifeless upon her shoulders, dark with sweat, and her robes were streaked with grime, clinging to her skin. Her breathing had become laboured, and she looked somewhat dazed. But she hadn't made a single complaint.

The forest had been too thick to ride this far, and so they had left their mounts tied to a tree. Robert had made sure to position them facing downhill, so that a quick getaway could be made, should they need one.

"What do you think?" Sarah whispered. Her eyes were wide, fixed on the sights ahead.

Nestled in the valley below was a small collection of buildings, laced with ragged concrete and rusted iron girders. Its borders had become shrouded by vines and a thick spattering of buckler ferns, but Robert still dared to wager that the complex had once been a remote business park of some kind.

The central building, an ugly maroon-bricked tower block, was nearing its end. The exterior walls on the upper levels had fallen away, taking with them cabling, piping and myriad office-room clutter. The resultant wreckage lay in the grass below, forming a rubble field that stretched for almost a hundred feet in every direction. In the harsh light of day, the building was rendered bare and cold, its cracked, grey pallor unwelcoming.

Running along the edge of the complex, beyond a small car park, was what remained of a chain-link fence, some ten feet high. Creepers had woven between the wire, obscuring its outline and engorging its apparent size. Heavily rusted in many places and torn away completely in others, it offered no protection to the complex's borders now.

Sarah shifted in the shallow well her body had created in the grass. She started forwards on her elbows, but succeeded only in digging herself deeper into the stinking mud.

"What are you doing?" Robert hissed. He pointed to the blades of grass above their heads, which were undulating at her every move.

"I can't see," she answered, squinting and darting her head back and forth. She jostled for a few seconds more, during which time Robert's gesticulations became ever more adamant, and the grass continued to sway.

He maintained his gaze upon her until her face had grown sheepish and her head still. He glanced down at the building, back to her questioning face, and then shook his head. "Nothing's moving," he whispered.

"Then why are we lying down?"

"We don't know who's down there. We have to wait until we're sure."

She cursed under her breath, pulling clods of sodden fabric away from her body. He watched her face scintillate with restless energy, and smiled despite himself.

"How much longer? I can't breathe down here."

Robert took another look at the building, seeing nothing of interest other than the outer door teetering in the lacklustre breeze. "I don't know," he said. "A little longer."

He made to shunt the duffel bag forwards with the utmost delicacy, but winced as Sarah turned her head to watch, blinded by a ray of reflected light from the rim of her spectacles. "Take those off, will you?" he muttered.

Sarah's eyes grew forlorn, and her head slid down to make contact with the ground. "I'm sorry." She paused. "I'm not like you. I can't do this. I shouldn't have followed you."

Her skin was now showing the first signs of sunburn, the delicate pallor of her thighs and upper arms taking on an angry pinkish glow. A lifetime with her nose in books had robbed her of any protection from the sun's rays.

He reached out, chancing an errant rustle, and gripped her arm. "It's okay."

They would have to leave. He'd get her back to the city and return to the clearing later with reinforcements. All they had to do was clear up a little recon now, and then at least the journey would not have been wasted.

He assessed the complex afresh as flies buzzed about his head. He was almost certain that this was the very same office building that the injured boy—Charlie—had mentioned. This was where he'd been held prisoner. And others had been held here too, entire enslaved families. Perhaps the nerve centre of the mysterious coalition Norman had spoken of. If this was indeed the place, they would have gained a major tactical advantage: they would have made the first step towards mounting an effective resistance.

If it was empty then they could set a watch and surprise the enemy when they returned. If it was occupied, they could saddle up every volunteer and storm the entire complex. Troublesome they might be, but a few marauders couldn't stand up to a hundred-strong cavalry charge. They could rid themselves of this scourge.

The tower block's door slammed against the outer wall, caught in a sudden gust of wind. He ducked instinctively, but forced his head back up and focused on the distant doorway. All was still. The wind died, and the door settled, squeaking.

Then a shadow moved inside. It was a mere blur of darkness against the concrete floor, but it sent a shiver down his spine nonetheless.

The heat suddenly seemed far away, the insects' chorus a distant nuisance. The doorway became scarred on his retinas, and he saw its frame even when he blinked, cast in glowing greens and neon purples.

The movement came again soon after. The shadow—that of a slouching man—slid across the floor beneath the open doorway. It was positioned some way inside, but from Robert's raised vantage point he could see some two metres into the building.

He froze in place and scanned the meadow by swivelling his eyes in their sockets, determined not to make a further sound. If the tower block *was* occupied then there might be others lying in wait, or patrolling the surrounding areas. The last thing he needed now was to be spotted because of his own carelessness.

Beside him, he sensed that Sarah hadn't noticed this turn of events. Her head still rested upon her arms. Sweat now ran in rivulets down her back, and she breathed laboriously in the heat. For the time being, Robert was glad for her exhaustion. As long as she remained as she was, they would most probably remain unseen.

The pair of legs passed the door again, stepping around debris and plant matter scattered on the floor. Robert almost cringed when the tip of a rifle barrel swung into view.

Moments later, another man came around the corner from behind the tower block, twirling a stunted pistol in his hand: a grizzled old goat with unkind Hispanic features and a long, grey beard. His skin was tanned a uniform bronze, weathered and pockmarked, and one arm was tarnished by deep scars that snaked from elbow to shoulder. Patrolling the edge of the rubble field, he didn't bother to look beyond the bounds of his path, making for a poor guardsman. Yet Robert wasn't fooled, sensing danger in the man's brutal face and lumbering gait.

Inside the doorway, the pair of legs passed into view again. This time they moved fast, with purpose. A few moments later a resounding clatter emanated from within the tower block.

Sarah jumped as though electrocuted. Robert reached for her arm to steady her, once again risking a stray rustle. She looked at him with wide eyes, but yielded under his soothing grasp, and settled back into the grass.

The banging grew louder, now accompanied by shouting. It sounded as though several people were fighting inside, and more were joining the battle by the moment.

The Hispanic man stood very still. He glanced about himself, then trained his gaze upon the wall closest to him, head cocked, listening. The pistol hung lame in his grasp, the hand twitching near the safety catch.

A single resounding rumble brought the scuffling inside to an abrupt end, leaving in its wake a deathly silence.

"What's going on?" Sarah whispered.

"Shhh." Robert didn't take his eyes from the Hispanic guard. "I'm not sure."

The guard remained frozen beyond the rubble field, patient and calculating despite his brutish visage.

The doors of the tower block flew open as a group of men burst outside. Two bore automatic rifles and sported dark, lank hair, their faces cruel and grimed. The other three stumbled some way ahead, arms folded behind their heads, unarmed, backing away. Those in the former group were dressed in ragged, shapeless shawls, while the latter were clad in somewhat cleaner work shirts and dungarees.

Two of the unarmed men were babbling, falling into a crouch before their captors, hands drawn up to their faces. Their companion stood erect and still, face set and expressionless, his blue shirt flapping in the wind. Even from a long way off, and with only the back of his head to go by, Robert could sense perseverant dignity and pride about him.

The Hispanic guard came striding forwards, his patience having vanished, waving his pistol and uttering rapid obscenities. He approached the two armed men and struck one of them across the head with the butt of the pistol without a break in his stride.

The three unarmed men glanced at each other, blinking in surprise. The Hispanic guard continued to berate the ragged pair, and struck them each a further two times. The unarmed men who had grovelled looked almost hopeful, but Robert saw a flicker of sorrow cross Blue Shirt's lips.

The armed pair threw off the Hispanic guard's assault with a barrage of their own obscenities, gesturing towards their prisoners with their rifle barrels.

The Hispanic guard turned slowly to the unarmed men and cocked his head; an almost childlike curiosity had infected his manner. Robert's gut twisted at the sight of it. The guard then sauntered closer, skirting around them, and said a few words. His voice was reduced to a near-inaudible hum by the intervening distance, but Robert picked up the tone: a faux-pleasant sigh far more sinister and blood-curdling than any bellow of rage.

The grovelling captors didn't answer, stood rigid—as one stands when confronted by a snarling hound—staring at the ground. Blue Shirt, meanwhile, hadn't moved. He still looked straight ahead, as though unaddressed.

The Hispanic guard nodded, as though to himself, and backed away. He and the ragged pair bickered with their backs turned while their prisoners waited in silence.

Sarah was tugging at Robert's cuff, her voice strangled and agonised. "What's going on?" She was once again darting her head back and forth, trying to see through the grass.

"They're just talking," Robert said, eyeing her carefully. He was now very aware of the rifle beneath him. He sensed that he should have it ready, as there wouldn't be time to prepare when the standoff broke. At least he'd positioned it so that it was easily accessible. Careful not to make a single rustle, keeping each motion fluid, he released the barrel from the duffel. Its size made it impossible to hide from Sarah any longer.

Her sudden outburst caught him off guard, and he almost lashed out, thinking her an assailant. He winced as she dug her nails into his shoulder and let loose an angry spiel from between gritted teeth.

He whirled, glaring. With as much delicacy as he could muster, he removed her arm from his shoulder, observing the blood welling up in the fingernail-shaped puncture marks in his skin. "Be quiet," he hissed.

He turned away, flipped up the tripod, and slid the barrel's length into the grass until the scope was positioned before his face.

"What are you doing? We can't, Robert. There are only two of us."

"I'm not doing anything. We're just here to watch. I promise."

"But we can't just let this happen, we have to help them. We have to go for help."

"We can't. We'll be spotted."

A pause. "They're going to be killed, aren't they?"

He swallowed. "I think so."

He tried to ignore the stifled noise in her throat, and peered through the scope. The men below ballooned to five times their previous size, revealing minute details that even Robert's hawk eyes hadn't been able to pick up before.

Sarah didn't answer, but he could feel her eyes burning a hole into the side of his head.

Shame festered in the seat of his loins. But not for a moment would he consider risking her. Not ever. If saving them meant living with the knowledge that she might have died through his doing, he'd watch them die a thousand times over.

The captors were now more animated in their speech, and the conversation was becoming heated. They hadn't bothered to glance over their shoulders to check on their prisoners for some time.

One of the men who had grovelled took a step forwards. He started babbling once more, hands clasped together, outstretched. Then he stumbled forth as his voice broke and he began whimpering, falling limp and cowering, as though recognising his terrible mistake.

The Hispanic guard turned to him, looking genuinely shocked at such audacity. He surged forwards, screaming, and began beating indiscriminately, sending both grovelers to the floor and plunging his fist into Blue Shirt's gut, doubling him up.

Sarah's exhalations shuddered. "What's happening?" she breathed.

Robert didn't answer. Though she didn't have the best vantage point, he knew that she'd caught at least a glimpse of it. And a glimpse would have been more than enough to see just how grave the situation was.

The three armed men by now stood before their prisoners, unmoving. Their weapons now seemed more obvious, more significant.

The prisoners visibly realised their imminent fate. They cringed unanimously and stepped back. The two who had begged before began in earnest now, sinking lower to the ground as they pleaded in high-pitched wails.

Sarah caught Robert's arm in an iron-fisted grip. He could feel her shaking. "Robert," she breathed. "Robert, kill them."

"What?"

"Kill them."

"They'll know we're here." The rifle wasn't silenced, and in the valley the sound of any gunshot would travel for some distance. If there were more men inside—and he suspected there were—shooting these three would be a deadly mistake.

"Well, do *something*." Her fingers dug into his shoulder with shocking strength, enough to make him wince.

"I can't."

"They're going to die unless we do something!"

"I know."

He could feel her eyes on him, and sighed. In any other circumstance, he wouldn't have hesitated. In fact, he was fairly certain that if he'd been alone, he would have intervened long before now.

But he wasn't alone, and his feelings hadn't changed. He would watch them die, if he had to. It would haunt him—the callousness of it would forever be a blight on his memory—but at the same time he knew it was indisputably just.

The Hispanic guard now approached one of the two grovelling men and flicked his pistol towards the floor in a quick motion. The meaning was unmistakable: Kneel.

The man responded by redoubling his pleading. Soon after, his companion joined him.

The three armed men shook their heads. One of them laughed openly. They waved their weapons at the ground imperiously.

Still, the two grovelled. Only Blue Shirt remained upright, his face grim.

The guards' amusement soon waned. The Hispanic then strode forwards, grasping the wailing pair by their collars and yanking them to the ground.

"Robert," Sarah hissed. Her voice was wooden, without intent, seeking comfort rather than attention.

Robert didn't look away. All his attention was focused on steadying the scope's crosshairs, each movement cold and fluid. Despite his certainty that he would watch—just let it all happen—he reached forwards and adjusted the magnification, bringing the Hispanic's head into sharp focus. Just in case.

Blue Shirt was still standing proud, staring at the tower block wall. He didn't acknowledge the guards' orders, or even their presence.

The Hispanic guard approached him, looking him up and down. The grey moustache above his lip bristled as his eyes constricted to fine slits. Then he spoke softly, a sibilant hiss of ill intent. Robert didn't need to hear the words to know what was coming.

Blue Shirt didn't answer. He still gave no indication of recognising anybody around him.

Then a scream rang out from the tower block, a feminine shriek laden with weeping shudders. Scuffling and grunts also issued from within, but were almost unnoticeable beside the volume of her piercing voice.

Blue Shirt's trance broke immediately. He surged forth, calling back to her, raising his arms, his set expression having dissolved into a mask of horror. Yet when he spoke, his voice was soothing, affectionate—dulcet tones of reassurance.

She answered, her cries interlaced with sobbing. She sounded young—Robert wouldn't have guessed any older than twenty.

Blue Shirt replied, his voice having exhausted its reassuring powers. He came to a staggering halt and hung his head, staring at the floor. He was shaking. Robert saw his shuddering shoulders and rapidly clenching-unclenching fists, and knew that his nerve had broken.

Through the scope, he saw the Hispanic's face crease into a wicked expression of satisfaction as he gripped Blue Shirt's collar and tugged him to the ground.

Blue Shirt, however, resisted. He threw off the Hispanic's grip and managed to land a single punch on his captor's face before being restrained by the ragged pair.

The woman still called out from inside, wailing with such pain and fear that Robert's chest felt as though a dagger had been thrust through it. Sarah whimpered beside him, cursing.

The Hispanic man roared, blood flying from his lips, waving the nose of his pistol and stalking forwards, striking Blue Shirt across the face with the sharp edge of the butt. An arc of crimson opened on Blue Shirt's face, right down to the cheekbone, exposing a streak of white.

"Why are they doing this?" Sarah shrilled.

Robert didn't dare look away now. The Hispanic visibly inflated as he took a deep breath, as though steeling himself. Then he raised his pistol, aimed at one of the grovelling prisoners, and squeezed the trigger.

The gunshot was deafening. It tore along the valley walls, returning from every direction in repeating echo, throwing a flock of birds from their nests in the nearby forest, scattering them into sky.

The prisoner flopped onto his side without a sound and landed in a heap amidst the dirt-streaked rubble, his hand twitching. The back of his head had been completely obliterated.

The woman inside let loose a spiel of unconstrained screams, choking on her own sobs. There were other voices in the building now, male and female. The sound of movement inside built as it had done before. Dozens of voices were suddenly ringing out, accompanied by as many sources of disturbance.

The Hispanic ignored the tower block, looking coldly at the remaining beggar. He dispatched him before a single plea could be made. The bullet caught the prisoner dead between the eyes. He fell beside his comrade, his arms splayed melodramatically across a jagged lump of concrete.

Sarah cried into Robert's shoulder, gripping his sleeve. Robert's curses intermingled with hers as he watched the Hispanic turn to his last prisoner.

Blue Shirt had struggled to his feet, and was staring forward once more. Though his eyes were wide, he trembled only slightly—it was only with the aid of the scope that Robert could see his shuddering knees. He called out to the woman, his voice raised over the increasing racket inside.

The message was apparently not to her liking; she immediately responded with an all-consuming screech of heartbreak.

The Hispanic raised his pistol to his last victim, a despicable smirk running rampant across his cruel features.

In his last moment, Blue Shirt's mouth drew tight, and he closed his eyes. He jerked as the gunshot exploded along the valley, plummeting straight down instead of falling backwards like the others. There, he lay still.

The Hispanic assessed the three corpses before him with a distinct air of satisfaction. He remained there as the ragged pair stepped forward to loot the bodies, simply staring. The murderous tool in his hand seemed to have been forgotten, hanging loose by his side.

Sarah pounded the dirt with her fist. Her sobbing was now an ugly concoction of furious snarling and muddled obscenities.

"We couldn't have done anything," Robert said. His voice ill-matched his wavering conviction.

She didn't stop beating at the ground until he gripped her arm and hissed, "*Quiet!*"

The ragged pair retreated to the tower block, leaving the bodies half-stripped. The disturbance inside was now more akin to the din of a full-scale riot. The wailing woman shrieked when a dull thud rang out, followed by a sound that dredged distilled dread from Robert's heart, one that unhinged his jaw and drew a gasp from his throat. Even the old Hispanic froze.

A baby was crying. Over the roar of dozens of screaming voices, it was unmistakable, sending Robert's stomach in a head dive for his boots.

He dropped the rifle and swung around, clamping his hand over Sarah's mouth just as she let forth a full-throated, anguished scream. He managed to stifle the body of it against his flesh, but he'd been just a moment too late to catch the initial piercing warble. He closed his eyes in dread as the noise broke out into the valley, rebounding from the valley walls for what seemed an eternity. Even the infant's wailing and the rancorous roar within the building failed to mask it.

Robert didn't need the scope to know that the Hispanic guard had heard. He had been hurrying inside, no doubt to quell the raging insurgence that awaited him. Now he stood perfectly still, facing the tower block door.

Sarah fought against Robert's grasp with stunning strength. To keep hold of her, he'd have to hurt her, and he'd never risk doing that—not for one second. And so, with a curse, he loosened his grip, and she wriggled free. "The baby," she choked. "Oh my god, there's a baby down there." She was too smart to try to stand, but still she cried out.

Robert was forced to take hold of her once more. The beginnings of genuine panic coursed through him. She was going to get them killed. "What are you *doing*?"

"We can't just sit here!"

"We have to." Robert pushed her head close to the dirt, shielding her as best as he could from his awkward position. He held his breath, muscles tensed, ready to make his move.

The old Hispanic's attack came with stunning suddenness. He turned so fast that any movement was lost in a blur of ragged tunic—it appeared as though he had turned one hundred and eighty degrees in a single instant. Robert now stared down the barrel of his pistol.

He broke cover and leapt upon Sarah just as the grass began surging back and forth and clouds of dirt were kicked up by a searing volley of bullets. Sarah screamed beneath him, shuddering as he forced her further into the dirt with his bulk.

The riot inside the building was interrupted by an outbreak of machine-gun fire. Battle cries gave way to unbridled screaming. The volley of bullets stopped, and Robert chanced glancing up just in time to see the Hispanic turn his head ever so slightly, distracted.

A flash of rage arced behind Robert's eyes, and he dived for the rifle. He landed with such momentum that he and it were carried end-over-end through the grass as he swung the barrel around. The moment he came to a stop, his eyes reached the scope, and his finger came to rest against the trigger. Before he even had time to register the magnified image, he had fired. The rifle bucked in his hands, slamming into his shoulder.

He immediately knew that the old Hispanic had been killed. His torso had been reduced to chum, an amorphous mass of bright-red jelly. He didn't fall for several moments, just stood there with an expression of frank disbelief spreading across his face. Then he plummeted to the ground, as though pulled by unseen wires.

The machine-gun fire continued in the tower block as Robert cast the rifle aside and dived back on top of Sarah. Men and women were shrieking inside, screaming for their lives, but to no avail. The infant hadn't made a sound for some moments.

"Come on," he yelled, pulling Sarah up.

She struggled, wild-eyed, and for a moment tried to surge forth down into the valley.

Inside, the prisoners were still screaming. While the sound of droves being cut down rang out, Robert grappled with Sarah, certain that they were far too late. What might have been hundreds of voices had become no more than a few dozen in mere moments.

Robert grasped her around the waist, hauled her around in a half-arc, and planted her upon the other side of the summit. "Run!" he bellowed.

"*We can't just leave them—*"

"Go now. GO!"

Dragging her in tow, he ran for the safety of the trees. As he bounded over fallen logs and past snagging roots, pulling Sarah beyond the first sheltering trunk, he felt a dagger twist in his heart.

The screaming echoed in the valley long after they had reached their mounts.

FOURTH INTERLUDE

The baby had changed everything. The despair, hopelessness and apathy that had lingered since the End had finally broken, giving way to bouts of feverish activity, debate, and hope. The adults had started leaving Lucian in charge of James and the baby while they went on lengthy trips in search of others. They talked, argued and bartered with strangers, suddenly filled with a will to act, to *do something.*

Vim and enthusiasm were rife.

Alex and James, having for so long struggled with their crop field singlehandedly, were besieged by helping hands. With the added help, they'd managed to rear a respectable garden of tomatoes, onions, potatoes, and even a tiny patch of strawberries in a matter of weeks. Their cows now produced enough milk to consider selling the surplus; they planned to make it their foremost icebreaker once trade negotiations started with their far-flung neighbours.

Today, James had already received plenty of help. Agatha and Oliver had risen before sunrise with him and taken the herd out to pasture. Though they'd soon retreated back to bed, haggard and bleary-eyed, he'd been nigh delirious with joy to have had them by his side.

It was now mid-morning, and he was getting stuck into preparing the earth for a fresh batch of barley. He stood back for a moment to observe the turned soil, his chest swelling with pride, then went back to pruning weeds alongside Lucian—who, at nineteen, could still easily sleep most of the day away, but had taken to work nonetheless. The two of them would work until breakfast, after which Lucian would often stay out to tend the animals while James went away to the classroom.

"Why don't you come in?" James said.

Lucian shrugged. "I won't like it."

"You've never tried it."

Lucian looked uncomfortable. "I don't read very well. I'm not like you, kiddo. I don't have the brains."

"You can still learn," James protested. "Learning is—"

"—the only way to save the world," Lucian said. His tone was far from the mocking slur it had once been. He now recited the mantra automatically, with force and familiarity.

James smiled. "That's what Alex says."

A shuffling made the two look up from their work just in time to see Paul shuffle around the side of the house. His gut had swelled to a size that could have rivalled Helen's at the height of her pregnancy, and he wobbled to and fro as he walked, his unshaven face bouncing atop his neck without control. A sickly smile grew on his face as he saw them and made a beeline for the crops, an ancient bottle of merlot swinging at his side.

"What you doing out 'ere, boys, eh?" he jeered, swinging the bottle to his lips. Most of the wine dribbled down his chin and splashed across the soil at his feet.

His drinking had taken yet another turn for the worse. The Sunday Mass with Agatha that he'd ritually clung to for their eleven years together had ended the night little Norman Creek had arrived. He no longer made any effort to help collect food or water, and disappeared for days on end, returning laden with rare alcohol and myriad injuries.

The boys didn't answer. He didn't press them or repeat himself, but James could feel his gaze on the back of his neck. He worked faster and kept his eyes on the ground, hoping that Paul would become bored and drift away. Instead, he lingered to watch them work, swigging away.

"Working in your fields, destiny child?" Paul said, laughing with great shuddering heaves. "Eh, destiny boy? You working to save us all, are you?"

James said nothing, feeling blood rush to his face until his cheeks glowed red-hot. Lucian hushed him and nudged him onwards, urging him to work faster still.

Paul receded into a deep silence, breathing with the harsh raggedness of inebriation, wobbling back and forth by several metres with each pacing stride. "It's over," he said eventually. His voice was low and laced with the tiniest of emotions, but James couldn't tell which.

Before he could think, wracked by a jolt of sympathy, he'd already replied, "What?"

He instantly recognised his mistake, and barely reacted to the impact of Lucian's fist against his shoulder, knowing full well that he'd doomed them both.

"Our time is up," Paul boomed. They both jumped at the sudden roar of his voice. "*Tribulation is at an end!*"

James and Lucian shared a glance, rose slowly to their feet and backed away as his face grew red and he began roaring, swinging the bottle above his head. A sudden, genuine panic threatened to break James's nerve.

Paul pointed a finger squarely in his direction as his eyes grew narrow and he bared his teeth. Saliva flew from his swollen lips. "The Antichrist is among us!" he screamed, stamping on the crops as he advanced, ripping up the stalks of tomato plants, cursing, "Rotten, stinking things!"

James stumbled back, but Paul was on him in moments.

"It's all your fault. You're Him—you'll kill us all!"

James blinked as Lucian threw himself between them, his fists raised. He made to strike at the drunkard, but his hand became lost in the all-encompassing palms of the enormous man. Before James could move an inch, Lucian had been lifted bodily into the air and sent sprawling in the dirt. There was a resounding thrum as his head struck the iron weed bucket. He moved no more.

James cowered, crying out and backpedalling towards the fence as Paul cast the wine bottle aside, his hands formed into outstretched talons. His chest shuddered with fright when his back made contact with the fence. There was nowhere to run. "Please, don't," he cried, scrabbling at the wood.

"Cursed boy!" Paul roared. He raised his fist, bearing down with murderous rage.

But his strike never came, because it was at that moment that another fist collided with his jaw, soaring in from somewhere over James's shoulder. Paul staggered sideways and fell into the dirt.

James blinked and let his arms drop, revealing Alex standing above him. His eyes were void of all but seething fury. His chest rose and fell as he strode forward and hauled Paul to his feet, hauling him up with apparent ease. He wrenched the drunkard around, manhandling him as though he was no more than a rag doll, striking him again and again.

Paul spat blood into Alex's face. Alex dropped him with a grunt.

Paul took the opportunity to crawl to his feet and stumble away. Then he'd taken hold of a pitchfork and swung around, his face a shade of puce, his eyes alight with feral malice. He advanced on Alex, who backed away on his haunches, hands raised.

"*Alex!*" James screamed. He made to surge forward, but Alex waved him back, his expression desperate. James hesitated, and cried out. There was nothing he could do.

"Dirty bunch of sinners!" Paul hissed and swung the pitchfork, bearing down on Alex with intent to maim.

The deafening roar of a gunshot, resounding and sudden, made them all duck. A flock of swallows exploded from a nearby thicket, filling the skies with wheeling silhouettes.

Oliver approached from afar with a rifle held tight against his shoulder, aiming straight at Paul's chest. His long coat was aflutter in the wind, his lazy eye was squinted shut, and the other was pressed against the rifle's sights. "Keep still, Paul," he called.

Paul froze, the pitchfork still held aloft, his eyes wide. He watched Oliver approach while Agatha and Hector came sprinting out from the house. Surrounded, with all eyes on him and with James cowering at his feet, he appeared to shrink and wither. "Where'd you get a gun?" he growled.

Oliver kept his gaze steady, coming to a stop at a distance appropriate to correct his line of fire, should it be necessary. "There's plenty lying around, if you know where to look," he said. There was no friendliness, familiarity, or emotion in his tone. His gaze was hard and watchful.

"Hector!" Helen cried from inside. "What's going on?"

Hector threw a hand up. "Stay inside. Don't bring the baby over here."

"Paul," Agatha hissed, agape. "What're you doin'?"

Paul gestured to James accusingly, as though pointing alone was sufficient to justify his actions.

James couldn't help flinching. Embarrassment coursed his veins as a whimper escaped his lips.

Agatha's eyes flitted from Paul to James, then to Lucian's static body, and finally the pitchfork, still hanging over Paul's head. She shook her head, almost imperceptibly. Behind her tense expression, James thought he could see deep disappointment—maybe pain.

"Tell 'em!" Paul yelled. Tears had formed in his eyes. "Tell 'em, Aggie! Tell 'em that it's Him!" He pointed his talons at James once more. His finger wavered wildly.

"He's jus' a boy," Agatha said.

"We talked about it, you and me! We talked about how this was our fault, how it was us being punished!"

Agatha's face remained blank, though a flicker of shame lingered on her brow. "All tha's changed with the baby. I don't believe tha' God would let a baby be born into this if it was nough' but punishment."

"The baby!" Paul laughed hysterically. "That baby's probably another one of *them*. Like *Him!*" he roared, rounding on James.

Agatha said nothing. She took a step back, causing Paul to gasp, his eyes suddenly wide and terrified. As she continued to back away, he took a step forward, dropping the pitchfork to the ground, his arm stretched out towards her.

"Aggie," he wailed. Fat tears spilled onto his unshaven cheeks.

Agatha shook her head and backed away still. Only when Oliver approached, ready to shoot, did Paul stop his advance. He whirled on the spot, staring around at them all, and appeared to shrink further. He now looked no more significant than a squirming child. He began to whimper quietly.

Watching him, James lost all power to describe his feelings. The closest he could get: a dash of sympathy, engulfed by an all-consuming hatred. He wanted to lash out, kick, bite and stamp, yet a strange lump had formed in his throat at the sight of the defeated creature.

Alex took a step forward. His gaze was even harder than Oliver's. "Leave," he said.

Paul didn't move for a while, while his eyes softened and grew wider. Then his lower lip began to quiver. "Where will I go?" he muttered.

Alex shook his head.

Paul took a step forward, unhindered by Oliver's warning, and clutched at Alex's coat with wringing hands. "Alex, please, don't."

Alex took a step back, but Paul followed, grasping and pleading.

"Don't make me go."

Alex shook his head.

Paul made to step towards the house, but Alex stepped aside to block his way. Again, Paul clutched at Alex's coat. "M-My things," he stuttered.

Again, Alex shook his head.

Paul stepped back, shrinking still, until his back was arched and he looked up at them all with one hand clasped over the other, his eyes red and puffy, his face sodden with tears and mucus.

"I don't have nowhere to go," he said. His voice cracked at the sentence's end. He looked to the others for help, seeking sympathy with waterlogged eyes.

But Hector was silent, and Oliver remained stoic, the rifle raised. Agatha's mouth was agape, and her own tears flowed across her cheeks. But she said nothing, and Paul's shoulders slumped.

Then he began to turn towards James. But before his gaze could reach him, Alex snarled, "Don't you dare look at him."

Paul froze, took a last sweeping look around at them all, and then—to James's shock—began to nod with sudden sobriety. He staunched his whimpering for long enough to mutter, "I'm sorry."

Nobody said anything. He looked forlornly at the house, and then began to shuffle towards the faraway road, hands clutched together.

Hector and Oliver watched him go until none of them could hear his sobbing any longer, then disappeared inside. Agatha and Alex went to Lucian, roused him, and pulled him to his feet. He looked dazed and his speech was slurred—James's heart skipped a beat at the sight of his lolling jaw—and so they carried him inside.

James, however, stood and watched Paul go until he was nothing more than a speck upon the horizon, slowly shuffling through the long grass. James knew there was nothing out there, not that way, not a stream to drink from, nor a single fruit-bearing tree. As he watched him go, though the knot in his throat refused to loosen, the fury in his gut matured, and grew.

*

Dinner was a quiet affair. Nobody ate with any enthusiasm, poking at their soup. Not a single conversation was struck up. They each remained at the table for long enough to take a few bites, then announced a loss of appetite.

With the Creeks tending to little Norman, and Lucian resting with a concussion, guarded against sleep by a watchful Oliver, the remaining three sat with their bowls pushed aside, twiddling their fingers.

James swallowed the last of his own soup with difficulty, glancing between Alex and Agatha, trying not to make a sound with the clink of his spoon. The silence in the kitchen was stretched tight as the drying deer hide on the back step.

Alex tapped the tabletop and stared into the candlelight with an ugly expression on his face. He hadn't said a word, nor moved from the table, since that morning.

James watched him for as long as he could bear, while the bulge in his throat grew larger still, then muttered, "You shouldn't have made him go away."

Alex started and glanced at James, as though surprised to see him. "What?" he said. The ugly expression on his lips was squeezed into a polite smile.

"You shouldn't have sent him away." James's voice didn't shudder as it had at first. Now anger had taken hold. Every fibre in his body wanted him to leap up onto the table, to shout and scream.

The polite smile on Alex's face slipped away as fast as it had come, replaced by a deep frown. "I had to," he whispered.

"He's going to get lost."

"He can't stay here, James." Alex sighed and slouched back. "He's dangerous, as much to us as himself."

"We can't just send him away!" James yelled. His chair flew back with a squeal, and then he was on his feet, fists clenched. The rage he felt for Paul came pouring out, directed instead at Alex. "He can't find food, water. He'll die."

Alex's tone remained even, but James saw his jaw tighten. "James, Paul isn't like the men you've read about in your stories. He's ill. He *would* have killed you."

"He'll starve out there, and you're just going to let him. You bastard!"

"*James!*" Agatha hissed. Open-mouthed, she drew her fingertips to her lips.

James paused. He blinked, then looked down at his clenched fists. The rage drained away at the sight of her, pooling down in his legs. He sighed, looked back to Alex, and pleaded, "If we're supposed to be saving the world, then how can we leave him? Aren't people like him the ones we're trying to save?"

Alex straightened. He said nothing. The ugly purse to his lips returned as he exchanged a look with Agatha. Then he began tapping the tabletop with his finger once more. "Bed time," he muttered.

"But—"

"Go to bed, James." Alex didn't raise his voice, but his brow had fallen low, and a dangerous rumble lurked at the back of his throat. He didn't turn to meet James's gaze.

James knew there would be no arguing.

He trudged away without another word and passed into the corridor. From the bedrooms he could hear the others whispering, but nobody came out to see what the commotion was about. He paused just beyond the kitchen threshold and hung in the shadows, listening.

"You're too hard on 'im," Agatha whispered.

Alex, loud and clear: "He's too young to understand."

"O' course he is—he's far too young to 'ave had to watch what happened today. But you can't leave 'im in the dark. If you want 'im to be the man he's goin' to have to be, you're goin' to have to let 'im live a real life. All he knows are words from books writ by dead men and women. It's all black and white to 'im, right and wrong, good and bad. We can't afford 'im to be like that."

"I'm trying to give him the best education that I can."

"Tha' won't be enough, Alex," Agatha hissed. "He's got to *live*. He has to feel and know wha' he's fighting for, not just be told tha' it's the right thing to do."

Alex sighed. "There's no time. There's never enough time."

A pause, then, "Sometimes I wonder if you put your dreams before 'im."

Neither of them said anything for a long time. Alex resumed drumming upon the tabletop.

James's heart hammered against the walls of his chest. His teeth were grinding together. He was desperate to run, to be gone from it all, and to forget that any of it had ever happened. Yet he stood his ground. He had to hear the last of it.

"I love that boy," Alex whispered.

"We all love 'im," Agatha said. "But do *you* love 'im more than that picture in your head?"

Alex didn't reply. Over a minute of silence ticked by, but the only sound emanating from the kitchen was the rattle of fingers upon the tabletop.

James slid away into the corridor, his gaze fixed on the floor. He entered his bedroom—still cluttered with myriad children's toys that he hadn't touched in years—and climbed into his bed without saying a word to Oliver or Lucian. He stared at the ceiling until morning.

*

They found Paul's body three days later, not far from the house, propped against the trunk of an old oak. His unseeing, dead eyes still bore traces of sadness. His body was slumped, an empty bottle of bourbon held in a claw-like grip. His legs, stuck out in front of him, were clad in only a thin pair of trousers.

He had been banished without a coat, undergarments, or socks, and died of exposure. James couldn't help imagining him looking over at the house, the drink dulling the cold, as he had slipped away.

Alex didn't speak for two weeks after his funeral.

For the first time in his life, James found himself doubting not only his destiny, but that of all things.

XXV

"I'm not going," Robert said. He'd just spent the last hour bringing Alexander and Lucian up to speed on what had happened in the forest. Now he'd retreated to his front doorstep and squeezed into the threshold so that he filled the entire doorway, determined not to give anybody so much as a hint of an invitation to follow.

"We need you," Lucian said.

Robert merely shook his head and repeated, "I'm not going. I'm staying right here." He paused, listening to the minute noises emanating from the living room. "We both are."

Twenty men on horseback had gathered in the street just beyond his garden gate. All of them now wore frowns of acute disquiet. Lucian and Alex stood only a few steps from his door, neither of them bothering to conceal their crestfallen expressions. They didn't argue or protest, but still they stared, planted to the spot.

"We don't know where to go," Lucian said.

"We've stationed everyone we could get up there." Robert looked over his shoulder at the ancient windup clock upon the wall. "The next changeover is at thirteen-hundred. I suggest you get up there and wait for them to break cover."

He leaned past the threshold so that the house no longer obstructed his line of sight, and pointed towards the hilltop. "Up there," he said.

Alex turned away without a further moment's pause. Lucian's brow flickered, and for a moment he looked close to saying something. Then he followed suit, shaking his head. They retreated to their mounts, their faces stolid, and wheeled to face along the street without a word of protest. Yet Robert sensed anger in the vehemence of their nods of salutation.

Lucian led the group away without looking back. The rumble of hooves upon muddied tarmac filled Main Street, heading for the city's edge.

Alex, meanwhile, lingered beside the garden gate. "Lucian and I will be heading back to London before dusk. I'm leaving everyone under your command." His eyes were hard as diamonds, devoid of any trace of charm. Here was the real Alexander, without his mask, the man behind the messiah. Robert knew that he was one of the few people who would ever see it. His voice was cold and harried. "Things in London aren't good. We might not be able to get back. I need you to hold the fort."

Robert bit back a hasty retort. There were people counting on him. "I'll do my part."

"Are you sure you're up to the job?"

"Is there anybody else?"

Alex's gaze flickered. His mask had already returned, his voice wrangled back to an even keel. He cleared his throat. "Good luck."

With that, he kicked at his mount's sides and raced after the others.

Robert retreated inside once he was out of sight and hurried back to the living room. Every candle in the house had been lit and flung into myriad corners. The sheer number made the room seem ablaze, lining its periphery, balanced upon books and teetering on the mantelpiece.

Sarah's voice sounded from the room's depths, hollow and toneless. "Are they gone?"

He caught sight of her figure amidst the sofa's shadows, her knees drawn up to her chin, rocking back and forth. Her eyes were fixed on the fire in the grate, wide and unblinking. She had barely spoken since he'd dragged her from the forest; hadn't eaten, nor slept, despite Heather's insistence that she rest.

"Yes." He manoeuvred around candle-laden trestles and discarded comforters, trying to reach her. The stifling heat rose up in waves, bringing a film of perspiration out on his skin before he could take even a few steps.

Heather sat with her arm draped over Sarah's shoulder. He couldn't be sure, but he suspected that she'd been awake since the day before. From what he'd seen of the traffic flowing back and forth between Main Street and the clinic, she'd been dealing with clamouring patients without pause.

After the attack on the wind farm, people's curious range of ailments had increased tenfold. Most were headaches and muscle pains, while some complained of difficulty breathing. But nobody could fool even themselves. It was a thinly veiled exercise in seeking comfort in any way they could. Affecting a dicky hip was a small sin if it meant half an hour of attention and a sit-down with somebody who cared.

It was harmless, but still Robert admired her for holding out so long. Now she looked utterly defeated, her hair wispy and lank, her white coat splattered with sputum and other body fluids.

Robert came to a standstill beside them and gritted his teeth against the tense silence that followed. There was nothing to be done. They couldn't leave the house, not now, not even for some air. Everyone had been ordered to stay inside, like rats holed up in the floorboards beneath a tabby's basket. Yet he couldn't let them stagnate. They needed to keep moving, to maintain an even state of mind. "We should open the curtains," he said. "We're safe here."

Heather looked up at him, baggy-eyed and ashen-faced. "Not from what you've told us," she muttered.

Robert took a step closer to her, moving as delicately as his lumbering body would allow. "We're safe," he repeated. Despite being in awe of her steadfast work at the clinic, he was almost snarling through bared teeth. "I've got half the city on watch. Nobody's getting through."

He ambled over to where Sarah sat and crouched before her, taking her hands. Her deathly white palms were dwarfed by his, yet still he gasped at how cold they were—like slabs of ice. "Are you alright?" he said.

Sarah looked at him as though from very far away, as though she couldn't quite see him at all. She nodded, and attempted a smile, but her lips wobbled and tears seeped from the corners of her eyes. After a moment she fell forwards and threw her arms over him. She began to shake as soon as her head came to rest on his shoulder, muffling fresh sobs against his shirt.

He brushed her hair and hushed her as the fire crackled and the candles danced. "It's going to be fine," he whispered. As he spoke, though he would never show it, his own conviction withered. The wolves were circling closer, and now there was blood on the air.

XXVI

The thumping of twenty steeds' hooves upon hard soil, combined with as many war cries from the men astride them, echoed within the confines of the valley, amplified to a thunderous rumble. To anybody in the surrounding area, the party would have sounded ten times as large.

Alexander led the charge over the crest of the hill, rifle balanced atop his saddle. Six riders banked away to either side, while the rest stayed their course, following him into a headlong descent. The group enveloped the office complex, each rider poised to open fire at a moment's notice, orbiting the chain-link fence.

Yet, as they reached the valley floor and the horses' hooves ceased to resonate, the resultant silence was deafening. Not a thing stirred amongst the tower block's remains. The entire valley was still and quiet, dead as the darkest Old World wreckage.

Alexander blinked, casting wild glances around at the surrounding hilltops, half expecting to see their enemy lining the tree line, ready to strike. For a moment he cursed himself, convinced that he'd led them into a trap—

onto low ground, where they could be picked off without trouble.

But there was nobody there.

The others' war cries trailed off without dignity. They slowed to a canter, then a trot. Then each rider stopped dead and exchanged disconcerted glances with their neighbour.

Alex had been sure that they would be met by an immediate volley of defensive gunfire. But after a further minute of half-hearted circling, nothing had stirred. The building sat derelict, nestled amongst overgrown layers of nettles and ferns.

Quiet as a tomb.

Alexander called a halt, and any residual movement died away. As one, they stared at the main entrance, which had been riddled with ragged bullet holes. A small, crimson lump lay nestled in the grass before the doors, unmoving. Beside it was the unmistakable profile of a stunted pistol.

"What do you think?" Lucian said, close behind Alexander's shoulder.

"They're gone." Alexander urged his mount forwards with a kick of his spurs.

The other men followed suit cautiously. From every direction, they drew closer to the concrete walls. Alexander listened all the while with one ear cocked, and still heard nothing from within the building except for the monotonous whistle of a stray breeze.

But the hairs on his arms and the back of his neck stood on end all the same.

He and Lucian were the first to dismount. They alighted on tiptoes and flattened themselves against the edge of the building, beckoning for the others to follow. The ragged hole left in the tower block's side by its fallen wall was only feet away—a gaping, unstable maw that looked ready to collapse at any moment.

Alex approached it nonetheless. Taking a deep breath, he leapt up onto a slab of fallen concrete. His feet met the surface with an unexpected lack of traction, and he wobbled momentarily before pitching himself towards whatever lay beyond.

He landed with a hollow clatter, squinting amidst inky blackness, and managed to pick out the edges of what looked to be a stairwell. It was cool and damp. A pervading odour rose up in waves, musky but sweet, catching at the back of his throat.

Lucian had leapt in behind him by the time his eyes had begun to adjust, and he could see well enough to tell that they stood upon a narrow landing. One flight of stairs down was a rusted 'G', which he guessed indicated the ground floor. The flight above them, however, led to nowhere; the upper landing had fallen away along with the outer wall.

Down was the only way.

With a clatter, three more men joined them upon the crumbling platform. Elsewhere in the building they could hear similar clatters as the others invaded through alternate entrances. They descended towards the rusted 'G' and passed through the doorway beneath it. Beyond, the darkness seemed to grow only thicker.

Alex remained upon the threshold for some time, uncertain. Craning his neck, desperate to catch even the smallest detail, he placed his hand on the wall nearest to him for support, and cried out: it was slicked with something akin to treacle.

He drew his hand away, but it was too dark to see even his own palm. Cursing, he stepped through the doorway, nearly yelling in fright when his foot hooked on something lying across the threshold. Freezing in place, he stroked the trigger of his rifle while his eyes roamed the blackness, fumbling with a small torch attached to his belt.

"Think that's a good idea?" Lucian uttered. "If we're not alone, we'll be made."

Alex held the torch aloft. "There's nobody here," he said, and thumbed the switch. A beam of light burst from its tip and pooled against the wall ahead, revealing what lay before them.

Revealing horror incarnate.

"Jesus," Lucian whispered.

Every wall was dripping with streaks of blood, every surface, every pane of glass and rotten furnishing, contrasting to such an extreme with the grey walls and drab plywood that it seemed to scream out at them. Alex dipped the beam as fast as he could, but still the others' rush of gasps and bouts of disgusted gagging deafened him.

Turning the torch beam upon the floor, he saw that his foot was wedged beneath the torso of a young woman. Half her face was calm and untroubled, as though she merely slept. The other half had been cleaved away, right down to the naked skull.

A curious mixture of fury and paralysing shock came over him. He turned around as his stomach churned. As though from afar he heard the others retching and reeling away from the carpet of bodies that lay in every direction.

Other shafts of light were spearing into the darkness elsewhere on the ground floor as the other teams reached the lobby. Each revealed only more bodies, carved up and motionless on the ground.

From somewhere across the lobby, Lucian's voice rang out, "Anybody find any survivors?"

A few nauseated grunts issued from each corner. All reported in the negative. A series of booming footsteps heralded Lucian's approach. A moment later he was once again at Alexander's side. "Robert said they tried to fight back," he said, and shook his head. "Look at these people. They're wives. Kids. Old folks. They didn't stand a chance." He shone his own light on the girl at Alex's feet, and closed his eyes against the sight of her face. "These people were executed. None of them were armed."

He fumed. "They were kept here for"—he paused—"what, insurance?"

"That's what Charlie said."

"If they went through the trouble of enslaving all these families, how could they afford to kill them?"

"Maybe they were too much trouble. Either that, or it's an example."

"To whom?"

"To us."

Alex left the room without another word, and set about searching the nearby offices, holding a hand to his churning gut. The corridors were empty, dank and rotten. Shining his light on the floor, he saw the remains of a great many pitiful meals, little more than bowls of gruel.

The last room along the corridor was the smallest, and had been swept and neatened. It contained only a desk, upon which lay something he recognised from profile only: a single silver-grey feather. Beneath it was a brown envelope.

A shiver coursed along his spine. He looked over his shoulder and saw that he was alone. Pushing the rickety remnant of the door ajar and stepping inside, he took the rifle from around his neck and leaned it against the wall.

He sat on the chair, cradled his head in his hands, and remained there in silence for a long time. Only when his hands had ceased to shake did he train the torch beam upon the envelope and reached out towards it.

XXVII

Billy was crouched amidst leaf litter. The branches of trees that had survived the year's strife danced overhead, having recently taken on a new lease of life. The grass underfoot was shedding the last of its desiccated, straw-like texture, and once again reached for the sky. Green shoots budded amidst the morning dew.

Life was returning to a world that had come so close to cataclysm for the second time in living memory. Birds once again twittered in the trees, and deer once again frolicked beneath the canopies of the land's youthful forests—forests still growing up around the remains of villages, towns and cities. Even a few hardy flowers had dared to rear their beauteous heads.

Billy had been sitting beneath the sun-dappled fronds of the sheltered copse for over an hour. It offered her all the cover she needed to remain hidden from any onlooker. A tawny owl had remained close by for some time, hooting somewhere out of sight, rustling buckled undergrowth.

Below her, perched upon a rocky incline that led down to a dense scatter of lean-to shacks, were the carcasses of ancient mobile caravans. Around them was what had been a halo of camping tents. The tracks that the newcomers had made in the earth as they'd arrived were still fresh.

She had found the settlement after the last of the food stores in the cabin had run dry. Daddy no longer noticed when she strayed from his beside unless he was sitting up for their daily meal—which now only lasted a mere handful of minutes, due to the pitiful size of their rations. The rest of the time he lay in a daze, slowly fading, growing further from her and the world with each passing day.

Sometimes he spoke nonsense, mumbled about a tower, a city, and a Dark Man. At first it had only scared her, and she had thought it meant Daddy was going to die soon. But then she had started having dreams too. Most of the things she saw were confused, just blurs, but through it all she could make out three men. One was blonde and old, another brown-haired and young. Her waking thoughts were of these strangers. She could have sworn she knew them, but had never laid eyes on either.

Then there was the third: the Dark Man. She didn't want to believe it was the same man Daddy saw, but when Daddy woke and talked about his nightmares, she knew it was. It was all the same, every detail. The pale young face, the dark cloak, and the strange marks over his cheekbones…

But there hadn't been time to dwell. They needed food.

Her first foray outside had been fraught with false starts and frightened tears, but after an hour she'd managed to brave the small distance to the cliff side. There, she had discovered that the cliffs formed a ridge, several hundred feet above the inland basin, leading down towards a vast expanse of fields and scrubland, all wild and unpopulated.

She had expected, and secretly hoped, that Daddy would wake and scold her for daring to wander away without his knowledge. But he had still been dazed and only semiconscious when she had returned.

She'd endured a night's hunger and growing thirst before daring to go out once again, straying into the nearby forest from whence they had come. That time she'd brought back stream water and berries. The water had unsettled her stomach, and Daddy had been furious when she had tried to feed him the berries—for, unbeknownst to her, they had been of a bad kind—and admitted what she'd done. But, despite his anger, he had taken her into his arms and thanked her.

That night he had laboriously sketched and described the safest and most likely things to eat that could be found in the forest, and sent her back the following day, with strict orders to stay close.

And stay close she had, that day. She'd brought back a few handfuls of blackberries and a canteen of water, which she had then boiled under his instruction. They had eaten together after nightfall, and Billy had felt stronger —not only in body, but in mind. She had done something herself. She had taken care of them.

She had, for the first time, taken the edge off the fear boiling away in her gut.

But her newfound strength had been cut down by the fact that, despite her efforts, Daddy had weakened only further by morning.

From then on she had strayed farther and farther into the woods, gathering the items that Daddy had described. Unfortunately, the woodland was too young for very much of anything to have grown to maturity. She was soon forced to stray even farther, far enough to have stumbled across the travellers' settlement.

From her vantage point in the copse she had watched them a little more each day.

At first, she would never have considered approaching them. Although Daddy now spoke almost constantly of leaving him alone—of leaving him in the cabin and finding people elsewhere—she refused to entertain the idea.

She didn't mention her discovery. Daddy would only want to investigate himself, something she was sure was now beyond him. Instead, she had merely watched, and waited, as a sense of the ragtag microcommunity had formed in her mind.

They, too, were new to the basin. That much had been immediately obvious. Still very much embroiled in the tasks of tying guy ropes, unpacking their belongings and felling nearby underbrush, their malnourished bodies and travel-weary faces had betrayed their true identities: nomads, forced away from their homeland—just like her, and Daddy…and Grandpa.

They, however, had clearly developed a few skills along the road, and had had more success at gathering than she. Each day they managed to acquire a mouthwatering array of fruits, root vegetables, berries, nuts, fish and smoked meats. As though only to taunt Billy further, they piled their spoils in the centre of their circle of makeshift homes.

While Billy had visited more often each day, and the sparse offerings of the forest had thinned to the point of mere morsels, she had watched them with a sense of overwhelming desperation growing inside her.

This morning, she had awoken with no pretence about the purpose of her visit to the copse: she would have to steal. She would take only enough to see her and Daddy through the next few days, and then she'd be strong enough to brave the scrubland farther afield. But today, there was no choice.

What she had seen once she'd arrived, however, had driven all thought of food from her mind. She'd fallen upon her haunches amidst the ferns, unable to move, staring down at where the settlement had been, until the wind had kicked up nearby leaves and twigs into the deep pile now nestled against her thighs.

It had clearly burned some time during the night. All that remained of the tents were their blackened profiles against the ground, and a few skeletal support wires. The caravans had been rendered buckled shadows of their former selves, their walls blistered open, having spilled their contents onto the ground outside. Everywhere, myriad personal effects lay charred and unrecognisable beneath a thick layer of grey-white ash. The food was gone.

No effort had been made to put out the blaze. Nothing had been dragged clear of the flames. Not a single body littered the ruins. The campsite merely lay smouldering in the midst of the sapling forest, as though man had never passed this way. No cries of sorrow sounded from beneath the trees, and no trail of survivors graced the undergrowth.

They were just gone.

"Enjoying the view?"

The voice, low and smooth, trickled over her shoulder and into her ear, seeming almost to creep up on her from behind. Her heart skipped a beat as she whirled in the grass, ready to run or scream. But she was stilled by the sight of the figure standing over her. She knew his face. "You," she whispered.

"Me," he said.

"You…you're not here. You're the nightmare man. You're not real. You're a dream!"

A smile grew on the man's beautiful face, right below a pair of eyes surrounded by dark streaks. If those eyes hadn't been so razor sharp, he would have looked funny, like the Pandas that Ma had used to show her in picture books. But this man was anything but funny. "Do I look like a dream to you?" he said.

She flicked her head down to look at his long black overcoat, and his feet planted in the grass, which parted around his ankles. His overcoat fluttered in the wind. He was real, alright. She couldn't have spoken if she had tried, so hard had her jaw clamped shut, and so she shook her head.

He crouched down beside her and gestured to the conflagration. "I'm sorry you had to see this," he said.

"Did you do it?"

His eyes widened. "Me? No." Absurdly, he smiled with genuine good humour. "No, this isn't my style."

Despite the mirth in his eyes, Billy's guts quivered, and she cowered in the grass. "Who are you?" she said.

He shook his head, suddenly impatient. Urgency filled his gaze. "There'll be time for that later. I need you to listen close." He swept an arm at the camp. "You see this? It's just the start. If you don't do exactly as I say, there won't be a soul under these stars who can escape what's coming."

Tears were splashing from her cheeks without check. Though he spoke softly, he frightened her more than even the devil who had taken Grandpa. The air around him seemed alive. "Please go away!"

"Billy."

"I want my Daddy!"

His gaze bore down on her with such intensity that she froze in the grass. "Listen, child! Listen well. Or else your *Daddy* will be but one of countless to perish in fire. You're special, Billy. You can make all the difference."

"Me?" she squeaked.

"You."

Despite herself and all her writhing guts, she asked, "How?"

The Panda Man spoke fast, his voice having fallen to a whisper. "Something is brewing on the horizon, something you're a part of, something that will decide the fate of not only this world, but many. Maybe all."

She blinked. "I don't understand…"

He shook his head, ever more impatient. "There *will* be time for answers later. Right now I need you to find some people."

"Who?"

"I think you know."

For a moment Billy could only frown up at him. Then the faces from her dreams danced in front of her eyes; the two men who seemed to hover over her bed each morning.

The Panda Man nodded with a knowing glint to his smirk. "That's right. I need you to find them before it's too late to change what He's done."

"What who's done?"

He didn't seem to hear her, glancing away at the horizon. "He's upset the balance." A scowl brewed on his alabaster face. "So much depends on the here and now, yet all these silly men ever do is think of themselves. It needs to be put right. We have little time."

Billy hesitated. "I can't leave Daddy. He's sick. Please, just go away and leave us alone!"

"Your father will be fine, for a while. Right now, I need you to get up out of the dirt. There's work that needs doing." He straightened, his long coat billowing around him, and offered a hand.

Billy's breath shuddered in her throat. "No," she cried. "Leave me alone."

"If you don't, your father will die. I guarantee it."

Billy sobbed, but offered her hand. It was seized by a grip of immense strength, and the Panda Man's eyes glittered. "Good," he muttered. Then he hauled her up in a hail of browning leaves and set her on her feet.

Billy brushed herself down, dazed, and took a breath to steady herself. "Where do I go?" she said, straightening up to meet his gaze. But he was gone. All that remained of him was a fading rustle in the grass, a groan in the bark of the copse's trees, and a single departing whisper on the wind. "It'll come to you. Find them, Billy. Find them."

XXIX

Norman shuffled without pause, passing each guard yet again as he circled the catwalk, orbiting the tower. They paid him no notice, their eyes trained beyond the wall, but he was glad for their presence nonetheless.

The city's shadows seemed alive today, boiling away where the sun's glare couldn't reach, as though plotting, murmuring.

He kept his gaze fixed a few feet ahead of him. It was easier to keep walking that way—in a trance where time was unhinged, one which kept his thoughts and chest pain at bay.

By the time he came to a standstill, the sun had fallen low in the sky, and his ribs were throbbing, coupled with an icy pinch in his chest that had taken seat not long after Alexander had departed. The heat of the day was ebbing, but it was still far too warm to explain the chill that now seemed to surround his heart, a raw, gnawing cold.

He'd passed out by the stables after Allie and Richard had left him. It couldn't have been for very long, as he had still been alone when he'd come to, but it had been long enough to bring him back to his senses. By the time they'd returned, regret and deep shame had set his cheeks burning and his stomach tied in knots.

He'd said things he didn't mean, done things he shouldn't have in front of people who were relying on him. He'd made a fool of himself. And there was no way to take any of it back.

A few hours of rest—with Allie watching over him— had been enough to cement an even state of mind. But still the pain had persisted enough to drive him back outside—to pacing the catwalk—in search of distraction.

He wondered just how long it would take the pain to fade. He now suspected that it was down to more than just the broken ribs. Something told him that, somehow, it was connected to the nightmares, and the scar upon the side of his head.

But right now the pain seemed distant. His mind had turned elsewhere.

When he'd been resting, he had endured a bout of restless twitching, and dreamed a dream all too familiar: the city, the storm, the yelling young faces, and the leering figure.

Looking out at London's skyline now, there was no doubt in his mind that it was the very same as that city's. This time there had been nothing vague about the dream; every detail had been rendered in sharp relief. He had not only tasted the stagnant mud, but felt the grit between his teeth, felt not only the icy rain upon his skin but also the weight of his sodden clothes. The bolt of pain above his right ear had this time seemed closer to a white-hot steak knife embedded in his skull. The voices of those standing above him had reached his ears—still distorted and meaningless, but audible.

It had all been more substantial. More real.

But most noticeable of all had been His return: that strange, leering figure. The first time Norman had had the dream, he'd been standing off to one side, watching. This time, however, he'd been standing directly behind Alexander and Lucian, the dark marks beneath his eyes casting his face in shadow. He had leaned between the bellowing figures, smiling, and repeated the words that now haunted Norman's every waking thought: "Remember, Norman. Remember. You were all there."

Norman shuddered. There would be no more sleep for him today.

A noise finally drew him back to the catwalk: scuffling footsteps, approaching from the tower. At first he suspected it was one of the guards changing shift, but the silhouette passing over the catwalk was slighter, more feminine.

Allison materialised from the tower's shadow, approaching with unmistakable purpose.

He tried to smile, but faltered, the shame of his earlier outburst arresting his lips. Instead he turned away and waited, leaning against the catwalk. From here he was looking out across the Thames, which cast a silver-blue glare across the city, one that enamelled the crumbling shells of glass and steel behemoths. The monuments of long-dead men momentarily struck him dumb—as the Old World's remains had done countless times before, and would never cease to do—as Allison continued to grow closer, until her face was mere inches from his.

"Can't sleep?" she whispered.

Norman drew a great sigh. "It feels like the whole world is holding its breath," he said, "just waiting for something to happen."

She nodded. "I've never liked it here," she said. "It's too quiet."

"It's always quiet."

"Yes, but here it's different. Not just silence but…an absence. Like there's something missing that isn't quite gone…just a ghost of something greater."

"I suppose all that's left are ghosts of greater things."

She shrugged. Moments later, she sidled an inch closer. "Do you ever wonder where they all went?"

Her words died on the wind, and Norman couldn't help swallowing audibly. "Sometimes," he said.

She shook her head, her eyes glassy. "It's hard to think of so many people. And they all just… I can never begin to imagine what it was like for the elders, what it was like to watch it all go, and know that they had to carry on."

"Alex always said it happened fast," Norman said. He snapped his fingers—though they both knew the snap was coming, it made them jump—"Just like that."

She shook her head once more. "Why?" She paused. "Why them? Why then, and only then?" She shivered. "Why are *we* still here?"

Norman felt his mind grapple with the questions, but only momentarily. It was all too big, especially now. After a brief silence he said, "I don't know. It doesn't matter. Best just to do what you can with what you have."

She was motionless for a long time, her gaze locked on the long-dead city, but when she turned back to him she had regained a trace of vim. "We're trapped here, aren't we?"

He nodded.

"What do you think will happen?"

"I don't know, but I don't think there's any doubting why we got through London untouched. They have us all together now, in one place."

He heard her throat crack. "Things *are* better, now. Not everyone is starving. Maybe…maybe it'll all just blow over."

He smiled despite himself and gave her arm a squeeze. "Sorry, Allie, but I don't think so. This was never about hunger. There's something they're not telling us. I'm going to find out what it is, but I don't know if I can do anything to put it right." He paused, thinking of Alexander. "Our past isn't all roses."

"There's the radio message, too. Maybe there's someone out there who can help us."

"Maybe."

Allie sighed. "At least we have you," she said. "You and Alex."

Norman tried to keep an even expression, but couldn't stop his shoulders slumping. "Allie…" He looked into her eyes, and felt the weight of two cities press upon his shoulders. "I'm not the man you're looking for. I don't think I ever was. I'm just…" His scar throbbed, but he pressed on, "I'm nobody." He looked out across the river once more to hide his burgeoning grimace. "I can't save you."

They lapsed into a silence long enough for the city's skyline to become emblazoned on his retinas. A dark presence seemed to be exuding from its murky depths, one he felt all too often now. He saw it peering around every corner, felt it pressing in from all sides.

And he suspected that Allie felt it too. They all did.

Her delicate fingers twisted into his, and her voice washed over him from lips that had grown close to his shoulder. "You *are* that man. I know you are." She pressed her lips against his cheek, and whispered in his ear, "You might not believe it, but I do."

That same eternal truth still rang out at him: *I'm not Alex.* But now, cutting over it, the disembodied voice of that nameless stranger spoke even louder: *Tsk, tsk, Norman. Storm's on its way, and you need to be ready.*

He sighed. "Maybe I can change," he said. "Maybe I don't even have a choice." He closed his hand over hers, looking out over the ruins of the Old World metropolis. Despite the warmth of her skin, a splinter in his thoughts kept him frowning. They had reached a turning point, and there was no going back. Their lives hinged on the council convening. Though it was only hours away, it might be too late. Amidst the city's streets he sensed malevolence, and a great many eyes moving over his skin. "They're out there, waiting. I can feel them," he said. "Whatever happens, it'll happen fast. We're not out of the woods, yet. Not by a long shot."

XXVIII

Alexander waited until the others had taken in the horrors under the tower block's roof, and could bear no more. While he sat motionless in the gloom, he heard them traipse outside to gag and vomit, one by one. The sound of scuffling also reached his ears. A few must have fainted, and were being carried outside. Only a handful remained inside, who he glimpsed passing by at the end of the corridor, searching for survivors with rags held to their mouths.

They found no one.

Eventually, they too filed outside, cursing under their breath. So shocked did they seem that all pretence of keeping watch had been abandoned. Through the nearly opaque office window he could see them gathered on the outskirts of the rubble field, sitting atop boulders with their heads bowed, broken.

Alexander waited until all had grown utterly still and silent. Even then, it took him some time to muster the will to move. His knees felt heavier than blocks of lead, while his hands, moulded around the envelope, seemed stuck fast to its wrinkled surface.

It would have been so easy to stay like that indefinitely, devoid of thought or worry. The world seemed distant; the massacre outside could have been a mere figment of his imagination. He might not have been so very guilty—so very responsible for every single part of it.

He was finally on the verge of moving when Lucian appeared in the doorway. His cheeks were pale, and his fists bunched. Alexander's heart sank at the sight of his distant gaze.

"Nothing," he said. "There's nothing. They cleaned the place out." He glanced at the bloodied walls. "Cleaned it out, killed every last one of them, and left. And we've got *nothing*. We're still on square one. I..." He threw his bunched fists to his temples and grunted. "I don't know if we can ever come back from this, Alex. I don't see an end to it." His arms fell to his sides, and his jaw grew slack. For the briefest of moments, Alexander saw the eight-year-old boy he'd once met in a roadside warehouse. "What have we done?" he muttered.

Alexander swallowed, felt a lump of self-loathing pass along his gullet, and shook his head. "We survived, Lucian," he said. "All we've ever done is survived."

Lucian's shoulders slumped. He lingered for a moment longer, and the light in his eye—the one that Alexander and so many others had relied on for countless years— died, perhaps for the last time. He nodded, slid from the doorway, and disappeared from sight.

Alex was left alone once more. It was only after Lucian's footsteps had well and truly faded, and the office building was filled with the tell-tale whistle of total silence, that he brought the envelope from his lap and tore it open.

*

Lucian stumbled in darkness.

So it's come to this, he thought. *How? How has it come to this?*

The others' voices grew faint as he raced headlong into the building's bowels, desperate for shelter, for isolation. He wouldn't let them see what this was doing to him. They needed strength, and he was going to give it to them. But not now. He needed a minute. "Christ," he muttered and stopped in the gloom, leaning against the wall. He breathed deep and let his head fall back, staring up at the ceiling. "Forgive us."

A quiet *snick* was his only warning before a cold blade pressed against his throat. He made to struggle, but arms gripped him from behind, while the blade pressed hard enough to draw blood. Lucian stilled, gagging as an elbow wrapped around his throat. He looked over his shoulder, and was dismayed to recognise his assailant. "We let you go," he choked.

Charlie's face was murder. He still stank like a sewer, and was dressed in the very same rags as when they had last met. But there was something changed in him. The child was gone. It was written in his eyes. "Let me go?" he breathed. "Letting me go would have been letting me die in that sewer. What you did was worse. You took away the only thing in the world I had left and dropped me back in the world like an animal."

He brought the blade up to Lucian's eye. "My father deserves justice."

"We didn't know, Charlie," Lucian said. "I'm sorry, but I did what had to be done."

"Shh, quiet! I've got plans for you, but if they hear us, I have no problem ending this right here, right now." The knife grew closer, a mere centimetre from Lucian's cornea. But it wasn't the blade he was afraid of. What really scared him was how frightened the kid sounded beneath that angry scowl. In the corner of his eye he could see Charlie's face, and wasn't comforted to see tears in his eyes.

"You're a good kid," he said. "Think about this."

"Oh, I've thought about it. I've thought of nothing else," Charlie spat. He wrestled Lucian's arm back until it felt like it might snap, and clamped a cloth over his mouth. "I won't be denied what I deserve." An ugly sneer crossed his quivering lips. "Let's see how the wise and powerful messiah fares without his dog to do his dirty work!"

Lucian did something of which he would have thought himself incapable. It was only the thought of Alexander that spurred him on. He begged, not with his stifled mouth, but with his eyes.

Charlie's face filled with glee. "That's right. You're mine. Blood is coming, and there's nowhere to hide. For them, anyway…It's time they faced the music." His eyes darkened, and he hauled Lucian back into shadow, lips pressed against the flesh of his ear. "But not for you. You're coming with me."

*

The crumpled note tumbled onto the desk, landing amidst the dust. Alex didn't need to touch it, for it had landed right side up, and the flowing hand was cast into sharp relief by the torch-beam. He read it without moving an inch. All the while, boiling agony festered in his gut, stemming from long-repressed memories—memories of hope, of dreams, and of emerald eyes:

Know this, brother: if there had ever been a time in which you could have saved them, could have ever truly saved anyone, it was the last time you looked into my eyes—when you chose your dream over your family.

Destiny calls, Alex. I'll be seeing you, soon.

—J

Coming Soon

BRINK

Part 2 of the epic Ruin Saga…

Thanks for reading, folks.

I hope you enjoyed the ride. If you have a spare moment, I'd greatly appreciate it if you could drop by your retailer's website and leave an honest review. Every nugget of feedback helps me provide a better reading experience.

Subscribe to the newsletter

Can't wait for the next instalment? Sign up to the newsletter now and keep up to date on new releases!

Some of the things I'll send your way:

- The latest news on upcoming releases
- Sneak peeks at future instalments
- News on how the writing process is progressing
- Exclusive discounts and freebies

Interested in being an advance reader for future releases? Get in touch!

Click to join the list: http://eepurl.com/V4niL

A Pendulum Universe Book

Something has gone wrong. A pendulum's swing is dying. If it stops, everything stops. The fabric of all existence is in danger. Shadows are moving, long-sealed doors have fallen ajar, and the balance of an infinitude of worlds has shifted. On one world, something has gone very wrong, indeed: the End. Six billion people have vanished, leaving a barren Earth populated with scattered survivors. While man struggles with mere survival and the eternal plagues of betrayal and retribution lay waste to already crumbling cities, a much greater mission begins.

So opens a universe that stretches far beyond Earth, across deserts and tundra, kingdoms of past and future, and ancient forgotten worlds between the cracks. If there is any hope, it lies in a precious handful, creatures of destiny scattered across all of reality. The success or failure of their gathering will decide the fate of countless lives.

Bringing them together will cause destruction, pain and death. Some will run, some will fight, and some will turn to darkness.

Only one thing is certain: the End was just the beginning.

Acknowledgements

My eternal thanks go to my family and friends for their support, understanding and tolerance during the four years that this project has been in the works—during which I muttered and scribbled in the corner. Without them, this novel would never have made it out into the world.

My cover designer, Levente Szabo, produced some beautiful work, and has my thanks for being so accommodating throughout the design process.

My editor, Claire Rushbrook, made every difference in catching my varied blunders, and cleaning up after my bad habits. Proofreaders Claudette Cruz and Anne Victory also did a stellar job.

Special thanks to Auriane Desombre, Nick Tajudeen, Ventura Dennis, Mary Moore, Heather Bryant and Bob Ferguson for all their contributions.

About the Author

Harry Manners lives in Bedfordshire, England with his family. When he's not writing, he studies Physics at the University of Warwick, reads a ton-load of books, and generally nerds out—for which he is staunchly unapologetic.

Website:

www.harrymanners.net

Facebook page:

www.facebook.com/OfficialHarryManners

Twitter:

@harry_a_manners

Blog:

www.harrymanners.wordpress.com.